MURDER'S COMING

GRAVE WITHOUT GRASS

MURDER'S COMING

GRAVE WITHOUT GRASS

DONALD CLOUGH CAMERON

COACHWHIP PUBLICATIONS
Greenville, Ohio

Murder's Coming / Grave Without Grass, by
  Donald Clough Cameron
© 2021 Coachwhip Publications

Murder's Coming published 1939
Grave Without Grass published 1940
Donald Clough Cameron, 1905-1954
CoachwhipBooks.com

ISBN 1-61646-510-7
ISBN-13 978-1-61646-510-0

MURDER'S COMING

For Eva
who believed

1

From the train window, Abelard Voss observed with interest the variegated course of Mill River. Out of the hills to the north it came clean and cold, twisting its green and silver through fertile valleys and lush meadows. Out of Andor, to the south, it writhed sluggishly between banks of sticky clay, its complexion dark red, like the waste from a slaughterhouse. Voss studied the great mill building of smoky brick where the chemistry of change took place. High on one side of this structure, the river came to a shivering halt, waiting for the end; low on the other side it seeped out in a flat ribbon, limp and soiled.

Voss looked at his watch, then pulled from his pocket the envelope postmarked "Andor, Mass." which had reached him the previous day in New York. From the envelope he drew a newspaper dipping and a terse, typewritten note. For the twentieth time he read them through. The clipping, torn roughly so that only *"The Advertiser,* Ando . . ." still showed at the top, read as follows:

SYMPTOMS OF MURDER!
We quote this week from the latest book by Abelard Voss, the famous young criminologist:

"Behind every antisocial act there is a pattern which the act completes. The thief spies a valuable jewel and decides on the spur of the moment to steal it. The suspicious husband sees his wife alight from a strange automobile a block from home, and drops the sports section of his newspaper to seize the murder knife.

"Yet those things which the police term *motives* are only the *cues* in the drama. Each of the crimes is completely logical in a coldly analytical sense and each of the criminals has trod a carefully charted course to the doing of the deed. For every noteworthy act, violent or peaceful, that occurs today had its reason yesterday—or a hundred years ago. It is possible to trace every step of the criminal's path back to its innocent beginning; that, in fact, is the usual procedure of sociologists and psychologists in our big cities.

"But the criminologist of the future will not start with the crime and trail backward. He will act before the crime has been committed. Even now he is learning to watch for the symptoms. . . ."

Citizens of Andor, such symptoms are before you!! The very air we breathe is heavy with the taint of imminent violence.

To name names would be to bring down upon our defenseless head the law of criminal libel if not the hatchet of an assassin. In a town as small as Andor, however, names and situations are the common property of everyone.

Have we opened your eyes? Have we brought to light the hidden germs that will burst forth in an uncontrollable plague if allowed to multiply unmolested and grow virulent? Will you recognize the symptoms and so defeat them?

Or have we only wasted words and space? If so, obituaries are five cents a line.

The note was shorter. It said:

Abelard Voss:
How would you like to test your theory here?
A. V. Atkinson

Even the signature was typed. Voss shook his head and knotted his forehead once more over that name. Somewhere in the back of his mind something stirred, some vague memory was half prodded into consciousness, only to slip beyond his reach again, unrecognized. That vague stirring, more than anything else, had propelled him into Grand Central early that morning, and on to the first train for Andor. He wondered at himself. In this small industrial town, from the look of it, he would not find even a petty larceny, let alone murder—or a fee.

The train sighed to rest along the concrete platform of the station, and Voss rose to his full and startling height, somewhat as a carpenter's collapsible rule unfolds. He extended a thin arm horizontally to the luggage rack, lifted down a large cowhide valise, and covered half the length of the coach in four strides, ducking his head automatically as he passed through the door.

In the sunlight of the platform he made a gawky figure, with his broad-brimmed Panama, the linen suit that hung on his angular frame like laundry on a dryer, and the big hands idle at his sides. Rimless spectacles perched on his hawk-beak nose, obscuring the gray twinkle of inquisitive, calculating eyes. His ears were abnormally large, his mouth wide and pleasant, his chin long and pointed.

While three or four loungers under the station awning stared in awed silence, Voss ducked into the dim interior of the station. The thin-faced man behind the window gave him a querulous glance.

"I'm expecting a wire," the young man said. "My name is Abelard Voss."

The station agent frowned as though trying to remember something. He repeated, "Abelard Voss." Then he goggled and permitted his lower jaw to sag a full inch, while the second hand of the clock jogged around a half circuit. He replied, "No, Mr. Voss, there's nothing come in yet."

"Something will," said Abelard Voss. "Meanwhile, I'd like to leave my bag somewhere." He hoisted it effortlessly to the ledge of the window. "Is there—?"

"Leave it right here." The thin-faced man swung back the grille over the window and reached for the valise. He grunted as he felt its weight.

"Thanks," Abelard Voss said. "Do you happen to know a man named A. V. Atkinson?"

The station agent considered. "There was old Tom Atkinson, the shoemaker. He died last summer and didn't leave no kin."

"He'll hardly do," Voss decided, and turned away.

Along the other side of the station, whitewashed stones in a rectangular patch of vivid lawn spelled "Andor." Voss's lips twitched as he looked at them. His limber stride carried him swiftly past the lawn, to where, across one end of the rectangle, was Main Street, with black-and-white crane gates stemming traffic until the train should resume its run. Voss turned left along the sidewalk, his eyes ranging over the street with a curiosity faintly tinged by vigilance. He always felt a sharpening of his senses when coming to a new place and unfamiliar people. The habit of concentrated observation, of putting trifles together into a pattern of significance, was second nature by this time, and he was unexpectedly rewarded for it. Ahead of him, coming toward the tracks, was a gaunt man in a shabby suit. As Voss's eye flicked over him the man halted abruptly, stared back for a brief second, then turned sharply on his heel and hurried away in the direction from which he had come. Across the back of the man's neck was a smudge which could have been dirt, ink, or even shoe polish.

Voss frowned; he had felt the impact of that brief scrutiny as certainly as he would have felt the thrust of a hand. He looked after the man for a moment, noting the jerky gait and the wide swing of arms. Then, as though chiding himself, he shrugged and went on.

Parallel to the railroad and fifty feet from the station, Mill River slid under Main Street. There was a bridge with iron handrails protecting the footwalks at either side. A few rods from the bridge was the slatted water outlet from the mill, at the base of a six-story wall pierced by narrow windows like a medieval fortress.

Even before he reached the bridge, Abelard Voss felt that there was something unpleasant about the man who was hunched over the railing on the mill side. It was not that his clothes were ragged and visibly dirty, even at a distance. Nor that he was barefoot—though that would have been understandable only in a boy, and this figure, with the unkempt gray hair straggling out from under a greasy cap, was obviously no boy. There was a looseness in the way the man sprawled against the rail, an obvious absence of any kind of self-control or self-respect in everything about him, that offended Voss. Curious to know why a tramp on a bridge should affect him so strongly, he crossed the street and bore down on the idler.

In a moment he knew the answer. The man's face, seen close at hand, was empty of all humanity. Voss perceived that he was an idiot, and reflected that one difference between New York and a small town like Andor was that here a mindless creature like this was allowed to wander around, unattended and unconfined. Perhaps, after all, the Andor indifference was not unkind; the man was obviously enjoying the business of looking over the rail and into the roiled and tainted stream below him. Even when Voss approached him he did not look up.

That investigator's curiosity which was so much a part of him made Abelard Voss hesitate, slow down, and ultimately come to a halt against the rail of the bridge. It was strange how the man's eyes never moved away from the water. Voss leaned over and stared down at the river. The slick that filmed the surface of the water made it opaque; all that he saw at first was his own face haloed by the floppy brim of his Panama. Neither the river nor his own reflection pleased Voss; he felt impatient with himself for having stopped. Small boys and village idiots could lean over bridges, but he ought to have more sense. So he told himself.

Then the idiot made a liquid, chuckling sound and Voss saw that he was pointing with one stubby finger toward a spot just under the bank. What seemed to be a darker shadow in the shadow of the bridge was rising and falling under the surface with a slow rhythm dictated by some mysterious current. Suddenly Voss's eyes became intent. A section of the darker shadow swung away from the mass and reached toward the surface like an arm, and on the end of the arm was a white thing that looked like— that was—a human hand. Its pale fingers, stretched rigidly straight and apart, came within an inch of breaking the slick and the arm seemed to be straining desperately toward the light. Voss felt sure it was a man's hand; the fingers were too blunt and thick for a woman's.

After a motionless second the hand sank back. It became a shapeless blob in the dull water and was blotted out altogether as the arm merged with the larger shadow. There was nothing to be seen in the river but Abelard Voss's shocked face and the grinning features of the idiot.

Voss wondered if it went on like that hour after hour— the drowned corpse struggling toward the sun only to fall back defeated. Then he smiled to himself. Some towns welcome their celebrities with brass bands and speeches. Andor had prepared a more appropriate and a grimmer welcome. Was it a coincidence that the *Advertiser's* fateful warnings should have been justified at this moment? Or— and Voss frowned more intently at the red water below his feet—or had the writer's foresight been hindsight after all?

A clear voice said at Voss's shoulder, "It's only red dye from the woolen mill now, but it may be men's blood before another hour."

Voss started, straightened and turned. The third person to stop on the bridge footwalk was a slender young man in neat gray clothes with a clerical collar and vest. His brown wavy hair was bare to the hot sky. There had been something like bitterness in his voice and there was bitterness expressed in his very blue eyes and his delicate, discontented mouth.

"Why do you say that?" Voss asked.

"You'll see." The young clergyman waved his hand vaguely to indicate what lay invisible behind the mill. "The three thousand men, women and children who work for Wilton's Woollies are gathered there waiting for the one o'clock whistle to call them back to work. A certain zealous man—a preacher like me, but with a different master—is trying to coax them to join a union. Thirty policemen armed with guns and clubs and tear gas and fifty company guards are doing their best to incite a riot that will give them an excuse to murder the organizer."

"Is murder the word?" inquired Voss.

"It's the only word that fits. Oh, I'm no socialist, no great friend of either labor or capital. So far as I'm concerned Jared Wilton's benevolent despotism is all right for Andor. He kept his loyal serfs fed all through the depression.

"But violence and bloodshed are what Claude Sackett and Alfred Fleming are breeding, and violence and bloodshed are contrary to the laws of God and man. If only I could make those two see it!"

"Sackett and Fleming. I'm a stranger here. I don't believe I ever heard of them."

"Sackett's family once owned the Wilton mill. Now he's general manager for Jared Wilton and a harder, more ruthless man never lived. Fleming is our chief of police and he's Sackett's servant, body and soul. He has no brain or creed or conscience of his own."

"I understood Jared Wilton was absolute dictator here."

The loquacious one sighed. "He is. An honest and a good man, but blind to everything that would displease him. He visits sick members of his employees' families, pays their doctor bills secretly, presents parks and schools and monuments to Andor—and lets Sackett work injustice all around him."

"I'm looking for an A. V. Atkinson," Voss ventured. "Do you know anyone by that name?"

"There used to be a Tom Atkinson, a cobbler—"

"He couldn't very well be my man."

"Maybe he's somebody new at the mill. They get a certain number of drifters every summer."

The idiot giggled again. Out of the corner of his eye Voss could see the shadowy arm begin to detach itself from the shadowy mass.

"To get back to your first observation," he said, "I was wondering if there might not be human blood mixed with the mill dye already."

The young clergyman followed the direction of Voss's gaze. He was gripping the iron railing and his knuckles whitened. He did not move or speak until the hand had completed its ghastly salute to the world above the water and had disappeared.

Then he breathed, "Merciful heaven!"

"The body's caught on something down deep," Voss said. "I suppose we'd better hunt up your police chief and tell him."

"By all means," the other agreed. "Come—I'll take you to him."

Fewer than a dozen of Andor's twelve thousand-odd inhabitants were visible the whole dusty length of Main Street, and Abelard Voss understood why when the clergyman had led him to the next corner. A side street dipped down a hill into a shady green park before the main entrance to the mill and it appeared that every able-bodied person in town was there. Men and women stood shoulder to shoulder, hip to hip, under the big trees. Policemen in khaki uniforms with holstered pistols in their belts and long batons in their hands were massed in a group at one side.

The slope of the dam that trapped Mill River, as yet unpolluted, made a grassy wall at the rear of the park. Halfway up the slope a lean orator in shirtsleeves was shouting and gesticulating, his partly bald scalp gleaming. At his right stood a dark-haired young woman holding a small American flag; at his left a tall man lifted aloft a placard on which was neatly lettered in scarlet:

IN UNION
THERE IS
JUSTICE!

The speaker was shouting, "Fellow workers, don't let your welfare and your children's welfare hang on the whims of an old man! Don't—"

A mightier voice drowned out his words. "C'mon, guys—are you yella? Let's show these foreign Communists how we feel about their dirty talk! Let's throw 'em in the lake!"

Two or three men took up the cry hopefully.

"In the lake!"

"Let's show 'em!"

"All right, gang!"

Exhausted by his efforts to keep up with the long legs of Abelard Voss, the clergyman panted, "That's Vito Russo trying to start trouble. He's foreman of the mill guards. If murder is done, you can bet his hands will be red."

The two men were almost at the edge of the crowd when it happened. Even Voss, who could see over the heads of all the people, could not be sure what started it. Apparently someone had thrown a stone which struck the man who held the placard. He yelled the single word, "Coward!"

Instantly a shower of stones fell about the two organizers and the girl with the American flag. The forefront of the throng surged ominously forward. Coatless men scrambled up the grassy slope, cursing and shouting, brandishing clubs.

The bull-like bellow of the man Vito Russo rose above everything else. It was crying, "Get the rats! Don't let 'em get away!"

An uncertain rumble came from the crowd, but the great mass of people remained rooted, content to be spectators.

A chunky fellow grabbed the dark-haired girl around the waist. The flag she was holding fluttered to the grass and was trampled underfoot. Kicking and screaming shrilly, she was carried to the top of the dam. There was a splash and silver spray shot into view. Her screams ceased.

The man with the placard was defending himself with the long stick to which it had been fastened.

Scarlet letters torn from the placard sailed in the air around him. The point of the stick jabbed a man in the belly and he howled and rolled to the foot of the slope. Then another man got behind the defender and swung a club and the man with the stick fell on his face and slid downward. Five men clustered around him, their feet kicking, their fists flailing.

A short but enormously broad man had grasped the orator by the front of his shirt. The orator was on his knees, arms dangling limply at his sides, head lolling back upon his shoulders. The short man held him up with his left hand and slugged with his right again and again and again. The speaker's face was covered with blood.

A good-looking policeman, dapper in his khaki uniform, mounted the slope leisurely. He paused to watch the short man strike the unconscious orator yet another time, then he put his hand on the slugger's shoulder.

"All right, Russo," he said. "We've cleaned 'em up."

A jet of steam leaped from a valve at the side of the mill smokestack. The hoarse blast of a whistle shuddered through the air, ending all other sounds. The crowd put off its immobility with reluctance and, wooden-faced, surged toward numerous doors in the mill.

"See?" said the young clergyman. "What did I tell you?"

Abelard Voss apparently did not hear him. He was striding through the thinning crowd toward the man in the uniform and his lips made a straight line above his pointed chin.

The policeman had shaken the speaker into a state of semiconsciousness. In trembling tones he was demanding, "Do you understand? Either you leave town before sunset or you go to jail. We ain't standing for no Reds in Andor!"

But before Voss could reach the officer, a plump little man with gray hair and bird-bright eyes struggled up the slope with the aid of a yellow cane. He cried shrilly, "Nonsense, Fleming! Mr. Frank isn't going to leave town or go to jail either. He and his friend Mr. Unger are going to our hospital and get fixed up and then I'm going to have a talk with them. You had no business letting this disgraceful exhibition occur. I was watching from a window and the meeting was quite orderly until Russo made trouble. I have already given orders for his discharge!"

The police chief blinked in indecision. "I was only trying to do you a favor, Mr. Wilton," he muttered. "If he stays you'll have plenty of labor trouble."

"Nonsense!" the little man shrilled again. "Treat your workmen right and you'll never have trouble." He raised his voice. "Come here, some of you boys! Help these two gentlemen to the first-aid hospital!" He raised his face toward the top of the dam. "You, Miss—come here!"

But the girl who had been plunged into the lake had no intention of coming down. From below she looked like a thin, shivering reed against the bright sky, with dark hair plastered over her forehead and around her face and her soaked dress clinging to her small breasts and narrow hips. For a space of seconds she stood poised, watching the scene below, then she turned and sped along the top of the dam out of sight behind the trees.

Jared Wilton shook his head and picked his way cautiously to the foot of the slope. He limped a little with each step, and, leaning heavily on his cane, disappeared into the main door of the mill.

Police Chief Fleming's smooth face was flushed with anger. He was startled to find Abelard Voss's grave eyes on a level with his own although Voss stood several inches below him on the bank. He took half a step backward so quickly he nearly lost his balance and sat down.

"There's a drowned man in the river just below the Main Street bridge," Voss said. "I thought you'd be interested in knowing about it."

"Drowned man, huh?" Fleming rallied belligerently from his surprise. "And who in hell are you?"

"My name," replied the other, "is Abelard Voss."

Fleming's eyebrows lifted and his thin lips parted. Softly he said, "Oh."

The young clergyman, a foot below Voss, was more articulate. He tipped back his head and stared. Then he murmured, "Abelard Voss! Lord, Lord!"

2

Obviously the President of Wilton Woollies, Incorporated, was partial to yellow. The thick rug in his outer office was the color of sulphur and so were the great drapes at the windows. The fluffy hair of his pretty secretary was a brighter gold and her frock was pale lemon. The whole place smelled of money.

"I haven't any appointment," Voss told the girl, "but I want to see Mr. Wilton."

"He's terribly busy this afternoon," the secretary responded. "Who shall I say wishes to see him?"

The magic of the tall young man's name did not fail. The girl looked blank for the merest fraction of a second. Then she rose with alacrity and entered the inner sanctum. From behind the door came the hushed exclamation, "Abelard Voss, the criminologist!"

Voss smiled to himself, a smile of pure and unabashed pleasure. Conspicuous since early youth because of his abnormal height, he had earnestly decided, at eighteen, that people should learn to stare after him for what he was, not for the freak that nature had made him. Although he could look back now with amused and affectionate tolerance at that adolescent and his grim determination, emotionally his reaction was still one of swift and uncontrollable pleasure. He was adult enough, sufficiently matured and well adjusted so that once he was engaged upon a case he could forget his own reactions, and concentrate upon the criminal's. But he could no more shake off those momentary, egocentric preoccupations than he could alter the height that had engendered them.

"Mr. Wilton will see you," the golden-haired secretary said, and held the door open for him.

Voss entered a large, airy office where there were twice as many sulphur-yellow rugs and window drapes. Jared Wilton stood up behind a massive desk and put forth a pudgy hand. He wore thick spectacles in gold frames and a thick gold watch chain across his chest.

"Sit down," he invited cordially, indicating a leather chair at his side. "It isn't often we have famous detectives in Andor, but you come well advertised."

"I'm not really a detective," Voss protested, lowering himself into the chair. "I'm a criminologist. Yes, there's a difference. I'm less interested in finding the criminal than in finding out what made him commit the crime. Not that I don't enjoy the chase, of course—or the fee. . ." He smiled candidly. "But I'm one of those lucky men who have managed to combine in their work their means of livelihood, their hobby, their sport—and the vent for their own inferiority feelings." He cocked an eye at Wilton, and found the president of Wilton Woollies, Incorporated, bewildered, Voss smiled gently and explained, "Finding the criminal out is what I'm paid to do; finding out what drove him to crime is what I like to do; and tracking him down—well, the hunt is the oldest of sports, I guess."

Jared Wilton looked more at ease and happier. Voss rubbed one long hand along his cheek and continued, "It's a vicarious way, perhaps, of enjoying the privileges man theoretically surrendered along with his original creed of anarchy."

"Anarchy," Wilton said. "You heard of the little trouble we had here at noon?"

"I watched it."

"Ah!" Wilton pinched the dewlaps below his chin. "Disgraceful! It should never have happened. Tell me, did you see how it started?"

"I saw the beginning, but the cause was either very slight or very obscure."

"The three agitators didn't start it?"

"You mean, did the girl and the two men attack your fifty guards and thirty policemen? No, it was the other way round."

"That's how it seemed to me. Did you notice a short broad-shouldered man with swarthy features? He was beating the speaker, Leslie Frank, at the last."

"Yes. I thought he was anxious that there should be trouble."

"I thought so too. That's Vito Russo, one of Sackett's men. My general manager, Sackett. I never approved of Russo. Well, I've fired him."

"The police could have kept order if they'd tried," said Voss.

"Just so. I wonder if I ought to replace the chief of police. . . . You know, I'm mayor of Andor. Alfred Fleming is my appointee, but he's Sackett's man, too."

"It's none of my business," ventured Voss, "but why not go right to Sackett? If you don't like the policy his men are following he could correct it. He works for you, doesn't he?"

Wilton's colorless eyes flickered. "Oh, I couldn't do that. He's my general manager, but in a way he's more. His people owned the mill and when the depression came they couldn't hang onto it. I bought it from Sackett and his father, who died last year. A part of the purchase agreement was that Sackett should be general manager as long as he wanted the job and should attend to the actual running of the mill without interference."

"An unusual arrangement."

"Yes, but it works." For an instant a hard gleam appeared in Wilton's eyes. "Sackett and I have known each other since we were kids. We used to fight together—I mean against each other. But he knows the business and we make money. However, I'm more interested in the human element than in wools and dyes and looms. I fix the men's wages and see to their welfare. I do what I can to improve their working and living conditions. You see, the mill supports Andor and as sole owner I'm responsible for just about everyone in the community. I might add I'm rather proud of what I've done, on the whole."

A placid smile settled over his face. Voss saw that Jared Wilton liked himself in the role of absolute monarch and relished the knowledge that the wellbeing of thousands rested in his hands alone.

"I've heard a lot of praise for your methods," Voss observed. "You haven't had any labor trouble before this, have you?"

"I haven't," Wilton replied emphatically, "and I'm not having any now. No employer of labor would have trouble if he'd follow my method. It's inconceivable that my workers would turn against me. That's why I don't object to having outsiders try to organize them. I'm going to arrange for Frank to address my men without interference hereafter. I'm having him at my house for dinner tonight and I'd have Unger, the young artist, too, except that he seems to be injured quite severely." He frowned. "A nice chap, Unger, He's spent the summer here in one of my cottages for the last five years. I don't charge him any rent."

"Is that Thomas Oliver Unger, the Boston painter?"

"That's him. He's pretty widely known. He calls himself a . . . liberal, I believe. He knows Frank from Boston.

Unger painted that." Wilton nodded toward a framed canvas on the wall. It was the portrait of a pale young woman with gray eyes the color of mist. She looked like a lovely ghost in the frame, until you looked more closely and discovered that the deep eyes and the firm, straight mouth were human—had known pain and met it with courage.

A slit like a knife slash crossed a corner of the canvas and marred one white shoulder.

"It's a fine picture," Voss said.

"My brother's wife, Dorothea." A shadow came over Wilton's round face. "Carter—that's my brother—took a knife to it in a moment of childish rage, so I brought it here for safety." He kept his gaze riveted on the green blotter of the desk.

Taking advantage of the change of subject, Voss began, "About that bloodthirsty effusion in your local paper—"

"Eh?" Jared Wilton jerked his gray head erect. "Oh, that! Tommyrot and balderdash and—and bunkum! I hope that isn't what brought you to Andor. Kramer, our editor, is a bit touched. I can't do anything with him." His tone implied that Kramer was the only man in Andor in that category.

"I got the front page of the paper and a letter in yesterday's mail," continued Voss. "I didn't take it too seriously, but the name signed to the letter had a familiar sound. I ran up here because I had nothing else to do. I took it for granted you'd be in a better position to tell me about Andor than anyone else."

"To be sure," Wilton said. "Anything you want to know." Voss put the typed note before him, and Wilton read it aloud.

> Abelard Voss:
> How would you like to test your theory here?
> A. V. Atkinson.

Wilton shook his head. "Never heard of him. I doubt if he lives here, unless he's a newcomer."

"I thought he might be one of your more recent employees."

"We'll see." Wilton pressed a button on his desk and the secretary's yellow head appeared around the door with incriminating promptness. "Please check the payroll lists, Miss Rhinehart, for an A. V. Atkinson," he directed.

"The letter," pointed out Voss, "was mailed from Andor."

"Then there are two nuts in town. I thought Kramer was the only one, except for Clubfoot Crippen. He's the village idiot."

"I saw him. He's the one who spotted the body in the river."

"Eh? What's that? You say there was a body in the river?"

"A dead man. Just beneath the surface near the bridge on Main Street. It was almost the first thing I saw after I got off the train."

"Good heavens, man! What did he look like?"

"I couldn't see for the dye in the water." Voss was marveling at the rapidity with which the blood had drained from Wilton's florid cheeks, leaving them waxy. "There was only his hand reaching toward the surface and falling back again."

"Did you notify anyone?"

"Your chief of police. I suppose he's having the body taken out of the water now."

Wilton steadied himself with a visible effort. He took a silk handkerchief from his breast pocket and passed it across his brow. His lips twitched as though he wanted to smile and couldn't quite make it—or didn't dare.

He said, "Seeing that must have strengthened your belief in Kramer's—er—prognostications."

"It started me thinking. Of course, the man might have fallen in accidentally."

"Hardly in a river that narrow." Wilton hesitated, pressing his pudgy fingertips together. "I'm going to make a confession," he stated finally, "and then I'm going to ask you a favor."

"Go right ahead."

"This is the confession. Pop Kramer is all wrong about the shadow of murder hanging over Andor and he couldn't possibly know about my own case. But I have suspected for some time that my life might be in danger for strictly personal reasons. . . . I suppose I can trust your discretion?"

"Absolutely."

"I'm afraid," Jared Wilton said, "my brother Carter is toying with the idea of murdering me for my money."

The door opened a crack. The secretary's smooth voice announced, "We have no one named Atkinson on the payroll, Mr. Wilton."

"Very well," replied Wilton, his tone slightly irritated. The door closed again.

"Is it just a feeling you have or has he actually made some suspicious move?" Voss asked.

"I'm not sure." Wilton took a deep breath. "You could find out very easily, I imagine. The favor I want to ask is, Will you take the case?"

"You mean, will I find out if he really wants to murder you?"

"Yes," said Wilton. "And see to it that he doesn't—if he wants to."

"H'm," said Voss. "Aren't you interested in *why* he might want to kill you?"

"Yes, yes, of course," said Jared Wilton, too quickly, perhaps. "But you can readily understand that the most important thing—for me—is that he shouldn't; whatever his reasons."

Voss glanced idly once more at the lovely figure on the wall, then shrugged, and said, "Very well, Mr. Wilton. My fees are high—and they carry a condition."

"Condition?" Jared Wilton looked as though he were unused to having people demand conditions of him.

"Yes. I reserve the right to withdraw from the case at any moment I choose, if it seems expedient to me to do so. Should I withdraw, the fee, of course, will be refunded."

Jared Wilton pinched the loose skin under his chin and frowned.

"I guess that's all right, Mr. Voss," he said. "I guess I couldn't make you continue if you didn't want to. And the fee?"

"Two thousand dollars for a period of not more than one month. However, since I shall have to live at your home while I am working on the case, we'll subtract board and lodging. Shall we say five dollars a day?"

For a moment, Jared Wilton looked angry. Then he smoothed out the frown and nodded.

"And if you finish the case in less than a month?"

"The fee," said Voss, "is two thousand dollars."

Wilton nodded once more, and opening his desk drawer, took out a checkbook. While he wrote out a check to Abelard Voss for the sum of two thousand dollars and no cents, he said, "I'll drive you home at five o'clock. Carter and Dorothea live with me, so your task should be not too difficult." He blotted the check and tore it from the book. "We have dinner promptly at six. There'll be guests, but we're informal. Leslie Frank and Sackett will be there, so you'll be entertained; they hate each other." He stood up and handed the check to Voss. "Meanwhile . . ."

"Meanwhile I'd just like to drift around town." Voss folded the check and thrust it in his pocket. "New places interest me."

"Fine," exclaimed Wilton, relieved. "I'll expect you at five."

The young clergyman was loitering in the park, which was otherwise deserted except for a group of small children playing hide-and-seek in the shrubbery. He came briskly to Voss's side as the latter emerged from the mill.

"I've seen your picture in the papers, Mr. Voss," he burst out, as though he had been waiting only for this opportunity. "I'm surprised I didn't recognize you right off. I'm James Morgan, pastor of Andor Tabernacle."

Voss took the proffered hand. "Glad to know you, Dr. Morgan," he said.

The man muttered gloomily, "Not *doctor*. Not even *reverend,* to be technical." Voss looked a question, and the young minister explained, "After two years in a divinity school, I had to leave to support my parents. When they died I became an evangelist. I held some tent meetings here and Mr. Wilton took an interest in me. I preached several times in the Tabernacle, which is his church, and when old Dr. Woodruff died three years ago Wilton put me in the pulpit permanently."

"Without ordination?"

"Some of the congregation made a fuss about that at first, but Wilton fixed things up. It's embarrassing sometimes, not being able to perform marriages—although once in a while a couple will have me read the ceremony after they've had a civil marriage—and a lot of people don't think it's right for me to bury the dead. George Parker, the preacher over at the First Baptist, gets most of the fees. But my people like me, I guess, and lately there's been talk of the bishop planning to ordain me."

They went along Main Street toward the railroad station. The idiot had vanished, but an old man sunning himself on a bench in front of a hardware store told Morgan the police had taken the body from the river.

"Didn't so much as say who it was or anythin' about it," he quavered. "Time was, folks had a minute to spare tellin' the news around, but these days they're always in a rush. Hustle, hustle, hustle!"

As soon as the thin-faced station agent saw Voss he held up a yellow slip triumphantly. "Came in half an hour ago," he yelled. "Guess it's important, by the sound of it. I'd sent it to you right away, only I didn't know where to find you."

Voss thanked him and tore open the envelope. The message was brief. It said:

NEW YORK NY AUG 6—
ABELARD VOSS
ANDOR MASS
ANDREW VIVIAN ATKINSON CONVICT-
ED TRIPLE MURDER ESCAPED TOMBS
PRISON 1925 LETTER FOLLOWS GENER-
AL DELIVERY

SAINT AMOUR

3

"I suppose," James Morgan hinted, "your business in Andor is strictly confidential."

Voss drawled, "Why, no. I came here as a fugitive from a house party of idle people, partly because Andor is two hundred miles from New York—and partly because your local editor's prophetic powers interest me."

"Poor old Pop Kramer," sighed the minister. "I'm afraid he's given to wishful thinking. Ever since he started the *Advertiser* and ran Floyd Turner's *Clarion* to the wall and broke Floyd's heart, Pop has been predicting fantastic events that never happen, drinking disgusting quantities of beer and staying away from church."

"I'm looking forward to meeting him."

"His shop is just up the line. We'll stop. He does the printing for the Tabernacle and so he won't hide when he sees me coming. I used to stop in and wrestle with the devil for his soul till I learned it was hopeless. You'll enjoy him, though, and his better half. She was Ada Prentis, an old maid. When Pop advertised for a wife who wasn't scared of anything, she answered the ad." Morgan laughed quietly. "He claims it's proof of the power of the printed word—or, at least, the display advertisement. But a lot of people think differently; they call her the Witch of Andor."

"Has she the evil eye?"

"No, only the hooked nose. She isn't scared of anything, and she's really a decent sort. She feeds stray dogs and tramps. She's got a dozen cats around the print shop, some of them black."

They had gone half the length of Main Street with Voss timing his strides to accommodate the shorter legs of the clergyman. The sun had grown hotter and blazed down from directly overhead. Where the cloying smell of printer's ink overwhelmed more fragile odors an unwashed window bore the black-and-gold legend:

THE ANDOR ADVERTISER
Job Printing
Joseph Kramer, Prop.

Morgan stepped into the little shop, disturbing a horde of flies. In a back room a small press was clanking rhythmically. Behind a low counter two ancient desks rose out of a litter of paper and cardboard. At one of them sat a gaunt woman, her enormous nose bent above a ledger.

"'Afternoon, Reverend," the woman said in a voice deep as a man's, peering at them from beneath heavy eyebrows.

"Hello, Ada. I want you to meet Abelard Voss. He's looking for Pop."

Ada Kramer stood up. She was taller than Morgan and only three or four inches shorter than Voss. She put out a bony hand cordially and her smile made all the thousand wrinkles of her worn face change their direction.

"Not with a gun, I hope," she said.

Voss shook his head. "Hardly, Mrs. Kramer. I wanted an excuse to get away from New York. Your husband gave me one."

"Well, he'll be glad to see you. He's been praying for a murder for a long time and in all the books the corpse and the detective happen along about the same time. But Pop isn't here now. He might be finding out who was drowned in Mill River, he might be gathering personals in the tap-room of the Commercial House, or he might be trying to collect a bill. You can wait or you can come back."

"I'll come back. I'm looking your city over. How about an hour from now?"

"You can see all there is in half an hour. I'll have Pop here by then. He'll be primed to tell you who all's going to get killed if somebody doesn't step in and change things."

The two men left. Voss observed, "Wilton says Kramer is off center mentally. I take it that isn't the case with Ada Kramer."

"It isn't the case with Pop, either," Morgan declared. "The old sinner is smart as a whip. Jared Wilton merely wishes he was crazy. Really, he shivers all the way to his toes every time the *Advertiser* makes a blood-curdling pre-diction."

"Wilton shivers?"

"He pretends not to. He's full of resounding phrases and prides himself on nourishing serpents like Leslie Frank in his bosom. But what passes for his goodness, I think, is essentially his weakness. Did you see the yellow rugs and curtains in his office? His house is the same color, inside and out. I believe in the symbolism of colors, Mr. Voss. Yellow is the color of coins and cowardice."

"He didn't act yellow when he broke up that party in front of the mill."

"What was there to be afraid of? He's the mayor and the boss. Fleming is weak-kneed and everybody knows it. Russo wasn't within hearing, nor Sackett. I noticed he didn't come outside till the fighting was over."

"I got the impression that he likes to interfere with people's lives, but pays liberally for the privilege and on the whole does as much good as harm if not a great deal more."

"He's a pompous old windbag!" Morgan laughed apologetically. "That doesn't sound very Christian of me, does it, considering I owe my job and everything to Wilton? But it's the truth. There's a bad streak in the family. In Wilton it became an inferiority complex that drove him to get rich in order to lord it over the people who had lorded it over him. In his younger brother Carter the same thing showed up as just plain meanness."

"How did Jared Wilton make his money?"

"The way they do it in the movies. He saved four or five hundred dollars and speculated in some New Jersey oil land nobody thought much of. A big company drilled and Jared got a million. He stuck to oil operations till he'd made several millions and had been away from Andor four or five years. He never married. In nineteen-twenty-four he came back here, built his yellow mansion and began to take over the town."

"And Carter?"

"He never made money, but he stole some. He was in prison in New York for grand larceny when Jared got back here. When his term was up Carter started to sponge on Jared. He put up the money for a couple of shows in New York that lost a great deal, at least according to rumor. He organized a movie company that flopped. Then he came back here and started loafing. It's the only thing he's been successful at."

"He's got a good-looking wife. I saw her picture in Jared's office."

Morgan halted so suddenly that Voss went two steps ahead of him. When Voss turned there was an unfathomable expression on the minister's face.

"Something?" Voss asked.

"It's too hot." Morgan waved a hand toward his left down a shaded side street. At the end of the street was a little park with rustic benches and a view across rolling meadows to high hills. "How about a breather?"

They strolled into the shady street. When they reached the park Morgan selected a bench set before a concrete post supporting a bronze tablet which announced that this park was part of the private estate of Jared Wilton, set apart for the use of the public "for purposes of relaxation and contemplation of the worthwhile things in life."

"There," Morgan said, pointing, "is one nest of vipers Jared Wilton nourishes in his bosom." His tone was jocular.

Fifty yards away, Abelard Voss saw a small cottage surrounded by a low stone wall and partly screened by green bushes. In the yard, the girl who had been thrown into the lake was hanging a wet skirt and blouse on a clothes line. She wore a sweater and slacks and her hair stood out around her head in wild confusion.

"Her name is Ruth Taylor," Morgan volunteered. "She's a reporter for a radical newspaper appropriately called *Struggle,* which is distributed here every day. Her job is to report the labor situation here and, incidentally, participate in it. Her story of today's fracas ought to be worth reading. She and Leslie Frank stay in the cottage, which Wilton lets Unger, the painter, use every summer. I guess Wilton rather fancies that makes him a patron of art. The town is pretty excited about a girl living alone with two men. Pop Kramer tries to give the folks at least one shock a week in the *Advertiser* and last week's jolt was a diatribe against gossips and busybodies."

"Pop sounds more and more interesting."

"He keeps the town supplied with excitement. He hates a lot of people and a lot of people hate him. It would be pretty dull without him."

"Where is the Wilton house from here?" Voss asked.

Morgan waved an arm to indicate ground that rose in gentle humps, covered in places with trees and shrubbery, toward the summit of a wooded hill.

"It's less than a mile and a pleasant walk. There's a good path, if you'd care to try it."

"No, thanks. I don't want to miss Kramer."

Morgan glanced at his wrist watch. "It's been twenty minutes since we stopped. I'll walk back with you, but I won't go in. I've got to make some parish calls."

They strolled leisurely back to Main Street and parted at the door of the *Advertiser* office. Voss found Ada Kramer hammering the keys of an aged typewriter with two claw-like forefingers. She did not slacken her clacking pace or miss a key as she looked up and said, "Pop ought to be back right now. Make yourself to home."

Voss leaned against the counter and glanced at an open volume of bound *Advertisers*. The front page facing him was dated early in July and the bold-type editorial in the center—apparently a standard feature of the paper—was headed: Talk About Dictators. Voss was intrigued by its opening:

> Andor could teach a valuable lesson to Mussolini, Hitler, Stalin and the other iron-fisted czars of the new Europe. Andor's own private dictator could teach them: "Don't shoot your enemies—disarm them with kindness, soften them with ice cream and cake, scratch their backs till they forget how to do anything but purr. Never let them grow strong through encountering the slightest opposition—"

A footstep and a gruff voice interrupted his reading. Voss looked into the incredibly lined, wrinkled and ink-smudged face of the gaunt man who had stared at him and hurried away from the station. He felt his hand gripped by calloused fingers.

"Abelard Voss!" rumbled the man. "One more instance of the power of the press. The *Advertiser* shouts your name and lo! you answer."

It was impossible not to return Pop Kramer's grin in kind, although his black eyes were hard as glass and sharp as a surgeon's scalpel. He was a lanky man whose wrinkled clothes appeared to have been slept in often. His head, surmounted by a mop of dank black hair, rose only an inch or two above Voss's shoulder, but at a distance he gave the impression of height and power. His high, narrow forehead was beaded with sweat and he looked tired from hurrying or coming a long way.

"I came," Voss said, noting that Kramer's grip had left a leaden smear across his hand, "to check up on the symptoms you mentioned."

"Let's go into the back room," Kramer suggested, leading the way through a gate in the counter. "It's cooler and I have some cold beer there and Ada can't contradict me. We've got more than symptoms for you to study now; we've got the real thing. Murder has been done as I predicted."

The shop behind the office had a concrete floor. Bulky composing stones, cases of type, a linotype machine, two small motor-driven presses and a paper cutter took up most of the space. In a corner was an ice chest. Kramer slid back the cover, took out two wet bottles and twisted off the caps with an opener that hung by a chain. He handed one to Voss and tilted the other to his lips, swallowing thirstily.

"Who's been murdered?" Voss inquired, seating himself on the corner of the ice chest.

"Richard Patrick Stott. A thrifty, God-fearing citizen who never annoyed anybody with his troubles—except me. I understand you discovered the body, by the way—you and that young blatherskite of a preacher. That means you'll get your name in next week's paper, too."

"I'll be honored. Who was Richard Patrick Stott?"

"A dye mixer at the mill. Been there five years. Boarded at the Widow Weston's humble cottage and fought off her attempts to marry him with apparent success. Didn't have an enemy in the world, so far as anyone knows—nor a friend, either."

"How was he killed?"

"The side of his head was caved in. Thirty or forty feet of heavy chain was wrapped around his knees. He worked on the fifth floor of the mill right above the water outlet. He went home for supper last Monday night and told the Widow he had to go back to the mill to mix a new batch of dye for the next morning. He rang in at seven-thirty and didn't ring out again. The dye wasn't mixed. But he was so unimportant nobody missed him, except maybe the Widow.

"Someone must have been waiting for him up on the fifth floor. Someone must have socked him with a hammer or something, weighted him with the chain and dropped him out the window. The body was buoyant enough to float and roll along the bottom as far as the bridge and then the water had weighted it so much it stuck. The chains kept the feet against the bottom. One arm lay against the bank and the other kept waving around in the current. Otherwise it might have been months before the body was found."

"I can see next week's headline—'Mysterious Murderer Still at Large!'"

"He'll probably be at large, but you'd never make the grade on the *Advertiser,* Voss. We've got to give 'em better'n that. We've carried journalism to new heights in Andor."

"This is good beer," murmured Voss. "What do you think is happening in Andor and where do you think it's leading?"

Kramer smirked and reached for two more bottles. "Anybody can look at a man and tell he's sick, but it takes a doctor to tell what's wrong with him. I can smell murder on the way—there's a distinct stench which emanates from influences too angry to be stopped short of the ultimate outrage—but it's up to you to discover just what germ has started the rot and where to do the cutting. I can tell *what,* but you'll have to tell *how* and *why.*"

"But I came up here on a holiday." He thought about Jared Wilton's check in his pocket and grinned to himself.

"Sure!" the editor jeered. "The minute you see or hear of murder, you start right in to forget about it! You never solved a case in your life or wrote a book!" He wiped sweat from his forehead and left a streak of ink in its place. "Why—if you don't lay awake tonight trying to puzzle this thing out, I'll let you take a shot at me. And I hate being shot at!"

"You've had experience?"

Kramer nodded. "Twelve years ago in New York—the cops shot at me."

4

Jared Wilton had the air of a man from whose tired shoulders a crushing weight has been lifted. He said, "It's been a bad day for Andor. I'm glad it's over. I hate to think of what the Boston papers will print tomorrow about that unfortunate disorder. Kramer is their correspondent and he doesn't pull his punches. Sometimes I think he hasn't the best interests of the townspeople at heart."

Limping and leaning on his yellow cane, the president of Wilton Woollies, Incorporated, guided Voss through the first floor of the mill. A twisting aisle took them through a jungle of mammoth looms where countless threads ran from white cones of twine to close-set metal slots and emerged from a maze of complicated mechanism in six-foot widths of woolen cloth wound on rollers.

A few minutes before, the looms had been whirring and chattering and the great room had been filled with busy men and women, but the five o'clock whistle had ended that in a swift-descending hum of sound, a rise of voices and a long series of musical bell notes from time clocks. Now only the dead machinery and the heavy smells of chemically treated wool, oil and hot metal remained.

Wilton's expensive sedan stood among a dozen trucks and smaller cars in a garage at one end of the building. He drove himself. He said, "I walk for my health most of the time." He slid behind the wheel and started the motor.

"Did they find out anything more about the murder of Stott?" asked Abelard Voss.

The gray-haired man snorted and trod hard on the accelerator pedal. "Murder nothing! He was a morbid sort. It was suicide. I've convinced Fleming of that and Dr. Hughson, the coroner, will say the same."

"But I heard his skull was fractured."

"So it was. That doesn't mean he was murdered. As a matter of fact there couldn't have been anyone around to do it. We have two night watchmen and Monday night, when Stott was last at the mill, Russo worked late, and none of them saw anybody. Stott was crippled up pretty badly with rheumatism. It's my theory he decided to end it all. He put the chains around his own legs and dropped from the fifth-floor window. His head struck something on the way down and he was dead or unconscious before he hit the water. That's all there is to it."

"There wasn't any trace of blood on the fifth floor?"

"Not a drop. There's a repair bench near the dye vats, but none of the tools had been used to hit anybody, according to Fleming and Sackett. One of the repairmen said a small vise was missing and Fleming had the bottom of the outlet dragged, but it wasn't there, so it must have been moved to another part of the mill for some reason."

"Well, if there isn't any evidence, one man's guess is as good as another's." Stott's death, after all, was not his case. "At least, so far."

"There isn't any evidence at all," Wilton declared firmly. "You can look over the place any time you feel like it. I'm sure you'll agree with me. That man Kramer would like to paint Andor as a community of murderers, but as a matter of fact there isn't a man in town would kill anyone. That is, with the possible exception of the one I mentioned confidentially to you."

"Ah!" Voss said. "I've been thinking about that."

"So have I. What's more, I want to tell you a peculiar circumstance I didn't have time to mention before."

The sedan had reached the railroad station and Wilton stopped it and opened the door. Voss entered the station, got his bag from the thin-faced man and returned.

Wilton did not resume his talk until they had swung into a broad boulevard which bore the name Wilton Drive. Then he gestured toward a strip of woods not far from the road.

"Yesterday I was walking alone there, as I do frequently, when all at once the weirdest feeling of danger came over me. I looked back and my brother Carter was following me, trying to keep out of sight behind trees. I became suspicious and went directly to the house.

"Later our maid, Carmen Corsi, reported a large butcher knife was missing from the kitchen."

"That may be significant." Voss hoped his tone was deferential enough to encourage further confidences.

"I thought so, too." Jared Wilton guided the car into a winding gravel drive between square stone gateposts surmounted by light globes. Arched over the gateposts was an ornamental scroll of wrought iron with gilt letters spelling *Wiltonshire.*

The grounds of Wiltonshire were vivid green with creeper grass. Artificial terraces, lakes with bamboo bridges, stone statues of undraped maidens and iron stags peering from clumps of shrubbery recalled the extravagant banalities of the General Grant era.

The house itself was in a more gracious Victorian mood, although it had been built long after such designs had ceased to be fashionable. It was painted bright yellow with green trim and shutters. Its roof was gabled and its wings sprawled at either side, ending in wide verandas. Voss suspected the grounds and house were those of an old man carrying a boyhood dream over into a new age.

Wilton stopped the car beside the house and motioned Voss to get out. He followed, leaving the car in the drive. He seemed nervous.

"You'll meet Carter now," he muttered. "Don't let his good nature fool you."

James Morgan and a young woman were in a corner of the veranda side by side in a swinging seat. As Voss and Wilton neared them Morgan stopped talking to his companion and stood up.

"I guessed you'd be here for dinner," he informed Voss, "so I drifted around and wangled an invitation from Julia. She's so anxious to meet you she can hardly contain herself. Miss Bisbee is the name."

"My niece," Wilton supplied.

Voss bowed. Julia Bisbee looked as though she could contain herself admirably under any and all circumstances and wasn't anxious to meet anybody. She was darkly pretty with sullen eyes and a heavy mouth. She was about twenty-eight.

"From what I hear of today's happenings," she said, "you'll have an opportunity to try out your talents in Andor, Mr. Voss."

He laughed. "Not me. I'm on holiday."

Wilton inquired, "Anybody here?"

"Just Dorothea," replied Julia, and her eyes flashed indignantly. "She's ill again, poor thing!"

"Not more trouble, I hope?"

She shrugged. "I don't know. She was out— She just sort of folded up, I've put her to bed." She glanced swiftly at Voss to note whether he had marked her hesitation.

"That's too bad," Wilton said. "Where's Carter?"

"He went away this morning and hasn't come back yet. Probably hanging around with Unger and his friends all day." Her tone implied that wherever Carter had been she was vastly disinterested in him.

Jared Wilton led Voss into the house through luxury-crowded rooms that invariably had a touch of yellow somewhere in them. Upstairs he showed his guest the large bedroom and bath that were to be his quarters. Then they went down to a spacious library occupying the opposite wing.

One wall of the library was completely covered with bookshelves. Several tables were piled high with recent popular magazines. There was a large fireplace of Italian marble surmounted by a dull landscape in oil.

Wilton led Voss to a humidor. "I don't smoke or drink—don't believe in either of them—but I keep cigars for my guests. Help yourself."

"No, thanks; I don't smoke either." Voss saw the sudden gleam in Wilton's eyes and hastened to stave off the hoary witticism that had been hurled at him almost daily, since, at fifteen, he had topped seventy-two inches. "It stunts one's growth."

Wilton laughed feebly and looked disappointed. Voss lowered himself into a comfortable leather chair and stretched his legs in front of him.

"I see you've met our preacher," Wilton said. "What did you think of him?"

"He's entertaining. He's told me all about half the people in town. I don't feel like a stranger any more."

"I discovered him. He's a good youngster, well trained in spite of the fact that he was never graduated from his theological college. He's done a good job at the Tabernacle and hasn't complained because I've deliberately held down his salary and kept him from getting his ordination. That's an excellent sign. I intend to use what influence I have with the bishop to have him ordained, and I expect him to go far in the church.

"That's only one of my ways of doing good in the world. I help Morgan get his start, and Morgan goes through life helping others, even after I'm dead. That's real charity."

Before Voss could comment gracefully on his host's conception of doing good in this world by subsidizing a representative of the next, a man came unceremoniously into the library. He was of medium height, stocky, with grizzled hair and a pugnacious jaw. Voss knew at once who he must be; this was Claude Sackett, general manager of Wilton Woollies and, if Morgan was correct, as ruthless a man as the world contained. He barely acknowledged Wilton's introduction of Voss.

"Jared," he began explosively, "do you think it's wise to have these labor agitators in your house as guests? Do you want all our men to think you're in favor of unions?"

Wilton's eyes snapped. "I want them to think I'm not afraid of unions or anything else, Claude. I'm not, either."

Sackett flung himself into a chair, reached for the humidor without being invited and bit the end from a cigar. "Another thing," he said, lighting a match and puffing until he was almost hidden behind clouds of blue smoke, "you sent down orders to fire Russo. I want to hire him back first thing Monday morning. He's a good man and he was following orders when he broke up that meeting."

"Whose orders? I'm in charge of the mill."

"My orders; I'm responsible for the way things run. I don't want agitators interfering with our production."

"Well, I don't like Russo. He stays fired. He's nothing but a thug. I've heard that he served a term in Sing Sing for murder."

"Manslaughter, Jared. They're two different things. He was only given two years. Anyway, you've always believed in giving ex-convicts a chance. You've hired plenty of them."

"Not this ex-convict," Wilton repeated stubbornly. "He stays fired."

"All right—I'll give him a job around my place. Make him a chauffeur or a personal bodyguard." Sackett smiled brightly and turned to Voss. "Don't mind these fights. I have to get tough with Jared once in a while to keep him in line. Sometimes I get my own way. This time I don't."

Wilton stirred uncomfortably. "This time," he echoed, "you don't."

An apologetic cough sounded in the doorway. "May I come in, gentlemen?" The younger man who stood there had his forehead swathed in bandages. His eyes were swollen and his lips puffed. As he came into the room he limped. When he smiled, Voss saw that two of his front teeth were missing.

"Come in, come in!" Wilton rose and stepped forward cordially. "Mr. Frank, this is Mr. Sackett, my general manager, and Mr. Voss, the famous crime expert. We're all terribly sorry to see you banged up like this."

Sackett growled truculently, "I'm not."

Frank's grin was somewhat ghastly through his bruises, but it was genuine. He said, "I didn't think you'd be sorry, Sackett. To tell the truth, I'm not, either." He extended his hand to Voss.

"Martyrs are valuable, eh?" Voss murmured.

"Exactly. Why, on my way here—I walked, in spite of this hurt knee—at least a dozen of your men stopped me, Wilton, to say they were all for the union since we'd been treated so brutally. They were particularly angry because Miss Taylor was manhandled and thrown in the lake."

"You see?" Wilton demanded hotly. "That's what I told you, Claude. Your methods are the kind that will make trouble, not mine."

"Bah!" Sackett sneered. "If you'd leave it to me, there wouldn't be an organizer dare to come within five miles of the municipal limits."

"Anyway, Mr. Frank," said Wilton, "I've discharged the man who struck you."

"Why?" the labor leader asked curiously. "He was only doing what he thought was wanted. He's as much a victim of the system as you are."

Frank was very much at his ease. Even now when they were swollen and inflamed, he had friendly brown eyes in his lean, brown face. His hands were the hands of a work-ingman. He took a chair near Voss and made an effort to change the subject.

"What do you think of the murder?"

Wilton gazed at him indignantly. Before either he or Voss could speak, Julia Bisbee came to the door. A clock was chiming the hour of six.

"Shall we wait dinner for Carter?" she asked Wilton.

He transferred his indignation to her. "Of course not! It's high time Carter began to think of other people. We'll go right ahead without him."

As soon as they were gathered about the table Voss no-ticed the sudden unaccountable tension that had come over them all. He was assigned a place between Julia and Morgan. Wilton sat at the head of the table with Mor-gan at his left and Frank at his right. Sackett was beyond Frank. There were two vacant places and Voss assumed that Dorothea Wilton sat usually at the foot of the table and Carter at her left near the window.

A small, dark-eyed serving maid moved noiselessly about the table filling the water glasses—a worried-look-ing creature, plainly of Italian extraction.

Wilton reached for his glass and withdrew his hand as Morgan bowed his head. Everyone bowed his head, except Julia and Frank, who stared blankly at each other until the clergyman had finished with his brief, mumbled prayer.

The silence became strained, almost intolerable.

Wilton cleared his throat loudly. "Well, well!" he exclaimed impatiently, "let's get started." He lifted his water glass. "Nothing like good food to—"

A child's high-pitched scream broke in on him. Julia leaped to her feet; Voss almost stumbled on her heels as he made for the window. Through it, he could see a small boy running across the lawn from the stream, half sobbing, half screaming, as he came. At his heels a small dog raced and yapped in excitement.

Now Voss could make out the child's words. He was crying over and over, "Miss Bisbee! Miss Bisbee!"

Julia left the window. "That's what comes of feeding them jam and cookies when they play around the house," she said, her voice queerly flat. "Toby probably cut his finger or bruised his knee." She went out to the veranda and leaned against the railing, waiting for the child to come nearer.

Those at the table could see her through the window. Everyone watched, tense and unmoving. As the boy panted across the lawn, Voss saw that he was about seven, with golden curls and brown eyes.

The woman leaned far toward him across the railing. She called, "What is it, Toby? What's the matter?"

The shrill answer reached them all. "It's Mr. Carter, Miss Bisbee! He's down by the swimming hole. There's blood all over—and he doesn't move."

5

It seemed to Voss that the silence that followed was less one of shock or apprehension than of caution. They all looked at each other quickly, eyes traveling from face to face, and then, more quickly, out the window again.

Voss suggested at last, "We'd better go down."

"I know the way," said Sackett. "Follow me." He hurried out of the room, across the veranda and over the lawn with Voss keeping effortlessly at his side. Jared Wilton hobbled after them, flanked by Morgan and the bandaged Frank, who also limped.

Julia remained leaning against the railing, staring down fixedly at the curly-headed child. Toby and the dog stared back at her, panting with open mouths.

Where the lawn gave way to the knee-high grass of meadows a narrow footpath wound toward the trees that marked the course of the stream. The dark earth was hard packed, but here and there Voss's watchful eyes picked out the small imprint of the heel of a woman's shoe. They were daintier heels than those Julia was wearing that evening.

The path went through a corner of the woods into which Carter Wilton had followed Jared the day before. It rose to the crest of a low hill from which Voss could see Unger's cottage and the bench on which he had sat that afternoon with Morgan. Then it dipped to the water.

The stream, when they reached it, proved to branch away from Mill River above the dam. Its waters were untainted by chemicals. The only dye in them now came from the wound in Carter Wilton's throat.

Carter Wilton had been nearly ten years younger than his brother. He had been taller and leaner and his face, contorted as it was by agony and horror, nevertheless showed traces of a weak handsomeness. His hair was dark and straight and flecked with gray only at the temples. Across his upper lip was a thin black mustache, carefully tended. His eyes were slate gray; just now they were open, turned upward toward his arched brows.

He lay on his back, his arms and legs sprawled across the sand, his shoulders and head in shallow water that rose to the level of his ears. His muddy clothes were disheveled and stained with blood. The open wound in his throat had ceased bleeding and Voss noticed that there were flies crawling around its edges. Voss forced himself to look; the brutal, practical details of death never failed to shock him momentarily.

"He's dead all right," Sackett muttered. "So dead he'll never make any more trouble in this world."

Voss stooped and put the back of his hand against the wrist at the shaded side of the body. "He's been dead an hour or two anyway," he hazarded. "He's cold."

Beside the body was the single perfect print of a woman's shoe. Even as Voss studied it a foot descended and blotted it out. He glanced up to find Sackett apparently absorbed in the scenery across the stream, but Voss did not believe that the obliteration of that footprint had been accidental.

Jared Wilton came stamping up. He gazed at the body for a long minute and turned suddenly away. It appeared for a moment that he was going to be sick; then he walked to a big rock twenty feet back from the water and sat down and did not look at the corpse again.

Morgan said, "May God have mercy on his soul." He made an odd gesture like dropping a pinch of earth on a coffin at a burial. His face was pale and his forehead gleamed with sweat.

There was no sign of emotion in Frank's face unless his brown eyes looked a little sadder. It was hard to tell, they were so discolored. He asserted, "There was quite a battle. The sand is all plowed up."

"All plowed up by intent," Voss supplemented. "The killer's footprints were here. He obliterated them with that dead branch while standing in the grass."

Voss watched Sackett to see whether the latter would react to the use of the pronoun "he." But Sackett's eyes did not so much as flicker.

"The murderer must have been spattered with blood," Frank pursued.

"Not necessarily." Voss was peering into the limpid water, searching the pebbly bottom vainly for the weapon. "If the victim wasn't expecting an attack the killer might have made a clean cut and leaped clear. It would take the wounded man two or three minutes to die and during that time he'd struggle."

"Like a chicken with its head cut off," Sackett said with unnecessary brutality.

Voss was struck by a strange circumstance. None of the four men around him betrayed the slightest sign of grief at Carter Wilton's death. He even fancied there was a look of approval on Sackett's face.

A movement in the path attracted his attention. He turned, then astonishment held him motionless. Julia was coming toward them, her arm around the waist of a tall young woman in a pale blue wrapper.

The tall woman was white as death itself. Her level eyes were gray as mist and her hair hung around her straight shoulders like a storm cloud. Her lips were pale and when she stopped walking her breasts, outlined vaguely by the fleecy stuff of her wrapper, rose and fell with her breathing.

She said in a loud whisper, speaking like a person in a trance, "The child was right. Carter is dead. I couldn't . . . I had to see for myself. . . ."

And she turned and started back the way she had come, still erect, still supported by Julia's arm.

"His wife!" Voss told himself. It had been a fantastic, unreal moment. He was surprised to find her even more beautiful than Unger's portrait—more ethereal, less human.

Then he caught the expression on Morgan's face and was surprised again. If ever a man's soul stood naked in his eyes, Morgan's soul did at that instant. The young minister might worship the God he served in Andor Tabernacle, but he also worshiped Dorothea Wilton.

"Somebody will have to phone for Fleming and an undertaker," Sackett was saying. "And somebody ought to stay with the body till they get here."

"I'll stay," Frank offered. "Wilton's all in and had better be helped back to the house and the rest of you probably will want to be there, too. I won't intrude. When the police get here I can go straight home. It's close."

"All right." Sackett started toward Jared Wilton, then turned again. "I'll tell Fleming you're keeping watch for me so he won't be nasty."

"A good idea." Frank grinned wryly. "I've had about enough nastiness for one day."

Voss lingered with Frank a moment, taking a last look at the corpse and the sand around it. He asked, "You aren't squeamish?"

"I've seen plenty of blood. I've shed a little of my own and seen many others shed theirs. It's a tough calling, mine."

"And profitless?"

"No." The labor leader shook his head vehemently. "In the end we always win. The sooner people like Wilton and Sackett learn that, the better it will be all around."

Toby and the dog were sitting on the bottom step of the veranda when the men reached the house. Wilton limped past without noticing the woebegone youngster and was helped by Morgan into a chair. He seemed to have aged twenty years in the last half hour.

Sackett hurried into the house to telephone. Julia and Dorothea were nowhere to be seen.

Voss sat beside the urchin. "What's your name?" he asked.

"Toby, sir," the boy piped in a clear treble.

"Just Toby?"

"Toby Smith, sir. And this is Rags." The dog cocked an ear at the mention of his name.

"Do you swim pretty good?"

"No, sir. Aunt Clara tells me never to go where the water is deep so I have to swim where I saw—that man!" The child's eyes clouded. "Now I'll be afraid to go there again and Aunt Clara won't let me go where it's deep and the other boys swim."

"Aunt Clara. Is her name Smith, too?"

"No, sir. Some people call her Mrs. Weston and some people call her the Widow Weston when she isn't there. Only I call her Aunt Clara. She takes care of me."

"You're pretty lucky," Voss said. "Aunt Clara takes care of you and Miss Bisbee gives you cookies and jam."

"Miss Bisbee gives me more 'n that," Toby declared stoutly. "She gives me clothes an' toys, too. She comes to see me a lot. She's the nicest lady in the world—even nicer 'n Aunt Clara."

"You certainly are lucky." Voss brought a handful of change out of his pocket and picked out the shiniest dime of the lot. "Do you think it would give you a stomach ache if you spent this for ice cream or candy?"

Toby's eyes were brighter than the dime. "Course it wouldn't!" he hooted. Then his face fell. "Thank you just the same, sir, but Miss Bisbee says I must never take money from strangers."

"Miss Bisbee is exactly right. But I'm no stranger, Toby. Why, I was having dinner with Miss Bisbee when you came."

"That's right." Toby's face almost disappeared in his smile and he stretched out a soiled hand. "Thank you, sir, very, very much."

Voss wandered into the house. The sun was setting, no lights had been turned on and the rooms were filled with quiet dusk. He moved aimlessly toward the library and was well inside the door before a sharply drawn breath warned him of another presence. He saw Julia crouching in the light of a small fire on the hearth.

"I beg your pardon," he said and returned to the veranda.

A sedan came speeding along the driveway, throwing gravel as it skidded around the curves. When it slid to a stop, Chief of Police Fleming and a khaki-uniformed policeman and a tall man with a doctor's bag got out. Sackett went to meet them.

"Hello, Dr. Hughson," he said. The tall man nodded a greeting, his pale face serious and preoccupied. "I'll take you to the scene. Did you call the undertaker, Fleming?"

"Yeh," Fleming told him. "He'll be along in a few minutes."

Morgan trailed after Sackett and the others. Voss remained with Wilton.

He said, "Pretty much of a shock for you."

Wilton breathed deeply. Plainly he was feeling pangs of remorse.

"A terrible shock," he mumbled. "I wish I hadn't suspected Carter of wanting to kill me. The more I think about it the more I see how I could be wrong about that."

Voss chuckled inwardly. He was amused by Wilton's effort to clear himself by suggesting that he was not afraid of his brother after all.

But the young man's face was serious as he replied, "There was no harm done. You took care of him, didn't you—gave him spending money and all that?"

"Yes, I gave him a lot at one time or another. His business ventures cost me nearly a million dollars. Lately I'd cut down on him. . . . We had some words over that."

"Had he been married long?"

"Two years. Too long for Dorothea, I'm afraid. Everybody advised her against it, but Carter was a convincing talker and I guess she thought she could change his ways. I hoped she could, at one time. The marriage broke Morgan's heart; he was in love with her, but he took it like a good sport.

"Carter wasn't a model husband, though. He would disappear for weeks at a time. He liked to drink more than was good for him and there was always talk of his affairs with other women. He was hanging around that girl at the cottage, the writer for that radical paper, they told me. And he had fits of violence. He struck Dorothea once while Sackett was here and Sackett knocked him down. You saw how he slashed the painting in my office."

"Was there bad blood between him and Sackett after that?"

"Not especially. In his lighter moods Carter was a good-natured fellow. He laughed everything off. Even his prison record. You knew he'd been a convict?"

"How was that?"

"It was a long time ago. In nineteen-twenty-four and twenty-five. He was living in New York and he'd forged some checks. He was in for thirty or forty thousand dollars. They caught him and sent him to the pen for eighteen months.

"I'd have helped him, but I didn't have that kind of money in nineteen-twenty-four. I made it late that year and the following year. When he came out I gave him enough so he'd never have to do anything shady. The only other trouble he ever got in was woman trouble."

"Did he care a lot for Dorothea?"

A little flame appeared in each of Wilton's eyes. "He hated her as only a bad man can hate a good woman. He couldn't stomach her goodness for some reason. I think he was a little afraid of her, too."

"In what way?"

Wilton did not answer. He sat for a moment watching a long black car turn into the drive. Then he sighed. "But after all—he was my brother. The job I hired you to do has ceased to exist. Mr. Voss, will you take another in its place?"

"Carter's murderer?" asked Voss.

Wilton nodded "The same arrangements?"

"The same," said Voss. "And the same condition." Wilton turned his head sharply toward him, then nodded.

"That's all right," he said.

The long black car had come to a stop in front of the veranda. A brass plate on the side bore the legend: "J. T. Woolcott, Undertaker." A scrawny youth was at the wheel and a fat, jolly-looking man sat beside him.

"Hello," the fat man called to Wilton. He removed his hat and bared a hairless scalp. "Sorry to hear the news, Mr. Wilton."

"Hello, Jerry. You'll find them all at the end of the path." Without acknowledging the undertaker's expression of sympathy, Wilton indicated the direction with a tired nod of his head.

Jerry Woolcott and his helper climbed to the ground. The latter went to the back of the car and took out a long wicker basket with a cover. He balanced it jauntily on his shoulder and the pair started toward the path. Voss reflected that the police were going to have to work very much at second hand. But Wilton was the law in Andor.

Morgan appeared, coming toward the house, walking fast. He came up on the veranda, quite breathless, and flashed Voss a signal with his eyes. Voss strolled toward him.

"I decided you ought to know," Morgan whispered. "I don't think Fleming wants to get to the bottom of this murder."

"No?"

"No. They moved the body and there was some writing in the sand. Fleming saw it and mentioned it before he read it. Then he kicked up the sand with his foot so it couldn't be seen any more and said he guessed he'd been mistaken. But I saw the writing—four letters dug into the sand with a stick or a finger."

"What were they?"

"S—A—C—K—and a straight line that might have been part of an E."

"No imagination needed there. How large were they?"

"About three inches high."

"Under the body?"

"No. Close to the side of it. They were near the right hand."

"Did Sackett see them?"

"I don't think so. But Fleming will tell him first chance he gets. They're cronies."

"It's a good thing Fleming isn't a blackmailer. He might have covered up the letters and got a picture of them before he destroyed them."

"He wouldn't dare. Sackett's too tough to be handled that way."

"I wonder if Frank noticed anything?"

"I doubt it. He kept his mouth shut. He left for Unger's cottage as soon as the police got there. You see, Carter's coat covered most of the letters and nobody would be apt to notice them until he was moved."

"Hmmm. Thanks, Morgan. I'll remember that."

"You can remember, too, that I'm not afraid of Sackett. If a witness is needed to testify . . ." He left the sentence unfinished.

Voss nodded. His eyes were scanning the darkening hills where a peculiar figure was limping toward town. He said to Morgan, "There's Clubfoot Crippen, the idiot. Has he ever been violent?"

"Good heavens, no! He's harmless as a baby. He lives alone in a cave back in those hills—has lived there ever since he drifted to Andor, seven or eight years ago. He's never caused the slightest trouble."

Morgan went over to Wilton. He said something in a low tone about the ways of God being obscure, but always just.

Voss sat on the top step and watched the idiot limp through the lengthening shadows. Julia came out and sat beside him. Most of the strain that had been apparent in her face and bearing had vanished. Her forehead was smooth and her mouth was in repose. But her eyes brooded.

"I want to ask you something," she said. "When you came into the library and I was there, did you notice I was startled?"

"I heard a sort of gasp from you. I guessed you hadn't wanted anyone to come in at that time."

"I hadn't. Did you see what I was doing?"

"You were kneeling in front of a fire you had apparently just lighted. You were burning something."

"Do you know that, or is it a guess?"

"I know it. You were burning a piece of cloth. It looked like a white dress or a part of one."

"I'm not so sure you're right about that."

"I'm sure. It was pleated like a skirt and I think it was linen. The ashes would tell."

"Not if I powdered them and swept them down the chimney."

"Perhaps not then."

"Well, that's what I did."

"You were wise," he said. "Because I not only saw the dress—I saw what was on it. A big stain, brownish red. A bloodstain, I imagine."

6

The thin, straw-haired girl behind the general delivery window in the post office had been exercising her deductive and intuitive faculties. She gave Abelard Voss two letters and a languishing look.

"This one," she said, fingering the long thick envelope with the imprint of the Police Department of the City of New York, "came on the late train yesterday. It looks and feels important. And this one"— she altered her voice and flipped the stained envelope with its typed address—"was on the floor under the mail slot this morning, so it's only from one of the yokels. A fan letter, maybe."

Voss escaped before she could carry her deductions further. When he reached the sidewalk, he thrust the official letter in his pocket and examined the other one. The address had a familiar look—it had been typed on the same machine as the note inviting him to Andor. He recognized the broken spur of the capital "V" and the small "e" struck considerably below the level of the other letters.

Within the envelope was a torn slip of cheap paper bearing a solitary thumbprint, beautifully etched in black ink, and the words:

Abelard Voss:
Aren't you glad you took my tip?
A. V. Atkinson

Voss scowled, replaced the paper in the envelope and put it in his inner pocket. He strode without a definite destination along Main Street, so preoccupied that he was unaware of the sharp and curious eyes that followed his progress from half a dozen doorways.

He felt the welcome coolness when the awning of the Commercial House cut off the bright morning sun, however, and noted that the armchairs near the entrance were as yet untenanted and formed an orderly and inviting row. For the time being it seemed the most solitary spot in town. He sat in one of the chairs and extended his gangling legs across the sidewalk.

With less care than he had accorded the other envelope he tore open the fat one and withdrew the lengthy communication from Lieutenant Bob Saint-Amour of the New York Homicide Squad. As he perused the neat pages his eyes grew ever more thoughtful.

> Dear Ab [ran the letter]: I hope to God your interest in Andrew Vivian Atkinson is not merely academic. It would be worth plenty to turn him up, partly because he's the kind of guy that is likely to kill again and partly because Allied Chemical Industries will pay twenty-five thousand dollars' reward for him.
>
> He's strictly a nut of the brilliant, idealistic type. He went in for science because he wanted to serve humanity and turned sour when he discovered nobody had much use for idealism. He was doing laboratory work with Allied Chemical twelve years ago this summer and his boss, a man named Stone, put him and two other men experimenting with a new formula for wartime poison gas—the deadliest ever concocted.

Atkinson couldn't keep his mind on his work for thinking of the poor devils who might die some day because of it. He couldn't sleep nights. He brooded till his mind cracked completely.

One day he took a pistol to work with him. He killed Stone and the two men working with him, the only ones who knew the formula. He phoned the police and surrendered quietly, very proud of himself.

He was sure no jury would convict him because he had done a great service to mankind and as a matter of fact some other nuts succeeded in arousing considerable public opinion in his favor. But the public opinion didn't penetrate to the courtroom and the jury found him guilty of murder in the first degree and he was slated for the chair.

The day he was sentenced he bragged to the judge, "God won't let you electrocute me." He was on the second floor of the Criminal Courts Building next door to the Tombs and he made a dive for the window and jumped.

Cops shot at him from the windows and the street but he made a clean getaway. They said he limped as though one leg was broken. That didn't stop him from getting around a corner and into a car, though, and to this day nobody has ever heard from him.

I don't blame you for not remembering the name. I didn't, either, till I looked up the record. You were just a kid reading dime novels when it happened. But it's still a live case and the reward offer has never been withdrawn.

If you've got a line on Atkinson for Pete's sake let me in on it! I'll hop a rattler to Andor

—wherever that may be—or anywhere else. It's a cinch the guy will repeat some day if he's still alive. That variety of lunatic, as you know, sees injustice everywhere and can't help doing something about it, getting more and more violent as he goes along.

His description twelve years ago was: Thirty-five years, five feet eleven, a hundred and fifty pounds, dark eyes and hair, scar from acid burn on left forearm. There's more, but that will give you a general idea in case you think you may bump into him. . . .

A smooth and cultured voice broke in upon Voss's meditations. It inquired, "How goes the investigation?"

The young man glanced up from the letter to encounter the eyes of Dr. John Hughson. The physician was a distinguished-looking man with his graying hair and the tailored navy-blue suit that made his slender figure seem more so. He was carrying his medical case toward his office just beyond the Commercial House.

"Sit down," Voss said. "I was on my way to your place. Did you finish the autopsies on Stott and Wilton?"

Hughson nodded and seated himself beside Voss, balancing the case on his knees.

"They were both murdered just as it appeared at first if that's what you want to know. Stott had been in Mill River about four days, and Wilton had been stabbed at least two hours before I saw the body, and more likely three or four hours."

"There's no possibility Stott committed suicide?"

"None whatever. He was struck twice by a heavy metal instrument with a corrugated edge and either blow alone was enough to kill him instantly. There were flecks of iron rust in the wounds. Nothing he could have struck while falling would make the same kind of marks. Furthermore, he couldn't have wrapped the chains around his legs and fastened them as the killer did and he couldn't have jumped from the window trussed up that way."

"Jared Wilton will have to give up his pet theory, then."

"Jared already has. Since his brother was killed he's sure there's a homicidal maniac lurking in the vicinity. He called me last night after you'd gone to bed. Said his heart was bothering him and he was afraid of an attack, but he only wanted someone to talk to."

"He kept me up pretty late talking about everything except the murders."

"He's really scared—so scared you'd think his conscience wasn't easy."

Voss shrugged. "Is anybody's? Was Carter's, I wonder? By the way, did you run into anything there?"

"I found out he'd have been dead pretty soon anyway. He'd lived a fast life and his insides weren't pretty. Liver practically gone, heart enlarged, stomach ulcerated—"

"He couldn't have cut his own throat?"

Hughson shook his head. "Someone got him with a wild sweep from his left. His arm couldn't have swung the knife that way. Anyway, I understand no weapon was found near the body."

"I hadn't forgotten that. Only sometimes people find it worth while to make suicides look like murders."

"This wasn't one of the times. His left wrist was clawed, too, with small sharp fingernails. A woman's, I'm pretty sure."

"A woman's!"

A new voice above and behind them entered the conversation—Pop Kramer's. He was standing in the hotel entrance just within the screen door and appeared to have been standing there watching and listening for some time.

"He had a wrestling match with that girl at Unger's cottage," Kramer said. "I saw 'em after the riot yesterday.

I was walking along Main Street and when I got to Cherry Street I could see through to the cottage. They were in the yard."

Hughson rose abruptly. "You seem to see and hear everything that happens in this town," he observed coldly.

"Got to, to keep up with the gossips," Kramer said. "They're stiff competition."

The doctor nodded to Voss and went on toward his office without further notice of the publisher.

Pop Kramer chuckled deep in his throat.

"I scorched his hide once for not making the sanitary inspections he's supposed to as Health Officer. Best way to combat the germs he ignores is to start drinking beer early in the morning. Have one with me."

"No," said Voss, "but I'll go in and watch you."

He accompanied Kramer across the cracked linoleum of the lobby into the cool gloom of the bar. The editor lifted a smudged forefinger for the benefit of the white-aproned individual behind the polished mahogany.

"One, Pete," he ordered. "Our famous criminologist is nothing but an overgrown sissy."

"Hell," Pete rejoined, "he's got to keep his head clear for his job. Catchin' killers ain't like runnin' a small town newspaper; it takes brains."

"Brains be damned!" Kramer took a long swallow of the amber fluid and wiped foam from his upper lip with the smudged forefinger, leaving a blue-black stain that resembled half a mustache. "Who's your current suspect, Voss?"

"A man named Atkinson. A. V. Atkinson."

"Don't believe I know him." Kramer's shaggy brows huddled in concentration for a long minute then sprang apart and upward. "Yes, I do, too! I get it! The mad idealist ridding a community of its vermin! It fits right in with my work of prophecy."

Voss showed his astonishment. "You know about Atkinson?"

"Sure, I do. He was big stuff in the papers back in nineteen-twenty-five. Killed a gang of chemists to keep 'em from making some kind of poison gas or liquid fire. I always thought it was a good thing. Were you kidding when you mentioned him?"

"Maybe. Maybe not. I've been trying to make up my mind."

He was staring in fascination at Kramer's hairy, muscular forearm. On the back of it near the wrist was a smooth triangle of pink flesh puckered at the edges—an old scar that might have come after an acid burn.

Kramer had mentioned being shot at by New York cops twelve years ago. He was about five feet eleven inches and had dark hair and eyes. He would have been about thirty-five years old in the days when Atkinson was on trial for his life.

Kramer said, "Son, I'm a mind reader. I can see right through you like you were made of glass. You're not worrying about any fellow named Atkinson—you're worrying about *me*. I'll tell you just how you've got it figured out.

"You know a lot of people have got it in for me and I've got it in for them right back. You know I like to see the wicked come to grief whether the justice that overtakes them is legal or poetic. You know I've been prophesying hell fire ever since I started the *Advertiser* and folks have been kidding me about my stuff not holding water and I'd give my three remaining teeth to see things start to happen."

He propped his chin in the heel of his hand and looked straight into Voss's eyes.

"So when the kidding gets too much under my skin what do I do? Why, I start out to fulfill my own predictions and at the same time rid the town of a lot of people I don't like.

"Maybe you've discovered I had a quarrel last week with Richard Stott. He wanted to use the *Advertiser* to promote some of his own private ideas about social justice which didn't jibe with either of the schools of thought in Andor. I told him I was interested in the fights, not the theory. He was pretty mad at me. So I sneaked into the mill the other night when I knew he was at work—an easy thing to do with only a couple of watchmen on duty—and hit him on the head and dropped him out the window.

"Yesterday I happened to see Carter Wilton trying to steal a kiss or something from the Taylor girl and I decided to make him my second victim. I've hated his guts for a long time, mostly because I've known his wife since she was in pigtails and she deserves better than him. All the town was either at work in the mill or gossiping over back fences about the fight there and it was simple for me to follow Carter on his way home through that hilly country till I got him in a good spot for butchering. Then I hurried back to have a bottle of beer with you, laughing up my sleeve all the time."

He took another swallow of beer and sloshed the rest around in the glass to make it foam.

"Do you think I ought to kill a couple more right away?" he inquired innocently. "Or should I sort of string 'em out to keep the paper in news?"

Voss breathed deeply and shook his head a little.

"Impudence and imprudence are hard to tell apart sometimes, Kramer. If I were a cop and you gave me that kind of case against yourself I'd lock you up on the off chance you were telling the truth. As it is, I'm going for a walk and think things over. If I were you I wouldn't tell that to anybody else."

"Hey!" Kramer called after him in dismay. "Fleming will nail me down if you spill it to him! I was speaking confidentially. I've been in better jails than Andor's and haven't liked 'em."

"I won't tell on you," Voss promised. "Not today, anyway."

He went straight to the railroad station, though, and scribbled a telegram to Saint-Amour suggesting that the latter come to Andor as soon as possible and bring all available identification records.

7

Forty or fifty men were standing at Main Street and Wilton Drive talking and laughing in loud excitement. Some of them stood in the center of the street blocking traffic, to protect a length of canvas that stretched from curb to curb.

A man holding the end of a light rope in his teeth began to climb a telephone pole, his feet and hands slapping fiercely against the spikes that jutted from the wood. Opposite him a second man mounted a second telephone pole with the other end of the rope between his clamped teeth.

The strip of canvas rose into the air with its weighted lower edge sagging and its middle bellying with the breeze. Tall red letters were gay in the sunlight. When the rope was pulled taut and bent around the poles the letters came into line and formed the screaming sentence:

STRIKE NOW TO END WILTON BRUTALITY!

Forty or fifty husky throats emitted a ragged cheer that lasted ten seconds and trailed off in a series of cheerful minor whoops.

Leslie Frank stepped out of the group to meet Abelard Voss. The bandages around the agitator's forehead were soiled, the soft flesh around his eyes was a darker purple than it had been and his lameness was more pronounced. His smile, however, was confident.

He said, "Yesterday morning these men didn't give a damn for all my arguments, but the minute they saw blood spilled they began spoiling for a battle."

Voss said, "I see half a hundred of them. The mill employs three thousand."

"The thing is cumulative. Fifteen minutes ago there were only a dozen here. Tonight you'll see a thousand men in Main Street selling one another on the idea of unionism. When the mill opens Monday morning every man, woman and child will be ready to sign up."

"Then you'll strike the mill?"

Frank shrugged. "It depends on Sackett and Wilton. Personally I hope Sackett tries to make more trouble. There's nothing like a strike to solidify our ranks. But if Sackett takes the wiser course and recognizes the union we'll probably negotiate for some small concessions and let it go at that."

"Sackett impressed me as wise enough."

"He is, in a way. But he certainly doesn't understand the psychology of the American workingman. They are docile when handled right. These men can be led to hell and back, but they can't be driven an inch without plenty of whipping."

"Sackett was behind whatever brutality there was. Why not put his name on your banner instead of Wilton's?"

Frank gave Voss a keen look. "You know better than to ask that. These men are employees of Wilton Woollies, Incorporated, not of Claude Sackett. Because of his guise as a friend, Wilton's our worst enemy, just as Sackett is our best friend as long as he remains openly against us."

Voss laughed. "You play the game scientifically, don't you?"

"The rules were made centuries ago. Look at the history books and see how every battle between the classes was won. In every case you find a bullheaded tyrant flying in the face of common sense and an enlightened leadership taking full advantage of his bullheadedness. The masses who are to reap the benefits of progress follow the smartest ones blindly. They're saved in spite of themselves."

"And they talk of democracy!"

"It's the nearest thing to it on the globe today. Real democracy is a very distant goal. The end of the work I am doing is too far in the future for most people to comprehend. It isn't important in itself that we win perhaps five cents an hour more pay for the Wilton employees and perhaps an extra five or six hours of leisure a week. But it will be important to their children and *their* children that the victory was won.

"The worst thing Wilton could do from our point of view would be to build his workers palaces and pay each of them a thousand dollars every Friday night. That way he would help perpetuate a paternalism that must be scrapped. It would be a thousand times better if the men through their own efforts demanded and got a two-dollar, raise. Do you see, my point?"

"Oh, yes. You're using smart tactics, but you're also fighting smart men. Do you really think you'll win this particular skirmish?"

"We'll win," Frank assured him, "because we'll go further than Wilton or Sackett can go. There isn't any sacrifice too great for us to make."

The workmen had begun to move toward the mill end of town. Two men were carrying a second strip of canvas rolled up on their shoulders. A third had a coil of rope. All of them looked supremely happy.

Frank waved carelessly to Voss and joined them. He called back, "If you're near the cottage stop in and see my host. He's banged up so badly he can't get out of bed."

A solid wall of late-blooming rambler roses, white and pink and red, surrounded the neat brown house of Clara Weston, who had fed and sheltered Richard Stott during his five years in Andor. The flowery barrier came to the height of an ordinary man's head and effectively guarded the front and back yards from the casual observation of passers-by. Abelard Voss could just see over the top of it.

He could see a boy and a dog and a woman wearing a pink dress beneath a latticed arbor at the side of the house. The woman sat in a wicker chair leaning forward and talking and the boy and the dog sat in the grass on their small haunches and listened attentively, watching every movement of her face.

As Voss passed through the gate he could hear the woman saying, "And the littlest of the three bears began to cry because somebody had eaten all the porridge out of his bowl, and there wasn't another speck in the funny little house—"

The ancient tale came to an untimely end as the teller caught sight of Voss. She was Julia Bisbee and her dark eyes were somewhat misty and there was about her an appearance of untidy prettiness. A pink flush swept over her face in a slow wave before Voss's amused stare.

"Go right ahead," he urged. "I like stories."

"Go on, Miss Bisbee," Toby echoed. Both he and the dog glanced at Voss with solemn reproach reminding him that he should have known better than to interrupt.

But Julia did not continue. She was embarrassed. She twisted her hands and looked at them. She said, "Toby and I are pretty good friends. Sometimes I stop to see him when I'm passing."

"Sometimes!" Toby deprecated. "Yesterday you didn't come. You wouldn't seen me at all if I hadn't gone swimmin' and found that man an' that—"

"Hush, dear!" said Julia.

"—an' that white lady there—"

"Hush!" Julia commanded more sharply.

"White lady?" Voss asked.

"You mustn't pay any attention to Toby. He—he has the most vivid imagination you ever heard of. He had some kind of a silly dream last night about a lady in white."

"A white lady," Toby repeated. "An' the man carried her off."

Julia patted his curls. "Yes, I know. But we won't talk about it any more. We'll talk about nice things—"

"She's nice!"

"—about the three bears." Her eyes pleaded with Voss.

"I came to see Mrs. Weston," Voss said, taking pity on her.

"You'll find her in the kitchen. Go to the back door that way." Julia pointed.

As he walked away she took up the thread of the nursery tale where she had dropped it.

"And so the littlest bear began to cry."

The Widow Weston opened the back door, came out on the tiny porch, sat on a painted bench and seemed highly pleased at the prospect of having someone to talk to. She was small, birdlike, bright-eyed, with only a sprinkling of gray in her brown hair.

"What did you say your name was?" she asked. "Bross? Sloss?"

"Voss. I'm staying at Wiltonshire. I wondered what you could tell me about your late roomer Mr. Stott."

The change that came over Clara Weston was discouraging and bewildering. She had been smiling expectantly; in the space of a split second she was literally quivering with grief. Two big tears rolled down her faded cheeks and she fumbled in the pocket of her apron for a handkerchief. As soon as she found it the storm of weeping burst.

"For-forgive me, Mr. Goss!" she sobbed. "E-every time I hear his n-name it makes me behave like this!"

He was dismayed. He said, "I'm sorry. I didn't know."

She controlled herself with a valiant effort and blew her nose.

"He was such a fine man, so upstanding and kind! He reminded me *so* much of my poor dead husband. They were both true gentlemen."

The pangs of remembering both of them at once set off the tears again, a flood of them. Voss shifted uneasily on the railing of the porch.

"We needn't talk about it any more if you don't want to," he told her. "I only wanted to find out something about his life. No one seems to know much about what he did before he came here."

She seized eagerly upon the point, determined to talk about Richard Stott if her weeping drowned her.

"That's right—no one knows. He was a man of mystery, Mr. Ross. I think there must have been some awful tragedy in his life. He acted like a man whose heart had been broken—who had wandered all over the world trying to forget."

"Where had he wandered?"

"He never said. But I could tell from the way he talked he'd been in a lot of places. New York and Boston. Maybe even across the sea."

"You don't know where he came here from?"

"No. It was enough for me that he was a gentleman. A perfect gentleman, I'll have you know. He was always kind and respectful and for all I was alone with him hours on end there was never a suggestive word or action from him." She sighed. "He wasn't one of those soft-spoken fly-by-nights. When he didn't come home Monday night I knew something dreadful must have happened. He was thrifty—" She stopped herself suddenly.

"Did he have any enemies?"

"He shouldn't have had. I don't see how anyone could have hated him. And yet someone must have, to do that terrible thing—someone out of his past, perhaps. Of course it was mostly the fault of that man Kramer."

"How?"

"Always printing items about murder and death. Putting bad thoughts in people's heads. He's an evil person. I used to tell Mr. Stott he shouldn't spend so much time talking to him. He's never set foot inside a church that I can remember and I've lived in Andor all my life."

"You said Mr. Stott was thrifty. Could someone have been trying to rob him?"

She glanced at him sharply. "He didn't make much money. What I meant was, he didn't waste all his pay on foolishness like so many of these unmarried men who are too selfish to marry and settle down. I don't guess he left anything. I'm paying Mr. Woolcott for the funeral because it's the least I can do."

"What did he do in his spare time?"

Mrs. Weston waved her hand vaguely. "He worked around the house. He had a lot of queer things in his room he fussed with. He kept the garden and took care of the flowers. I don't know how I'll get on without him; I feel that losing him has made me a widow all over again!"

Once more the tears welled up in her eyes, but she dammed them long enough to clarify her last statement.

"Understand, when I say 'widow' I don't mean what most of the folks in Andor would think if they were to hear me. There was never anything between us the whole world couldn't know. I might have been really his widow, though, if this . . ."

The floodgates could withstand the strain no longer. They gave way explosively.

Voss waited till the attack of grief had worn itself out. He said tentatively, "I was talking to Toby. He's quite a boy. Your nephew?"

She fidgeted. "I—well, yes."

"Is his mother living?"

"No, thank God!" she cried. "She died when Toby was a baby—the wretch! She—she wasn't married."

"Oh," said Voss.

"Well may you say 'oh!' It isn't half what the women in this town said when the boy came. Think of my own sister disgracing me that way and never even telling who the father was! Of course," she added as an afterthought, "it isn't the poor child's fault."

"Of course it isn't!"

"And then Mr. Stott was so fond of him. Mr. Stott said it didn't make a bit of difference that Toby was a . . . wasn't like other children. I think that was noble of him."

"It was very sensible."

"He was *such* a good man—"

Voss left her sitting on the bench, quite incoherent with her memories of Richard Stott's nobility. He went back to the arbor and discovered that Julia had completed the story of Goldilocks and the Three Bears to Toby's and Rags' complete satisfaction.

"I'm just going back to Wiltonshire for lunch," she said. "Will you go with me?"

He nodded, clapped Toby on the shoulder, and fell into step beside her. They took the curving path that passed Unger's cottage. In the front yard Ruth Taylor was sitting under a twisted pear tree, her hair blowing, tapping the keys of a portable typewriter. Unger, his head a mass of bandages and his tall form bent painfully, was limping around the side of the cottage.

"Martyrs have a hard time of it," Voss observed. Julia started.

"What? Oh, I see. I don't think I'd waste any sympathy there. There are other martyrs, more innocent."

"You're thinking about Toby."

"Yes. I suppose Mrs. Weston told you his story. I don't know why, but she insists on telling everyone as though it were something that shouldn't be forgotten."

"It's the way she was taught. The sins of the fathers shall be visited on the children. . . ."

"She's good enough to the child. But as he gets older his life will be desperately unhappy. Already some of the other boys call him names. He's still too young, to understand."

"It's tragic."

"I'll never marry and have a home of my own," Julia said firmly, "but if ever I did the first thing I'd do would be to adopt Toby."

"It would be a splendid thing for him. I hope you change your mind about marrying for Toby's sake."

She laughed shakily. "It's not my mind. It's somebody else's mind that needs changing!"

When they reached the yellow mansion Jared Wilton was pacing the veranda. His hands were clasped behind his back.

"Wilton brutality!" he shouted at them. "After all my kindness—after all the consideration I have shown my people—they let those banners stay on Main Street! Why don't the workers tear them to bits? Why don't they talk about Sackett's brutality? He's the one who ought to be blamed for all this. He's caused every bit of trouble we ever had in Andor!"

Luncheon was a gloomy meal. Dorothea's eyes had a distant, abstracted look. She barely spoke to any of them and excused herself before they were fairly started. Through the window, Voss saw her crossing the lawn with a casualness that was too studied to be genuine.

Once or twice he tried with Julia's help to draw Jared into a conversation unrelated either to murders or labor trouble, but without success. The old man's blazing eyes were fixed on his plate as he chewed his food methodically.

"Wilton brutality!" he kept muttering.

8

The quaint stone cottage that by the grace of Jared Wilton was Thomas Oliver Unger's retreat—and by the grace of Unger sheltered Leslie Frank and Ruth Taylor likewise—was cool and surprisingly spacious inside. Two thirds of it was a pleasant living room whose smooth plaster walls were pierced at either end by casement windows embracing long and lovely views. At one side was a hewn stone hearth and mantel.

The delicate beauty of Dorothea Wilton filled the room like quiet music so that one was conscious of it always. Above the mantel she gazed down with a wistful smile from a framed canvas, her shoulders gleaming like ivory above the bodice of a blue gown. At the foot of the portrait a vase of blue and red flowers might have been a votive offering placed before the image of a goddess.

Dorothea in a gayer mood laughed out of a smaller frame in the center of the opposite wall. A third and larger canvas rested on an easel in a corner, not yet completed. It seemed to hold Dorothea's ghost. The face was a pale frightened thing seen through a fog, the figure a grouping of swirling masses of faint lavender and gray, misty and elusive.

Dorothea Wilton in the flesh sat upon the very edge of the studio couch beside the fireplace and looked through the window toward the wooded hill behind the cottage. She listened without expression to the soft, swift speech of the artist.

Unger lay back upon the couch, a convincing invalid, his face as white as his bandages and only his blue eyes lifelike beneath lowered lids. One arm stretched across the couch so that the restless fingertips could brush the cloth of her skirt.

"You've got to go away," he muttered. "It would be suicide to stay. In another place you can forget all about Andor and what has happened."

Neither of them was aware of Abelard Voss until he spoke. He stooped in the open door and said, "Would another visitor excite the patient?"

Confusion held Dorothea speechless for a moment. She moved hurriedly away from the edge of the cot and stood tall and pale and startled. She put one hand to her throat and stammered, "Mr. Voss! How . . . how very nice of you to call on Mr. Unger!"

She introduced them. Unger nodded none too graciously.

Voss helped himself to a chair. "Frank told me you were too badly hurt to get up. I thought I'd bring some sympathy."

Unger licked his lips. His eyes said, "What's your game? You saw me walking around an hour ago and you know I know you saw me."

He said aloud, "I'll have to stay in bed another day or two at least."

"I saw what happened yesterday," Voss told him. "It was a pretty senseless thing. The mill whistle would have broken up the meeting in another five minutes and everybody knew it."

"It's just as well it happened the way it did," Unger declared. "It will hurry whatever's going to come out of this mess. I don't mind a lot. I was looking for a new experience and I got it. I don't care much about social problems, but I'm interested in people's actions and reactions. The faces of those thugs as they came toward me were worth seeing."

"If I were an artist I'd prefer to study certain facial expressions at a distance."

There was a pause. Into it Dorothea flung the explanation of her presence in the cottage. She was frightened and eager for understanding. Voss surmised it went deeper than the mere fact of her being found alone with another man the first full day of her widowhood.

"Mr. Unger and I have been friends since he started coming to Andor for the scenery five years ago. He has made several portraits of me and I'm vain enough to think they're very fine. I was to have a sitting today—I didn't know he was too ill to paint—and now I've simply turned my visit into a sick call."

"She's my only patron," Unger said. "Once I did a study of her brother-in-law, but I didn't flatter him and he never came back for more. He likes landscapes, but lately I haven't been doing many. Human beings are more interesting."

"You've done very well by your patron." Voss looked again at each of the paintings. He knew Unger was an able painter and Dorothea a splendid subject, but he saw more than craftsmanship and artistic perception in the brush strokes. Unger had made of the young woman a creature of almost heavenly perfection, had put all of himself into every line of drawing and every inflection of color. Doubtless these were the finest pictures he had ever made.

Carter Wilton may have hated his wife, but she had certainly not gone unloved. James Morgan adored her with a passion that her marriage had never smothered; he had betrayed himself eloquently just by the way his eyes had followed her the day before. And Unger loved her with a love that could no more be concealed than his bruises could.

Neither man would grieve over her husband's death.

Ruth Taylor came into the cottage rattling a folded newspaper. She was not pretty, but there was extraordinary litheness in her small figure and smoldering fires glowed back of her dark eyes.

She smiled at Voss. "You're the big detective from New York, aren't you? Which of the three of us do you suspect of being the murderer?"

He said, "You've got the best motive. A man can get over a few punches, but I should think a woman would remember a ducking in the lake for a long time."

"I've got a clear mental picture of the man who pushed me in. He was short and heavy and had a round bald spot in the middle of his scalp. I'm just waiting to meet him again."

"I feel sorry for him. I understand you can take care of yourself pretty well."

Her eyes regarded him steadily. "How do you mean that?"

"I'd like to speak to you alone," he said. "Maybe you can tell me about something that's got me worried."

She led the way outside and perched on the edge of the table beneath the pear tree. She crossed her slim knees and lighted a cigarette.

"All right. What's the mystery?"

"I didn't want Mrs. Wilton to hear. Someone saw her husband around here yesterday a little while after the trouble at the mill and a little while before he was killed. Did you see him?"

"I not only saw him; I had a fight with him."

"That's what I was told. Someone happened to be looking."

"So Sackett has spies on the job! We're under surveillance. I should have known it. I suppose that makes me a suspect."

"Not necessarily. I take it you had good cause to fight with him."

"The best. He'd been hanging around here ever since Frank and I came to town. He was trying to make some kind of business deal with Frank—I never did find out exactly what kind—and he would have made another kind of deal with me if I'd let him. He's one of those men who is crazy about women and not particular about beauty.

"He didn't know about the riot till I told him. He wanted to see Frank. When I told him Frank was in the hospital he decided it was a good time to make a play for me. He grabbed me and tried to kiss me. Since the law is chivalrous about such things I guess that makes him the criminal—not me."

"Nice sort of fellow!" Voss commented.

"Yes. He didn't kiss me, though. I kicked his shins and slapped his face and he went away mad."

"You kicked Wilton and slapped him. You scratched him, too?"

"No, I didn't."

"There were the marks of a woman's fingernails on his wrist."

She held out her hands palms downward. Her fingernails were tiny and ugly and without points.

"I'm not proud of them," she said. "I've chewed them since I was a kid and I've never been able to stop it. It's a nasty habit. I guess it's an out for me this time, though."

"I guess it is. Now I've got to find another woman with fingernails. Not that it will prove anything—he may have tried to kiss half a dozen girls yesterday morning and someone else may have cut his throat for another reason entirely."

"Well, I hope you never find the right one. He deserved what he got and I'd hate to see anyone go to prison or the chair for it. If you want my personal theory Sackett had him killed to put suspicion on Leslie and me."

"That's a novel idea."

"Not so novel. Most of the labor leaders in jail today were framed."

"Sackett wouldn't do it himself, of course."

"It would be that fellow Russo, who started the riot. He'd as soon stick a knife into you as look at you."

"It would make a good story for your paper."

"It already has. I sent the story in last night."

"But suppose it isn't true?"

The girl shrugged and tossed her cigarette away. "I think it is. You'll probably find out it's the truth if you investigate impartially."

"The end," he murmured, "always justifies the means, doesn't it?"

"Always. We're fighting for the most important thing on earth—economic freedom, which is the basis of all freedom—and we can't afford to lose. Do you think I'd hesitate for a minute to take any advantage that might mean the difference between victory and defeat? The other side never hesitates. Do you think I would?"

"No," he replied thoughtfully. "I don't."

Dorothea came out of the cottage. She said, "I'm going for a walk, Mr. Voss. Would you like to join me?"

"Very much." He said good-by to Unger and Ruth. They took the path he had walked earlier with Julia. Dorothea was silent as they climbed the side of the low hill. She was still frightened, it was obvious—afraid, perhaps, Voss had heard things not intended for his ears, when he came to the doorway.

"I rather like your painter friend," Voss ventured.

It was a subject she welcomed. "He's a remarkable person. Besides being one of the best of the modem painters, he has a splendid mind. He sees things so clearly. Almost everyone likes him. Even Julia, though she hates Ruth and Frank."

"I've been thinking about Julia. It's remarkable, the attachment she has for that youngster Toby."

"She loves children. What she needs more than anything else in the world is a home and children of her own."

"She told me she would never marry."

"I don't think she ever will. In all her life she's had only one affair and that, believe it or not, was with Sackett! Three or four years ago everybody thought they would get married. Then Sackett and Jared had a particularly violent quarrel—they're always having them, you know—and somehow it spread to Sackett and Julia. They broke up and they've hardly spoken since."

"Neither will take the first step toward making up, eh?"

"Maybe it's that and maybe it's something deeper. Julia is funny; she never lets you know what's in her mind."

"I've noticed she's good at keeping secrets."

Dorothea turned startled gray eyes toward him. "What makes you say that? Do you think she's hiding something?"

"I wouldn't put it that way. I just thought she seemed entirely self-contained."

From the top of the hill they could see the country in all directions. At their right was the little valley through which flowed the willow-fringed stream where Carter's body had been found. Voss saw Dorothea's mouth tighten almost imperceptibly as she looked that way. Then her eyes, moving on, widened and she inclined her head.

"There's a mystery for you."

Voss saw a tattered, fantastic figure limping and hopping down the side of the hill across the stream. He carried a small object that made glittering arcs in the sunlight as his arm swung. Near the bottom of the hill he stooped, lifted a flat stone and put the object under it. He turned and started back up the hill laboriously, apparently not having seen them.

"What's his story?"

"Nobody knows," Dorothea said. "One day several years ago he appeared in Andor and he's been here ever since. He lives in a cave behind that hill. No one knows where he gets his food or the rags he wears. He's never spoken an intelligible word to anybody. Somebody even made up the name Clubfoot Crippen for him; it isn't his real name. They say he's harmless."

"I wonder."

A hail withdrew their attention from the distant figure. They saw James Morgan climbing toward them. The clergyman was smiling.

"Julia said you'd gone walking," he said to Dorothea. "She didn't say you were in good company, though. I was afraid you might have gone to see the godless Mr. Unger."

"I had," Dorothea said. "That's where I met Mr. Voss."

Morgan's face hardened. "You're spending a lot of time there, Dorothea. Aren't you afraid of what people will say?"

An expression of angry amazement came over her face. "Why should people say anything? Can't I choose my friends without being talked about?"

"Of course you can, Dorothea." The clergyman's smile returned somewhat sheepishly. "I guess I'm only jealous. Godless or not, Unger makes a beautiful portrait of you. If I was rich I'd buy them all."

"I'd like one myself," Voss said.

"Another rival!" Morgan made a grimace. "But perhaps you'll advise me just the same. I've got a legitimate excuse to preach a dramatic sermon tomorrow—a sermon about a murderer. Something has recently reached me that has some bearing, I think, on the things that have happened in Andor. Do you imagine people would accuse me of trying to borrow sensationalism from Pop Kramer?"

"What if they do? My observation has always been that in New York the preachers with the most sensational topics get the biggest congregations."

"That's true. You have to scare people or entertain them with vaudeville stunts to get them interested in Christ these days. Well, I'm going to take a chance and do both. The Tabernacle was half empty last Sunday. If word gets around that I'm going to talk about what everyone else is talking about there'll be a full house tomorrow."

"What is it that has given you the legitimate excuse?"

Morgan shook his head. "A secret's no good once it's told. Come around at ten o'clock and find out. The town's buzzing with talk about you, too—tales of your exploits that would amaze and astound you—and you'll be an added attraction. Take a front pew where everybody can see you. You could probably stand a good dose of preaching after having been exposed to criminals and their works for so long."

"You're an opportunist just like Leslie Frank."

"Saving souls is largely a matter of opportunism. All evangelists know that a scared person will embrace Christ without much coaxing whereas one contented with his lot can't be bothered even thinking about salvation. That's why hell fire and brimstone are so popular."

Voss left them together. He explained he wanted to see Jared Wilton and he walked in the direction of Wiltonshire until they were out of sight behind the hill. Then he circled and crossed the stream on a fallen log.

It took him ten minutes of casting about and getting his bearings to locate the flat stone beside which the idiot had stopped. Looking carefully around to be sure he was unobserved he hooked his fingers beneath its edge and lifted.

Where the stone had been thousand-legged worms wriggled and shiny slugs crawled. Among them a long-bladed kitchen knife with a wooden handle was pressed into the black earth. Wood and steel were stained thickly with dark blood.

9

Julia Bisbee said that evening, "Promise not to leap to conclusions and I'll tell you something."

"I promise," Voss agreed.

They were standing at the railing of the veranda watching the afterglow of sunset, alone after a glum dinner garnished with Jared Wilton's grumblings. Dorothea had complained of a headache and gone to her room and Wilton was sulking in his library.

"Carmen—the maid—has confided in me, so in a way it's her secret I'm telling," said Julia. "I'll expect you to keep it as well as you can. She's in love with the muscle man Uncle Jared fired yesterday, Vito Russo. She's going to have a baby in five or six months."

"A little muscle man?"

"That's the horrid part of it!" Her eyes flashed in the dusk. "It will be my precious Uncle Carter's!"

"Ah!" Voss forgot the subdued glory of the sky. This was a bit of sordid gossip worth knowing.

"Even though it's criminal for a person to be so stupid, I don't blame the girl so much. Carter was a man who could twist a dull-witted girl around his little finger and think it funny. He had a warped mind that rejected every idea of morality. He deserved to die for that if for nothing else."

"It's hard on Carmen."

"She's made her own trouble. I tried to fix it up for her. I advised her," Julia confessed shamelessly, "to arrange things so Russo would think it was his own child. They're going to be married. But young girls in love have absolutely no sense. Carmen confessed everything. I heard them quarreling in Italian in a corner of the garden this afternoon."

"You understand Italian?"

"I spent a year in Rome and Naples. Russo was in a towering rage and called Carmen names that made her cry. He said he'd marry her, but if he ever so much as caught her looking at another man he'd cut both their throats— 'like that fool's throat was cut.'"

"Now we're getting somewhere!"

"That wasn't all. Russo said, 'Do you think I am afraid to kill a man?' If he's innocent I'd hate to see him arrested because of what I've told you. But he didn't sound a bit innocent. He held a bully's position at the mill; he could easily have had some trouble with Richard Stott, some motive for murder we don't know about."

"Would his boss Sackett stand for murder, do you think?"

He heard the sharp catch of breath in her throat. "Why bring him into it?"

"Sackett's name, most of it, was printed in the sand beside Carter's body. Fleming obliterated it without saying anything. Morgan saw the letters and seemed to think Carter tried to write his murderer's name."

"Sackett didn't kill him. He has too much sense. It was a trick of the murderer to shift the blame."

"Yet Sackett is Russo's friend. Russo would hardly try to frame him."

"You never can tell where treachery will begin or end. Let me assure you Sackett is no murderer. He wouldn't kill or order anyone else to kill."

"I wanted your opinion about that. I don't know Sackett well. He seemed decent enough when I met him."

She warned, "Don't think I'm praising him. He's wholly ruthless in some ways. I never knew anyone more cold-blooded about the feelings of others. But he isn't crude."

"Brutal, eh?"

"Not altogether. He's—" She stopped and glared at him in accusation. "You're trying to make me put on an act. You've heard we were good friends once."

"Yes," he said.

"That's all finished. We thought we liked each other and found out we didn't. I find him very distasteful now. But at the same time I respect him for his good qualities. One of them is common sense. Sensible people don't cut other people's throats."

"Not as a rule."

"I hope nothing I've said has made you suspicious of him."

"It hasn't. I appreciate your telling me what you overheard. It may go a long way toward solving this. There's one more favor you could show me if you would."

"What kind of favor?"

"You could tell me what you were burning in the fireplace last night and why you were burning it. I'm quite sure it was a bloodstained dress and naturally that makes me curious to know more."

"I can't tell you. I'm sorry. I give you my word it wouldn't help you to know."

"We'll let it go at that, then. If you say it wasn't a significant act I'm inclined to believe you."

"That's a very nice compliment."

He said, "It doesn't stop me from wondering whether you could tell a lot more about Carter's death if you wanted to."

"Now you've spoiled it. I'm tempted to be angry, but I won't be because I understand your reason for wondering. I'd have been quite capable of killing Carter under the proper circumstances. I'm very glad he's dead for the sake of Dorothea and others. But I know no more about it than you do and possibly not as much."

He sighed. "My ignorance is growing every minute!"

Walking toward Main Street half an hour later Voss passed Andor Tabernacle and saw on a blackboard the title of the sermon James Morgan would preach Sunday morning—"A Message to a Murderer." The chalked letters gave a grim look to the snowy edifice with the slender spire.

But all Andor seemed grim and excited this sultry Saturday night. The people on the sidewalks seemed to be waiting tensely for something to explode. Automobiles were angle-parked fender to fender the whole length of Main Street and the bright shop windows illuminated rude jostling throngs.

At the corner of Wilton Drive men's voices were raised in hoots and catcalls, good-natured enough until one sensed the undertone of savagery. Over their heads hung the scarlet-lettered banner Voss had seen put up that morning. A policeman in khaki clung near the top of one of the telephone poles that supported it; his free hand stretched out with a penknife and the rope parted. One end of the heavy canvas swung downward as men and boys scurried out of the path of its weighted lower border. A second later another policeman, atop the telephone pole on the opposite side of the street, chopped with a knife blade and the defiant strip lay in a crumpled pile in the street.

Men snatched it out of the hands of cops who would have captured it. They ran clumsily along the street disrupting traffic. A hoarse cheer arose and spread. The cops grinned nervously and wiped sweat from their faces. At the next corner men swarmed up other telephone poles to stretch the banner to the breeze again.

Pop Kramer elbowed his way through the crowd toward Voss. Kramer may have washed his face and hands since morning, but if he had, the day's labor in the print shop had decked him out with new ink smudges.

"It's a new game," the editor said. "All afternoon the cops have been tearing 'em down and the men have been putting 'em up again. The cops are getting tired, but the others love it. So far it's been good clean fun, but wait till somebody gets hurt or a cop gets sore and begins swinging his club."

"It would break Wilton's heart to see his men acting like this."

"He ought to give orders to leave the banners alone. The crowd thinks he's responsible for the cops being out, but Sackett started it. I was at the police station talking to Fleming when he came in and gave the order. He warned Fleming to lay off rough stuff, though."

"If a fight started that mob would wreck the town."

"You're damn' right. It's a union town tonight. Not that the boys have really been converted; they've just discovered a new way to enjoy themselves."

"What's Fleming doing about the murders?"

"He blames Frank. He wants to arrest him, but Sackett says to wait till Frank breaks a law and can be arrested for something else. Frank is smart enough to mind his own business for the time being."

He nodded toward the other side of the street. Leslie Frank sat there with three or four other men on the steps of the brick Town Hall. The men were smoking and talking quietly. Catching sight of Voss's lanky figure and seeing the direction of his gaze, Frank waved.

Morgan came along the street. He paused and ran a finger around the inner edge of his reversed collar. He looked hot and uncomfortable in his clerical garb.

"The devil's weekly protest against the Lord's Day," he observed. "Swanson's Bar and the Commercial House are packed. A lot of people who ought to be in church tomorrow will be sick in bed instead."

"It won't be your fault," Kramer averred. "I saw the sign in front of the Tabernacle. Folks will be accusing you of stealing my stuff if you start preaching about things like that."

"I know it. But I've had a call I can't refuse."

"A letter from the murderer himself, I'll bet."

Morgan's look of surprise was equivalent to an affirmative answer.

Vito Russo elbowed his ponderous way out of the Commercial House. He was staggering drunk. He grinned greasily and bellowed, "Hi, Rev'rend! How's about takin' a li'l drink with me?"

Morgan's glance was severe. "One look at you would make me a teetotaler for the rest of my life, Russo. It's a vice I hope never to achieve."

Russo chortled, "He don' wanna vice! But he's gotta vice jus' same! I seen it with m' own eyes!" He laughed foolishly and reeled past them.

Morgan flushed. "Filthy stuff!" he said. "I didn't believe in prohibition when we had it; now I'm almost convinced we need it back. Probably I've got a great many vices, but that's one I don't want."

"Maybe you'd like it if you ever tried it," Kramer suggested, his eyes twinkling. "Look at me—I thrive on beer!"

Voss missed the clergyman's reply. A hand plucked at his sleeve. He looked down into the pretty face of Jared Wilton's yellow-haired secretary.

"May I see you for a minute?" she asked.

"Certainly, Miss Rhinehart." He moved with her into a sheltered doorway.

"It's about something that happened yesterday morning, Mr. Voss. I thought it might be important. Mr. Wilton sent me with some papers to Mr. Sackett's office. Mr. Sackett's secretary wasn't there and Mr. Carter Wilton was in the private office.

"I waited for Mr. Carter to come out and all at once both of them started to talk very loud. I don't usually listen to other people's conversations, but I couldn't help hearing every word. I didn't think much about it at the time, but I've been wondering ever since—"

"What were the words?"

"Mr. Carter said, 'You'd better play ball with me or I'll tell everything to my brother and both you and Russo will be looking for new jobs.' And he swore, but I won't repeat that."

"You needn't. What did Sackett say?"

"He said, 'You do that and I'll make so much trouble for you you'll wish you'd never been born. He was real mad and he swore, too."

"Did you hear any more?"

"No. Before that they had been talking softly, and right after, Mr. Carter came out looking quite angry."

"You haven't any idea what it was all about, have you?"

"I'm only a secretary. I do my work and try not to pay attention to anything that's not my business. I'd never have mentioned this if there hadn't been a murder. If you let it out that I've told you I'll probably lose my job."

"I won't. If I mention you to anyone it will only be to tell them you're my idea of the perfect secretary. Thanks for taking me into your confidence. If it helps catch the murderer I'll see that you get the credit."

Her cheeks were pink with pleasure as she left him.

Morgan had gone on. Kramer seized Voss's elbow and piloted him toward the bar entrance of the Commercial

House. The editor said, "Talking to preachers dries up my tonsils. I bought this morning so it's your turn to set 'em up. It isn't my fault you didn't take advantage of me."

They had to wedge their way into a place at the bar. Voss ordered two glasses of beer. He inquired, "Why would Vito Russo want to kill Richard Stott?"

"I don't know," Kramer replied innocently, "Did he?" Then he slapped the bar impulsively. "By God, I believe he did! He went to the mill Monday night around eight o'clock and left about nine."

"How do you know?"

"Ada and I live on Lincoln Avenue two blocks from the mill. I was sitting on the porch when Russo passed. I know it was Monday because the Sunday *New York Times* reaches me in the mail that day and I was reading it. I didn't see him go into the place, but I watched till he was close to the building. There's nothing else in that part of town except the mill. Russo isn't the sort to just sit in the park."

"He might have done it, at that," mused Voss.

"You think so? Then you *were* kidding when you mentioned that guy Atkinson."

"That's the only thing that bothers me. I wasn't kidding. This letter is the one thing that makes me think Russo may be innocent." He handed Kramer the envelope he had received that morning. "Russo wouldn't write a thing like that."

Kramer studied the envelope before he drew forth the torn slip of paper. He read it carefully. His dark eyes glittered and his mouth curled downward at the corners.

"Damn it," he said, "now I'll have to leave town! Somebody is trying to frame me and I wouldn't stand a chance once they arrested me."

"What's that?" Voss asked.

"This was written on my typewriter. The 'V' is broken. There aren't a dozen other machines in town and it's a cinch none of them has a busted 'V.' Anyway I know the look of that type as well as I know my handwriting."

"Furthermore you've made me a present of your possible motive," Voss reminded him.

"You think I've forgotten? And if you need anything more to hang it on me—here!"

Angrily Kramer rubbed the ball of his left thumb across the moist top of the bar. He pressed it firmly against the slip of paper beside the thumbprint that was already there. Ink and moisture left a perfect etching. He studied the result and thrust the paper at Voss.

"I didn't kill Stott or Carter Wilton," he declared, his teeth clamped tight together. "I didn't write that note. But look!"

The two thumbprints were identical.

10

At nine o'clock Sunday morning the bell of Andor Tabernacle began a dramatic double toll for the murdered men. *Bong-bong!*—and then the deep reverberations shivering over the town, rolling out into the peaceful countryside in far-reaching waves—and after the space of a full minute *bong-bong*! again.

Jared Wilton glowered and fidgeted and had difficulty with his collar buttons and refused everything but orange juice at breakfast. He told Abelard Voss fretfully, "I'll have a talk with the young jackass! Parker is going to conduct the funerals, not Morgan—let Parker do whatever tolling is necessary. If I'd known before Morgan posted his announcement that he was going to preach about the—the deaths—I'd have put a stop to it in a hurry. It isn't decent!"

Dorothea, who had not spoken beyond her first greeting at the breakfast table, came unexpectedly to the minister's defense. "He has a reason for doing this. He told me about it yesterday. He thinks perhaps he can make the murderer confess."

"Tommyrot!" Wilton exclaimed. "If he wants to do police work I'll get him a job with Fleming. If he wants to preach the Gospel he'd better forget all about crime."

Julia said, "I haven't read my Bible in the last few days, but I seem to recall a lot of references to sin in it."

"Even my own family is against me!" Wilton appealed to Voss. "What do you think?"

Voss kept his eyes carefully on his second plate of ham and eggs. He said, "I'm trying not to form any definite opinions till I have more to go on. I understand Morgan has something up his sleeve, though, and I'm curious to know what it is."

Wilton grunted. "He's a fool!" He winced as the bell tolled again.

Notwithstanding her defense of Morgan, Dorothea was not going to the service. She explained she had slept badly and the violet shadows under her gray eyes bore out her words. Wilton gave her a sympathetic glance.

"I don't blame you. You've gone through enough without having it thrown at you all over again from a pulpit. I wouldn't go, either, if people didn't expect to see me."

Wilton intended to drive to the Tabernacle and Julia wanted to walk. Voss chose to escort Julia.

They left the big yellow house when the bell had been tolling for forty-five minutes.

Before they were halfway to their destination Voss realized that James Morgan was going to have a congregation far greater than his most optimistic expectations. People were converging from all directions upon Andor Tabernacle. Each street had its spaced procession moving purposefully beneath the booming and the murmuring of the bell.

"The church won't hold a third of them," Julia declared. "Even the theater wouldn't hold them all. I didn't know that many people in Andor cared about salvation."

"It isn't salvation they're after." Voss was watching the faces of those nearest him. They were all eager and expectant. All were stamped with a common mark; all were engrossed with a single terrible idea.

Murder.

The bell moaned and people stood uncertainly on the church steps and on the lawn, unable to get inside. The benches had been filled long since and the aisles and the space at the back of the auditorium were jammed. Worried ushers in white gloves squirmed in and out of the crowd on pointless errands.

Snatches of conversation reached Voss's ears.

"I heard Morgan is going to name the murderer!"

"They say the one who done it will get up and confess and ask everybody to pray for him."

"They certainly ought to take up a good collection!"

Eyes, curious and speculative, fixed on Voss's ungainly figure as he piloted Julia through the crowd and made a path into the church. Jared Wilton had a private pew near the front, an entire bench protected by a blue velvet rope and a sign reserved. An usher unfastened the rope and held it aside for them and replaced it.

Julia whispered, "There's Toby and Clara Weston across the way. Clara's a devout Baptist; I doubt if she's ever been here before."

There was a commotion in the center aisle. "Morgan's done more than raid the Baptist fold," Voss said. "He's gathered in the heathen."

Pop Kramer and his gaunt wife Ada reached the Wilton pew. Kramer had scrubbed his face and hands nearly clean and wore a white collar. Ada looked exactly as she had in the printing shop two days earlier. Kramer winked at Voss and unhooked the velvet rope and stood aside to let his wife precede him into the pew. He took down the reserved sign and put it on the floor.

"Jesus didn't play favorites," he announced to no one in particular, but loudly enough so that people three rows ahead turned around. He seated himself next to the aisle.

Encouraged by his example some of the men and women standing in the aisle edged into the pew and sat down. An usher watched with agonized eyes and twisted his gloved hands, but did not interfere. In a moment the pew was filled.

"Uncle Jared will be furious," Julia predicted. She was smiling and wanted to laugh. She looked around and met the eyes of Claude Sackett at the other side of the church. Sackett smiled back at her.

"Is he a regular here?" Voss inquired.

"Goodness, no! I don't think he believes in much of anything, but he goes to the Baptist church because Uncle Jared comes here and he contributes heavily to all Mr. Parker's pet projects because Uncle Jared contributes to the support of the Tabernacle."

"Murder," said Voss, "is a wonderful thing for bringing all kinds of people together."

The oppressive tolling ended. Like a live thing set free from long bondage the bell pealed and caroled gaily. Men and women sighed audibly and visibly with relief. The pipe organ began to rumble "He Leadeth Me." Six men and six women sidled into the narrow choir loft above the altar.

There was another commotion in the aisle as two ushers broke a path for Jared Wilton. They paused forlornly at the pew that had been guarded by the velvet rope. Wilton stood there for a long moment glaring at the usurpers. Kramer gave him a pleasant nod.

"You've got my seat," Wilton said.

"Unh-unh," Kramer denied. "I'm sure it was empty when I came in. You should have got here first if you wanted it."

Wilton's face turned the red of musty port wine. He compressed his lips and shrilled, "Someone will have to get up. I always use this pew. I support the Tabernacle."

A rawboned youth near the center of the bench arose. He said, "Sit here, Mr. Wilton." He made a clumsy exit, tripping over Kramer's feet, and Wilton made an entrance just as clumsy. Across the church Sackett looked at Julia and smiled again.

The organ had come to the end of a verse. There was a pause in which the members of the choir waved their hymnals in languid rhythm. A warning note rumbled loudly and that part of the congregation which was sitting got unevenly to its feet and commenced to sing.

James Morgan emerged from a door at the side of the platform. He wore a dark suit that made him appear taller and more slender and his face was as white as his clerical collar. He moved to the center of the platform and laid his left hand on the lectern and tossed back his wavy brown hair. He looked out over the congregation with eyes that seemed impossibly blue and bright. He did not sing. He only stood there dreamily absorbing the collective stare of the expectant faces and listening to the slow words of the familiar hymn:

> He leadeth me! O blessed thought!
>   O words with heav'nly comfort fraught!
> Whate'er I do, where'er I be,
>   Still 'tis God's hand that leadeth me.

"He's an angel," Julia breathed. "He couldn't look like that if he wasn't."

He had the makings of a great preacher, anyway, Voss thought. His personality held the congregation spellbound even during the first formalities of the service—the opening prayer, the announcements, and the collection.

Patient as the people were—and not twenty of them had come to hear prayers and hymns!—one could feel suspense building up like a tangible thing. By his very casualness Morgan heightened it, drawling his words a little, slowing his motions. Only once did Voss glimpse emotion in his eyes and that was when Morgan looked toward the Wilton pew and scanned the faces of all who sat there. Voss fancied the clergyman was disappointed in that searching scrutiny—that in this his hour of importance Morgan would have been better pleased if Dorothea had been there to watch.

The offertory finished, Morgan straightened beside the lectern. He took an envelope from his pocket, opened it and studied the sheet of paper it contained. The church was so still that the singing birds in the trees outside seemed almost rowdy.

"My text," announced the minister, "is taken from the first chapter of the Book of the Prophet Isaiah. Perhaps you have read it once or twice or ten times, but you must have heard it quoted times without number. It is the most miraculous promise to be found in all the Bible—one that makes life and death alike worth while.

"*'Though your sins be scarlet, they shall be as white as snow; though they be red like crimson, they shall be as wool.'*"

In the silence someone—it might have been Kramer—whispered, "They shall be as Woollies!" A woman tittered. A fat lady in front of Voss turned around and registered indignation.

Morgan declared sonorously, "Today I come to preach to one man among you—to a man who has set aside the Sixth Commandment and has taken the lives of two of our beloved townsmen—who is here today within the sound of my voice, unrecognized and unsuspected. Can you feel his presence, brethren? Listen while I speak to him!"

There were gasps and a craning of necks. Voss could feel distinctly the electric thrill that flowed through the assembly. He saw that even Wilton was impressed and leaned farther forward and gripped the head of his cane tighter.

"In my hand," continued the minister, "I hold a letter from that man. 'Tell me,' he asks, 'is there any salvation for a murderer?' In the words of our Lord I have answered that question. There is the same salvation that awaits you and me and every, man born of sin and reared to suffering.

"There is more to the mighty sermon contained in the first chapter of Isaiah. Listen to the flaming sentences the prophet wrote.

"'Hear the word of the Lord, ye rulers of Sodom; give ear unto the law of our God, ye people of Gomorrah. To what purpose is the multitude of your sacrifices unto me? saith the Lord: I am full of the burnt offerings of rams, and the fat of fed beasts; and I delight not in the blood of bullocks, or of lambs, or of he-goats. . . .

"'Wash you, make you clean; put away the evil of your doings from before mine eyes, cease to do evil; learn to do well; seek judgment, relieve the oppressed, judge the fatherless, plead for the widow. . . .'

"These are the things that are required. Put away the evil of your doings. Seek judgment! *Then,* saith the Lord, 'Though your sins be as scarlet, they shall be as white as snow.'"

Morgan's blue eyes swept the sea of faces before him— puzzled, excited, frightened faces. Voss wished he could see what the clergyman saw. Of the faces he knew only half a dozen were within the range of his vision—Julia's, taut with concentration; Wilton's, startled and loose-lipped; Ada Kramer's, inscrutable as the visage of the Sphinx; her husband's, humorously scornful; Sackett's, frowning and speculative; Clara Weston's, gray with fear.

Was another face somewhere in the crowd betraying guilt? Perhaps in analysis the argument from the pulpit was not powerful, but the words were thunderous and stirring and the atmosphere was more emotional than any words could have made it. The solemnity of the tolling bell seemed to hover yet in the air like a sound of doom. Morgan's voice rose suddenly, rang out like a clearer bell, pierced like the note of a silver bugle through the auditorium.

"Won't you let God be your judge? God, Who maketh the burden no heavier than the servant can bear? Won't you come up before us now and cleanse yourself by confession? Won't you wash your sins as white as snow and claim the mercy that knoweth no stint?"

He waited, hands outstretched, eyes roving over the people before him. Perspiration gleamed on his forehead. Breathlessly, the congregation waited with him, its collective will strengthening his. The men and women—yes, and the children—wanted someone to rise and confess. Their desire mounted, became unbearable, stretched into a full minute—two minutes—

A woman moaned, "Oh, my God!" A baby started to cry.

The spell was broken. There was an uncomfortable shifting of bodies.

After that emotional pinnacle the rest of the sermon and the service was flat and sterile. Morgan declared, "Perhaps we have saved him, even so. Perhaps we have sown in his heart the seeds of repentance that will burst and grow and flower and redeem him. Perhaps our murderer will yet confess and seek a place in heaven."

He wiped the sweat from his brow, blessed the congregation and retreated wearily to a chair and sat down near the rear of the platform. The organ pealed a shuddering note and the choir arose. The closing hymn could not rise above the noise of the departing hundreds.

Kramer grinned at Voss and shouted, "Makes me think of a Broadway show flopping the first night out. Wait till you see my dramatic criticism!"

Wilton looked at him as he might have looked at a rattlesnake. "It was disgraceful," he snapped. "The only thing I can think of that would make it more disgraceful would be to have you write about it in the *Advertiser.*"

In the aisle, inching his way toward the door, Sackett appeared pleased about something. At the rear of the church Unger, the artist, his forehead still bandaged, was watching the crowd with thoughtful, observant eyes.

Julia touched Voss's arm and said, "Everybody will be laughing at him, but I think he deserves credit. He tried his darnedest. That ought to mean something, oughtn't it?"

11

The portly man did not awaken when the twelve-fifteen paused at Andor. He snored gently in his seat, his round chin pillowed in its own fat, his manicured hands folded across his stomach. His felt hat had fallen off and was crushed between his shoulder and the window and a fly skated confidently across the bald spot at the crown of his head.

On the station platform the gray-haired conductor glanced along the length of the train and signaled to the engineer. Abelard Voss raised his eyebrows and shrugged his shoulders and turned away.

The bell on the locomotive clanged and the conductor picked up the portable step he had needlessly placed on the concrete and swung aboard. As the train creaked into motion he entered the coach and looked at the sleeping man. An expression of consternation came over his face.

Lieutenant Bob Saint-Amour regained consciousness under the frantic manipulations of the conductor's hand. He heard the conductor scolding, "I called out Andor a mile back. Are you deaf?" He opened one eye just in time to see the sign on the station glide past the window.

Saint-Amour stood up, smoothed the wrinkles out of his gray suit and regarded the conductor with heavy-lidded agate eyes. He inquired placidly, "So what?" He picked up his hat and restored it to an approximation of its original shape and walked unhurriedly toward the vestibule. He climbed down to the lowest of the three steps and grasped the iron handrail.

"You can't do that!" the conductor shouted, "She's going too fast. You'll have to go on to the next—"

The New York homicide detective swung off into space. His feet scattered gravel. He took three running steps and halted. With his back to the rushing train he looked out over Mill River, stained a poisonous purple this Monday, and back fifty yards toward the station. When he saw the tall ungainly figure under the flopping Panama he made a megaphone of his hands and bellowed, "Abelard!"

Voss waited for him, his eyes glinting with amusement behind the spectacles. When Saint-Amour's leisured gait brought him near enough he said, "You were sleeping."

"Amazing!" growled the detective. "How do you deduce those things?"

"You forgot your bag."

Saint-Amour looked at his empty hands and considered. He shook his head. "No, I didn't bring one." He opened his coat to show a toothbrush in a transparent case. "I figured we'd clean this up right away. If I get stuck for another day I can buy a shirt and a pair of socks and charge it against my share of the reward money."

"There's a train back to Boston in three hours," Voss said. "Shall we hurry so you can get back to New York by midnight?"

"Never mind. I've got four leave days coming and I'm taking them all in case Atkinson refuses to waive extradition and delays things. Where've you got him?"

"I haven't got him. If I had why should I send for you? But we've got two murders in this town and I have a hunch others are planned. It's barely possible your man Atkinson figures in the case somewhere. Until I find out for sure I'm suspecting everybody for miles around."

Saint-Amour half closed his eyes. "It's lucky I came," he averred. "It would take you weeks to get to the bottom of it with your books and your psychology."

"Want to bet?"

Saint-Amour said, "Unh-unh. It's illegal and immoral. But you can tell me what has happened. I saw the papers, but they just had squibs."

They were on the bridge over Mill River. Voss pointed out the spot where he had seen Richard Stott's gruesome salute.

"He was killed a week ago tonight," he explained. "He was mixing dye in the mill. The murderer fractured his skull with a heavy instrument as yet undiscovered and weighted him with chains and dropped him out of that middle fifth-story window."

"Why?"

"I wish I knew. He was boarding with a widow who wanted to marry him. He had some ideas about the rights of workingmen that didn't agree with either the union men or the mill gang that is fighting the union. He had a spat with the local editor when he tried to get his ideas into print."

"Pretty weak motives. But if a nut like Atkinson did it that wouldn't matter. A guy with a cracked mind makes big things out of little ones. How about this other dead guy?"

"He got a knife in the throat sometime Friday afternoon over on the other side of town. It looks like everybody who knew him had a reason for killing him."

"Name me some of the important names."

"His brother Jared Wilton—my client. He owns the mill and most of the town. The first time I met Jared he told me he thought his brother wanted to kill him and asked me to find out if he was right. They'd quarreled about money and about the way Carter Wilton treated his wife."

They were strolling along Main Street. They had reached a point where they could see into the park in front of the mill. The scene was very like the one that had greeted Voss the day of his arrival. The open space was packed with workers. This time, however, the bandaged agitator stood alone on the side of the dam with an American flag on a pole thrust into the earth at his side and only three or four uniformed cops were visible.

"I guess Wilton has given strict orders to the police and his private guards to keep their hands off," Voss said. Briefly he told of Friday's riot and Wilton's disapproval.

"Do you reckon the old guy would commit a murder?" Saint-Amour asked.

"He would if he was scared enough. Otherwise no. He doesn't like messiness. He takes great pains to avoid trouble. He likes to think of himself as a minor god in Andor and he kids himself into thinking everything runs smoothly under his benevolent rule. He's generous to a fault and pleasant to everybody till he thinks he's being crossed. Then he can be mean."

"Where was he Friday afternoon?"

"I tried to check on him and couldn't. He was in and out of his office several times. He spent part of the time in the first-aid hospital at the mill where the two injured in the riot were treated. It would have been possible for him to slip out of the mill and drive or walk through back streets and across country to the place where Carter was murdered."

"Then we'll suspect him slightly," Saint-Amour decided.

Voss grinned wryly, "I have to return his fee if he did it," he said. "I couldn't charge a man two thousand dollars for sending him to the chair."

"What the hell," said Saint-Amour. "When we find At-kinson, you'll get half the twenty-five thousand reward—that ought to be enough for you. Who's next?"

"Vito Russo. He's foreman of the guards at the mill and he started the riot, probably at the instigation of Claude Sackett, the general manager. He served time in Sing Sing for manslaughter. He was in the mill the night Stott was killed.

"He's going to marry the maid at Wilton's home and the maid is going to have Carter Wilton's baby. Russo knows about the baby. Jared Wilton fired him right after the riot and he spent the afternoon wandering around by himself."

Saint-Amour sighed. "A guy like that couldn't very well be Atkinson, but we'll keep him in mind."

"Sackett's next on the list," Voss said. "Sackett would have owned the mill if it hadn't been for the depression and Wilton's childish desire to humble him. He hates all the Wiltons. Russo is his man and so is Fleming, the chief of police. Friday morning Carter Wilton threatened to tell some dark secret to his brother unless Sackett paid him money or did something for him. Sackett threatened right back, 'I'll make so much trouble for you you'll wish you'd never been born.'"

"Has Sackett got a pedigree?"

"A long one. He couldn't possibly be Atkinson."

Saint-Amour sighed again. "Get on with the roll call."

"Julia Bisbee. She's Jared's niece and a nice person, but she'd be quite capable of killing a man if she considered it necessary. She has nerve and the courage of her convic-tions. She knew Carter was worthless and was ruining his wife's life. Julia thinks a lot of Dorothea Wilton. After we found Carter's body I caught Julia burning a white dress that was stained with blood, and she wouldn't talk about it."

"Julia Bisbee. It's surprising how many murders are committed by nice women. Will you go on, or shall I just take a look at the city directory?"

"There isn't any. The next most logical suspect, I guess, is Carter's widow, Dorothea. She's so swell and so deserving of sympathy I'd like to leave her out of it. But Carter treated her like a galley slave, knocked her around and cheated on her and made her life hell. There were prints of a woman's shoes on the path leading to Carter's body, and the measurements match her shoes. Of course, she may have used the path before Carter was killed, but—I've got a hunch Julia was burning her dress."

"You get me up here on the pretext of hunting for Atkinson, and you drag in women!" Saint-Amour complained.

"I thought about James Morgan, our handsome young minister, who is in love with Dorothea and might therefore have had a motive for killing Carter, even though he's always preaching against violence. Unfortunately, there isn't a thing to connect him with Stott and he was with me about the time Carter was murdered—although the doctor can't fix the moment exactly."

"Thank God, you've managed to eliminate one of the citizenry! Haven't you got anybody who could be a homicidal maniac?"

"I've been saving an idiot for you, but I doubt if it's a case of dementia praecox or psychasthenia, such as Atkinson must have had; it looks to me like plain imbecility dating from infancy or else caused by syphilis. He's a nasty-looking fellow who might be anywhere from thirty to fifty. Came here six or seven years ago and lives in a cave. He's never told anybody his name, so they call him Clubfoot Crippen. He wanders around like a spook. He called my attention to Stott's body, and I happened to see him hiding a bloody knife—undoubtedly the one that killed Carter Wilton, and certainly the one stolen several days before from the Wilton kitchen."

Saint-Amour took a cigar from his breast pocket and sank his teeth into it. His eyes seemed sleepier than ever.

He said, "That would be Atkinson. God probably told him to be a hermit and live in a cave. He's smart enough and knows enough about the brain and its diseases to play the part perfectly. Why bother with the others when you've got him?"

Voss said, "I'd expect to find Atkinson quietly doing some kind of useful work in his own line. He had a mission—why should he cut himself off from the world entirely? If he was so sure God was looking out for him, he wouldn't bother with an elaborate disguise. His very vanity, I should think, would keep him from masquerading as a mental defective."

"You can keep your other suspects. I'll take the idiot."

"You're welcome to him. I've got plenty more. It won't hurt to count them off. . . .

"Thomas Oliver Unger, an artist, is also in love with Dorothea, and he lives near where her husband was killed. A girl reporter and the labor agitator are staying in Unger's cottage; the day of the murder Carter tried to get fresh with her and got slapped. Leslie Frank, the agitator, might have done the killing, or the girl, Ruth Taylor, might have. I suspect Frank of writing Sackett's name in the sand beside the body, obviously to put suspicion on Sackett.

"There are three, all living together. In addition we have Carmen Corsi, the maid, whom Carter had loved and left, and a few others I'll skip for the moment.

"Last but far from least I'd like to call your attention to Joseph Kramer, better known as Pop, the editor of the *Advertiser*—"

"Please!" Saint-Amour protested, raising a plump hand. "You're snowing me under. I don't want to hear about this fellow Kramer at the moment or anyone else. I'm concentrating on the idiot."

They had turned into a side street and were abreast of the cemetery, Voss paused and looked over the green iron fence at two brown mounds close together. That morning he had seen Richard Stott and Carter Wilton buried there in black coffins that were almost identical. The Reverend George Parker had conducted brief and unimpressive services.

Voss murmured, "Wreaths for the vanquished." He inclined his head to indicate the battered little truck of Jim Schmidt, the florist, just entering the gateway to the cemetery. "Wonder why flowers are being sent after it's all over?"

He moved toward the gate and was halfway to the hummocks of fresh earth when he got an unobstructed view of one of the wreaths being lifted from the truck. His head jerked in surprise and he shouted, "Wait!"

Jim Schmidt waited, mildly annoyed, holding the wreath in his two hands. It was almost as high as he was.

"Who told you to bring them here?" Voss demanded. In the truck he could see that the other wreath was identical with the first, a huge disc of red roses with white blossoms forming letters.

Schmidt laid the wreath on the ground and brought from his jacket a soiled envelope which he handed to Voss.

The moment he saw the typewritten address Voss knew where the letter had been written. He took out the sheet of paper, unfolded it and read:

> Dear Mr. Schmidt: Enclosed find a $50 bill for which kindly arrange two large wreaths of red roses for the graves of Stott and Carter Wilton. Each must bear in large white letters the word "AMEN" and the signature "AVA." Place them over the graves an hour or two after the services.
>
> J. Wilton

Schmidt said, "Ava. I guess it's Latin."

Saint-Amour read the note over the crook of Voss's elbow. He said, "Unh-huh. It's an old Latin word meaning Andrew Vivian Atkinson. Now just why should Jared Wilton do that, Voss?"

"He didn't. Notice his signature is only typed. The note was written on Pop Kramer's typewriter, which has a broken capital 'V' and a twisted small 'e,' the same machine that wrote all the notes signed 'Atkinson.'"

"Pop Kramer's typewriter, eh? Why didn't you tell me about him?"

"I was trying to when you shut me up."

"That's right—the editor. Is he a nut by any chance?"

"Either he's crazy or he's one of the most whimsical men I ever ran across," said Voss. He turned to Schmidt. "Don't place those wreaths. Someone's playing a joke on you. Call Wilton and ask him about it."

Schmidt looked sad and let his shoulders sag. "After all that work!" he moaned. "What is only fifty dollars when one must destroy the work of his hands and heart?"

Voss and Saint-Amour left him displaying more genuine sorrow than the place of burial had seen that day.

The New York detective was deep in thought.

"This Kramer," he asked finally, "is he a religious man?"

"Decidedly not!" Voss replied.

"What does he look like?"

"He looks," Voss said, "just about as I should think Atkinson would look, even to the scar on his left arm. Twelve years ago in New York he was shot at by cops. When I mentioned Atkinson's name he knew all about that case. He deliberately gave me a convincing lot of circumstantial evidence against himself, all in fun. He predicted these murders—or *some* murders at any rate—the middle of last week. His left thumbprint was on one of the letters supposedly written by Atkinson."

"Holy mackerel, Abelard! Do you think he's our man?"

Voss shrugged. "I named twelve suspects and put Kramer last to give him a place of prominence. So far I haven't formed any definite opinion about any of the twelve. I'm looking for a thirteenth suspect—one who resembles each of the others in some part, has some of their qualities and motives, and may be one of them or may be someone I haven't noticed. He may be A. V. Atkinson. Certainly Atkinson fits in here somewhere, in the flesh or in the spirit. I doubt if anyone snatched his name out of twelve years of obscurity just to mystify us."

Saint-Amour chewed his unlighted cigar. "The way we solve most of our murders in New York," he said, "we make up our mind a certain one did it. We bring him in and put him through the works and if it turns out he didn't do it we make up our mind all over again and drag in the next most likely one. Sooner or later we get the right guy and he gives himself away.

"While you're fussing around being careful not to make up your mind I'll take a look at your editor with the scar on his arm. If he didn't do it I'll go after the idiot. Then if I have to I'll go right through your list.

"After that maybe we'll find time to worry about this imaginary bird you've invented—this thirteenth suspect."

12

The Proprietor and Editor of the *Advertiser* was alone in his littered office when Voss and Saint-Amour found him. His chair was tipped perilously and his scuffed shoes rested on the edge of one of the desks.

"I'm trying," he told Voss without moving, "to think of words appropriate to yesterday's occasion and its presiding genius. My thesaurus suggests mountebank, charlatan and posture master, witling, dizzard, jobbernowl and mooncalf, but they aren't equal to my sense of indignation. I loaned my Rabelais to a sweet young lady school teacher last June and haven't been able to get it back. How's your stock of adjectives and epithets?"

"You've already got me punchdrunk," Voss said. "Aren't you being a little unsympathetic?"

"It's the artist in me." Kramer lowered his feet to the floor one at a time and flexed his arms. Then he turned his muddy eyes upon Saint-Amour. The latter was scrutinizing Kramer carefully from toe to head, taking note of all the crooked seams in his face and neck, of his height and build, of the scar on his wrist. Pop bore the scrutiny with fortitude. He reached for a pencil and a slip of paper.

"A stranger in our midst," he observed. "That's worth a paragraph in 'Random Jottings.' What's the name, residence, business and purpose in coming to our fair town?"

"The name is Bob Saint-Amour," Voss said. "He's a detective lieutenant attached to the homicide squad of the New York City police department. He came here hoping to pick up the trail of a fugitive from justice named Atkinson, a convicted murderer—"

"And he thinks I'm Atkinson." Kramer shook his head sadly and laid down his pencil.

"Not exactly. That can be easily established. But we'd both like a talk with you."

Kramer sighed. He got to his feet. He said, "Last time I was in jail I swore never to go back, come hell or high water. I hope to God you two don't make a liar out of me. Come out in back where there's beer and where Ada won't discover the cops are after me if she comes in. There'd be the devil to pay if she knew."

They walked through the shop past the small presses and the linotype machine. Kramer produced a chair and a high stool for his guests. He slid back the cover of the ice chest and brought forth dripping bottles.

Saint-Amour accepted a bottle with a pleased grunt. He took a sip, leaned back in the chair and closed his eyes. He said, "We know Atkinson's pedigree and everything about his life up to twelve years ago. He was never in the printing business unless he picked it up after we lost track of him."

Pop said, "The lucky devil! I was never in anything else. I used to take my afternoon nap in the hellbox in my dad's print shop out in Arizona. That was when men toted guns and used 'em. My old man shot his way out of many an argument with his subscribers. They used to think it was a capital offense if their names weren't spelled right.

"One day the old man was slow on the draw and after that I ran the paper myself for two years. Then there was an important election and I backed the wrong side. After the voting, the winners from the governor to the sheriff got to thinking over what I had printed about them and I had to get out of the state.

"I drifted east working my way on small papers and stopped a while in Chicago. About twelve years ago I came on to New York and got a job with a Broadway scandal sheet called *The Whisperer*. I did so well there that pretty soon my boss was arrested for criminal libel with a dash of blackmail.

"When they came to arrest the boss they wanted to take me in, too. I went down the fire escape and ran till a cop shot me—that's how I got this scar on my left arm—and then I gave up. They kept me in the Tombs for six weeks as a material witness.

"I landed in jail the same day this man Atkinson escaped from the courtroom across the Bridge of Sighs. The papers printed millions of words about it and while I was waiting to be turned loose I didn't have much to do except read them.

"That's as close as I ever got to your murderer. I never saw him. After I left New York I don't think I ever heard his name till Voss mentioned it the other day. Then I remembered."

"Looks like you're not going to be a big help," Saint-Amour remarked. "Why did you pick this town to settle in, anyway?"

"I often ask myself that question." Kramer poured the last of his bottle of beer down his throat and smacked his lips. "I guess I was getting tired of drifting. I was getting close to forty and decided I'd get a little paper of my own and a wife and settle down.

"Andor already had a paper, but there was room for two and Floyd Turner and his *Clarion* didn't look like too much competition. Folks say I ruined his paper and broke his heart and hastened his death and maybe they're right, but it wasn't my fault entirely; if he'd had brains and guts he could have licked me at my own game because he knew everybody in town and I didn't—then.

"If I had it to do over again I guess I'd pick Andor, ugly as it is, or a town like it. Find a factory community dominated by a single man and you generally find a weak-kneed populace. Then you can cut loose and be yourself. Out in Arizona I'd have ridden a rail for some of the things I've printed. Here people grumble and talk about stopping their subscription, but they don't miss a line of what I write."

Saint-Amour opened his eyes a slit. "You can get away with murder, can't you?" he said.

He said it so casually that the editor grinned and nodded. Then he realized the significance of the words and his face became grave.

"I believe I could if I wanted to," he stated. "I haven't been trying to, if that's what you mean."

Voss put his empty bottle in the case of empties beside the icebox. "Bob is thinking about the editorial you ran last week," he said. "The one that was headed 'Symptoms of Murder.'"

"I could guess that one." Kramer's face remained serious. "I wasn't kidding the customers when I wrote it. I was in Boston three or four weeks ago and I picked up your book, Voss—the one I quoted from. I agreed with most of it. I saw how your theory might be applicable to the situation here.

"I'd have bet money there'd be blood shed soon. Only I didn't look for poor old thick-headed Stott to get it or even Carter Wilton. I looked for either Jared Wilton or Claude Sackett to be killed and for the other to go to the electric chair for doing it. The way those two men hate each other it will happen yet.

"Look at the way they're fighting now. Wilton is scared to death of unions; he wants to keep on being the big I Am in this town and he couldn't if his workmen were telling him what to do. So he takes the smartest course and makes a pal of the union organizer. He has him at Wiltonshire for dinner and the average mill worker says, 'What the hell! This red-hot from Boston is just another phony. He isn't a worker like me—he's a chum of millionaires. Why should we line up for him as long as Wilton is paying us good wages?'

"So what does Sackett do? He'd love to see Wilton take a beating. When he realizes Wilton's strategy is succeeding he gives Russo orders to play right into the union's hands by starting a fight. He gives the men something to get really excited about—Wilton brutality. He hopes the men will organize and tell Wilton where to get off and he doesn't give a damn if they wreck the mill!"

"I suppose it all dates from the depression when Sackett lost the business?"

"It dates from the time they were kids. Sackett used to drive a Shetland pony through the streets and sneer at Wilton in his patched overalls. Wilton swore to himself that some day he'd be rich and lord it over Sackett. They're both ambitious men and just now Wilton is riding highest. It wasn't so long ago he broke up a love affair between Sackett and Julia Bisbee. Do you think Sackett would cry if Wilton should stumble and break his neck?"

"Probably not."

"You've been up here three or four days, Voss. I've been here seven years. I've felt the hatred between those men growing all this time. Most of it comes from Wilton. It's too big now to be held in check. Maybe what has happened already is one result of it."

"Suppose all the people in town were lined up in front of you," Saint-Amour asked Kramer, "and you had to make a guess at the slayer to save your own neck. Which one would you point to?"

"Morgan."

"The minister? Nonsense! Why?"

Kramer's grin had returned. "Because," he said, "having no idea who could have done it I'd embarrass the one I liked least. But if you gave my artistic sensibilities time to get over that bit of juvenile playacting yesterday I might pick either Wilton or Sackett. Wilton could be trying to get rid of some people he didn't like and frame Sackett at the same time. Sackett could be trying to scare Wilton to death—"

Kramer broke off suddenly. He called, "Hold on, Saint-Amour!"

The detective had left his chair and was ambling around the shop. He had stooped and picked up a smudged slip of paper and was putting it in his pocket with an innocent air.

"You don't have to do that," Kramer said. He strode to one of the presses, put the fingertips of both hands against the ink plate and placed them over a sheet of glossy white paper. He handed Saint-Amour a perfect set of fingerprints.

"Thanks," Saint-Amour said quietly, waving the sheet to dry it.

"If you go picking up every inky sheet of paper in the place you'll get prints of Ada and Bert Walker, my helper," the editor told him. "A printing shop is a dirty place. You'll find all our fingerprints on everything and a lot of other people's besides.

"But that set isn't going to do you any good. They won't be Atkinson's prints because I'm not Atkinson. The mark of the left thumb will match the mark on the letter Voss got the other day, but all it will prove is that somebody sneaked in here and used my typewriter and a sheet of paper I had handled. Anybody could get it at night. Years ago I lost the only keys to the front and back doors and both Ada and I use hairpins to get in every morning."

"What do you think?" Saint-Amour asked Voss when they were back in Main Street.

"I think Pop's saner than most people," Voss said, "and more adult—and he's got a sense of humor. I like him."

"I could like him myself." Saint-Amour began chewing a fresh cigar. "But it wouldn't stop me from sending him to the chair."

"Do you think he's Atkinson?"

"I've got pictures of Atkinson and he could be. Twelve years can make a lot of changes in a man. Kramer isn't lame, but that doesn't prove anything; Atkinson might have broken his leg when he jumped out of the window, but it could heal straight, couldn't it? And even if he's not Atkinson he could be guilty as hell of these murders."

"What do you want to do about him?"

"I want to have him watched. Have you got a drag with the chief of police?"

"He wouldn't be the man to see. We'll drop in on Sackett. While Wilton thinks he's running this town Sackett really does the job. Fleming will listen to what he says, but he wouldn't pay much attention to either of us."

Sackett's office was on the first floor behind the general offices of the mill. There were no rugs on the floor and no curtains at the windows. A middle-aged secretary with frowsy hair admitted Voss and his companion at once. The general manager was going through a sheaf of papers with every appearance of industry. Clouds of blue cigar smoke hung in the air. His cold eyes greeted his visitors not unpleasantly and signaled them to chairs.

"What can I do for you?" he growled.

Voss introduced Saint-Amour. He said, "He's checking up on Kramer's past record and would like to have him kept under close surveillance for a day or so. There's no particular reason for thinking he'll run away, but there's no sense in taking chances either."

Sackett thrust out his lower jaw. "I'll tell Fleming. I'd give a year's pay to see the old trouble maker get in hot water. I'm afraid he didn't kill Carter Wilton, though."

"Whom do you suspect?"

Sackett put through his call before he replied. He got Fleming on the line and gave him terse orders. He warned, "If you lose track of him I'll get a new man for your job and make you come back to the mill."

He cradled the receiver and watched Voss unblinkingly with his narrowed eyes. "I suspect Leslie Frank most of all. Carter was trying to force him into a crooked deal, I believe, and was annoying his girl."

"What kind of a crooked deal?"

"Carter was starved for money. He had expensive tastes and his brother kept him broke. He wanted me to pay him ten thousand dollars to get rid of the union gang—said I could take it out of my private expense account. I'm pretty sure he offered Frank a cut of the money if he'd go in on the deal; I don't know of any other way he could get Frank to quit. I presume Frank told him to go to hell like I did."

"And that led to murder?"

Sackett said, "You've got to remember Carter's temper. You've got to understand how keen Frank is to organize this mill. It would be to Frank's interest to throw a murder scare into the town. Agitation always gets better results when people are afraid of something."

"Did Frank kill Stott, too?" Saint-Amour asked.

"All I know about that is that Stott was trying to convince Frank that the workers ought to form an ideal community here in Andor, a sort of miniature Utopia, and let the national union and the rest of the world go hang. Stott didn't bother other people much as a rule, but he could be crusty and vindictive when he thought he was right and the other fellow was wrong. Maybe you can make something of that situation."

Voss told him, "We've got clues and motives that point to a number of people. You're one of them. The most direct clue points to Julia Bisbee. After we found Carter's body I found her burning a bloodstained dress."

Sackett's features altered just a trifle as though a shadow had descended over them. His eyes left Voss's face and focused on a corner of the ceiling.

He said, "Julia Bisbee! You're crazy, man! She wouldn't have anything to do with killing anybody."

"She's willing to admit she was burning a dress, but she won't say why."

"Forget about it. She's got brains and she knows better than to get herself in a jam. You'll waste time if you worry about the possibility of her killing Carter."

Voss smiled. "She told me the same thing about you when I mentioned that your name was written in the sand beside the corpse. You knew it was, didn't you?"

"I knew it, but I didn't think you did. That was Frank's doing; there wasn't any writing when you and I looked the ground over at first. It was dumb of Fleming to destroy the marks; we might have proved something by them."

"Then there was the footprint you destroyed—"

Sackett asked innocently, "Did I? It must have been accidental. I wonder if it could have been left by that girl—what's her name?—Ruth Taylor. Leslie Frank's girl."

"I wonder," Voss echoed drily. "I think we ought to let Saint-Amour talk to the people at the cottage; he's got a way of smelling guilt. Being a New York cop he has no rating here, but I don't suppose Fleming would object."

"He wouldn't. He hasn't got brains enough to object to somebody setting the town hall afire. I have to do everything for him except change his diapers. Saint-Amour will be welcome and will have every assistance we can give him as long as he wants to stick around.

"I'd like to see this mess cleaned up as soon as possible because murder's a funny thing. If a man gets away with it once or twice he generally wants to do it again. And it gives other people ideas; it's catching."

Sackett shook hands with both of them when they left. They went to the Commercial House and Saint-Amour got a room. Voss walked up the creaking stairs with him to the dismal cubicle with its threadbare carpet and sagging bed.

"I don't like these junkets to crossroads towns," Saint-Amour complained. "Give me the Parker House in Boston or the Book-Cadillac in Detroit and I think I'm getting a break."

He produced a thick envelope from his coat pocket. Out of it he took photographs and cards and papers. He unfolded a large card across which were spread the prints of a man's ten fingers. He placed it on the dresser and laid beside it the inked paper Kramer had given him. He compared the markings on the two sheets and looked disappointed.

"So far," he said, "Kramer is a hundred percent in the clear. The loops and whorls say he isn't Atkinson and he never was."

13

Morgan had been at Wiltonshire for dinner. Jared Wilton was inclined to be peevish, but the young minister's assurance kept him out of difficulties. He produced an elegant argument in defense of his "Message to a Murderer."

Morgan posed the rhetorical question, "Would a man have written a note like that to me if his conscience wasn't troubled?" He argued, "An aching conscience cries out for expression. No man who knows that he has done wrong can get rid of his sense of guilt without confessing to someone. Wise men have known that for centuries; the confessional is one of the sturdiest pillars of the Church of Rome.

"What if I did fail? Trying is always worth while. The guilty man may have lost courage at the last minute and stayed away from the service. But if he was there he must have been tempted powerfully to reveal the whole thing and have it over with. Anyway, the thought of confession is in his mind; he may decide at any moment to avail himself of the divine mercy I promised him."

Wilton took up the challenge. "I don't agree with this soft way of telling people, 'It's all right whatever you've done; just say you're sorry and no matter what the law of man decides, God will pardon you.' It encourages wrong-doing. I can imagine the man who wrote that note saying to himself, 'If the promise of forgiveness is true to-day it will be true ten years from now. I'll wait and maybe kill some more people meanwhile. When I'm ready to die I'll confess.'"

"It isn't likely," Morgan said. "If he's remorseful for what he's done he won't want to add to that remorse. If he's afraid of being caught now he won't put himself in triple jeopardy by committing another offense against the law. If he's neither remorseful nor afraid it's a different matter; but in that case why did he write?"

"I think someone was playing a joke on you. I'll bet that man Kramer wrote the letter. He was in church for the first time since he's been in town, snickering and whispering beside me."

Morgan's face tightened. "Kramer is capable of almost anything, but even he wouldn't do a thing like that. It's worse than blasphemy. He'd like to make a fool of me—he seems to hate me more than anyone else in Andor—but he wouldn't dare go that far!"

The phone rang and Carmen answered. It was Saint-Amour calling Voss.

The detective said, "Damn it, Abelard, we could probably get indictments against pretty nearly everybody in town. Not one of the people you mentioned as suspects seems to have a decent alibi for all of Friday afternoon. Sackett was on a mysterious errand. Nobody knows where Russo was spending his time. Frank and Unger got out of sight as soon as they left the hospital. Kramer claims he was in the bar at the hotel, but the bartender told me he only spent about half an hour there."

"How about the idiot?"

"I found his cave. It's a filthy place. Nothing there but a lot of rags for a bed and two or three rusty pots and pans and a pile of garbage. It's hard to picture a human being living in a hole of that kind.

"The nut was there, but he beat it when he saw me coming. He went about a hundred yards up the hill and watched me and wouldn't come down when I yelled at him. I got his fingerprints off one of the pans, though—dusted them with black powder and managed to get a fairly good direct copy on a piece of paper because the pan was thick with grease. They aren't at all like Atkinson's prints, but one of them matches the only print I could find on the knife you gave me."

"Do you want him arrested?"

"God, I don't know. He carried that bloody knife between his thumb and second finger. The marks show it. But when the murderer slit Carter's throat either he didn't leave any prints because he wore gloves or he was damned careful to wipe 'em off.

"Maybe the idiot's as harmless as folks say and somebody's trying to make him the goat. If that's the way of it he might do us more good outside of jail than in. I don't guess he'll run away. He went back to the cave when I left, moving when I moved and keeping the hundred yards between us all the time."

Voss said, "Leave him alone for a while. He can't possibly be Atkinson. Your pictures of Atkinson prove it as well as the fingerprints. A man can't grow a hump between his shoulders and change the shape of his skull."

When the conversation was ended Voss could hear Wilton and Morgan disputing about morals and theology in the dining room. Julia Bisbee had already left the table and Dorothea was just leaving. Voss wandered through the front door and down the flagstone walk that halved a lush lawn flanked at either side by tall ornamental hedges.

The last dull crimson traces of the sun had disappeared and dusk was thickening. Muffled thunder sounded in the distance and there were occasional faint flashes of lightning on the horizon. By all the signs it would rain in a little while and rain hard.

Voss was not aware that Dorothea had followed him until she spoke at his side. She said, "I've got a confession to make—one very much like the kind Morgan was speaking about, only it wouldn't help me to tell it to him. Will you listen to me?"

He looked down from his awkward height. Beneath her words he caught an undertone of sharp earnestness. He told her, "I'm a pretty good listener."

They went a few paces without speaking. Her face was like a pale flower in the dusk. The heavy air held the scent of some delicate flowerlike perfume she used.

She said, "I guess I killed Carter."

The silence came down again broken by their soft footfalls and the rustling of leaves as a breeze arose. He waited a moment before he prompted, "You *guess?*"

"If I were judge and jury I'd convict myself. I had every provocation. He hated me and made my life miserable. He got drunk and cursed me and struck me frequently. He tried to make me beg and steal money from Jared. He behaved disgracefully with other women. I used to pray sometimes that he would die and set me free."

"I don't know of any penalty for praying people to death," Voss said. "If it was a sure method a lot of people would be guilty of murder."

She explained, "I was only trying to make you see that if I killed him I was justified to some degree. And if I did it I was out of my head. I don't remember anything about it. I suspected myself as soon as Carter's body was discovered, but I wasn't sure till I heard Julia and James talking just before dinner. They were in the swing on the veranda and nobody was around. I heard them when I came around the corner of the house and when they mentioned my name I listened."

"Do they think you killed Carter?"

"They're sure of it and they're trying to shield me. Julia has always been my best friend and James—well, he wanted to marry me once. But I don't want them to shield me at the risk of getting into trouble or having someone else suspected and persecuted. If I did it I'll take the consequences. I'm not afraid."

"You shouldn't be. You'd have the full sympathy of any court. Suppose you tell me the whole story."

"There isn't a great deal to tell. After lunch Friday I started out to see Thomas—Mr. Unger. He was doing a portrait of me and I didn't know then that there had been a riot at the mill. Carter had forbidden me to see Tom any more, but I didn't think he had any right to order my life after some of the things that had happened. I have always considered Tom a good friend.

"I was about half way to the cottage when I saw Carter go into the yard. Ruth was there alone. They talked for a minute and Carter put his arms around her and tried to kiss her. She struggled with him and he let her go and started toward Wiltonshire by the path that runs along the stream.

"I was angry. I didn't care what he did as long as he didn't embarrass his brother or me publicly, but I thought he was doing that in this case. Someone else could easily have seen him with Ruth."

"Someone else did," Voss said. "At least one other person."

"Well, I went down by the stream to meet him. He got there first and stood watching the water. He had a furious expression on his face and I should have known better than to speak to him, but I was too upset to think clearly.

"I went close to him and said, 'Carter, you should be ashamed of yourself!' He hadn't heard me coming and he jumped. Then he swore and came toward me doubling his

fists. I remember his hitting me in the breast and the chin.
I fell down and must have struck my head against a stone.

"The next I remember I was undressed in bed and Julia
was bathing my face with a cold cloth."

"Had you walked home?"

She shook her head. "At first I thought I must have,
but this evening I learned the truth. James came to the
house Friday afternoon and Julia told him I had gone for
a walk. They went looking for me. They found me lying
beside Carter's body and my dress was covered with blood.
Julia smoothed the sand where it was trampled and James
carried me to the house and so far as they know no one
saw us. He and Julia agreed to say nothing. Julia burned
my dress and some of my other clothes that were stained."

Voss stopped walking. A hundred feet ahead of them,
almost invisible in the gloom, the figure of a man was
crossing the lawn. He was moving rapidly toward one of
the hedges which in a moment would screen him from
sight.

"That's Russo," Dorothea informed him. "He comes almost every night to see Carmen. He meets her a little way
from the house because Jared doesn't like him."

"Clandestine love, eh?"

She wasn't interested in Vito Russo. She said, "They
couldn't send me to the electric chair if I stabbed Carter
without knowing what I was doing, could they?"

"No, they couldn't. You needn't worry about that at all.
Will you promise me something?"

"Anything within reason."

"Don't mention a word of what you've told me to anyone."

"But I'd like to talk to James and Julia about it."

"That would be all right. But don't talk to anyone else.
Ask them to keep the secret a while longer, too."

"But—wouldn't it be better to make a clean breast of it? Think how much worse it would look if it was found out that I knew I had done it and had tried to cover it up."

"I doubt very much if you did it," Voss said. "It's possible, but highly improbable. Where would you get a knife, and what happened to it later? There's no telling who might have seen Carter at the cottage and followed him to the place where he was killed, or perhaps just come upon him there by accident. While you were lying unconscious someone could have killed him and left you to take the blame."

"But who?"

Voss sighed. "Carter had so many enemies it will be a hard job to answer that question. I've got enough circumstantial evidence to take half a dozen people into court. But it couldn't have been all of them. . . ."

A hoarse cry broke the quiet. It was followed by a crashing in the bushes behind which Russo had vanished, and then a sound that was half moan, half sob.

"Go to the house!" Voss commanded Dorothea, and ran toward the sound. The bushes were thicker than he had anticipated. Branches tore at his coat, scratched his hands and face. It seemed hours before he had battered his way through.

A brighter gleam of lightning and a louder peal of thunder greeted him as he emerged, and then an uneven beat of limping footsteps rose above the sound of the rain. Crouched against the hedge, concealed by its foliage, Voss held his breath. His body tensed as he caught a glimpse of a vague shape hurrying toward him—a shape bent almost double, the face concealed by an upturned coat collar or a strip of dark cloth. That would be Russo, he guessed.

When the figure was directly in front of him, almost within reach of his long arms, Voss sprang. He tried for a flying tackle that would hurl the other to the ground. But the soft earth beneath the hedge played him false; his foot slipped, he staggered off balance, and his shoulder only struck the man's hip a glancing blow.

From the man's throat was wrenched a surprised cry that might have been an oath or a sob. He fell to the ground, and Voss sprawled face-downward beside him. The other man recovered first; he scrambled to his knees while Voss was still gasping, and his fists thudded against the back of Voss's head and neck. They were clumsy, unskilled blows, but there was strength behind them and they hurt. Voss put up his hands and arms as shields, trying to roll away, and then his antagonist's knee drove against the hinge of his jaw with numbing force.

Voss lay motionless and stunned on his back, the sound of ill-matched footsteps growing fainter in his ears. With a tremendous effort, he thrust himself erect, leaned to run after the vanished man and opened his mouth to shout a warning.

He neither ran nor shouted. There was a dark form against the grass, twenty feet from him in the direction from which the limping one had come. He strode toward it, clamping his teeth grimly.

It was Vito Russo, and Vito Russo was dead. It was not too dark to see, at close range, the thing that had been done to him. A tiny hatchet, a child's toy with a dull-edged blade hardly larger than an oak leaf, had been driven into the skull with such violence that the metal was half buried in the brain.

Voss knelt over the warm corpse. The coat had fallen open to reveal an automatic pistol holstered beneath the left armpit. Russo had been given no opportunity to draw the weapon; apparently the killer had been pressed close against the hedge, lurking in ambush, and had struck without warning.

The rain was coming faster. Even if the lush grass or the soft earth had taken footprints, they would be washed out in no time.

Voss went to the house. Morgan and Julia were on the edge of the veranda, watching for him through the storm. Dorothea had just joined them. The rain spattered from the railing of the veranda, wetting all of them.

"What was it, Voss?" Morgan asked, his voice oddly tight. "We thought we heard a yell."

"That was Russo," Voss said shortly.

"Russo! What's the matter with him?"

"He's dead."

Jared Wilton overheard him. He stood just within the doorway, as though he had come from the library. He was panting and his face was ghastly white splotched with purple.

"My God!" he gasped. "What did you say?"

"Russo has just been killed. His body is beside the hedge. Someone did it with a toy hatchet and got away from me."

He thought Wilton was going to faint. He took a step toward the old man, but was waved back. Tottering and limping heavily on his sore foot, Wilton made his way to a chair and sat down. He faltered, "Get Dr. Hughson for me. My heart—"

By the time others arrived on the scene the rain had become a cloudburst. Voss had found a slicker several sizes too small for him, but Saint-Amour huddled unhappily beneath the nearest tree, his soaked garments clinging to his rotund body.

Alfred Fleming was frightened. He said to Dr. Hughson, "Great Scott, he was Sackett's right-hand man! Who'd have dared—?"

Hughson interrupted with heavy sarcasm, "I suppose if Sackett hadn't liked him, it would be all right! Since it was this way, though, we won't suspect you."

"Now, listen—" Fleming protested, shivering in the wet.

Saint-Amour beckoned Voss beneath the tree. "It's only a little damper than out there," he muttered. "You said the killer limped when he ran away, and yet he was husky enough to knock you out. That could be the idiot, couldn't it?"

"It could," Voss replied. "I've been thinking about him. But it could also have been Wilton, Frank or Unger, all of whom are temporarily lame. Besides, even you could limp if you wanted to."

"I will tomorrow, with rheumatism. Now we've got three murders—three angles we can take in getting to the guy we want, presuming one person did them all. Who hated Russo the most?"

"I could give you a long lecture on that subject. Russo started the riot at the mill and so was responsible for Frank and Unger being beaten and for Ruth being thrown in the lake. I've heard of murders being committed for no more reason than that.

"Then, Sackett may have wanted him out of the way because of what he knew and might tell about secret goings-on at the mill. There were some— Carter Wilton had threatened to expose something that would involve both Sackett and Russo.

"Jared Wilton hated Russo and had forbidden him to come here. He got Russo fired from the mill, but Sackett was going to give him a job on the outside, the inference being that Russo would continue to do his dirty work. Wilton may have had some very good reason for wanting him out of the way.

"Russo was having difficulties with Carmen, the maid, too. He was mad at her for having had that affair with Carter. And while I don't think of any more details at the moment, I have no doubt I could discover excellent reasons why he might have been murdered by Kramer, the Widow Weston—"

"Or anyone at the house."

"Yes—except Dorothea. She was walking with me. She didn't do it."

"You aren't falling in love, are you, Abelard? Is romance blossoming in this blood-soaked soil?"

"It's blossoming fast," Voss stated, "but I'm not in on it."

"It's early for Dorothea to pick herself another husband," said Saint-Amour, "but when she does it had better be Morgan. He ran into me this afternoon and introduced himself and showed me the sights. A nice guy; but long-winded. I took occasion to pump him, and when her name came up he positively glowed. He's got it bad."

"I can't blame him much."

"He's got it so bad," Saint-Amour went on, "I figured I'd better get his fingerprints checked. I let him handle my watch."

"Yes."

"He doesn't look old enough to be Atkinson, but you never can tell about those things, so I compared his prints with Atkinson's. And what do you think I found out?"

"I think," said Voss, "you found out the young fellow is entitled to a clean bill of health."

Saint-Amour nodded glumly. "And I'm just as glad. There's always a lot of grief when a preacher gets pinched. Let's make a dash for the house; this rain's getting worse."

They raced for the veranda. Hughson and Fleming and all but one of the four policemen who had come with the chief had preceded them. They made a group in one corner of the porch. Fleming was telling Jared Wilton how it must have happened and Morgan hovered near, listening.

Julia stood a little apart from them. She came up to Voss, acknowledged his introduction of Saint-Amour with a nod, and said, "I just saw the hatchet the murderer used. Fleming has it. There may be dozens of them in town, but it's exactly like one I bought at the ten-cent store a month ago."

"What did you do with it?"

"I gave it to little Toby. He used to carry it around stuck in his belt. He always had it with him till two or three days ago, when I noticed it was missing. He said he'd lost it."

"Anyone could have found it," Saint-Amour remarked, "but who'd have chosen a thing like that as a lethal weapon?"

"Pop Kramer spoke of the possibility of his defenseless head being made the target of 'the hatchet of an assassin' if he mentioned certain names in certain connections," Voss recalled. "It was on the front page of the *Advertiser* in bold type."

"Then, damn it, Abelard—"

"No use getting excited. It's a common enough expression. Pop could use it without thinking. But it might have put an idea in someone else's head. Everyone in Andor reads the *Advertiser,* so you've still got the field to choose from."

"That," said Saint-Amour, "is the trouble with these small-town cases. The hard part is to find somebody who couldn't be guilty!"

14

Chief of Police Fleming telephoned Voss while breakfast was in progress at Wiltonshire. The summons interrupted a bitter harangue by Jared Wilton, who had just learned from Julia that murder would once more be discussed from the Tabernacle pulpit at the Wednesday night prayer meeting.

"He said last night," Julia reported, "that what happened to Russo made him more than ever convinced that there was no sense in trying to ignore unpleasant subjects even on religious occasions. He said the town would be terrified and he must do what he could to reassure and comfort the people."

Wilton did not agree. He fumed, "The young whelp's had his last chance! I put him where he is and to show his gratitude he insists upon talking about things he knows are distasteful to me! He makes open scandals out of things that should be hushed up as quietly as possible. All right—I'll call a meeting of the vestry and see that they fire him and get someone else in his place. I've threatened to do it before and this time I'll keep my word."

Julia protested: "There's no harm in it. I'll admit he gets pretty dramatic, but I don't believe in ignoring unpleasant things even in church. As long as they exist they've got to be considered.

"Besides," Julia pointed out, "if you fire James there'll be talk and scandal about that. He has a lot of friends."

"Let there be talk, as long as it's the last time. When it's over we'll get some Gospel on Sundays instead of penny-dreadful pipe dreams. What do you think, Voss?"

The telephone spared Voss the necessity of taking sides. He went to the instrument and was surprised at the new note of humility in Fleming's voice. Sackett must have given him a first-rate dressing down, he thought.

"Mr. Sackett wants me to have a talk with those Reds at the cottage and get them to make definite statements about Russo, Stott and Carter Wilton," Fleming said. "He told me I'd better take you and Lieutenant Saint-Amour along. Will you come?"

"You can pick me up any time," Voss said. "I'll give Saint-Amour a ring and we'll get him at the hotel."

"There's another thing." Fleming hesitated. "The man we had outside Kramer's house last night phoned in and said he'd lost Kramer somehow. He isn't home or at his office. Sackett's pretty mad about it, but I think we'll find him around town somewhere."

"I hope so." Voss hung up and gazed out the window. The downpour of the previous night had become a bleak drizzle that gave no promise of ending and all the world seemed gray and sodden. He got Saint-Amour on the phone.

"Hell!" the detective objected. "It's a perfect morning for staying in bed. Besides, my clothes aren't dry."

"All right," Voss told him. "Go back to sleep. I'll wake you up when we've finished with them and located Pop Kramer. By the way, you didn't know the cops lost track of him last night, did you?"

Saint-Amour yelled, "What? Our hatchetman gone? I'll be ready for you in fifteen minutes—no, ten!"

Voss returned to the table and finished his coffee. Wilton had dropped the subject of Morgan and was berating Sackett.

"Everything would go along smoothly," Wilton was saying, "if I could keep Sackett from making trouble. He won't have a chance today because the rain will prevent a meeting at noon, but if he can manage it he'll start some trouble before Friday, when the workers will vote on striking for recognition. He'd like nothing better than to see the mill ruined and the whole town starving."

Julia got up abruptly. She said with more than a trace of warmth, "If you'd try to get along with Claude Sackett instead of fighting him all the time your mill would be a lot safer and better off. If anything happens to it because of your silly quarrel it will be as much your fault as his!"

She walked from the room, leaving Wilton to stare after her in shocked astonishment. He wailed, "My own niece!"

Voss saw Fleming's sedan in the drive. He made a hasty excuse and got his hat and hurried through the rain to the car. Fleming gave him a sheepish smile.

"I'm sorry about Kramer," he said frankly. "I hope he hasn't taken a powder. Sackett was sore and told me I didn't have the brains of a caterpillar. Maybe I have and maybe I haven't, but I couldn't very well watch Kramer myself and how was I to know my man would go to sleep?"

"Did he?"

"He doesn't admit it, but he followed Kramer home at six o'clock last night and didn't see him after that. He sat in front of Kramer's house in an automobile till six this morning, when another man relieved him. Do you think he stayed awake all that time?"

"I hope he stayed awake till after Russo was killed. I'd like to know whether Kramer was out of his house after dinner."

"I asked about that. He said he didn't see Kramer go out, but that he might have sneaked out the back way. He was so uncertain I don't like to depend on his word. I think he must have sneaked home for dinner or something and is afraid to admit it. We could ask Mrs. Kramer if her old man went out—"

"Don't. If Pop hasn't left town already he probably won't unless he figures we're anxious to grab him. We'll let it rest for a while."

"That's what I thought, but after my talk with Sackett I don't know whether to trust my own judgment or not. He wants you or Saint-Amour to do the questioning at the cottage. It's all right with me because I realize you and he have handled more murder cases than we ever hear about in Andor."

"Saint-Amour is one of the best cops in the country," Voss told him. "I'm no policeman—but I'd like to hear what they have to say—find out what makes them tick."

"Huh?" asked Fleming.

"Nothing," said Voss. "Just thinking out loud."

"I hope you can figure this thing out," complained Fleming. "If you don't I'll lose my badge. I'm sure Frank is guilty, even if it does look a little bit funny about Kramer, but how we can pin it on him is more than I can see."

Saint-Amour was waiting for them under the awning of the Commercial House. His gray suit was a damp mass of wrinkles and his lids drooped listlessly over his round eyes.

He did not mention Kramer. He grumbled, "I should never have left New York. If I don't get a piece of that reward after going through all this misery I'll break down and cry."

He climbed into the back seat and slumped in a corner and proceeded to doze off.

Ruth Taylor spied the car from the doorway of the cottage. She came out on the tiny porch. They heard her call back into the house, "Get up, comrades! They've sent a cop apiece for us! Now we'll eat on the town for a while."

Voss left the car and ducked under the low roof of the porch. "Not this time," he corrected her. "This is just a friendly visit."

Ruth said, "You aren't eligible for the union. If you don't want to pinch us what do you want?"

Fleming replied tersely for Voss. He wasn't in a jesting mood.

"Information."

"Okay, chief. What do you want to know?"

Fleming looked expectantly at Saint-Amour. He stood more in awe of the portly lieutenant than he did of Voss. But Saint-Amour failed him; he seemed asleep on his feet and said nothing.

"Uh—what do you know about these murders?" Fleming demanded.

She brushed the dark hair back from her eyes and smiled. "If you'd read my paper you'd find out not only what I know, but what I think about them."

Voss interrupted, "Miss Taylor and I have been through that already. We won't go over the same ground. Only one important thing has happened since then. Miss Taylor, I suppose you have heard about Russo's death?"

"Last night," she said. "Leslie and I were drinking a coke at the drugstore and everybody was talking about it."

"Where were you at the time he was killed?"

"Not so fast," she countered. "How would I know just what time he was killed? But I can account for the whole evening.

"We had something to eat about half-past six and sat around talking till eight. Then Leslie and I took a walk up

Main Street and Unger said he was going to get some rest. Leslie and I went to Lucas's grocery and Williams's meat market. Leslie stopped in front of the Commercial House to talk to some men.

"We got to Carpenter's drugstore just after nine and heard the happy tidings at the soda fountain. From what was said I judged Russo had just been killed. Does that clear us?"

Saint-Amour opened his eyes a trifle. "You Reds will probably have an airtight alibi the day you blow up the world," he said.

Ruth flashed, "And you big-bellied New York cops will frame us anyway, so what's the difference?"

The lieutenant grinned. "I can understand your reference to my waistline, but how did you know I was a New York cop?"

"I've done organization work in New York. I've been arrested there. All the plainclothes cops I saw were fat and sloppy and sleepy."

Saint-Amour laughed and slapped his leg. "You and I could get along," he chuckled. "I'm kind of anxious for the revolution to come myself. Abelard, she didn't kill anybody; if she had she'd be proud of it."

She agreed seriously. "I would. If I had reason enough to kill anyone, I'd want the world to know the reason. But these people . . . our fight isn't with people like that; it's with the bosses."

"Sackett and Wilton, you mean?"

"Only in a narrow sense. They aren't really the bosses. Our enemies are men in Wall Street and Washington and Pittsburgh who control basic industries and raw materials. It wouldn't do any good to kill them, either, because the ideas that keep them alive would remain and other men would step into their shoes. We've got to do away with the old ideas."

"Well said!" Saint-Amour exclaimed. "You get a high mark for that recitation. Now if we could see Leslie—"

Frank showed up in the doorway. He said, "Any time." He was in his bare feet and was tucking the ends of his shirt into his trousers. His dark hair stood up in wild disorder and he had taken off the bandages from his forehead. There was a nasty unhealed cut in his left temple. The flesh around his eyes was still purple.

Voss said, "Ever since Friday I've been wondering why you wrote Sackett's name in the sand beside Carter Wilton's body."

Frank was startled. He asked slowly, "What makes you think I did?"

"It's plain enough. There was no writing in the sand when I made my examination. If Carter had written anything the killer would have erased it as carefully as he erased all other marks. And Carter couldn't have made those neat block letters; he was strangling and choking to death."

"It was a foolish thing to do," Frank admitted. "I didn't really think it would get Sackett into trouble, but I thought it might worry him. Let's just call it an unhappy impulse and let it go at that."

"We'll call it impulse," Voss consented, "but I'm not so sure about letting it go at that. And I'm curious about another thing. What sort of proposition had Carter made to you?"

"A very stupid one. I meant to mention it to you before this. He thought he could talk Sackett into paying money to get me to leave town. He wanted to make a deal with Sackett and give me a share of the money—two thousand dollars was the sum he mentioned—if I'd leave voluntarily and let it appear that he'd scared me out. I told him to go to the devil."

"Did he threaten you or make you angry?"

"He threatened me and made me indignant. But he didn't give me a motive for murdering him."

"How did you feel about his attentions to Miss Taylor?"

"I didn't know about them till after he was dead. Ruth didn't tell me. If I had known I would have ordered him to keep away from her, but I wouldn't have cut his throat."

"You'd had a disagreement with Richard Stott, hadn't you?"

"A disagreement—yes. He tried to convert me to a plan to make Andor a self-sufficient anarchy based on brotherly love. He talked my head off. It was a pretty and an idealistic scheme, but it wouldn't work anywhere. I'm a fanatic in my way and he was one in his and we didn't get along. I tried to avoid him because his mind was completely closed to new ideas, but he insisted on arguing and got to the point of calling me names and saying I was a menace to humanity."

"What did you do?"

"Walked away from him."

"And later?"

"We met on the street once or twice and didn't speak."

"Then you didn't murder him."

Frank twisted his mouth into a patient grin. "I didn't murder anyone. Not Stott, who didn't mean a thing to me one way or another; not Carter Wilton, who probably had a great many enemies besides me; not Russo, toward whom I felt no ill will even after the riot.

"Besides, Ruth has already told you where we were last night. You can make inquiries of the people we saw."

"Unfortunately," Voss pointed out, "that alibi isn't sufficient. She said the three of you were here from six to eight. Russo died at seven-twenty. One of you could have slipped over to Wiltonshire and used the hatchet on him."

"That's bad." Frank frowned. "We could testify for each other, but it wouldn't be the same as having disinterested witnesses."

"No, it wouldn't," Saint-Amour interjected. "How old are you?"

"Forty-seven."

"Twelve years ago you were thirty-five. You're five feet eleven, weigh around a hundred and fifty and have hair and eyes of the right color. You're lame. Do you know anything about chemistry?"

"I wasn't lame before Russo got hold of me Friday. Chemistry was one of my subjects in college, but I've forgotten most of it."

"You look like an escaped criminal I've been hunting."

Frank said, "I guess I'm an ex-criminal. I've served time in Boston and New York—for picketing; in the days when that was a crime. But I never escaped. The police have my record and my fingerprints."

Saint-Amour decided, "I won't pester you any more unless I get some evidence tossed at me. Right now I'd be inclined to give you a clean bill of health. Where's the other one who lives here—the artist?"

Ruth called, "Your turn, Tom!"

Unger's sullen voice replied, "If they want to see me they'll have to come in. I'm in bed and I'm staying here till noon."

They trooped into the living room. Unger lay beneath blankets on the studio couch. His blue eyes resented their presence; they particularly resented Saint-Amour, who gazed at the three paintings of Dorothea and whistled.

"Feeling better?" Voss asked.

"I'm all right, thanks. A little tired of all this question-and-answer business. If you let me talk I can save you a lot of asking."

"Go ahead; I'd rather you did."

"All right. In the first place I'm not particularly interested in the labor movement. Leslie Frank and Ruth are my friends and they're sharing my diggings and I hope they stay a long time, but I'm neither for nor against their work. I went to that meeting Friday because I wanted to look into a sea of faces of men and women hearing exciting talk and because I wanted to help Frank if I could. Maybe you could call me a lukewarm well-wisher of the champions of labor.

"As for the three murdered men, I didn't know the man Stott, not from Adam. I'd seen quite a lot of Carter Wilton and I didn't like him, but we were neither friends nor enemies. I barely knew Russo; after his gang beat me up I might have taken a punch at him if I'd met him on the street, but I'd never have used a knife.

"Finally, I'm not a murderer by inclination or circumstance. I didn't kill any of them."

Voss said, "That's practically all we want to hear. Just one question—did you ever talk with Clubfoot Crippen, the idiot?"

"You can't talk with him. He makes sounds, but they aren't words. He passes every day and once I got him to stop by giving him some candy. I made a couple of sketches of him and when he saw them he laughed. From the sores all over him I'd say he belongs in a hospital."

"And I've got a question," Saint-Amour said. "When Carter Wilton's wife was posing for you did she ever say anything—?"

Unger's teeth came together with a snap. He lifted himself on one elbow. He spaced his words carefully.

"Never. I told you I wasn't the murdering kind, but I'll kill the man who tries to drag her into this."

"I didn't mean to say anything against her." Saint-Amour's eyes were wide and innocent. "I only wondered."

He started for the door. Fleming moved with him uncomfortably. Voss said, "Thanks, all of you," and trailed them.

When they were in the car Fleming's obvious disappointment broke the surface. "I still think we ought to arrest Frank," he said.

"For what?" Saint-Amour demanded.

Fleming subsided, and pressed the starter button. He had the car in gear when Ruth came running out. She clambered on the running board. She said, "Unger's a swell fellow. Don't go away with the notion he had it in for Carter Wilton because of Dorothea. He's in love with her, but while Carter was living he kept it to himself. Just in the last two or three days he's begun to let her see it.

"You know when he was pretending he was sicker than he really was Saturday—making believe he couldn't get out of bed? Well, that was to get her to spend more time with him. He wasn't being selfish about it; he wanted to get her mind off what had happened."

Voss smiled at her. "Don't worry. We aren't going to build a frame for him. Personally I think he's all right."

The car moved forward. Saint-Amour, already nodding in the back seat, spoke up, "I think they're all all right. I'd join their damned union if they'd let me."

Fleming's face was grim. He drove fast to the Commercial House and let them out in the drizzle. When he told them good-by his manner was shorn of much of the awe that had characterized it.

Saint-Amour sighed. "We've disillusioned him. He thought we were going to pick up a murderer like a magician pulls rabbits out of a silk hat. It was his first workout with city slickers and it didn't come up to expectations!"

15

"Pop is a Blowhard," Ada Kramer said. "He howls for blood but he wouldn't hurt a fly. Now he thinks he's getting deep into this murder business he runs away."

Beneath heavy brows the gaunt woman's sharp eyes peered at Voss and Saint-Amour good-humoredly. When she saw Saint-Amour's hitherto serene countenance turn grave she warned, "Now don't go getting notions. I been married to Pop more than five years and watched him get into all sorts of trouble, but I never yet caught him so much as thinking about killing anybody. No telling what he's been up to, but it's probably nothing I can't take care of myself when I get my hands on him."

Voss asked, "When did he leave, Mrs. Kramer?"

"He went for a walk after supper and heard about Russo and sat up late writing a piece for the paper. He left a note for Bert Walker to set what he'd wrote in type the first thing this morning. After I was in bed he told me he was going to light out for parts unknown. I was too sleepy to pay much attention—he's always talking about things he's going to do and never gets around to—but he was gone when I woke up this morning."

"Can we see what he wrote for the paper?"

Ada Kramer yelled into the back room, "Bert, bring out a proof of the galley Pop was so anxious about!"

"The local cops did a fine job of watching him!" Saint-Amour observed with ponderous sarcasm.

"He knew you'd put the police after him," Ada revealed. "He thought it was funny because one of them was parading up and down the street all day yesterday, peeking in the window and following Pop when he went out. I guess another one must have been outside the house in an automobile all last night; at any rate he was sleeping behind the wheel when I woke up at five-thirty."

"That's why Pop lammed," Saint-Amour decided. "He figured we were suspicious of him in spite of all the slick talk he gave us and he was afraid of getting tossed in the can. That's what we get for trusting things to these hick cops."

Bert Walker came out of the shop carrying a damp sheet of paper. He warned, "It's wet—and sizzling!"

Voss spread the sheet on the counter. Beside him he heard Saint-Amour's amazed whistle. The story

Kramer had written for next day's paper, topped with stilted headlines, said:

GOOD NEWS! YE ED IS GUILTY!
(But Only in the Eyes of the City Sleuths)
Actually He's Gone to Catch Murderer!
Circumstantial evidence stacked up so high against Joseph (Pop) Kramer, fearless editor of Andor's fearless newspaper, that he went into hiding yesterday to keep from being jailed for the murders of Richard Stott, Carter Wilton and Vito Russo—and incidentally to show up the detectives from the big city by tracking down the real murderer himself.

In the pallid light of dawn the editor crept past the slumbering form of Patrolman Anthony Budd, ace shadow of Chief Alfred

Fleming's alert police department, who had
been detailed to watch him. He vanished into
a thin drizzle of rain, leaving consternation
and suspicion behind him. . . .

And in highly convincing style Kramer had gone on to
list all the causes anyone might have for suspecting him of
guilty knowledge of the slayings. He concluded:

And so in self-defense Pop Kramer has decided to solve the mystery himself. He has given
himself forty-eight hours to scare up the real
culprit. Failing that, he will probably grow
whiskers and change his name and move to a
city where he is not known, supporting himself henceforth by authoring ponderous tomes
on the psychology of criminals and instruct-
ing others how to catch them, which is always
easier than catching them yourself.

Saint-Amour breathed, "He's referring to you, Abelard."
Voss laughed. "I don't mind. Remember that song,
'They all laughed at Christopher Columbus'? In my own
muddle-headed way, I'm beginning to get at the underly-
ing facts in this case. I don't think I'm going to like them,
either." He was no longer laughing. "There's something
. . ." Voss paused and wrinkled his forehead, "something
particularly unpleasant—yes, I know, murder is never
pleasant. But when some poor devil finds his wife in bed
with his best friend, and shoots them both, because his
world has suddenly gone out from under his feet—or a kid
who was educated in the reformatory gets the jitters in a
holdup and shoots the one he wants to rob—well, that's
murder, and it's no fun. But it's—well, it's natural, if you
follow me."

Saint-Amour pursed his lips and shook his head. "I don't," he said.

Ada Kramer looked at Voss and nodded.

"'There but for the grace of God, go I,'" she quoted.

"Exactly," said Voss. "The betrayed husband or the lost kid—that could be anyone—you, Bob, or I. . . ."

"Not me," said Saint-Amour. "I can't move quickly enough to act on impulse."

Voss grinned. "H'm, yes—perhaps I shouldn't have included you in the category of normal human beings. Anyway, what I'm getting at: underneath these murders there's something strange—something that hasn't anything to do with the way you or I would react. Something odd—not quite decent. But I'm getting down to it. I'm going to point my finger at the murderer before very long."

"You can keep your hands in your pockets. Why should you have to point out the murderer to me after he's practically confessed? Mrs. Kramer, if you know where your husband has gone you'd better let us in on it. Loyalty is a fine thing, but there are times when it's out of place."

Her face, that had relaxed for Voss, tightened again, and her eyes were as expressionless as polished stones. "I don't know where he is. I know you're barking up the wrong tree. If you name him as the guilty one you'll only have to come around and apologize later."

"The man's sheer nerve is what gets me!" Saint-Amour was shaken out of his customary matter-of-factness. "He'll go down in the records as one of the most arrogant criminals in history!"

"There's an arrogance that often goes with innocence, too," Voss murmured. "I've seen accused men—"

Ada Kramer said, "You better go, both of you. If I stay here listening to you run down Pop I'll get mad and do something that will get me arrested."

"We aren't running him down," Voss told her, "In his own way Saint-Amour is complimenting him and I'm trying to point out the probability of his complete innocence."

They went out. The rain had dwindled to a fine mist that floated in the air like damp smoke.

Voss said, "I wish Kramer hadn't been so cagey and secretive, so insistently individualistic. I never could figure out what kind of thoughts were running through his head. Now I suspect his disappearance is a preliminary to something that may turn out to be mighty important and I can't figure out exactly what it is. If I could, I'd feel easier about the next couple of days."

"You can feel easy," the detective boasted. "While you're doing your figuring I'll be hunting Pop. If I catch him we'll both be home in the next couple of days."

"Luck to you," Voss said. "I'll let you hunt alone. I'm going to shut myself up and think. Believe it or not I've got the pattern of this murder spree pretty nearly complete. There ought to be at least two more murders—"

"Run along! There's liable to be a dozen more if that guy stays on the loose. Call me tonight at the hotel and I'll tell you the answers to your problems."

Voss hurried along Wilton Drive, his long stride bridging puddles, his head bent in thought. He had reached the point opposite the wood in which Jared Wilton had first feared death at the hand of his brother when a voice filled with fear shrilled, "Mr. Voss! Mr. Voss!" He halted and strained his eyes through the gray haze toward the darkness of the trees.

A brown figure was running awkwardly out of the wood, stumbling over the rough ground. It was a full minute before he recognized Dorothea Wilton. Then he vaulted the low stone wall that bounded Wiltonshire and ran to meet her.

She was dirty and disheveled. Her cloudy hair swirled around her terror-filled face. Her dress had been drenched by the rain and was encrusted with mud and dead leaves as though she had been lying on the ground. Her eyes were staring and she breathed in great gasps through her open mouth. Blood had spread over her left cheek from an ugly scratch and her throat was covered with dark bruises.

"Jared has been killed!" she babbled. "We were walking in the rain—" She leaned against him, half fainting. He gripped her shoulders to steady her.

"Easy," he said. "You're hurt, too. Who did it?"

She began to cry. "I don't know. Someone—back in the underbrush—was waiting for us. Something hit me hard—and I fainted. When I came to—he was dead!"

Voss's eyes were glittering slits. He put his arm around her waist. He said, "Show me the place. I won't let you get hurt."

They went into the wood and reached the hard-packed stony path that ran through its center. They followed it into a gulley, along the bottom of which raced a rivulet gorged with rain. Across the narrow stream Jared Wilton lay prone with one side of his face pressed against the path and the lower part of his body forming a dam over which muddy water leaped. A jagged stone had torn a gash in his scalp above one ear. Blood had flowed over his forehead and dripped upon the earth.

Voss dragged the limp form out of the water. He put his hand over the heart, inside the vest. His eyes, which had been troubled, widened with relief.

"He isn't dead," he told the girl. "I'll get him to the house and we'll call a doctor. You need attention, too; it's a wonder you weren't choked to death."

He lifted Wilton in his arms. The little old man was heavy, and his weight made walking difficult. When they reached the edge of the wood and were close to the yellow mansion, Dorothea ran ahead.

Julia met Voss at the door. Her face was pale and frightened. "I've called the doctor and the police," she said. "Carry him into the library and I'll see what I can do while we're waiting."

Once stretched on the leather sofa, Wilton moaned and opened his eyes. His gaze came to a slow focus on the ceiling, shifted to the anxious faces of Voss and Julia and gleamed suddenly with memory. He cried weakly, "Dorothea!"

"Dorothea is all right." Voss moved aside to let the injured man see her huddled in one of the chairs. She made a feeble effort to smile.

Wilton closed his eyes again and breathed deeply. After a minute he looked at Voss. "Who was it?" he asked.

"I didn't get there till it was all over," said Voss. "The path was too stony to take footprints."

Wilton's jaw dropped. "Didn't Dorothea see him?"

"She was knocked out before she had a chance to look around. When she came to, no one was in sight."

"Good heavens! We were strolling along, talking about nothing in particular." Wilton stopped for breath, but waved aside the water Voss held out. "Once I noticed the bushes moving. Thought it was an animal—didn't worry. We went down—into the ravine. The undergrowth—is thick there. All at once—something struck my head. That's the last thing I remember."

He lifted a shaking hand toward his scalp, where the blood was clotting.

"Where were you going in the rain?"

Wilton did not reply, and Dorothea smoothed her skirt and looked embarrassed. "I—I often walk in the rain," she said. "I like to put on old clothes and get wet and smell the wet earth and the leaves. Today I was going to meet Tom for a stroll. Jared came home from the mill early and saw me leaving. He caught up with me, and—well, we just started talking. He was worried—he thought it was dangerous for me to go out alone."

"He wasn't far wrong," Voss observed.

A door banged. Alfred Fleming came into the library, panting. James Morgan followed him closely. At the sight of Dorothea smeared with blood and dirt, Morgan crossed the room and took both of her hands in his. He whispered, "Thank God you're safe!"

"We'll get him," Fleming promised grimly. "I'll send every man on the force out looking for him. If we don't round him up before dark, I'll swear in a posse."

"Whom will you get?" Voss inquired.

Morgan answered before the chief could speak. "Crippen, the idiot. It came to me last night that he must have been the one who killed Russo and fought with you, grunting meaningless sounds instead of talking or swearing. An hour ago I saw him scurrying toward the wood, grinning to himself like a devil. I hunted up Fleming to tell him. I was in Fleming's office when Crippen tried to murder them, and when Julia phoned there I guessed what had happened."

Dr. Hughson entered, brisk and dapper, as Fleming left the room to telephone. The physician stared at Dorothea and Wilton keenly, but longest at Wilton. He said, "Jared, that scalp wound doesn't look bad, but you do. I've brought some medicine for your nerves. You're supposed to take a teaspoonful every night at nine and another an hour later if it doesn't make you sleep. Take a dose right now and go to your room and lie down. I'll come in and patch you up in a couple of minutes." He took a black bottle from his pocket and handed it to Wilton.

"And now, young lady, your throat," he said. "It's sore and it will get sorer. Those are the marks of strong, desperate fingers. . . ."

A spasm crossed Morgan's white face and he clenched his fists tightly.

By eight-thirty that evening Voss had his thinking finished. His boyish face wore an eager expression as he closed his notebook and started downstairs. He encountered no one on the way from his room to the front door. The entire household had retired except for Julia, who had gone out immediately after dinner.

The only people Voss saw all the distance to Main Street were a couple loitering in the shadows of a row of maples across the street. He noted that the man had his arm around the woman's shoulders protectively and that they were engaged in talk so interesting that they did not hear his footsteps. The man was Claude Sackett; the woman, Julia Bisbee.

When he reached Main Street there was no sign of the throbbing excitement that had filled that thoroughfare Saturday evening. Most of the shop windows were dark and the pavements, gleaming after the shower, were all but deserted.

Saint-Amour sat in one of the armchairs in front of the Commercial House, chewing an unlighted cigar. He rose and came ponderously down the steps to join Voss. They moved along the street.

"I've soaked up all the gossip of Andor," Saint-Amour reported. "Everybody knows the most intimate secrets of everybody else around here and I've gathered them all in and considered them with care. and I haven't learned a damned thing! How did you get on with your figuring?"

Voss said, "Nicely, thanks. I figured out a man's secret all by myself—one that only a single other person in the world knows. I'm going to let you in on it."

"Will it get me anywhere?" the lieutenant wanted to know.

"It may give you a claim on that reward of twenty-five thousand."

Saint-Amour said, "Umm!" He threw away his cigar and spat and walked faster.

Voss led him into a dark side street and up a low hill, to the fence enclosing the cemetery. Voss stopped at the locked gate.

"Over you go," he directed.

Saint-Amour drew a deep breath. "I don't like it," he muttered. "If you're playing a Hallowe'en joke I'll break you in two. You'll have to give me a hand."

Voss steadied the portly man as he hoisted himself to the top of the gate and dropped heavily on the other side. Placing both hands on the gate Voss swung his feet over. He walked straight along the cinder drive between gray monuments to a white-painted board shack. He took a screwdriver from his pocket and pried away one side of the padlock fastening.

The door swung open and he disappeared inside the shack. His voice echoed strangely. "Here are some of the sexton's overalls for you. I'll bring the spades. We're going to open a grave."

"God, Abelard—why?" Saint-Amour's accents were taut. "What's the matter with getting a regular exhumation order?"

"No good. It would spoil everything if it got around that we'd been looking at this corpse. These overalls are only half big enough!"

"I wish I'd gone to bed." The New York detective extracted another cigar from his vest pocket and clamped his teeth on it hard before he began to struggle with the earth-stained garments tossed at his feet. "These are only half big enough for me, too—only in the other direction!"

Voss emerged with two spades, a scarecrow figure in the darkness. He crossed the soggy grass to one of the bare mounds that had been fresh the day before. He gave one of the spades to his companion and sank the blade of the other into sticky clay.

"Heaven help you if you're wrong in your figuring!" Saint-Amour whispered. "Is it Carter Wilton?"

Voss deposited a neat spadeful of earth on the grass beside the mound. He replied tersely, "Stott."

When the steel of the spades scraped the outer box of the coffin, Voss descended into the grave and cleared the earth from its surface. He used a pencil flashlight to locate the screwheads, which he attacked with his screwdriver. It was tedious work in the narrow space, opening the polished, inner box.

When the yellow light fell on the rigid face of the murdered man, discolored by four days in the sluggish waters of Mill River and ghastly despite Jerry Woolcott's powder and rouge, Voss wiped the clay from his hands carefully. He reached into his pocket and brought forth an ink pad in a flat tin box. He raised the stiff arms a little and pressed first the pad and then a sheet of glazed cardboard against the cold fingertips. He passed the cardboard up to Saint-Amour.

"Clear enough?" he asked hoarsely.

Saint-Amour's voice had a catch in it. "Clear enough," he said.

Voss replaced the covers and made the outer one tight with the screwdriver. He lifted himself out of the grave and wiped slippery perspiration from his brow. He stared at Saint-Amour.

"Well?" he inquired.

Saint-Amour had stooped behind a broad tombstone to light a match. He compared the dead man's fingerprints with others on a card he had in his pocket.

He said quietly, "I don't know how you guessed it, but you're right. Richard Stott was A. V. Atkinson. Now can we get out of here?"

They filled in the grave, obliterated the traces of their work, replaced the spades and the mud-caked overalls in the sexton's shack and repaired the door fastening. They clambered over the gate and went swiftly through the shadowy streets like two thieves.

16

The thin blonde in the post office trilled, "Good morning, Mr. Voss. You've got more fan mail from the same party." She slid a limp envelope beneath the grille of the window. It had been addressed on Pop Kramer's typewriter.

"Much obliged," Abelard Voss said. He took the letter and moved with some discomfort toward the door. All his muscles ached from their labors in the cemetery and he had lain awake long afterward. His gray eyes were as clear as ever, but fine lines of weariness surrounded them and his shoulders drooped.

The day was cool and sunless. The hard light struck the folded paper Voss took from the envelope and brought out the typed lines clearly. They were brief and to the point:

> Abelard Voss:
> You have had your chance and failed. My work will be finished tonight. Then I will go elsewhere.
> > A. V. Atkinson

Voss's face was troubled as he walked to the Commercial House. He found Saint-Amour in the bar, bedraggled and worn-looking, his eyes bloodshot and his suit stained and shapeless. A hoarse croak was his greeting.

"Some fun! I ruin a sixty-dollar suit and get the galloping pneumonia. If Pete doesn't hurry up with that hot lemonade I'll drop dead here and now."

Pete said, "Coming up!" He slid a steaming glass across the bar. He placed a whisky bottle and a smaller glass beside it. "It will cure anything."

"I've got lots wrong with me," Saint-Amour growled. "I can't sleep, I can't walk, I can't think. I've got a headache."

"I've got a warning," Voss said. He handed Saint-Amour the note.

The detective read it and nodded grimly. He lowered his voice. "Kramer sent it. He wrote it just before he skipped. Wonder if it's his idea of a joke or if he's got another killing up his sleeve?"

"I'm not sure it was Kramer, Bob. It's shaped like a piece of the puzzle I'm trying to put together. Kramer didn't make the puzzle."

"If he didn't he sure is complicating it! The way you storybook detectives go around trying to find a pattern to fit every crime you'd think all murderers sat down and drew maps before they started out. But they don't; they wait for their chance and work up an alibi if they're smart and go to it."

"The patterns I look for and write about aren't deliberate designs," explained Voss. "The person who makes them is hardly ever aware of them. They're the product of his particular type of personality and psychology. Very often his subconscious mind drives him to seemingly trivial acts of detail that fill out the picture. Like this note."

"You don't think it's a rib?"

"I think it's a genuine warning. Tonight he expects to have finished off his other victims."

"I suppose you've got it all figured out who the victims will be?"

"I've got a pretty good idea."

"Would they be Wilton and Dorothea?"

Voss smiled without humor. "You'll see."

The detective pushed his empty glass away impatiently. "All right. You were here first and it's your party, so I'll wait till you get ready to tell me what's on your mind. After all I can't kick; you found Atkinson for me and the reward notice reads Dead or Alive. What dirty work have you got cut out for today?"

"We're calling on the Widow Weston. Richard Stott lived at her house."

"Let's go. Only don't try to tell me she killed him. I've seen her and she's not any bigger than a grasshopper."

They went along Main Street to the corner of Cherry. Saint-Amour was as preoccupied as his companion during the first part of the walk. Suddenly he burst out, "Look here—they didn't catch the idiot. Fleming had men hunting and hanging around the cave all night. That means he's run away. And if he attacked Wilton and Dorothea it's a pretty safe guess he did the rest of the blood-letting, isn't it?"

"If he attacked them."

"That's right—they didn't actually see him," Saint-Amour admitted. "Okay—I'll keep my mouth shut. Only remember, if I act dumb it's because you haven't told me anything."

"I'll tell you the minute I've got it all straight. I'm feeling my own way right now, Bob. I need lots of information."

They turned into Clara Weston's neat yard and circled the house. She came to the back door and eyed them with undisguised apprehension. She asked Voss, "Is this the detective they sent up from New York?" Her voice trembled.

"This is he," Voss told her. "Lieutenant Saint-Amour of the homicide squad. He's got the mystery almost solved."

Mrs. Weston lifted the corner of her apron and dabbed at her eyes. She sank down upon the bench on the porch.

Saint-Amour fixed her with a stern gaze. "A very great deal depends upon what you tell us, madame," he said.

She broke down utterly. Tears spouted from her eyes and streamed down her cheeks. She moaned, "May Heaven forgive me!"

The plump detective backed away from her, embarrassed and repentant of his gruffness. He stammered, "There, Mrs. Weston! Don't take it so hard."

She wailed, "I knew I shouldn't have done it! But I was desperate and—and—what else could I do?"

Saint-Amour's mouth opened. A frosty gleam came into his eyes. His embarrassment vanished and he glanced triumphantly at Voss, who blinked in bewilderment.

"You knew it was against the law, didn't you, Mrs. Weston? You were aware that the law of this state—ah—Massachusetts—has fixed the most severe penalties for crimes of that kind?"

"Oh, my stars! Yes, I guess I knew it. But I didn't think."

Saint-Amour's tone was weighty with disapproval. "And you knew it was against the law of God, Mrs. Weston? It is expressly forbidden in one of the Ten Commandments—I forget just which one."

"The Eighth. Yes, I knew. But I can make it up! I won't have to go to prison if I give it back, will I?"

Saint-Amour spluttered, "What—what can you give back?"

Voss said drily, "You might have saved yourself a lot of trouble if you'd remembered what you learned in Sunday School. Do you know the wording of the Eighth Commandment?"

"Of course I do. 'Thou shalt not kill.'"

"That's the Sixth. The Eighth is 'Thou shalt not steal.'"

Saint-Amour closed his eyes and took a deep breath. He said, "Madame, forgive me. Whatever it is you have stolen

you may keep for all of me. I thought you were confessing
to three murders."

Indignation dammed her tears. "You thought *I* killed
poor Mr. Stott? How *dare* you? I—I've never been so in-
sulted in my life!"

Voss hastily intercepted the impending storm. "He was
a God-fearing man, wasn't he, Mrs. Weston?"

"Indeed he was. Why, he was positively holy! All hours
of the night he'd pray out loud in his room. He was the
most religious man I ever met. . . ."

"Mr. Stott was a member of the Tabernacle?"

"Yes, I'm sorry to say. He used to have the true faith till
he quarreled with the Reverend Parker over some of the
tenets of the Baptists and renounced them. But Mr. Parker
won out in the end; he had the burial service.

"Mr. Stott used to say young Mr. Morgan had a great
deal of sense and would be a fine preacher when he got
older. He talked with Mr. Morgan a lot. For all I know he
may have been right; I'm open-minded about religion and
I believe even the members of the Tabernacle will be received into heaven if they repent in time, and anyway . . ."

"Perhaps you'll let Lieutenant Saint-Amour look over
the things in Mr. Stott's room. The lieutenant is deeply
interested in Mr. Stott's past and is overlooking no clues."

"I'm sure he's welcome. But there won't be any clues;
I've gone all through the things that were there. There's
a case full of bottles of chemicals and a lot of funny glass
globes and jars he was using to try to invent a new kind
of dye. There's his Bible and some of the manuscript of a
book he was writing about the meaning of Revelations.

"But if it will help catch the poor benighted creature
that did the murders I'll be glad, and I hope they hang him
higher than the moon and refuse him a Christian burial. I
still can't get over how he thought *I* was the guilty one. At
first I thought he meant—that is—"

"You don't have to be afraid to tell us, Mrs. Weston. We're only interested in the murders. Did you keep something of Mr. Stott's for yourself?"

She hung her head. "Well—not exactly. I just didn't say anything about it. It was six hundred and fifty-four dollars and a half he asked me to save for him out of his wages. I paid a hundred dollars for his funeral and was going to pay another hundred for a nice stone for the grave and I thought probably he'd want me to keep the rest if he could have the say. I'm a poor woman and even now that I'm not going to have to take care of Toby any longer—"

"Toby's leaving you?"

Clara Weston tightened her lips. "I shouldn't have said anything about that. Nothing definite has been arranged."

"Then we'll forget it. About the money, perhaps you could keep it by putting in a claim with the public administrator. If Mr. Stott hadn't any near relatives and didn't owe any money—"

"Oh, I'm sure he didn't." Clara Weston's teary smile was like the sun breaking through a summer shower. "I'll see a lawyer about drawing up a claim this afternoon. If you'd like to see his room, Lieutenant, I'll take you right up."

Saint-Amour said, "I'll meet you at the hotel later, Abelard." He winked, and followed Clara Weston into the house.

Julia and Toby and Rags were coming along the street from town. The child's eyes were sparkling and he laughed as Voss came near.

"Lookit my new sweater!" he cried, grasping the front of that shining red garment and stretching it out while Rags leaped against him and barked joyously. "Miss Bisbee got it for me."

"It's a fine sweater," Voss said. "It's certainly nice to have someone buy you things, isn't it?"

"It sure is!" Toby agreed. "An' that isn't all. She's going to build me a new house right on the corner we just passed an' there's going to be a little house out in back for Rags an'—"

"Toby!" Julia scolded, her face pink.

Toby looked soberly at Voss. "I wasn't to tell," he said. "I forgot."

"Then I'll forget, too."

The youngster nodded. "Then it will be all right, won't it, Miss Bisbee?"

She laughed nervously. "I hope so, dear."

Voss suggested, "He won't be calling you Miss Bisbee much longer, will he?"

"Why—why shouldn't he?"

"I happened to see you walking with Sackett last night. You had the look of young people making plans for the future."

"It was your fault we were together! You got me so excited with your talk of being suspicious of Claude that I had to warn him. And you had him all worked up about my burning that dress and he decided he'd better warn me. He didn't want to come to Wiltonshire and I couldn't very well go to his house so we met on the corner."

"By that vacant lot. Does Sackett own it?"

She nodded.

"I suppose he'll have the foundations put in before winter?"

Her expression was compounded of shyness and happiness. With the loose tendrils of her dark hair escaping from the pins and falling around her face and her color heightening to scarlet she was so radiant that Toby stared at her in wide-eyed wonderment.

"After all there's no reason you shouldn't know. We're going to slip away to Boston and be married tonight. It's a secret nobody else has been told."

"Tonight!" A troubled furrow creased Voss's forehead. "Isn't that pretty sudden? I mean—it's all very nice, and I'm glad you both got rid of the stiff-necked pride that kept you apart so long, but—"

"We've waited four years," she said. "Considering that, our new plans aren't so sudden."

"I wish I could get you to change them just a little."

"How?"

"I wish you'd ask Sackett to wait till Friday instead of whisking you away tonight."

"But I couldn't do that without a very serious reason."

"I'll give you one confidentially," Voss said. "The person who has committed all these murders is going to strike again tonight. I hope to trap him, but he may be cleverer than I think. I'd—well, I'd feel better if I knew Sackett was going to be on hand tonight and tomorrow."

The blood ebbed from her face, leaving it white and strained. She whispered, "You think Claude is involved?"

"I haven't said that. I think he'll be of considerable help in solving the case. I haven't told him so, of course—he'd like to wash his hands of the whole thing, I suspect—and I'd just as soon you wouldn't tell him."

"I won't. I'm willing to trust you to the limit. But what excuse can I give for wanting the wedding delayed?"

"Give him any excuse except the real one. Say your Uncle Jared's physical and mental condition is so bad you don't want to upset him any more until after Friday, when the labor trouble at the mill will reach a crisis."

"I'll find a way," she promised. But her eyes were troubled.

"And now since we're exchanging secrets there are others you don't have to keep any longer. Did Dorothea tell you I knew the truth about the dress you were burning?"

"Yes. I was horrified when I heard she'd told you. You—you don't suspect her?"

"Not a bit."

"I'm glad. I suspected her. I thought she did it when she was out of her mind and I wanted to spare her as much as I could. I'm awfully relieved to know she didn't. So will Morgan be; he always insisted it must have been someone else."

"She was Toby's white lady, wasn't she?"

"Yes. Toby didn't see what happened at first. But he saw Morgan carrying Dorothea away. Toby was a little distance upstream from where Carter lay and it wasn't till he had finished paddling in the water that he found the body. By the way—I don't know whether it will be of any help to you—but Toby lost his toy hatchet the same day he saw the white lady. He isn't sure, but it's likely he dropped it by the stream when he undressed to go into the water and forgot about it afterward. Anyone could have picked it up. Clubfoot Crippen would have if he'd seen it, I imagine."

"That helps. Thanks."

Toby said, "Good-by, sir. You can come and visit us in our new house when it's finished."

17

The unionization of the down-trodden workers of Wilton Woollies, Incorporated, had taken a place of secondary importance in the minds of the populace now that a man hunt was in full cry. The new crimson posters went unregarded as men stopped on corners and in doorways to discuss the possibility of their women and children being slaughtered in their homes while they went about their business. Even the boldest were pleasantly and indignantly scared.

In front of the Commercial House a salesman whose wife and children were safe in Buffalo held forth on the merits of summary justice.

"They've got the right idea in the South. I'll admit there's a lot to be said against stringing up Negroes and burning 'em when there's a chance they're innocent, but if you've got the goods on 'em it sure teaches the other Negroes to be good. Now this nut that's running around killing people will probably get a nice home in an asylum with three meals a day and pretty nurses to pamper him and all the other nuts in this part of the country will say, 'If he can get away with it so can we.' But if he was whipped and strung up by the thumbs and sprayed with gasoline and burned the rest of 'em would think twice before they killed young widows and such like."

"What we should of done," gravely declared a pimply youth, "we should of got a gang and rode him out of town on a rail soon's he showed up."

"Fleming sent over to the county seat for sheriff's officers to help beat the country," stated Perry Williams. "I hope he shows up before they get here. I got a shotgun loaded with buckshot in my store and the little woman's got another all ready at home and the minute either of us sees him we're going to let fly."

Bob Saint-Amour came to the end of his patience. He got out of his chair and glared at the half-dozen of them. He rasped, "You make me sick! You'd lynch an imbecile and think you'd settled everything. Did it ever enter your heads that somebody a lot smarter than the nut might be behind all this? If he should get lynched it would just make four murders instead of three."

All the men looked at him in sullen silence excepting Len Farrell, the white-haired proprietor of the hotel.

Farrell said, "I been thinking the same thing. I don't like to talk about a neighbor and a lodge brother, but I hear Pop Kramer dropped out of sight just at his busiest time of the week. He done more talking about killing than everybody else put together 'way before a single thing happened. I always thought Pop was a nice guy in spite of what other people said, but I'd like to know where he went and why before I make up my mind anybody else is guilty."

The youth's eyes grew solemn. "Gosh!" he recalled. "Remember last Hallowe'en at the Lion's Club masquerade Pop dressed up like a cave man with that wig and whiskers and some of the women went home because all he wore was that tiger skin rug? He looked a heap like the idiot that night; folks were kidding him about it."

"Come on, Abelard," Saint-Amour urged. "I'm only making things worse staying around here. I try to save the idiot from getting lynched and now they're going to grease the rope for Kramer."

When they had gone a little way from the hotel Saint-Amour said, "Murder is just a little crime compared to stupidity. A smart man could stir up a mob in no time and turn it loose on anybody he didn't like in this town."

"In any town," Voss amplified. "It's being done every day. It's a favorite political stratagem."

"Here comes Frank. By the look of him," hazarded Saint-Amour, "he wants to see us." He called, "Hi, comrade! I see you're all healed up!"

Frank didn't smile. There was a queer intensity about his dark eyes, nearly normal again after the pounding they had received, and a grimness in the set of his mouth. He said, "Somebody doesn't want me to heal up. I wonder if you'd come over to the cottage. I've found something pretty serious. I don't want Fleming because I mistrust both his brains and his motives."

"What did you find—a bomb?" Voss asked.

Frank jerked his head around. "Are you guessing or did you know? I've found as nice an infernal machine as any nihilist ever contrived. It was under the stones of the hearth."

"That ought to let the idiot out," Saint-Amour mumbled.

The agitator scoffed, "Idiot my eye! Every one of the crimes has been directed against me. Whoever planned them thought I'd be suspected from the beginning and either arrested or lynched. The thing that saved me was the beating I took; it won me the sympathy of the workers and I've managed to keep it."

"In other words," Saint-Amour said, "in trying to work against you Sackett actually did you a favor."

Frank snapped, "Sackett staged the riot, but not the killings. He isn't the type for underhanded work like that.

He's hard-boiled and believes in direct action. Given a free hand he might hire a gang to chase me out of town and throw stones at me if I tried to come back for my hat. He might be capable of having Stott and Carter and Russo killed, but he wouldn't do it solely to frame me."

"So what?" the New York cop inquired, puzzled.

"I'm not in a position to accuse anybody. If I was I'd single out Wilton as the master mind. I could see through him all the time he was trying to prove his broad-mindedness by inviting me to dinner and guaranteeing that his guards wouldn't make any more trouble. He works best in underhanded ways. God knows what kind of grudge he had against Stott, but it wouldn't be hard to give him motives for the other murders."

They had reached the cottage. Frank led them through the open front door. Two flat stones had been pried up from the hearth and beside them lay a small cardboard carton. Packed neatly in the carton were four yellow sticks the thickness of a man's thumb and eight inches long, wrapped in oiled paper, two dry cell batteries, a spark coil from an automobile, a brass detonating cartridge and the dial and mechanism of a cheap alarm clock ticking blithely. Copper wires connected the batteries to the clock and the coil and the cartridge.

"Someone made a bad job of planting it," Frank said. "Ruth and I went for a walk this morning and when we came back Unger had gone out, too. There was dirt on the floor and I could see where the stones had been loosened. I pried them up and found the time bomb with the clock set to explode it at eight tonight. All three of us would have been blown to pieces. I left the wires connected, but I guess it's safe for now."

"Do you know where Unger went?" Voss asked, examining the hearth.

"Probably to meet Dorothea Wilton; he's started to teach her to paint. Someone brought this in after he went out. The door's never locked."

"What happened to Ruth?"

"I wanted to get hold of you right away. I thought maybe you could get fingerprints from the bomb; a man who expected his handiwork to be blown to bits in a little while might not be careful about things like that. I sent Ruth to Wiltonshire looking for you while I tried town."

Voss decided, "We'll take this out of the house and hide it where it can't do any damage. There won't be any prints, and maybe we'd better let it explode on schedule. You'll be safe till eight tonight, if you don't tell anyone about this, and I've got other things to do meanwhile."

"Neither Ruth nor I will say a word; I've got to hurry to talk to the workers when they come out of the mill at noon, but I won't mention this."

Saint-Amour inquired, "Comrade, don't you ever get tired of slinging propaganda?"

The organizer grinned. "Don't you ever get tired of chasing after murderers?"

"You're damned right I do!" said the detective.

"We're about halfway to Crippen's cave, aren't we?" asked Voss, gazing up at the hills.

Saint-Amour heaved a patient sigh. "I'll show you the way. This is your sixth day in these parts and Crippen has moved to another state and thirty cops have trampled over everything, but maybe there's still time for you to pick up a clue."

"I was twelve years late finding Atkinson," Voss reminded him.

"And it will be twelve more years before you tell me how you did it!"

"I'll tell you now. Starting with the assumption that he was to be found somewhere in this case I merely figured out which man in Andor looked and acted as I thought Atkinson would look and act. Kramer came closest to filling the bill, physically, but his hard cynicism didn't fit what I knew of Atkinson's mysticism and his fingerprints eliminated him. Stott was the only other possibility. His past was a mystery; he knew a lot about dyes, which are an important province of chemistry; he was religious and dreamed of an idealistic society on earth; he was as old as Atkinson would be and about the right size and he had a limp which he blamed on rheumatism."

"Simple, eh? Only most people wouldn't have thought about Stott as anything but a victim. It's barely possible, Abelard, there's something to be said for your method of keeping an open mind and forming no opinions beforehand.

"Finding Atkinson has put me up the air higher than ever. According to all the rules he ought to have done these killings, but he couldn't have done any of them."

"He could have inspired them," Voss said cryptically.

They took the path that led to the stream and crossed precariously on the fallen log.

Saint-Amour said, "You know, the evidence against Crippen is too good to be true. If we found him this afternoon we could put the blame for everything on him and call the case closed. He couldn't defend himself. The authorities would clap him into an asylum for the criminally insane and everybody would be satisfied."

"Excepting me," Voss objected.

"And me, Abelard. I've been thinking maybe you aren't as crazy as you look. I've even been writing things down in a notebook like I've caught you doing. My newest bright thought not yet jotted down is that Frank could have planted that bomb to remove suspicion from himself—or Unger could have."

"What are your other jottings?"

Saint-Amour produced a dog-eared notebook and thumbed through scrawled pages. He found the place he wanted and began to read.

"A—The three murders were all committed by the same person. All were acts of violence apparently done at the first opportunity. All required a certain amount of strength."

"So far," commented Voss, "you're a hundred percent right."

"B—It is unlikely that a woman did them. A woman would have been spotted around the mill at night and anyway she wouldn't have been strong enough to throw Stott out the window weighted down with chains. That eliminates from the original list of suspects suggested by A. Voss the following: Ruth Taylor, Carmen Corsi, Julia Bisbee and Dorothea Wilton."

"That's correct."

"C—Since the same person did all the murders, Vito Russo is also eliminated."

"Very definitely."

"D—The notes signed 'A. V. Atkinson' are so timely they must have been written by the murderer. That would eliminate Crippen because it seems impossible his imbecility and illiteracy can be phony. It is probable the murderer planted evidence pointing to Crippen to throw the police off the trail and make the idiot the goat."

"That's more than a probability; it's almost a certainty."

"I'll change it. E—The six remaining suspects are Jared Wilton, Claude Sackett, Leslie Frank, James Morgan, Thomas Unger and Joseph Kramer. The first three seem to have the strongest motives, and it would have been possible for Wilton to have faked that attack on himself, but Kramer looks guiltiest either because he deliberately invited suspicion for reasons best known to himself or because some one of the others is trying to frame him."

"You haven't forgotten our thirteenth suspect?"

"Give him a name, Abelard, and I'll mark him down. Or give me his height and weight and the color of his hair."

Voss said, "I can give you an idea of his mentality and psychic makeup. He's a slightly smeared carbon copy of our late friend Atkinson."

"Whose spirit is marching on," Saint-Amour muttered, closing his notebook with a snap. "And am I glad we didn't meet up with it last night. I had about all I could stand as it was. What do you mean, carbon copy? And why smeared?"

Voss said, "He's idealistic, too. And a fanatic about what he believes, convinced he is right, just as Atkinson was. Smeared? Because I think he's let his ideals be clouded by emotions more personal. Or rather, I think he's using his ideals as an excuse to himself—rationalization, it's called. Before and after the act . . . who's that?"

"One of Fleming's cops. That's Crippen's cave behind him. If they'd pull the cops out of here for a while and then sneak back they might catch him. But maybe it's just as well if they don't, seeing how upset the town is."

The cop was tired and irritable. He growled, "Make yourselves at home, you two. I been here since midnight without relief and it's real comfortable. It was specially nice when it was raining."

The cave was a shallow depression against a huge boulder that thrust out from the side of the hill. Trees and bushes came close and screened it from the wind and the idiot had built a crude lean-to of boughs almost covering the entrance.

Voss thrust his head inside and encountered an unpleasant animal smell. All he could see in the gloom were a couple of pots and pans in a corner and a pile of sodden rugs and blankets. Outside were a heap of ashes where a fire had been kept and a heap of rotting odorous garbage.

Saint-Amour shuddered. "A dog would keep his kennel cleaner. It will be a break for Crippen if they send him to an asylum."

Voss looked at the cop. "Nobody's been around today?"

"Only the artist fellow and Mrs. Wilton. See that clump of bushes down there? They're behind it."

Voss began to descend the hill. The New York detective trailed him, protesting, "Why don't you give young love a chance?"

The artist's easel came into sight facing a rolling panorama of low. hills, but neither Dorothea nor Unger were near it. Unger had moved his folding chairs back a little and they sat almost hidden by the bushes. Dorothea was leaning against him and his arm was around her and her face was lighted by a strange brooding smile.

"See?" said Saint-Amour. "Two's company."

They heard him and started apart. Unger released Dorothea and frowned and said, "Hello. Are you hunting that poor devil, too?"

"No," Voss said. "I was—just looking." He stopped and stared at the tripod supporting the canvas on which Unger had daubed raw greens and browns. The leg farthest downhill was braced by a rusted piece of iron.

"It was under a stone I happened to step on," Unger told him. "The stone rocked and I turned it over. It's no good any more."

Voss found another stone and set it to brace the tripod. He picked up the iron object. It was a small machinist's vise weighing four or five pounds, hardly bigger than a man's fist.

"How could a thing like that get up here?" Saint-Amour wondered.

"The man who killed Richard Stott could have brought it here," replied Voss. "This is the weapon he used; it was taken from the fifth floor of the mill."

Unger breathed, "Good Lord!"

Dorothea put her hands to her throat where the bruises were still plain. She said, "It seems so horrible that a poor helpless creature should be driven to do things of that sort!"

"He's become a mad beast," said Unger. "They'll have to put him away before he depopulates the town."

"Do you expect to be home tonight?" Voss asked him.

Unger was surprised. "So far as I know. I always am. It's dark by seven-thirty and there's nothing to be out after dark for."

"I might just possibly drop in between seven-thirty and eight," stated Voss. "I'd like to talk with you some more."

"I'll be glad to see you. Why not come earlier and try Ruth's cooking? It isn't half as unsettling as her philosophy."

"I can't tonight. I've got to—" Out of the corner of his eye Voss saw a sudden movement in the valley. He said, "Look!"

In a little clearing surrounded by thick bushes Clubfoot Crippen crouched like a wild animal and peered around him with a terror that was apparent even to the watchers two hundred yards away. His rags were like shaggy fur and his tufted hair like a mane.

Saint-Amour gasped. "You use black magic to locate 'em, Abelard!"

"I didn't spot him first. One of the cops did. See!"

A short distance from the clearing a figure in khaki was circling warily, holding a pistol uptilted in his right hand. He reached a point where he could see the idiot and shouted something. Instantly Crippen darted away, swift as a rabbit despite his misshapen foot.

Voss started running, bellowing to the cop as he ran, "Hold it!" The cop didn't hear him, and a second later the *crack-crack* of shots floated up the hillside. The first khaki figure was joined by a second and there was the sound of two pistols.

The idiot ran about fifty feet. Then as though his feet had been yanked from under him he went down on his face and sprawled full length. He pressed his face against the earth and clasped his hands behind his head. His feet kicked like an angry child's. The cops kept shooting and ran toward him.

Voss was still running, still shouting, "Hold it!"

The men in khaki did not hear. One of them stopped, took careful aim and fired at the prostrate figure.

Saint-Amour uttered an oath and whipped a short-barreled revolver from a holster beneath his left arm. He pointed it skyward and yanked the trigger three times in quick succession. The reverberations were like thunderclaps against the hillside.

Both cops halted. They stared at the running figure of Voss and at Saint-Amour frantically waving his arms. They looked at one another and put their guns in their holsters. They walked slowly toward the idiot, who lay motionless now.

18

The jostling men and women from the mill were not giving their best attention to the union orator this noon. They had something more stirring to think about, something that warmed them like strong whisky and made them feel agreeably cruel and ferocious. They had questions to ask one another and opinions to compare.

"Do you think they'll ever catch the so-and-so?"

"How many more do you reckon he'll kill if he stays free?"

"No use locking up a guy like that; the nearest lamp post's good enough for him!"

Ruth Taylor was at the edge of the crowd, leaning against a tree, watching Frank and smiling encouragement. He stretched himself an inch taller and raised his voice.

"Fellow workers . . ."

In the front of the throng some of the men and women listened dutifully to every word. In one of the windows of the mill Jared Wilton watched everything that went on, his eyes expressionless. But the mass of the crowd was bored and restless.

From his niche in the wall of the dam that held back Mill Lake the speaker could see up the hill to Main Street. He saw a man run out of a store and pause on the corner and run on, waving his arms. He saw other runners follow the first.

In a dramatic pause at the end of a particularly effective question, Frank's ears caught a sound above the subdued chattering of the workers, a distant babble of yelling and hooting. A group of thirty or forty men came into sight on Main Street. They were milling around and shouting and policemen were holding them at a distance from something.

A man at the edge of the crowd shrieked, "They got him!"

The cry leaped through the crowd in a chain of individual voices lifted now at the left of the orator and now at the right. "They got him! They got him!" Incredibly, in a single instant every throat in the throng threw out the words at once so that a treble shudder shook the trees like an earthquake.

"They got him!"

The fringe of the crowd flowed like a torrent of bobbing corks into the street that ran up the hill. The body of it heaved convulsively and surged after. Men and women pushed and were pushed, tripped and fell and cried out in pain as feet trampled them. In less than a minute the park was empty of people except for Ruth leaning against the tree and Frank watching from the dam. After a moment Jared Wilton came limping out of the mill.

Frank scrambled down from the niche. Ruth went to meet him and he put his arm around her waist. Both their faces were pale.

She said, "The beasts! Isn't there anything we can do?"

"We'll see," said Frank. "I doubt it."

They started up the hill. . . .

The cops had been taking Clubfoot Crippen to the mill hospital, the only one in town, in spite of the strenuous remonstrances of Voss and Saint-Amour. Fleming and several of his men had joined them and they had made a clumsy stretcher out of a tarpaulin and two clothespoles. The stretcher sagged in the middle and Crippen lay in a slopping puddle of blood that had streamed from wounds in his shoulder and thigh.

The idiot had lain staring up at the sky with cloudy brown eyes. Under the dirt and sunburn and festering sores his face was a dull gray. His tattered garments were soaked from sleeping out in the rain and his dark hair was a tangled knotted mess intertwined with twigs and leaves. His wounds were hurting and he made a continual whimpering sound like an injured puppy.

At the edge of town men had joined the little procession one and two at a time till there were fifteen or twenty at Main Street. Before the stretcher bearers reached the turning to the mill the number had more than doubled and included many housewives. Some of the group were yapping loudly for summary punishment, the housewives loudest and shrillest. The cops had little trouble keeping them back from the stretcher, however, and only a few spat and threw stones. Fleming was flushed with victory and confident that his difficulties were at an end.

Then the roaring wave of mill workers engulfed them.

Voss saw them coming and jumped in front of the stretcher and tried to make a barrier of his long arms. The tide swept him aside as though he were a puny child. He doubled his fist and swung at a sweaty face in front of him just as the face went down, thrown off balance by pressure from behind, and his fist hit another man's shoulder harmlessly. A stone struck his forehead and for a moment he was dazed.

One of the cops drew his pistol, but Fleming swore at him and he put it back in its holster. Workers shouldered aside the stretcher bearers and they dropped their burden on the pavement. Heavy work-shoes kicked at the wounded prisoner.

The plump Saint-Amour was the hapless center of a moiling snarl of men. He used his fists well, but briefly, then he was sitting in the street with only one sleeve of his coat left to him.

A thin rope appeared from nowhere. A noose dropped over the head of the idiot and he was dragged across the street and jerked upright by two men. A third man climbed a telephone pole and leaned far out to pass the rope over a thick cable. Hands were waiting to grasp the loose end of the rope; they tugged mightily.

The idiot rose six inches into the air. His legs thrashed, the toes of the whole one extending downward trying to find support. One hand went to his throat and plucked feebly at the rope; the wounded arm hung useless at his side. His face purpled and his mouth opened horribly and the tongue stuck out.

Then the rope broke where it chafed against the cable and the squirming creature fell to the pavement in a quivering heap while men howled and women screeched.

Before they could raise their victim up again Voss stood over him, more furious than he had ever been in his life, driving hard fists into the faces and bodies of men. A little distance from Voss, on the running board of an automobile, James Morgan was crying frantic words that could be heard only in snatches. "Brethren, remember the words of the Lord . . . let the law judge . . . though he seem guilty as Judas . . . I beseech you . . ."

Voss could hear Saint-Amour at his side panting, "You lousy sons—! Take that and that!"

They couldn't stop it. Already Voss was being forced away from the crumped figure. In another ten seconds they would be hoisting the poor devil into the air again. . . .

Something was happening back in the crowd. Men and women were leaping aside to make an aisle. Down the center of the aisle marched a lean figure grasping one of the clothespoles which had been left on the farther sidewalk. He swung it right and left like a two-edged sword and men and women dodged and sprang and fell. Behind him Ruth Taylor stepped over the forms of the fallen.

The aisle extended to Clubfoot Crippen and to Voss. The latter lowered his aching arms. He stared in amazement at Leslie Frank, who stopped in front of him and faced the mob, his eyes no longer gentle, his face terrible to see.

"Fools!" he bellowed. "Slaves! Listen!"

Silence began around him and spread in a slow wave to the farthest reach of the mob. At first it seemed there was no sound left, only a deep pulsing vibration everywhere. Gradually came the realization that the steam whistle atop the mill was calling huskily and had been calling for minutes past. Men looked at one another and then uneasily away. Women tightened their lips and cast indignant glances at the men nearest them. A girl started to bawl loudly. Feet shuffled as bodies turned in the direction of the mill.

Then three thousand men and women, boys and girls were marching all at once back to their looms and tables and vats, docile as three thousand sheep.

Two cops in stained and disheveled uniforms lifted Clubfoot Crippen by the shoulders and legs and began to carry him as gently as they could toward the mill. His eyes still watched the sky vacantly and the whimpering still came from his chafed throat and his blood dripped over the legs of his bearers. Fleming watched them dully; all the elation had gone out of him.

Frank smiled wanly at Voss. His eyes were gentle again and his face was sad. He said, "That's their real master. They live and die by the whistle."

Sackett pointed out, "We're about the same height and breadth. You've got more belly than I have, but it won't hurt you to squeeze it a little." He went to a closet and brought out a brown suit.

"I hate to take it," Saint-Amour said. "But I hate to run around naked, too."

"You're welcome to it. I'd give more than that to see the two of you fight again as you did up on the corner."

"How about Leslie Frank?" Voss asked. "He saved the day."

"Frank could have anything he wanted from me; I like him so well for what he did I've even quit suspecting him of Carter Wilton's murder. I'd run him for mayor against Jared and win, if he'd let me. But he doesn't want a thing except a union."

Saint-Amour looked up from his struggle with Sackett's trousers. "The one thing you don't want him to have, eh?"

"Hell," Sackett said, "I've been on his side from the first! Do you think I had Russo start that trouble last week for any other reason than to speed up unionization? I didn't expect Russo to go as far as he did. Let the men organize; I can still handle them. We pay fair wages; there'll never be a strike unless Jared asks for it."

"Then why in the name of—?"

Sackett told them, "I'll come clean. I don't really give a damn what happens here. I planned to go out of town tonight and stay till everything was settled. I've put off my trip till the week end for certain reasons, but I still feel the same way.

"If Jared has his way about the union, all right. If Frank has his way it would please me even more. I don't bear anybody a grudge, even though I've been expecting Jared to murder me for the last few years.

"But last week, and until yesterday, I was holding a grudge. I wanted Jared to lose his precious power over the people of Andor and break his heart grieving. With union leaders telling him what he could do and what he couldn't do, he'd curl up and wither away. That's why I deliberately played into Frank's hand.

"That's what Carter was threatening to tell Jared the morning of the day he was killed. Carter overheard me telling Russo what I wanted him to do and why. Carter said I'd have to buy his silence and I kicked him out."

"I guessed a lot of this," said Voss. "I'm glad you've had a change of heart. Jared is a sick old man not worth hating. You'll win your feud with him inevitably because he won't live long."

Saint-Amour had succeeded in buttoning the waistband of the trousers around his stomach. His face was red with exertion.

He puffed, "This suit—won't be much good to you—after today. I'm stretching the seams a mile. Were you serious when you said Jared wanted to murder you?"

"Stretch away," Sackett told him. "I was serious in a way. I knew Jared would like to murder me. I didn't think he'd have the nerve—till lately."

"He was the first name on our list of suspects," Voss said. "You ran third. We haven't eliminated either of you."

Sackett said, "Of course, Jared never got along with Carter. He was afraid of Carter. He was ashamed of Carter's actions and hated him for the way he treated his wife."

"So I gathered."

"He was scared of Russo, too. He acted bold as a lion when he gave orders to have him fired, but I know he worried about Russo's revengeful temper." Sackett frowned. "About Richard Stott I don't know. He was a good worker and minded his own business. He had some queer ideas, but he didn't pester many people with them. In all fairness I can't imagine Jared wanting to harm him."

Voss murmured, "Umm."

"But—" Sackett shrugged his big shoulders. "I'll let you fellows worry about that. I don't believe the idiot did the killings—Hughson tells me he isn't going to die, which may or may not be a good thing, and that there isn't any question but that he can be sent straight to an asylum—and I don't want to worry too much about Jared. We've hated each other too long. I think it's time both of us adopted a little of the Christian charity that fool Morgan prattles about."

"It wouldn't hurt either of you. If you'll tell me one thing I'll leave you to your work. How do you spend your evenings?"

"The night Russo was killed I was in my study working."

"I don't mean that night in particular. I mean every night."

"I spend them all the same way. I don't go out more than two or three times a month. I read and do a lot of my work in the study. I'm all alone; the housekeeper leaves right after dinner and goes to her own home."

"Will you come to Andor Tabernacle tonight?"

"And listen to a lot of unholy drivel about repentance?" Sackett shrugged. "If you think I ought to, I suppose I can."

"Good," said Voss. "I'll be seeing you there."

When they were outside Saint-Amour pleaded, "Don't walk me any more than you have to. Sackett is generous, but too skinny. It's lucky he has his clothes made of good material; the strain on these pants is terrific."

"Go on up to the hotel and unbutton," Voss suggested. "I've got things to do."

"Getting tickets home?" Saint-Amour asked hopefully.

"No. Getting some information about vice."

The detective elevated his eyebrows. "Vice in Andor?"

"Not the kind they talk about in New York. Viciousness is private and pretty ordinary here. But a certain person's vice may have a lot to do with clearing up our difficulties."

Saint-Amour said, "Go ahead; I'll trust you. The word 'vice' has only one connotation in my cop brain, but maybe you're one of them who can take it or leave it alone."

19

Bob Saint-Amour accepted one of Jared Wilton's cigars and crammed half its length into the pouch of his cheek, waving away the proffered lighter. He said, "I don't smoke, thanks." His teeth sank contentedly into the tender tobacco leaf.

Wilton slumped back in his chair. His fingers drummed against its leather arms. He muttered, "All this excitement must have done something to Morgan's mind. Quarreling with me—telling me his call to the ministry was more important than my wishes, and that I had no right to advise Dorothea not to see too much of him! He never dared do that before, the ingrate!"

Abelard Voss prowled the library with a restless tread. The clock on the mantel showed five minutes before seven. He and Saint-Amour had dined with the master of Wilton-shire and Dorothea and Julia, who had gone upstairs to dress for the service at the Tabernacle.

They had watched and listened all through the meal for some warning that death lurked near. There had been no slightest sign.

In desperation Voss asked finally, "Mr. Wilton, how could you be killed most conveniently?"

Wilton was startled. His mouth opened and he said, "Eh?"

"I don't want to alarm you, but I have cause to suspect someone may make an attempt on your life this evening— probably has already set some trap for you. How do you think he would do it?"

"If my nerves get any more shocks," Wilton quavered, "I'll die within an hour. How would anybody want to kill anybody? A gun, a knife, poison—"

"We can rule out the gun and the knife because they could be too easily guarded against. Poison wouldn't have been administered in the food at dinner because it would have killed everyone; I was so sure of that I didn't have any qualms about tasting everything."

Saint-Amour exclaimed, "So that's why you were a bite ahead of us all the time!"

Voss nodded seriously. "I have a good sense of taste and smell. I've made a study of poisons and can detect most of them, no matter how they're concealed."

"Damn me for a fat kangaroo!" Saint-Amour said. "There I was stuffing myself till I was sure these pants would split."

Wilton glanced at the New York detective in cold reproof. Then suddenly his face paled and he seemed to have difficulty breathing.

"Poison!" he whispered. "But—but—even if it wasn't in the food . . ." He struggled to his feet. "Get Dr. Hughson!" He was purple in the face now. "Get him right away."

Voss took him by the arm. "What is it, Wilton?"

"My medicine," Jared Wilton's voice rose to a shriek. "No one else takes my medicine . . . there could be poison in that."

"When did you take it?" snapped Saint-Amour.

"I haven't—yet," moaned Wilton. He sank slowly into his chair again and his eyes avoided theirs. Now that his panic was wearing off, he seemed ashamed.

"Where is the bottle?" asked Voss.

"Behind the clock," said Jared, and wiped his face.

Voss reached out a long arm and took the bottle. He held it beneath his aquiline nose for a long instant. He drove the cork firmly into the bottle neck.

"Nice guessing, Mr. Wilton," he said. "That smell is very like bitter almonds."

"Cyanide!" Saint-Amour cried.

Voss nodded. "A spoonful of that medicine would kill a man in a matter of seconds. No—don't get shaky now, Mr. Wilton. The danger is past."

Wilton steadied himself with palsied hands on the arms of his chair. He sank back into the cushions and let his head droop.

"Claude Sackett," he mumbled. "I've feared him for years. Now I'm done for. He's really made up his mind to kill me and sooner or later he'll succeed. We use potassium cyanide for some of our dyes and there's any amount of it in Sackett's keeping."

"You needn't be afraid of Sackett," Voss said. "He's stopped hating you. As far as the quarrel between you is concerned he's ready to say 'uncle'—literally. He and Julia are going to be married."

"They're going to be married," Wilton repeated. The two men could almost see him shrink like a toy balloon with a slow leak. He was savoring the fullness of defeat and its flavor was not agreeable.

He said, querulous as a sick child, "I'm losing my people at the mill, Voss; they're joining the union and all I've done for them will become merely a basis for new demands. I've already lost control of the village affairs; Sackett has been running things under my nose to suit himself, even though I'm mayor. Now I've lost my niece to him and he'll own the mill after all, just as he did at the beginning when I couldn't sleep for thinking of all he had and all I lacked."

"You're still in the saddle," Voss comforted. "Take a grip on yourself and remember you've grown up since those days. The mill will be yours as long as you live and your life will be what you make it. Sackett has quit hating you; quit hating him for Julia's sake and your own and you'll be surprised how good you'll feel."

A forced grin crooked the old man's lips. "You sound like that fool Morgan. But I guess it makes sense. I'm fond of Julia. Maybe I'd better go to the prayer meeting with her and Dorothea in spite of my fuss with Morgan. After nearly sixty years of hating it won't be easy—"

"You'll manage. Meanwhile Saint-Amour and I will get around to your real enemy, the one who tried to poison you. I think we've got him stopped everywhere."

Saint-Amour asked as the pair of them were leaving the house, "Who is he, Voss? The doctor? He could have fixed the medicine."

"The medicine was all right last night."

"I suppose it wasn't any of the three women in the house. The bomb pretty well eliminated Frank and Unger. You've given Sackett a clean bill of health. Unless Wilton poisoned his own medicine, the only live suspect we've got left is Kramer."

Voss grunted. "Kramer knew Stott and he knew Atkinson's story, but did he ever connect the two?"

"Don't make me play guessing games, Abelard. You know the guilty man. Tell me who he is and we'll go and get him."

"He's a man whom Atkinson felt impelled to take into his confidence. We know of several with whom he spoke at length. Mrs. Weston told us that he spent a lot of time with Kramer—and Kramer himself said Stott had 'pestered' him. Leslie Frank admits that Stott tried to convert him to his own ideas. Mrs. Weston told us Stott attended the Tabernacle. Then I thought of the doctor, who might

have got close to him while Stott—or Atkinson—was sick.
I thought of Wilton, who believes in giving ex-criminals a
chance. I thought of Fleming, who sees thousands of circular photographs of criminals, and of Sackett, who likes
to have tough customers like Russo work for him—only
Atkinson wasn't a tough customer; in a way he was a very
gentle murderer.

"Finally I decided who the only man was who could
fill the bill and, sure enough, all the pieces of the puzzle
fitted together one by one until the picture became plain.
He was at the Tabernacle last Sunday, when Morgan delivered his 'Message to a Murderer,' and I was too blind to
see him. He'll be at the prayer meeting tonight, flattering
his vain soul. . . ."

"I get you!" Saint-Amour said wonderingly. "Damned
if I don't!"

At a quarter of eight Voss and Saint-Amour walked into
the police station and found Chief Fleming in his cubby-
hole of an office turning the pages of a detective story
magazine. Fleming looked up without enthusiasm. He
mumbled, "Now what?"

"Now we're going to give you a chance to grab yourself some glory," Saint-Amour announced. "Not that you
deserve it—but this is your territory and I haven't any
authority to make a pinch. We're going to take you to the
guy who did the murders."

"We've got the guy in the hospital under guard," Fleming said. "I think everybody in town is screwy, including
the pair of you. Guess what we got now. Ghosts!"

Voss asked, "Whose ghosts?"

"Richard Stott's. The Widow Weston called up in hysterics and said she saw him floating out of her window
big as life when she was coming home from the store. Five
minutes later Mrs. Simcoe phoned from her house three

blocks away to say she saw the same thing and I asked her if she'd been talking to the Weston woman and she said no. I'd planned on going to the church to see what Morgan's got up his sleeve this time, but now I got to run this place all alone."

"You mean you've got to let the place run itself," Saint-Amour contradicted. "You're going with us to the prayer meeting."

"I wish you'd gone there instead of coming here. Do you expect to find the murderer saying his prayers?"

"We sure do. The meeting started fifteen minutes ago and he's likely finished most of them by now."

Fleming was outraged. "You better both go back to New York," he advised. "If you go trying to make arrests in church you'll have old Jared throwing you in the can. He thinks that place is sacred."

Voss was impatient. "You don't have to come if you don't want to, Fleming. Saint-Amour and I can't waste time. Morgan is probably halfway through his talk on the murders. The killer expects to finish his job tonight. He thinks four or five more people will be dead. If that doesn't interest you, we'll be going."

Fleming got up. He took his cap from the desk. He warned, "I'm taking your word for it. This isn't my idea; it's my duty. If anybody has to take any blame, it won't be me."

"But if there's credit to be had," sneered Saint-Amour, "that's different, hey?"

They got into Fleming's car and rode down Main Street to Wilton Drive. The machine had turned the corner and was almost at the lighted Tabernacle when Fleming shoved his foot down hard on the brake pedal and the tires whined against the concrete.

"God damn!" he shouted. "That *is* Stott!"

Out of the corner of his eye Voss had a momentary
glimpse of a limping shadow moving along behind houses.
The dusk kept him from getting a good look before the
shadow vanished behind a barn.

Fleming yanked the gearshift lever into low, jammed
down the accelerator and pulled at the wheel. The car
leaped into a driveway and charged through a back yard
into an alley, jouncing through the soft earth of a vegeta-
ble garden. The alley was deserted.

"He couldn't get far," Fleming cried. "We'll get out and
hunt."

Voss looked at his watch. "No, we won't. It's seven minutes to eight. If that was a ghost it has vanished into thin
air; if it was a man I've got a hunch we'll find him where
we're going."

They climbed out and walked to the front door of the
Tabernacle. Voss gave whispered directions as they mounted the steps. They went abreast into the auditorium where
the benches were three-fourths filled with intent men and
women.

Morgan stood erect and confident at the lectern, his
blue eyes shining and his voice vibrant with emotion. He
was saying, "The Lord has visited his anger upon Andor."

Just for a second the young clergyman's glance rested
on the three men as they entered together and separated,
Fleming moving along the left aisle, Saint-Amour taking
the right aisle and Voss striding down the center. They
chose seats near the platform while Morgan's listeners, re-
sentful of the interruption, stared and fidgeted.

Opposite Voss, in the pew with the blue velvet rope
guarding its entrance, sat Jared and Dorothea Wilton with
Julia and Sackett. Jared's cheeks were the color of put-
ty and he glared angrily straight ahead of him. Dorothea
looked frightened; she turned her pale face toward Voss

for an instant and her eyes acknowledged his presence, then looked down again at her folded hands in her lap.

Morgan was saying, "The Lord has seen fit to put a murderer in our midst. But I have had a divine message from heaven, telling me the good people of Andor need fear no more for the future. All the evil that has threatened them will be uprooted and destroyed!"

The people shifted uncomfortably. They did not know whether to discount the terrifying words of this seemingly inspired man or to fear them. They were fascinated and thrilled and annoyed all at once.

Voss glanced down at his watch. One minute before eight. The minister's slim figure seemed to grow taller.

"God is watching over Andor!" he cried. "Can you feel Him in your hearts? His ways are mysterious, none knoweth how He moves, but His justice is righteous and His anger terrible. At any moment, the doom from the skies may strike the evil-doers who have brought sin to Andor and the Lord's wrath. Divest yourselves of sin, people of Andor, open your hearts toward God, lest His vengeance be visited upon you."

He paused dramatically. In the silence all could hear the clock at the First State Bank begin its mellow chiming. Someone gasped audibly and someone else smothered a giggle.

Morgan screamed, "Do not laugh! God will not forgive you for laughing at His holy works! Pray, rather—pray for your souls—"

There could have been no more dramatic moment for the mighty crash that shook the church and the town and thundered against the heavens, smiting the eardrums again and again as the echoes rolled and rebounded. People were stunned into motionless silence or hurled to their feet shrieking. All senses save the sense of fear were shocked into temporary oblivion.

Above the tumult the voice of Morgan soared like the blast of a brazen trumpet. "Pray, children of sin! Pray for your lives and your souls! Now is the moment for confession, sinners of Andor!"

His pale face glowed and his eyes were flashing torches, as he turned them toward the Wilton pew, whose occupants, almost alone of the congregation, were not standing or kneeling.

A tall, stooped man limped from the doorway onto the platform. He wore shabby, ill-fitting clothes. In the shadow of a drooping hatbrim his eyes gleamed piercingly through shell-rimmed glasses. A corner of his harsh mouth twitched with a nervous weakness. Morgan, still facing his audience, did not see him.

Fleming breathed, "It's Stott! No—yes, it is, too!"

In one movement, Voss flung his long body into the aisle. To his right, Saint-Amour pounded heavily. On his left, Fleming dashed down the aisle. All three of them had to push their way through the crowd of men and women, swearing, praying and screaming, who were fighting their way in the other direction, toward the door.

Morgan stood erect, still unconscious of the man behind him, but the fire had gone from his eyes. Fleming darted around him, flung himself on the limping man, and then, at a gesture from Voss, stood there silently, clutching the man's arm.

"We have found the murderer, Morgan," said Voss.

"Have you?" said Morgan. "Are you sure? Can you prove it in court, or is it only another circumstantial case, a fuse for lynching, like poor Crippen's case?"

"No, this time we can prove it," said Voss. "This time we have our man. Turn around, Morgan."

The young man turned, questioning Voss with a glance, and saw the figure of the limping man. Fleming let go his grip, and the figure took a step forward.

Morgan backed away slowly as the grim figure advanced. His lips worked, shaping barely audible words. "Atkinson—Stott—whatever your name is—you said you'd come back. I killed you once. I can destroy you again—I can call upon God—"

His shoulder struck the corner of the lectern upon which rested the huge Bible, rocking it. He put out a hand to steady himself and his elbow gave impetus to the rocking. The lectern toppled with a tremendous clatter and the book thudded in a broken heap on the floor, its glazed pages fluttering.

The noise seemed to recall the minister from a dream. He sagged and then shivered and looked down into the Wilton pew, past the ashen face of the old man huddled there.

He whispered, "Dorothea!"

She would not look at him. And bowing his head in his hands, he let them lead him from the Tabernacle.

20

Pop Kramer brought a dozen bottles of beer in a sack from the store next to the police station. He closed and locked the door of Fleming's office behind him, shutting out the excited crowd that milled about in the main room. He extracted wads of cotton from his nostrils and cheeks, took off the spectacles and the battered felt hat that had belonged to Richard Patrick Stott and shrugged his shoulders, letting a small cushion drop from between them beneath his coat. He lifted four bottles from the paper sack and produced an opener from his pocket.

"Since you insist on holding the post mortem here we might as well have all the comforts of home," he said to Fleming, opening one of the bottles and passing the opener to Abelard Voss. "It's been two long days since I had a decent drink, hiding in that shooting shack in the woods."

"What was your idea?" Saint-Amour asked. "If you watched and saw Morgan sneak into your office and use the typewriter Monday night, why didn't you grab him or call Voss or me? It would have been evident that whoever wrote the notes knew plenty about the murders."

"I had a lot of ideas. I was sore at all of you for setting the cops to watch me. You might have thought I was trying to frame the reverend. He might have known a way to squirm out of it, being a tricky customer. I thought if I waited for the prayer meeting and scared him in front of the crowd he might give himself away. I knew I could do a fair job of impersonating Stott, since we looked so much alike to start with. I hid to keep you dimwits from arresting me and this evening I sneaked into the widow's house while she was out and helped myself to Stott's clothes and spectacles. When she saw me jump out a window and fainted I knew I was good."

"You fooled Morgan," Voss conceded. "Catching him off guard when he was scared already, you broke him down. We might have had a hard time convicting him if he hadn't blurted out the truth in front of three hundred witnesses."

Kramer drank deeply, smacked his lips and chuckled. "It worked better than your new-fangled theories."

Voss smiled and traced designs with his finger on the blotter on the desk before him. "I was doing just what I wrote about in my book, which you quoted so impressively a week ago and sneered at so insultingly in today's *Advertiser*. I was discovering the basic situation, uncovering the murder pattern."

Fleming said humbly, "If you don't mind, Voss, I'd like to hear the whole story."

"I'm a little in the dark myself," confessed Saint-Amour. "Come clean, Abelard. If Fleming and I are going to claim a share of the credit we'll have to know how it was done."

"It isn't very complicated," Voss said. "When you get the picture you'll all wonder why you didn't lock up Morgan at the beginning. He gave himself away by just being himself, as is usually the case.

"Think of him as he really was—a brilliant, ambitious and unstable young man living for the most part in the idealistic world a good many preachers inhabit and compelled to rub elbows with the unappreciative, materialistic little world of Andor. Jared Wilton was his benefactor, but at the same time he was a hard taskmaster.

"The one important thing in his life—the single driving force, the supreme tragedy and the paramount motive for all his shedding of blood—was his love for Dorothea Wilton. It was an obsession that colored everything he saw or heard or thought. He had wanted her more than anything else in the world at the time of her marriage to Carter Wilton, and probably he thought he would have won her if Jared Wilton hadn't interfered on the theory that marriage was just what his harum-scarum brother needed.

"Morgan pretended to be a good sport about the marriage, but actually he brooded and multiplied his bitterness. He went quietly insane seeing Carter mistreat his wife. He must have felt a powerful and growing urge to kill Carter for a long time.

"But in all probability Morgan's dream of murder would never have reached the stage of actuality if it hadn't been for Richard Stott. Driven by a troubled conscience and believing he had found a spiritual kinsman in the fervently religious minister, Stott confessed that he was really the fugitive A. V. Atkinson. Morgan was entranced by his story and immediately imagined a parallel adventure with himself as the hero. As Atkinson had killed for the good of mankind, so might Morgan kill for the good of Dorothea in particular and a lot of other people incidentally. Like most persons who contemplate crime, he deliberately forgot his basically selfish motive in his anxiety for self-justification."

"He thought he was inspired!" Fleming muttered.

"He was a weakling," Voss said. "If the matter had rested there, he would have been content with dreaming. Atkinson forced his hand. Atkinson got suspicious and afraid when Morgan refused to let go of the subject of murder. Having received a confession one should forget it and help the confessor forget. But Morgan talked and talked on the forbidden subject and Atkinson came to the conclusion that he would have to kill the minister for his own safety."

"I thought Atkinson was just an idealistic killer," Saint-Amour frowned. "I thought you said he wouldn't kill for personal motives."

"I did," said Voss. "But remember what I said about rationalization? Atkinson firmly believed, I have no doubt, that if Morgan revealed his true identity, Andor would lose the benefit of the Utopian schemes he was planning for it. Morgan, too, to Atkinson, became an obstacle in the path of truth. So, a week ago Monday night, as Morgan has confessed, Atkinson invited Morgan to the mill, where he was working. He planned to kill Morgan and throw him into the river. But Atkinson was old and lame and clumsy and the minister was strong and quick. Morgan killed Atkinson instead."

"In self-defense," Saint-Amour grunted, "He could have beaten the rap."

"He got panicky, Bob. No one had seen him go into the mill and there were no witnesses. He wasn't sure he'd be believed, and he knew that even if he kept out of prison or the chair, his career would be ruined. So he weighted the body with chains and dropped it into the river, hoping it wouldn't be found until it was too late to tell how he'd died; and he carried away the blood-stained vise.

"Leaving the mill, he met Russo. It gave him a bad scare, but he took a chance on Russo being too dumb to connect him with the disappearance of a dye mixer."

"He must have changed his mind about Russo later," Kramer said, reaching for another bottle.

"He did. I'm coming to that. Meanwhile he spent a couple of days getting over his scare and deciding that murder was easier to get away with than he had thought. Nobody found the body in the river and nobody worried much about Atkinson's disappearance. Lacking a balance wheel, Morgan is a creature of mental extremes. When he stopped being afraid he became overconfident.

"He heard that Carter Wilton had struck Dorothea. For the first time he made up his mind definitely to realize his dream of murdering Carter. Your 'Symptoms of Murder' editorial, Kramer, appeared almost at the moment his mind was made up, and he thought it too good a bet to overlook.

"He picked you to take the blame, Kramer. You had prophesied terrible things to come and, being without honor in your own country, had made enemies of half the people in town, including Carter. Morgan hated you like the very devil because you had poked fun at him, perhaps not realizing how thin-skinned he was. He saw a way to make use of your prophetic writings, your reputation, your typewriter and your carelessly scattered fingerprints to put investigators on your trail."

Kramer shivered. "I could almost feel the nippers."

"As a second choice, he picked Clubfoot Crippen for a scapegoat. The idiot couldn't possibly defend himself if, say, a couple of murder weapons were found in or near his cave. Failing to pin the crime on you, he knew the police would be sorely tempted to send Crippen to an asylum and call the affair closed."

"Or kill him and call it closed!" Saint-Amour growled, eyeing Fleming until that individual squirmed in his chair.

"Atkinson was a third possibility," continued Voss. "If neither you nor Crippen suited the authorities, Morgan intended to contrive to have Atkinson's body found in a month or two. By that time no doctor would be able to say exactly when he had died. It would be natural for detectives to conclude, once they discovered Atkinson's identity, that he had gone on a second killing spree and had drowned himself. That's why he put Atkinson's name on all the notes—if Kramer was to be the goat, it would seem that he'd tried to obscure his trail by using the name of a known killer, and if Atkinson was blamed and it was assumed he was alive after Carter's death, people would marvel at his arrogance in using his own name."

"If the idiot had taken the rap," Saint-Amour said, "I suppose we were all intended to think Kramer had sent the notes just as a joke."

"It would have looked that way. Morgan would have suggested it to me himself. He counted on me to help him a lot. When he clipped the editorial and sent it to me with the first note in New York, he knew the signature would bring me here. He counted on meeting me and seeing that I stumbled on the proper clues and became suspicious of the right persons. He probably thought it unfortunate that through a freakish coincidence the idiot showed me Atkinson's body almost as soon as I got off the train, but even so, he felt perfectly safe.

"His chance to murder Carter came that same day, just after he had met me. He had gone to Wiltonshire looking for Dorothea and was strolling along the path through the hills when he saw her beside the stream and saw Carter strike her. He was already armed with a knife he had stolen from Wiltonshire, where he came and went almost as a member of the family. He crept up on Carter and slit his throat while Dorothea lay unconscious, and in his struggles the dying man splashed her with his blood. Then Morgan obliterated all traces of a struggle except a single one of Dorothea's footprints, which lay so close to the body he didn't notice it, and went to Wiltonshire ostensibly looking for Dorothea. The rest of that episode you know. He knew Julia could be counted on to keep the secret if she thought Dorothea had killed her husband.

"While making sure he had left no traces at the scene of the crime, Morgan found the toy hatchet Toby had lost.

Later he hid the bloodstained knife and the vise that had killed Atkinson in Crippen's cave, and for some obscure reason the idiot hid them again beneath stones. And when Sackett saw Dorothea's footprint beside Carter's body he blotted it out, perhaps because he thought it might have been Julia Bisbee's footprint."

Fleming said, "I can figure out the next step. Morgan got afraid Russo would mention seeing him at the mill the night Stott—Atkinson—was killed."

"With good cause," said Voss. "Russo made a bad joke, one night when he was drunk, about 'seeing the minister's vice.' He hadn't connected it in his mind with the murder yet, but Morgan couldn't count on his continuing not to. Knowing that Russo sneaked around the hedge every evening to see the maid, Morgan simply laid for him and socked him with the hatchet. He was close enough to the house so that he could get back in the darkness before he was missed, even though I almost had him for a moment. But finding the body gave Morgan an extra respite, of course."

Saint-Amour snorted, "Anybody can take it from there. Jared Wilton was slated next."

"Yes," said Voss. "Jared had become his enemy because he objected to Morgan's sermon addressed to the murderer. Morgan knew Jared planned to have him fired. But more than that, Jared had forbidden Dorothea to see too much of him and he thought that was why she was spending time with Thomas Unger. He had started all of this because of her; if she turned against him, everything he had done would have been done in vain.

"He tried to kill Unger with that bomb because he realized the artist was winning Dorothea. He could have stolen dynamite from any of the farmers around Andor; they use it for clearing their land of stumps and rocks. He was so desperate he didn't hesitate to jeopardize the lives of Ruth Taylor and Leslie Frank, too. Very likely he considered them unworthy citizens who ought to be killed anyway."

Fleming said, "All right; we know what Morgan did and why. Now how did we—did you get wise to him?"

Voss's keen eyes twinkled behind the spectacles. He said, "We—I didn't have a single definite clue till Saturday night. Then I was talking with Kramer and Morgan in Main Street and Vito Russo came along and gave the preacher away with the pun on the vise. Only I didn't start thinking about that until yesterday." He frowned at this lapse.

"Once I started theorizing about Morgan, he filled out the picture himself. I recalled how he had collared me as soon as I stepped off the train, as though he'd known I was coming—how one of his very first words was *murder*. His love for Dorothea was apparent from the start; his very efforts to seem casual when her name was mentioned showed how important she was to him. I hadn't known him an hour before I realized he was playing a role and that under the surface he was bitter about a lot of things.

"His real character took shape in everything he did. He pretended humility, but his arrogance was too great to remain hidden. Last Sunday, when he seemed to be pleading with the murderer to surrender, he was really pleading *for* the murderer; he was passing out broad hints that murder was justifiable under some circumstances and shouldn't be condemned hastily. The very fact that he talked about the murders at every opportunity was against him.

"Then, when we found the poison in Jared's medicine, I was sure. There were only six people present besides Saint-Amour and myself when Dr. Hughson prescribed that medicine for Jared. No—five—Fleming had stepped out of the room to telephone. The five were Jared himself, the doctor, Dorothea, Julia and Morgan. The doctor was in the clear because the first dose was all right. And we had already decided that no woman had committed the crimes. Jared might have done it himself, to throw suspicion from him, just as he might have faked the attack on himself for the same reason. But Jared didn't fit the psychological picture of the murderer. And although his terror at the mention of poison was so exaggerated that it looked faked, I knew it wasn't. Jared had already shown me indications of cowardice. But I knew more definitely than that. You can fake lots of things—you can ape the sound and movement of fear—but you can't control the blood vessels nor the sweat glands. And Jared was dead white, and then purple, and his face was wet.

"So that left only Morgan. That last note setting the deadline for tonight was his idea of a filial bit of cleverness. I was supposed to say, 'Only a crazy man would give a warning like that; it couldn't be Morgan, because he isn't crazy, but it could be Kramer. . . .'"

Kramer said, "That entitles me to another bottle."

"All that I had to do was make up my mind who his victims would be and take steps to protect them. It wasn't difficult. Frank's discovery of the bomb made it unnecessary for me to worry about Unger. Wilton's medicine practically suggested itself as the agent of death. I thought Morgan might possibly have added Sackett to his list of victims, because they hated each other, and I arranged to get Sackett out of his house for the evening. Even though it seems now he would have been safe at home, I wanted him to witness the showdown. Andor's police department is going to have to take this case to court, and I guess even Fleming will agree it's really Sackett's police department.

"And I was pretty sure Morgan's nerve would last only as long as he believed himself safe. I'm glad the ghost of Atkinson showed up to scare him at the psychological moment, though—"

Saint-Amour said, "I get it, all but one thing. How did our final suspect ever dare put on a show like he did to-night? What made him think he could get away with it?"

"He was drunk, Bob—drunk with victory and pride and self-importance. He visualized his enemies defeated, his ambitions realized, the woman he loved delivered to him. He felt eloquent. He was sure he could convince his congregation that he had received a message from heaven."

Pop Kramer pried the cap off his fifth bottle of beer. It made a hissing sound and he grinned mawkishly.

He suggested, "Let's add it up. A. V. Atkinson, insane killer, dead; Carter Wilton, thief and wastrel and poten-tial killer, dead; Vito Russo, hireling thug and convicted slayer, dead; James Morgan—

"Say, it's got a happy ending after all, hasn't it?"

"It could have had a very different ending," Voss re-minded him.

"Not with you around," Kramer said expansively, "The *Advertiser* will apologize for its late sneers at you and praise you to the skies, come another Wednesday. It will also point out the romantic aspects of the case—how the misguided minister gambled and lost all for love and how the law-abiding young artist won the girl."

He scowled and shook his head. "But it wouldn't be the *Advertiser* if it was all sweetness and light. We've got to give the customers some serious stuff."

He took a pencil and a folded piece of paper from his pocket and wrote rapidly. He held up the paper.

On it he had printed:

VOSS PREDICTS MORGAN'S EXAMPLE
WILL BRING NEW WAVE OF MURDERS

"It will uphold tradition," Pop said proudly. "It will—"

He subsided. Lieutenant Bob Saint-Amour had also uncapped another bottle of beer. He had arisen and was pouring it solemnly over the editor's head.

GRAVE
WITHOUT
GRASS

GRAVE
WITHOUT GRASS

Counting myself
I have killed everyone
who knew about it.

DONALD CLOUGH CAMERON
AN ABELARD VOSS MYSTERY

1 BREWSTER LYONS SHOT HERE
  7 YEARS AGO
2 JENNY MIDGE'S HOUSE
3 BREWSTER LYONS' GRAVE
4 BAY VIEW INN

5 WALDHAM GOLF CLUB
6 SUE LYONS' HOUSE
7 TERRY WHITCOMB'S HOUSE
8 CYNTHIA CARRINGTON'S HOUSE
9 DR MANNING'S HOUSE

10 DALE PARS
11 CANNING FA
12 ELITE CAFE
13 CITY DRUG
14 AMANDA HO

LONG ISLAND SOUND

WALDHAM BAY

CEMETERY

BAY STREET

HILL STREET

FRANKLIN STREET

For
My Father
And Favorite Critic

1

Abelard Voss knew that he was observed the instant he came within view of the small brown house. The sway of a sheer curtain in a window, the immobility of an erect shadow behind the curtain, betrayed a watcher. He was pleased to have made the discovery so promptly; his gray eyes twinkled through the rimless spectacles that straddled his aquiline nose and his wide mouth twitched at the corners.

Strolling unhurriedly along the shaded village street, Voss bore the furtive scrutiny without resentment. Strangers were forever staring at him for reasons that were quite obvious. His height was incredible; his clothes—tan tropical worsteds this warm midsummer afternoon—fluttered loosely about his angular frame; his long narrow face was a study in rough-hewn flesh and bone obscured somewhat by the flapping brim of an enormous Panama; his taste in shirts ran to awning stripes and his necktie of the moment was a stunning mixture of magenta and purple. When experimentation had convinced him that no skill of tailoring or subtle blending of hues could produce upon his awkward body the effect of neat grooming he would have preferred, he had characteristically divested himself of all sartorial worries and wore what he pleased, providing it was convenient.

Now that he had reached the maturity of his early thirties he was cynically tolerant of the glances of the curious. But he could never forget the period in his gangling 'teens when self-consciousness had been an unending agony and a dark conviction of inferiority had driven him to seek compensation outside the conventional pursuits of men.

Out of that painful period, with its brooding hours of introspection, had emerged his absorbing interest in the obscure motives that shape human behavior and his inspired resolve to make that interest the means of causing the world to stare at him for what he really was, not for the gawky caricature that nature had made him. Already a large part of the world had learned to appreciate Abelard Voss, the successful young criminologist, for his uncanny solutions of crime problems and his extensive contributions to the literature of scientific detection.

He reflected with a tinge of pure pleasure that, soon enough, the citizens of this Long Island town of Waldham would be regarding him with more of awe than amusement.

The person who kept vigil in the window of the brown house had heard about him. Vague as the shadow was against the curtain, Voss was certain that its contours were feminine. Sue Lyons lived alone there and according to the local chief of police she had said she would be glad to discuss that old matter of her brother's mysterious death with Voss. Of course "glad" was a word people often used without meaning it.

He wondered what emotions stirred within Sue Lyons as she watched his approach, fancying herself unseen behind the curtain. Perhaps she would be angry because he had arrived seven years late to awaken tragic memories. She might easily be contemptuous of his unofficial intrusion so long after official activity had ceased. Possibly she was fearful of what he might unearth in the way of family skeletons if he dug too enthusiastically.

On the other hand, it was conceivable that she had planned far ahead for his coming—even that she had been the one to send that urgent summons, with its grim suggestion of murder accomplished and murder to come, which had brought him here.

He drew from his breast pocket the unsigned letter that had reached him in New York earlier in the week. The envelope bore a Waldham postmark. Slowing his pace, he read the typed lines again:

Dear Mr. Voss:

Your outstanding record as a practicing criminologist has convinced me that you are the one man to whom I may reasonably address this unusual appeal.

Will you come to Waldham immediately for the purpose of ascertaining the true facts about the fatal and mysterious shooting of Albert Brewster Lyons in 1932? So doing, I firmly believe you will not only expose a murderer, but save an innocent life as well.

Unfortunately I cannot reveal my identity at this time. I ask you to undertake this venture on faith, and enclose to stimulate that faith the sum of five hundred dollars, which should more than cover your expense.

Should you discover the true facts together with reasonable proof, tell no one, but insert in the classified columns of the Waldham *Courier* the words "Report ready." I will then make myself known to you, acknowledge this letter and be prepared to pay whatever fee you may fix.

Meanwhile it would be better if you pretended to be interested merely in the surface facts of the case, which is well remembered here, with the idea of writing something about them.

Voss scowled. In a way it was an unfair letter, giving him no opportunity to refuse, no way to return the five crisp hundred-dollar bills that reposed in his wallet. He had never before entered blindfolded upon an investigation. Yet the letter had come at a time when he was chafing against idleness, with his newest book completed and no fresh task in sight, and he had concluded finally that it would do no harm to look the ground over and decide whether it seemed worthwhile to gamble on an anonymous client.

Three hours ago a train had deposited him at the edge of Waldham. He had gone by taxi to a sprawling frame hotel that clung to the lower slope of a hill overlooking Waldham Bay, and thence to the dingy office of the local newspaper. A cheerful youngster named Eddie Braithe, who proved to be owner and editor of the weekly *Courier,* obligingly produced tattered files containing the story of the seven-year-old shooting.

From the newspaper office Voss had gone to the police station in the town hall where Cornelius Proctor, the bluff chief of the department, had been largely impressed both by his caller's appearance and reputation. Proctor had been delighted to provide Voss with much inconclusive information which the *Courier* had not recorded for reasons readily understood.

Proctor had telephoned Sue Lyons. "She's the girl to see if you really want to write it up," he declared. He drummed on the battered desk with his thick fingers and looked at Voss keenly and repeated with heavy emphasis, *"If* you really want to write it up." He had given Voss directions for finding her house—one block out Main Street to the Victory Monument and two to the right, toward the edge of the bay.

Voss folded the letter and replaced it in his pocket. He was close to his destination. The watcher had left the window; there was no sign of life about the place. But when Voss turned into the flagstone walk between clumps of flowering hydrangea a woman appeared on the screened porch and stood waiting within the door.

He removed his Panama, uncovering dank black hair that would never stay properly combed. "Miss Lyons?" he inquired.

She inclined her head stiffly. Through the screen Voss saw that she was about thirty-two, taller than most women and handsome without being in the least beautiful. Her face was framed in soft brown hair, loosely bound; her eyes were watchful and secretive beneath heavy brows; her mouth was wide and her chin square. A plain dress of rough linen hung straight on her spare figure.

"I'm Abelard Voss," he told her. "Chief Proctor phoned about me. I hoped we would have a chance to talk."

Her head was only an inch or two higher than his own as he stood at the foot of the two steps that went up to the porch. Her look was deeply searching. She made no move to open the door.

"Cornelius Proctor said you were interested in what happened to my brother," she remarked, her tone even and colorless. "I can't understand why you should be at this late date."

He was ready with an explanation. "My work deals with crimes of violence. I am more or less interested in every case that comes to my attention. It was only recently that I heard that your brother's death had never been fully explained. As soon as I had some time free I came out from New York to look over the police records on the chance that I might learn something of value."

"Who told you about it?" she asked.

Voss found the question disconcerting. He thought swiftly and skimmed close to falsehood. "The New York police keep records of all unsolved homicides in this part of the country. This case is among them. I was looking through the files in Centre Street a few days ago." He let it go at that.

Sue Lyons was trying to make up her mind about him. That much was evident in the way she kept looking at him and the careful way she chose her words. Voss realized that he was dealing with a clever and cautious woman.

She said, "It's rather ghoulish, you know, digging up the dead past to get material for sensational books and articles."

"An unsolved case is never dead," Voss said. "No statute of limitations applies to murder. I'm not at all sure I'll write about your brother's death, but if I do it will be to educate people, not to entertain them." His manner became slightly pedantic. "I spend most of my time investigating cases, but I write only about a few—those which illustrate a point or teach a lesson. I'm not interested in the sensationalism of crime so much as in the machinery that makes criminals tick. I have been making that clear to your chief of police, who is reading my syndicated articles in the *Daily Record*. He's quite concerned about this case."

"He's more concerned about you. He was out of breath when he phoned to say the great Abelard Voss was in town." There was no mockery in her voice; she seemed friendlier than she had been. "I told him that since you're here I'd rather show you around myself than have someone else do it. I . . . I loved Brewster, Mr. Voss, and I wouldn't have his death distorted to make a good story. He didn't kill himself."

"As I understand it he couldn't have. There were no fingerprints on the gun and the wound was not one a man could have inflicted on himself. At least, if it was suicide, your brother—or someone—went to some pains to make it look like murder."

"It wasn't suicide. You'll see that it couldn't have been when I'm through showing you. I suppose you would like to see where it happened? I used to go there and pray that the murderer would be found. I still do, but not so often. But if I thought you could find the guilty person . . ."

"I'm not exactly a detective, Miss Lyons." Voss's smile crinkled the corners of his eyes. "Finding the criminal out is what I'm frequently engaged to do, but I accomplish that through finding out what made him a criminal, which is what I like to do. Not that I don't enjoy the excitement of the chase. But it is in the recognition of the psychological pattern which all crimes have that I please myself esthetically and inflate my downtrodden ego."

She did not respond to his mood, possibly because she did not understand the candor of his self-revelation. She pushed the screen door open and descended the two steps to the flagstones. She said, "You know this is the anniversary of the day he died, don't you? I was getting ready to go to the cemetery when Cornelius phoned. We can walk that way to the place where . . . he was shot . . . if you don't mind."

"Not at all," Voss murmured.

Sue Lyons walked beside him with the free stride of one used to the outdoors, swinging her arms. In motion, with the slanting rays of the sun making glints of red and gold in her hair, she came to life and lost the air of austerity that had seemed so much a part of her in the beginning.

They went back one block over the course Voss had traveled and turned right. A hundred yards ahead of them the street became a gravel drive beyond stone pillars that marked the entrance to a cemetery, where trees arched over white headstones that were vivid against the green sweep of tended lawn.

Sue Lyons reached a point directly between the pillars and halted abruptly as though she had come against invisible gates. The sun struck her shoulder and made of her shadow an elongated arm pointing across the graves. Her eyes looked steadily where it pointed and she spoke in a tense whisper.

"She's here!"

Voss gazed with quickened interest among the orderly rows of monuments. He saw an old woman kneeling beside a rectangle of newly turned earth a dozen yards from the gravel drive. She wielded a gardening trowel, stirring the earth near the roots of flowering plants. Her stooped body was hidden in part by the grave's squat shaft of dark marble, pointed at the top.

Even in the sunlight the woman appeared uncommonly repulsive to Voss, who had trained himself to look for more than surface details. A gray shawl was drawn over her head and shoulders. Despite the heat of the day she wore a sweater of dirty white, broken through at the elbows. Her skirt bulged over shapeless hips bolstered by many layers of petticoats.

"Who is she?" he asked.

"Jenny Midge." Her voice retained its hushed quality. "She was Brewster's nurse and mine when we were children. She stayed with my people till he was . . . till he died."

"And the grave?"

"My brother's." She was silent for a space before she added vehemently, "Jenny Midge has no business here. She's demented, Mr. Voss—she's stark mad."

The woman could not have heard, yet she raised her eyes at that moment and stared at them. Voss received an indelible impression of an ancient face, bloated and wrinkled, wreathed with snaky strands of yellow-white hair, pitted with caverns from which murky eyes peered. He could *feel* the repellent impact of her look.

Sue Lyons gasped.

Jenny Midge watched them, unmoving, for slow seconds. Then she got to her feet laboriously and walked with a curious hitching of her left leg and shoulder, not quite limping, to the driveway and across it toward the sagging wire fence that marked the western boundary of the burying ground at the foot of a wooded hill.

Her departure was like the lifting of a pall. Sue took a deep breath and Voss noticed that her strained face lost some of its tautness as the old woman drew farther away. Sue's low-heeled shoes scuffed the gravel.

Voss tried to shrug away the feeling that he had looked upon something altogether evil. He reminded himself forcibly that there was a rational and scientific explanation for Jenny Midge and her unwholesomeness—for all men and women and all that was good or bad about them—if one troubled to seek for it.

Sue moved silently to the spot Jenny Midge had quitted. The dark monument was inscribed simply:

ALBERT BREWSTER LYONS
June 4, 1906
July 7, 1932

Voss read the dates and was conscious again of that vague inconsistency which he had sensed in the unsigned letter. Seven years had gone by, to the day, since that last tombstone date—and now the broken ground was like earth over a new grave. Seven years—and the scarlet and pink roses that balanced on their thorny stems were as dewy as the first offerings of a fresh grief.

"Seven years," Albert Brewster Lyons's sister said, echoing his thought, "and no grass grown. Grass grows on every grave in Waldham but this one, Mr. Voss. She won't let it grow—not a blade."

Voss's eyes narrowed against the sun for a last glimpse of the witchlike creature. Presently he smiled, and the smile erased an expression of grimness.

"No wonder people haven't forgotten!" he said.

She faced him. "Brewster's funeral will be seven years ago Sunday, the day after tomorrow. There was a terrible storm, but most of the village was there. . . ."

She went on telling about the funeral. Cynthia Carrington had not been present; she had been at home having hysterics and Dr. Manning had attended her. Terry Whitcomb was alone in his sloop on the Sound, alive by a miracle. Jenny Midge had made a scene at the grave, swearing awful oaths of vengeance.

From his talk with Cornelius Proctor and his perusal of Eddie Braithe's newspaper files Voss was able to fit the names into niches in his orderly mind. Cynthia Carrington had been Brewster Lyons's sweetheart seven years ago. Dr. Garth Manning, the present chief medical examiner of the county, was suspected to have fallen in love with her about that time and to all appearances was still in love with her. Terrence Whitcomb had been Sue Lyons's fiancé and Brewster's best friend, a rich and irresponsible fellow who spent most of his time sailing; now he was a solitary drunkard, keeping to his fantastic house at the edge of the bay, often sailing alone on moonless nights.

The years—something that had persisted through the years—had changed them all. That was the really significant thing, Voss told himself—the thing he had sensed behind the urgency of that unconventional letter, and was beginning to see more clearly, and hoped with all the enthusiasm of the born investigator to fathom.

"It happened up there, didn't it?" He pointed toward the top of the hill, massed with green trees through which showed patches of gray rock and the brown thread of a winding path.

"I'll show you." Sue turned and retraced her steps. Voss followed her slowly.

Where Franklyn Street met Hill Street at the cemetery entrance, a dirt road began looping northward and westward around the foot of the hill close to the shore of Waldham Bay. A quarter of a mile along the road could be seen a corner of Bay View Inn, where Voss had taken up his temporary abode. A fingerpost announced that somewhere beyond the inn lay the Sea Crest Golf Club.

Just past a clump of leafy alders, a stocky man in white overalls was painting one of the gray outbuildings of the inn. Voss watched him sweep the heavy brush in a practiced rhythm.

A tall man accompanied by a slender woman in a flowered frock came out of a pathway near the alders. They strolled arm in arm, talking together—or rather the man talked and the woman listened somewhat listlessly. Voss heard the hiss of a sharp indrawn breath from Sue. She said, "Cynthia. Cynthia and Garth Manning."

"Is it so strange to see them out walking?" he inquired.

"This time it is. It's unbelievable. They've been on the hill."

Still he did not understand. "It must be a pleasant walk."

"The last time Cynthia Carrington was on the hill," Sue said, "was the evening Brewster was killed. No one could coax her near the place afterward. She never so much as mentioned it."

"But after seven years—"

"It's the anniversary. No woman would forget that."

Voss watched the couple with his lively eyes. The distance was not too great for him to see that the woman was beautiful. Her dark hair was bound closely about her small head and the firm lines of her bosom and hips were youthful. She looked like a slim girl, yet she must have been past thirty.

Garth Manning would be about ten years older. He wore gray trousers and a white jacket and carried himself with easy dignity. At intervals he slashed casually at weeds before him with a yellow cane.

They did not look toward Sue Lyons and Voss. They cut across a corner of a field toward the heart of the village.

"The doctor may have prescribed the walk," Voss said half to himself. "Getting rid of the secret terror by facing it is good psychology."

It was then he noticed that the stocky man had put down his paintbrush and was looking after the strolling couple with a queer fixity, not moving a muscle. The distance was too great to read the expression on his face, but a glare of hatred would have gone well with the pose.

As they passed beneath the alders and began to climb the stony path Sue spoke with a trace of bitterness, her face holding a wistful, hungry expression.

"Cynthia and Garth should have been married years ago. They would have been if Garth hadn't got mixed up with a girl who used to work in the canning factory. He was her doctor. The girl was going to have a baby and she went into court and made him pay for its support. No one believed Garth was responsible, but you know what the courts are like and what a tremendous advantage a woman has in those cases. The baby died, but the scandal didn't."

Voss nodded. That was another thing he had learned from Chief Proctor. Evelyn Lister, the girl's name was, and she was the bad girl of Waldham. She had red hair, dyed, and green eyes, the chief had said, and was "just about the prettiest trick in town, which explains why all the women hate her."

Halfway up the hill the path swung to the edge of a bluff. One could see the northern edge of the cemetery through the trees and, below, a rickety, unpainted house with boarded windows. The walls of the aged structure leaned crazily, the roof threatened to collapse at any moment and the rotting shingles had scaled away. But, amazingly and pathetically, a trim and weeded flower garden bloomed red and yellow and blue beside it.

"That's Jenny Midge's house," Sue informed Voss. "That is, the county took over the title for taxes long ago, but no one else ever bothered about it. People say it's haunted. Jenny was born there. One spring before my time typhoid killed her father and mother and two brothers and Jenny came to stay with my parents and work for them. She takes care of the old garden and they say she sleeps there sometimes, although she keeps house for Terry Whitcomb and has a room there, too."

"There are people who won't let go of tragedy," Voss said, pausing to stare at the place in fascination. "They think only of death in the midst of life. They're like toadstools fattening on decay in darkness."

"Jenny's like a toadstool," Sue agreed. "Like a toad, too." She pointed. "We're almost at the place where Brewster was found."

The path was cool. Green twilight filled the space between the interlacing branches. Undergrowth was dense at either side, making it difficult to see more than a few yards. The twittering of birds was loud and suddenly the woods vibrated to the high-pitched whine of an outboard motor in the bay.

They rounded a curve in the path, their feet making no noise against the packed earth, and came in view of a place that was like a dusky grotto hollowed out of the greenery. Slabs of rock carpeted with moss floored it and from a wall of stone at one side a thin trickle of sparkling spring water splashed musically into a tiny pool. In the center of the tiny recess was a natural stone bench.

"This is where . . ." Sue began, and then fell silent.

Twenty feet away a girl and a young man sat on the stone bench with their backs to the path. The man's hair was dark and carefully combed and he wore slacks and a sport coat; the girl had red hair and her dress was a pale green cotton print. They sat close together, deep in conversation, and what with that and the tinkling of the spring and the whine of the motorboat they seemed utterly unaware that they were observed.

Sue touched Voss's arm and together they moved along the path. Before they were quite past the grotto, however, Voss saw the young man's head turn and recognized his face. He did not pause. He was aware that Sue Lyons's mouth had become a thin bloodless line.

"I know that fellow," he remarked a few steps farther on. "He's a writer for the wood-pulp magazines—George Thael. He grinds out mystery and horror stuff by the bale. I've run into him at writers' meetings."

She said harshly, "I know the girl. I wish I didn't. Seeing her always makes me feel that the world's an ugly place."

"Evelyn Lister?" he hazarded.

She bent her head affirmatively and lengthened her stride.

The path led ultimately to a round platform of rock that formed the summit of the hill. The trees were spaced farther and between their trunks ahead of him Voss could see nearly the whole shining expanse of Waldham Bay, with its sailboats and motor cruisers moored off the yacht club and along the shore. Beyond the bay was the deeper blue of Long Island Sound, with a white steamer creeping along the invisible line that was its center, and beyond that were the dark line of the Connecticut shore and the crimson and gold of a gorgeous sunset. At his right the colored rooftops and snowy church steeples of Waldham village thrust upward through venerable trees.

"It's beautiful," he said.

But Sue Lyons's mind was not dwelling on beautiful things. She barely looked at the panorama. She said dully, "Brewster was found back there at midnight by my father. He was lying behind that stone seat out of sight. He had been shot while he was sitting up and had lain for some time on the rock bleeding. The gun was ten or twelve feet away and the police couldn't trace it. The shock killed my father within the year and my mother died three months later."

The twanging song of the outboard motor reached them again. Until that moment Voss had not realized that it had stopped ten minutes or so ago. He went to the edge of the rocky platform and looked down, but the contour of the hill hid a part of the bay beneath him where the boat evidently was.

"You can see from the last turn," Sue called. She darted back along the path out of sight so quickly that Voss blinked.

He watched the changing colors of the sunset for two or three minutes, wondering what secrets and guilty consciences and impending tragedies were hidden in the peaceful-looking village. Who down there knew the real answer to the mystery of Brewster Lyons's death? Whose innocent life was in danger if the writer of that unsigned letter had been right? What was the name of that writer, and what had been his innermost purpose?

He turned to follow Sue and met her climbing back, out of breath. Her pallor startled him. "It's getting cool and I've tired you," he said. "We'd better go down."

She waited for him. The twilight of the path had deepened and the chirping of the birds had all but ceased. The noise of the outboard motor was mellowed by distance.

"I could see the boat," Sue said, "but I couldn't tell who was in it. The sun blinded me."

No one was sitting now on the rock bench by the spring. The water clattered merrily, but the place had an empty, mournful appearance. A scrap of white cloth lay on the green moss carpet.

"Come," urged Sue, plucking at his sleeve as he lingered. "I should have gone home before this. That's only a handkerchief the girl dropped."

Voss was not looking at the handkerchief, however. He was looking beyond it where a spatter of red stained the stone of the seat. The spatter was fresh and glistening.

Moving cautiously, he picked up the handkerchief, noted the embroidered "L" in one of its lacy corners and put it in his coat pocket. He trembled a little with excitement. From where he stood he could see a small white hand extending beyond the end of the stone.

The hand was Evelyn Lister's. She lay huddled behind the rock where Brewster Lyons's body had lain seven years ago. Her hair was stained a deeper red than any patent dye could make it. The jagged rock that had battered her skull, a rock larger than a man's two fists, lay near her. She was dead.

2

Abelard Voss was unfavorably impressed by Sue Lyons's reaction. She followed him with reluctance as far as the stone. The break in her breathing told him when she caught sight of what lay behind it. She recoiled a step, drawing her thin shoulders erect. Her attitude was defensive.

"She deserved it!" she cried, her voice unnaturally harsh. "It was bound to happen sometime. One can't ruin other lives without paying for them."

"What other lives?" Voss asked, his eyes glittering down upon her. "Garth Manning's? Cynthia Carrington's?"

She made an impatient gesture. "God knows what lives," she said. "You do something wicked to a person and you never know how far that wickedness will reach or how many it will touch. She was all bad. Everything she did hurt someone."

He frowned thoughtfully. Angry hatred lay behind Sue's words where he would have expected to find nothing more corrosive than contempt, leavened perhaps by a touch of pity. Evelyn Lister might have been bad in life, but in death she was none the less pathetic.

He looked down again at the dead girl's rouged cheeks, the moist lips curling away from small teeth, the dilated eyes rolled back in their sockets. Horror was graved in the hard lines of the face, but it did not obliterate the facile prettiness of which Cornelius Proctor had spoken.

The shadows were darkening. A wide circle of stillness surrounded the spot where they stood as though the odor of death had spread like a noxious vapor over the hillside. Birds chirped and sang at a distance, a far-off squirrel chattered and down in the village a dog howled. But nearer at hand not so much as the snapping of a twig or the rustle of a leaf rose above the monotonous melody of the spring.

"You'll walk back with me?" Sue said. "I'm . . . afraid." Her anger had vanished and her glance shifted fearfully to the dense wall of the woods.

Voss took her arm and they went out of the place of death and down the twisting pathway. There was no way of telling whether the slayer of the red-haired girl still lurked near, whether desperate eyes watched them go. Voss knew that he should have stayed with the body, but Sue's terror was too real to ignore.

"I'll take you to the street," he said. "You'll be perfectly safe there. You can go home and call Proctor. I'll go back up to—"

Her foot turned on a rounded stone. She gave a little scream and clung to him and he put a strong arm around her shoulders. A spasm of pain contracted her face.

"It isn't anything," she said after a minute. "I broke that ankle playing tennis last year." She tried her weight on it tentatively. "I guess it's all right now." But she limped, nevertheless, and held tightly to his arm until they reached the bottom of the path.

The man who had been painting the white outbuilding of the inn had gathered up his buckets and brushes and departed. Some children were playing in Hill Street and three or four grown-ups strolled beneath the arching elms. Across the vacant lot where Cynthia Carrington and Garth

Manning had walked the gables of the Lyons house were visible past the stone corner of the Waldham Yacht Club.

It was ten minutes after eight by the wrist watch Voss wore. Less than half an hour of fading daylight remained.

"Can you walk from here?" he asked Sue. "Do you think I ought to stay with you or call someone?"

"I can walk. I'll hurry. You or Cornelius Proctor can find me at home whenever you want me. If you don't, will you phone me in the morning?"

He promised. He watched her swing down the street, striding like a man, without any trace of a limp. He lingered a moment in indecision. Then he went back up the path.

The ramshackle structure where Jenny Midge's father and mother and brothers had lived and died was indeed like a haunted house squatting at the foot of the bluff, with the eerie dusk dimming the splendor of its ordered garden. Something moved in the garden and Voss could make out the old woman's stooped figure beside rose bushes spattered with blossoms that reminded him of tiny drops of blood. She was a gray ghost in a place of ghosts; her trowel rooting up grass and weeds was a dagger opening wounds that should have healed years ago.

The symbolism appealed to him.

The grotto where the dead girl lay was as Voss had left it—*or was it?* All at once he sensed an indefinable difference. It might have been only that birds sang again in the branches overhead as though a malignant presence had removed itself. It might have been only the subtle alchemy of the waning light.

The huddled body had not been moved a hair's breadth. The length of white ash where a cigarette had burned itself out on an uncovered patch of rock, and the brownish wad of another half-smoked cigarette defiling the clean pool, had been there earlier. The thick moss showed no footprints and was spotless. The girl's outflung hand . . .

Voss leaned closer, looking at that hand. A furrow appeared between his brows. Funny he hadn't noticed before this the crumpled piece of paper almost hidden by the clenched fingers. Had it been there when first he saw the hand? Had the fingers been clenched then or had they been lax?

He grasped a corner of the paper with the tips of his thumb and forefinger and drew it free. He shook out the folds and saw that it was an ordinary sheet of linen notepaper torn from a tablet on which a dozen printed words, cut individually and carefully from a column of a newspaper, had been pasted.

The words were:

> I was only fifteen
> when it happened
> but I knew too much

Voss sat on the extreme end of the stone bench. His mind, unbidden, conjured up a picture of this sylvan retreat seven years ago, a picture that might have been caught back from the hurrying stream of time. Dusk was at hand as now. Birds were making a great fuss about finding satisfactory perches among the green leaves. On the rock sat a solemn-faced young man resembling pictures Voss had seen of Brewster Lyons, and beside the young man sat a demure girl. In the screening underbrush lurked a long-legged schoolgirl, her jade-green eyes alight with mischief and her hair—*had* it been red in those days?

The picture was fogged with distance and twilight and Voss could not see what happened very clearly. But there was a shot, quite sudden, and a dissolving puff of white smoke, and the solemn young man jerked and sagged upon the stone. His startled companion sat still as the rock.

The schoolgirl clapped her hands over her mouth to stifle a scream. She watched for a minute more, unable to tear her scared eyes away. Then she crept back through the woods until she reached a loop of the path farther down. When she felt the hard earth under her feet she ran as fast as she was able all the way home.

It could have happened that way, Voss thought. And yet seven years was a long time for a girl like Evelyn Lister to keep that kind of a secret. Unless—and Voss's eyes sharpened as the notion came—unless she had been paid to keep it.

Someone was coming up the path fast, his panting breath louder than the scuffing of his feet. Voss arose as Cornelius Proctor charged into the grotto and stood blowing like a winded horse.

"Sue called me; where is she?" he said all in a breath. He wiped his wet forehead with a broad palm and ruffled his sparse, graying hair. His colorless eyes spied the outstretched hand before Voss could answer and he went to the long stone.

Cornelius Proctor was a large man. His face was rugged and his jaw heavy with folds of flesh that overhung his limp collar. He was fifty-odd and fat was beginning to conceal muscles that must have been lean and hard in their better years.

He looked at the body a long time without saying anything. He straightened, took a fat cigar from the breast pocket of his blue serge coat and fished vaguely in other pockets.

"Match?" he mumbled.

Voss did not smoke, but he found a packet of matches in his pocket and gave it to Proctor. He said, "Miss Lyons and I came up here about seven-thirty and the girl was sitting with George Thael, a young fellow who writes. Know him?"

Proctor inclined his head, exhaling blue smoke. "We make you crime experts right at home in Waldham, don't we? Thael came to see me a few days ago about the Brewster Lyons case. Thought he might get an idea for a story out of it."

"We came back," Voss continued, "ten or fifteen minutes later. Nobody was in sight, but I noticed what looked like blood on the stone. I saw . . ."

He was reaching into the pocket where he had put the handkerchief which he had picked up. The pocket was empty. He stiffened, remembering how Sue Lyons had stumbled and clutched at his coat. He had taken it for granted that the "L" in the corner of the handkerchief had stood for "Lister." But it could have stood for "Lyons."

"You saw. . . ?" Proctor prompted.

"I saw her hand," said Voss. "This paper was in it. I didn't notice the paper at first, but when I came back it was there. The murderer might have been hiding close by and put the paper there when I took Miss Lyons to the foot of the hill. Of course that's just a possibility. I might have missed it the first time."

Proctor read the words pasted against the paper. "Believe it?" he asked.

"I don't know." It was a provocative picture, that one his imagination had painted so neatly, and he hated to let it go. "How about the girl? Did she live here seven years ago? Would she blackmail a man or a woman?"

Proctor grunted. "She was born here. Her ma and pa split up and went away and a no-good uncle raised her. She's been on her own since she was fourteen or so. Even when she was a kid in grammar school she was bad and I guess pretty near all the boys learned the facts of life from her one time or another.

"She tried to blackmail Doc Manning two years ago when she got in the family way, and she backed it up by

going to court and having the doc declared the father. He'd
been treating her for something or other. I don't think the
doc was responsible—even in this town a good-looking
medico doesn't have to depend on girls like her for you-
know-what—but the woman's word usually goes in cases
like that."

"I wouldn't say I believed it, then, but I'd think about
it a lot. Unless the one who killed her is plain crazy he left
that note for one of two reasons—to throw us off the track
or to warn somebody."

"Just a gesture," the chief suggested.

"Then he's crazy. Not necessarily raving, but overbal-
anced by thymus. Thymocentrics kill and leave notes."

"Thymo— How do you tell 'em, Voss?"

"You don't always. The thymus is one of the ductless
glands we all have—the gland of childhood, it's sometimes
called—and a majority of murderers and practically all
geniuses are largely controlled by it. Particularly the murderers who leave notes like that one and invent intricate
plots and leave false trails. But glands are funny. Sometimes they put plain labels on people and more often they
don't. I can send you a book—"

"I wish you wouldn't," Proctor hastened to interrupt.
"Books get me all mixed up. I'd rather sort out the suspects in the old-fashioned way. We've got this Thael fellow. See anyone else?"

Voss told him about Cynthia Carrington and Garth
Manning and the policeman's bushy eyebrows jumped.

"Cynthia here!" he marveled. "Now I'll believe anything. You know last time she was here was with Brewster
the night he was bumped off. A lot of people thought she
did it. A lot of others blamed Manning. I was pretty sure
neither of them could have."

"If Manning did it and Evelyn knew about it and was
blackmailing him—"

"He'd have two damn' good reasons for killing her. If it was me that baby business alone would be reason enough. Anyway, the doc'll be here. He's county medical examiner and I called him right off. Got track of him at Cynthia's. He'd gone from there to the golf club to see Ralph Decker. Ralph's taking shots in the arm for hay fever. Hell of a thing for a golf pro to have."

"A man in overalls was glaring at the pair of them," Voss said. "He was painting some of the buildings around the inn. He was short, heavy, bushy-haired—"

"By God!" Proctor smote his left palm with his right fist. "You got something there. That's Art Dawson, the Lister girl's real sweetheart. Both of 'em have been living in Jack Miller's boarding house on Walnut Street. Living together, folks say. Dawson's got a temper. Had him in jail three times for fighting when he was drunk. He's jealous, too. Once he went after the doc with a gun." He reflected. "Say, if he'd seen Thael and Evelyn together he could've sneaked up here and killed her. It would be like him, only I'd think he'd try to kill Thael, too."

"And there's Jenny Midge."

Proctor considered. "Never could make her out. Maybe she had it in for the Lister girl. She's got it in for everybody else. But, damn it, you can fire questions at her all day without getting a sensible answer. She had us running in circles and tearing our hair when Brewster was killed."

"That's the list. We didn't see anyone else." Voss debated whether he should mention that Sue Lyons had been out of his sight at about the time the murder must have been committed, and certainly had picked his pocket of the handkerchief that might have developed into an important clue. He decided to wait.

"Irv will be along right away," Proctor said. "I left word for him. Irv's my boy. Knows fingerprints and all that stuff as well as any of the experts in New York. We'll put a watch on Thael and Dawson right off and call out Gardenia."

"Gardenia?"

"Hell, haven't you heard? This is one police department that's got everything. Gardenia is a purebred bloodhound from some kennels over in Connecticut. Ben Thoad bought her when she was a pup and trained her out of books. She's an old girl now, but she could trail a man clear across the Sound."

"It's a good bet," Voss said.

"Wait till you see her." He paused, listening. "Here comes Irv now."

A husky fellow of twenty-five came up the darkening path. He wore slacks and a sleeveless sweater and walked swiftly and lithely, carrying a tripod and a big camera case. His eyes were the hard gray of the chief's and he had the same rugged features on a more youthful scale. His uncovered hair was black and straight.

He looked at the body and said quietly, "Evelyn Lister, eh? Got anything to go on?"

"Just what Abelard Voss tells me," the chief said. "You've heard plenty about him, Irv—shake hands with him. Then hustle back to headquarters and send Backus to keep an eye on that writer fellow Thael. He's boarding at Amanda Holmes's house on Taylor Street. If he isn't there tell Backus to find him and keep him in sight. No arrest unless he tries to leave town."

Irv Proctor's handclasp was firm. He asked his father, "Think Thael did it?"

"We don't know. Might have been him or Art Dawson. Have one of the other boys locate Dawson and watch him without letting on. Then find Ben Thoad and tell him to bring that hound of his up here. Tell him to stop at the Bay View Inn and get some of Dawson's work clothes—a shirt or a shoe. Then you can come back and put your college education to work."

Irv said, "Oke." He was gone with astonishing speed, leaving his paraphernalia behind.

"A good boy," Proctor murmured. "Young, but smart. You'll find him a lot of help."

"Me?" Voss looked blank. "You're the crime expert here, Chief. I just ran up for the week end to look around. Naturally I'm interested, and if I can help . . ." He stopped talking because his audience was smirking at him in open disbelief.

"We'll see," Proctor said. "Maybe what I heard about you wasn't true. Maybe you're just one of those guys that always gets in the way, like reporters. And then again maybe you're a pretty good detective who came up here for a more important reason than you're letting on." He looked over his shoulder. "Speaking of reporters . . ."

Young Braithe—Eddie Braithe, who had inherited the Waldham *Courier* when his father died a year or two ago— came into view, towing by the hand a slim, pretty girl. Both wore immaculate white linens and were alike enough to be taken for twins, brother and sister, with their light brown curly hair, blue eyes and delicately carved features. They were about twenty-three, Voss guessed.

Braithe introduced Voss to the girl. Her name was Dale Parsons. Braithe said, "We drove to headquarters to find out if anything was doing and Backus told us. I thought it was luck, getting a good yarn like this right after the *Daily Record* made me its correspondent here. Then I remembered about you, Voss."

"It's your story," Voss said. "The *Record* only buys my syndicated stuff. I don't write for it."

"I know. But they won't miss a chance like this—you on the scene and your name so well known. They'll offer you plenty to cover it."

"It will still be your story, Braithe. Once I tried to get a job on a New York newspaper and every city editor in town looked at me once and said no. So I don't belong to the Newspaper Guild and I don't scab. I don't need money badly enough to pretend to be a reporter when I'm not one."

Eddie Braithe's face crinkled in a grin of delight. "You mean it? Zowie! This is the biggest day of my career in Waldham." He brought a pencil and a sheaf of paper from an inner pocket and held the pencil with his left hand. "I'll start by interviewing you. 'Abelard Voss, noted criminologist, who discovered the body while investigating another murder that occurred under almost identical circumstances in the same spot exactly seven years ago, said—' What did you say, Voss?"

"I said," Voss told him with firmness, "'it's Chief Proctor's case and no doubt he will solve it without any amateur assistance. When it's all cleared up I may look over the reports and write something."

"Pretty smooth," Braithe said admiringly. "Chief, you could learn things from him!"

3

Garth Manning arrived soon after Braithe. He glanced at them all without speaking and approached the body with a curious rigidity, his arms stiffly at his sides, his knees scarcely bending. His eyes were bleak and harassed and his every movement seemed forced. He had come up the path empty-handed, without his yellow cane or the leather kit medical men usually carry.

Braithe had brought a flashlight. He held it over the dead girl and flicked the switch with his thumb. Voss had not realized how dark it was until he saw the blood-clotted head floating in the puddle of brilliance.

Dale Parsons made a choking sound and turned away. Proctor sucked in his breath audibly. Manning snapped, "Turn that damned thing off!" Braithe muttered an apology, the light vanished and shadows leaped to soften the horror.

Manning leaned forward to examine the body, but did not touch it. His scrutiny lasted less than half a minute. He looked obliquely up at Voss while he spoke to Proctor, his voice low and rapid.

"Fractures, bad ones. They'd have killed anyone instantly. I guess you know the time of death."

Proctor cleared his throat. "Half an hour after you and Cynthia were up this way, near as I can tell."

"She was all right then," Manning declared. "We came this far and turned around and went back. She was with a young fellow I've seen around the village two or three times."

"Anything about your walk we ought to know?"

Manning regarded him nervously. "We didn't notice anyone else, if that's what you mean. If you want to know why we walked up here I—I'm not at liberty to say just at present."

Proctor glanced toward the path. He raised his voice. "Didn't waste any time, did you?"

Voss had heard no one. He was startled to see Irv Proctor with another man and a dog, a large black-and-tan bloodhound bitch whose long ears drooped at either side of a doleful head protruding from folds of loose-wrinkled flesh. The animal's shoulder muscles quivered and her bloodshot eyes beneath a furrowed forehead remained fixed on the stone seat.

The man with Irv resembled the dog comically. He was older than Proctor and wore an unpressed uniform that had lost half its brass buttons and hung shapelessly on his pudgy frame. His nose was long and sad, his head quite hairless, his ears were large and his eyes round and dark.

"Thunder!" he rumbled without enthusiasm. "How d'you expect me and Gardenia to go through the woods in the dark?"

"We'll manage," Proctor said. "Ben, this is Abelard Voss, the murder expert I was talking about. Voss, this is Sergeant Thoad, the veteran of the force."

Voss offered his hand. "She's a nice-looking animal," he observed.

Ben Thoad seemed not to notice the hand. He gave Gardenia's leash a petulant jerk and Gardenia turned upon him a gaze eloquent with reproach.

Proctor was at Voss's elbow. He whispered, "Ask him why he named her Gardenia. It's his one joke and it's lousy, but he loves it."

"A beautiful animal," Voss repeated with emphasis, "but an unusual name. How did you happen to pick that name for her, Sergeant?"

Thoad's eyes puckered suspiciously. He growled, "Because she smells so good." For a second his face was forbidding, then it displayed evidences of strain and finally it contorted amazingly into a smile of blissful happiness.

Eddie Braithe snickered. Dale frowned. Proctor grinned indulgently. Manning fidgeted. Irv pursed his lips indelicately and gave vent to that salute known the earth around as the Bronx cheer.

"That's pretty good," lied Voss, chuckling.

Sergeant Thoad expanded visibly, "Trained her myself," he volunteered, "on boiled liver and old shoes. She's followed trails five days old smack to the man we wanted. She's found burglars, runaway kids, nuts from the lunatic asylum—"

"She's got to catch her first murderer now," Proctor broke in. "Did you get those work clothes?"

"Shirt and shoes both," Irv said, tapping a paper-wrapped bundle under his arm. He kept looking at Dale Parsons out of the corner of his eye. "Everything's set. Thael was running a typewriter in his room and Backus could see him through the window. We went past Miller's boarding house and Dawson was sitting on the front steps talking with Jack Miller."

"We'll get started then. When we've finished with Dawson's trail we'll see what Gardenia can tell us about Thael. For the time being we know Thael was here, but we don't know what Dawson was doing all the time. Ben, you and Gardenia do your stuff."

"You watch," Thoad said to Voss. "You'll see what a smart bloodhound can do. Smarter'n any human detective, by thunder!"

He took a glass jar from his capacious pocket. Dale had been petting Gardenia and Gardenia had been wagging her tail and sniffing the girl with approval, meanwhile ignoring Braithe's friendly overtures. The jar put an end to the exchange of compliments. Gardenia promptly forgot the girl, the corpse and all else excepting the object Thoad held in his hand.

"Boiled liver," Thoad said. He unscrewed the top of the jar and extracted a pinkish scrap. Gardenia's head lifted, her ears cocked, her tail lifted and her mouth drooled.

Irv unwrapped the paper parcel and dumped a pair of paint-spattered shoes and a shirt on the ground. Thoad put the jar back in his pocket, let the dog smell the morsel of meat and then tossed it on the clothing. He let Gardenia strain at the leash for seconds and released her. She lunged and the boiled liver vanished. She sniffed frantically at the clothing, seeking more.

"It's like candy to her," Thoad explained. "She's been raised on patent dog food, healthy, but not so tasty. She'll trail to heck and back for liver. She knows she'll get more if she finds the one who wore these clothes."

He picked up the garments and shook them in front of the bitch. He wrapped the end of the leash tightly around his hand. He tucked the shirt and shoes under his arm.

"Find 'em, Gardenia," he commanded.

Gardenia knew the game. She lifted her muzzle, turning it this way and that, and lowered it to the moss. She started around the little clearing and Thoad, who limped with his right leg, let her drag him after her. At the point farthest from the path she turned abruptly into the woods.

"So Dawson *was* here," Proctor said, his voice husky. "Coming, Voss?"

Voss followed into the gloom beneath the trees. The others remained behind. A thin branch bent by the chief's passage whipped across Voss's cheek, stinging like the lash of a whip, and he put up his left arm as a shield.

"Thunder!" Ben Thoad boomed, ahead of them, as he floundered over a fallen log.

For the most part the trail was through comparatively open places between the trees. It was a steep way leading downward, but not too difficult for one who wanted to climb or descend the hill without being seen by any person who might be on the path. They touched the path at only one point, crossing it at right angles and plunging immediately afterward down a steep embankment where heavy shoes had left scars in moist clay.

"Two different sets of footprints," Proctor said, puzzled, flashing the light he had borrowed from Braithe over the hillside. "Both going the same way."

Gardenia led them presently out of the woods and to the building Dawson had been painting that afternoon and thence to a second outbuilding where she sniffed about the door.

"Tool shed," Proctor stated. "That would be where he changed clothes. Once we find out just how he moved around we'll have a pretty good idea how much truth there is in what he tells us."

The trail swung back from there straight to the juncture of the path and the dirt road, where four cars waited. There they met Braithe, Dale and Manning.

"Nothing I can do," Manning told Proctor. "I'll send Tom Wilkins up for the body. Irv is staying with it. Tomorrow will be soon enough for an autopsy." He climbed into a battered Buick roadster.

"Tomorrow will be plenty soon," said the chief. "Not much question about the way she died."

Braithe's Zephyr sedan was new and shiny. He held the door for Dale and went to the other side to get in behind the wheel. "We'll follow in luxury," he said. "Irv is going to make a couple pictures up there for me. I'll get on the phone and gift the *Record* the story soon as you make a pinch."

Gardenia plodded east on Franklyn Street past the cemetery gates, her nose a good ten inches from the sidewalk. Thoad leaned backward against the leash and sweat ran down his cheeks and over the bulging flesh above his collar.

Voss said, "Jenny Midge." His hand indicated the gray blob in the cemetery moving among the solemn tombstones with that curious hitching gait, coming toward them. The shawl was drawn closely over her head and her face was obliterated by shadow, but he was conscious again of that first impression of malignant evil.

"Come on," Proctor said roughly. "Jenny gives me the creeps and I've got enough to worry about without having nightmares. One of the things on my mind since we saw those two sets of tracks is a hunch that Eddie Braithe isn't going to have any pinch to report tonight—not unless I decide to take that writer fellow in. Whatever Dawson's alibi, he'll have a witness to back it up."

They walked along Franklyn from Hill to Main Street and from Main to Walnut, where Jack Miller and his wife kept boarders in the big yellow house that was second from the corner. Braithe paced them in his Zephyr, one gloved hand holding the wheel, one arm thrown carelessly around Dale's shoulders.

Gardenia led them straight to the steps of the Miller house and straight to the stocky man who sat alone on the steps glowering at them. Voss recognized the painter, out of his overalls, dressed in a decent brown suit and washed and combed. The bitch looked from Dawson to Thoad confidently and wagged her tail and Thoad patted her head and reached in his pocket for the jar of liver.

"You lookin' for me?" Dawson challenged, including all of them in his surly glance.

"Yep," said Proctor. He took a cigar from his pocket and bit the end from it. "Match?"

Dawson extended a packet of matches ungraciously. Proctor lighted the cigar and put the remaining matches in his pocket with the matches Voss had given him.

"It's about Evelyn," Proctor said. "She's not here?"

Dawson's voice was a waspish snarl. "Don't ask me about that tramp. Ask any of the young loafers around town, but don't ask me. I been tryin' to be on the level with her, but every time I turn my back she's off with some other guy."

"Who, for instance?"

Braithe had got out of the sedan and strolled over to the group, leaving Dale behind. Dawson said, "Ask him, why don't you? He's the demon reporter. He keeps tabs on all the society doings in this town. Me, I work too hard to notice things."

"This is serious," Proctor declared. "We want to know who she's been chasing around with besides you. If you don't want to tell us here and now I'll have to take you in."

The painter's manner changed. "Something happened to her?"

The chief nodded. "Something serious. You've got to do a lot of explaining."

"You got her in jail?"

"We're taking care of her," Proctor replied evasively.

Dawson turned pale. "Listen—" he said, his voice hoarse, "whatever she says, I didn't have nothin' to do with it. I didn't ever want her makin' trouble. But she—she's always thinkin' who she can get money from. She's caused trouble before and she'll cause trouble again. I made up my mind I was through with her when I seen her with a strange guy this afternoon."

"You're through with her, all right," Braithe said softly.

Dawson sensed a hidden significance behind the words. He cried, "She ain't dead?"

"Who was she trying to get money from?" the chief asked.

"First you tell me," Dawson insisted. "She's dead, ain't she?"

Braithe said, "Yes, she's dead."

Dawson stared at him. He stared at all their faces.

He read the truth in the annoyed expression in Proctor's face. He took a deep breath.

"So she's dead," he said simply. "Okay, I'll tell you all I know. I seen her this afternoon walking up the hill and then I seen a guy going up after her. He's been around town about a week. I seen him before and I'd know him if I seen him again. Maybe he's the one who killed her."

"How did you know she was killed?" Proctor demanded.

"Why . . . why, I was just guessin'. All you cops here . . . And then it's hard to think of her dyin' natural."

There was truth in that last statement, Voss reflected. If any person ever created the forces of his or her own annihilation, Evelyn Lister must have done just that. She might almost have been born to be murdered.

"Was she trying to get money from that fellow?" asked Proctor.

"Money?" Dawson frowned. "Oh, hell—I don't know. I thought maybe you'd pinched her on Doc Manning's account. He always claimed he didn't have nothin' to do with that baby of hers and some day he'd find a way to prove it. I thought he'd finally got around to doin' somethin' about it."

"Something like claiming she'd been living with you?"

Dawson fidgeted. "I thought he might be claimin' that. She wasn't. We always had separate rooms. I never was that way about her. I'd married her if she'd been on the level, but she wasn't."

"You don't know what happened while she and that fellow were on the hill?"

"How could I know? I was paintin' at the foot of the hill. I seen 'em walkin' up, but I couldn't see where they went. The trees was too thick."

Proctor looked at Ben Thoad, who was feeding boiled liver to the delighted Gardenia a tiny scrap at a time. He asked, "Bring your handcuffs, Ben?"

Thoad looked up. "Sure I brought 'em. Brought a gun, too. We going to take Dawson to the cage?"

"We are if he doesn't stop lying." Proctor faced Dawson squarely. "You were up by the spring where Evelyn was killed. You saw Evelyn and that fellow sitting there. You went through the woods where nobody could see you. The dog trailed you all the way from the body and we found your tracks besides."

Dawson wet his lips with his tongue and dried them with the back of a hand. He looked at the sidewalk, at the trees that lined the street, everywhere but into the chief's eyes. Reading his bafflement, Voss waited alertly for the painter's next words.

Dawson mumbled, "I went right up and right back. I seen him foller her up and I didn't like it much, but I kept on workin'. I seen Manning and the Carrington lady go up and come back and then I seen Miss Lyons and this big guy." He pointed to Voss. "By that time I'd done a lot of thinkin' and I wanted to see what was goin' on. So I sneaked up and looked where the guy and her was sittin'. That's all they was doin'—just sittin'. I kind of eased up when I seen it wasn't any worse and wasn't likely to be, but I was still a little sore."

"What were they talking about?"

"I didn't get close enough to hear. I was about twenty feet away. I'd been there about two minutes when Athens Jackson came along and seen me. He'd been out to that

farm behind the golf club gettin' milk for Miss Carrington,
and he always cuts across the side of the hill. He's scared
to go through a cemetery, like most black folks. And I
walked back down with Athens Jackson and put away my
stuff and changed my clothes and came home. And if you
don't believe it you can ask him."

Proctor looked at Voss. If Dawson's story were true
there was no longer any mystery about the second set of
tracks descending the hill. If Athens Jackson, the Negro,
substantiated the story it would give Dawson a fairly good
alibi.

Proctor blew out cigar smoke meditatively. He said,
"Dawson, I'm going to leave you here till I talk to that fellow who was with her. If you decide to tell the whole truth
when I come back maybe I won't take you to jail at all. Just
remember we'll find out everything anyway and the more
you hold back the worse it will be for you."

"I've told you everythin'," Dawson declared. He stood
up. He asked rather humbly, "Could I see the—her?"

"Later," said Proctor. "I'll stop by for you."

Thoad put the empty jar back in his pocket and Gardenia licked her chops regretfully as she watched it disappear. She shied impatiently from Braithe when he tried
to pet her. Thoad waved his hand and limped toward his
home around the corner with the bitch padding at his
heels. Braithe drove away with Dale toward his Main Street
office presumably to telephone the *Daily Record*.

Voss and Proctor walked back to the foot of the path,
got into Proctor's shabby touring car and drove around
the block toward the house in Taylor Street where George
Thael was staying.

"Maybe I should have pinched Dawson," Proctor said,
"but I hate to go off half-cocked."

"I've noticed that the best detectives go slow in making
arrests," Voss told him.

"Then I ought to be a good one. I never lock up any-body unless I have to. In the first place a fellow can make a lot of trouble in a small town like this if he gets locked up by mistake. In the second place I always feel sorry for somebody who wants to get out and can't. There's excep-tions, of course."

"What kind of exceptions?"

"A man who beats his wife or kids can rot in jail with-out spoiling my sleep. A drunk ought to stay put till he's all sobered up. And whoever killed that little Lister girl—well, I wouldn't trust myself once I got my hands on him. What difference does it make if she didn't go to Sunday school?"

"No difference," said Voss.

As the car drew to the curb a man in uniform detached himself from the shadow of a tree and came up to them. He was young and thin and sallow and walked with his hands in his pockets and his shoulders slumped.

"Chief," he said, "I been worrying about this bird Thael. That front window is his. The light went out half an hour ago and I ain't seen him since. Not likely he'd go to bed this early."

Proctor swore. "If you let him get away, Backus . . ." He left the sentence unfinished and got out of the car. Voss went up on the porch with him.

A plump, middle-aged woman answered the thud of the knocker. She beamed at them. "Why, Cornelius," she gushed, "I thought this would be your busy night. But come right in. . . ."

"I'm terribly busy, Amanda," he interrupted, flush-ing with embarrassment. "Busy as all get out. This is Mr. Voss—Mrs. Holmes. We'd like to see your boarder, Mr. Thael."

"Mercy sakes! He was here till fifteen minutes ago writ-ing. Then Betty Wilkins phoned to tell me about the awful thing that happened to the Lister girl and I went upstairs to tell Mr. Thael, thinking he'd be interested because he writes stories about murders. I guess I shouldn't have bothered him while he was working. He didn't say much, but he looked mad and pretty soon he went out the back way. . . ."

"Golly," Proctor muttered. "Listen, Amanda—if he comes in don't say anything to him, but phone me at the station right away. If I'm out leave a message with whoever's there. I've got to see him about something important."

"You said *if* he comes in. Cornelius, he isn't—?"

He said clumsily, "Certainly he isn't. Now don't worry about anything."

He turned and went down the steps hastily. Voss said good night to Amanda Holmes and followed.

Proctor vented his wrath on the luckless Backus. "Of all the dumb excuses for a cop!" he raved. "Letting a murderer walk away right under your nose. Why, if your old man wasn't on the town council I'd have your badge and buttons so fast . . ."

4

George Thael came back Saturday morning. He awoke Abelard Voss by a stealthy knocking at the door of Voss's room in the Bay View Inn. The sun poured dazzling rays through the windows and Voss was briefly blinded by them as he rolled out of bed, an awe-inspiring figure in his striped pajamas, and opened the door a crack. He did not recognize Thael standing with his shoulders hunched in the darkness of the hall. He said sleepily, "What do you want?"

"You," Thael said. "Let me in, for God's sake, before someone sees me." He put a hand against the door and pushed and Voss moved back, wide awake all of a sudden.

"What a week end!" Voss said softly. "I spend half the night hunting for you and when I finally get a chance to sleep you come around and spoil it. The chief of police thinks you stole a boat and put out to sea, possibly with the idea of drowning yourself."

He sat on the edge of the bed and felt with his feet for slippers, remembering the long tramping of the night before. Proctor had routed out Ben Thoad again and Gardenia had been acquainted with the scent of some clothes from Thael's room. The bitch had followed an invisible trail to the end of the yacht club wharf and there the scent had given out. They had tried the shore of the bay for two

miles in either direction without interesting Gardenia and
Proctor had been made to back down from his boast that
she could trail a man across the Sound.

Thael dropped into a chair and ran nervous fingers
through his oily hair. He was younger than Voss and heavier,
though of medium height. His bright greenish eyes were
sunken in dark circles and his face was pasty. His clothes
were wrinkled and the open collar of his sky-blue shirt was
soiled.

"Give me a cigarette," he said. "I ran out during the
night. I can't talk without a smoke to steady me."

"I'll get you some." Voss went to the telephone and
ordered cigarettes, orange juice and coffee. Leaving Thael
in the chair he went into the bathroom and ran the shower.
He was bathed and partly dressed when there came a tap
at the door and Thael scuttled into the bathroom to hide.
It was the bellboy with a tray.

Thael lit a cigarette, when the bellboy had departed,
and inhaled smoke hungrily. He said, "So they think I
killed the girl."

Voss stooped in front of the mirror, knotting his tie.
"Why shouldn't they? You were with her. You ran away before they could get to you."

"Do you think I did it?"

"Maybe. I wouldn't bet on it. There are a lot of things
in your favor."

"I'm glad someone thinks so. What are some of them?"

"You're a stranger here. You hadn't known her long
enough for tension to develop in an ordinary way. You
knew you had been seen with her, therefore you wouldn't
be likely to kill her when and where you did unless some
sudden need or insane urge arose. You ran away, but now
you've come back again. Of course, a man would have to
know a lot of things I don't know before forming a definite opinion. Why you were interested in her in the first
place . . ."

"Why is an unattached man in a strange town usually interested in the woman with the spiciest reputation?" Thael countered bitterly. "At that I wasn't interested enough to care a snap of my fingers whether I met her or not. I don't go in for tarts as a rule. But I heard some of the young bloods snickering about her when she walked past the Elite Café and I thought she was pretty."

"How did you meet her?"

"In the traditional way. I was out walking and she dropped her handkerchief."

"A handkerchief with an initial?"

"I didn't notice. I handed it back to her and she asked me if I wasn't new to Waldham and we got talking. She walked on after a minute or two and took that path up the hill—I thought it over and decided to follow her—I'll let you guess why—but when I caught up with her she didn't seem glad to see me."

"She might have had another date there."

"That's exactly what I thought. When I saw she wasn't in the mood for me I only stayed a few minutes. We were talking about a man who was killed on the hill six or eight years ago."

"Did she know much about it?"

"She remembered it pretty clearly. She was only a kid when it happened. She said she knew a lot about it and so did some other people, but it was being kept quiet."

"She didn't mention any names?"

"No. I fished around, but she shut up like a clam. I decided she didn't really know anything. She might have had a suspicion of some sort."

"What else did you talk about?"

"Well, one of the local medicos—Manning, his name is—and a swell-looking woman came up the hill to where we were sitting. They turned back the minute they saw us. Evelyn got pretty excited. She said Manning was a louse and had made all kinds of trouble for her and one of these days she was going to get even with him in a big way, I'd heard the story about him—you'd be surprised how much gossip I've picked up in six days at Amanda Holmes's house—about Evelyn's baby and how the medico was the goat, although everybody knew a doctor would have been careful and it could have been sixteen other guys. We were still talking about him when you came past. Evelyn didn't seem to care much about that Lyons woman with you, either."

Voss's eyes narrowed. "What did she say about Sue Lyons?"

"Only that she was stuck-up and snobbish and thought she was better than everybody else. Said she was really as bad as anyone and carried on a secret affair of her own with Manning, but pretended to be holy and pure."

"And after I passed you?"

"I beat it," Thael said, grinding out his cigarette in the tray. "I could see I was out of place and I'd begun to think about my reputation. You and the Lyons woman made four who had seen us sitting together and that's enough to start talk in a burg like Waldham. I meant to spend the whole summer here and I really wasn't awfully keen about making her. I didn't want to be talked about for something I hadn't done. I told her I'd see her again and left her sitting there."

"You didn't see anyone else?"

"I was going to tell you. I heard someone moving in the woods down toward the bay. I got a quick look at a man in white with his right hand up to protect his face from the branches. I thought maybe he was the one she was waiting for—some married man sneaking out to forget his wife. I didn't see him clearly and I doubt if I could recognize him again."

That man in white could not have been Dawson if Dawson had told the truth, Voss thought. Dawson had climbed the hill and descended while Thael was still with Evelyn.

He said, "Why did you run out? When you heard about the murder why didn't you tell the police about seeing that man?"

Thael lighted another cigarette. "I came to this town for peace and quiet," he said. "I was a nervous wreck in New York. I was batting out too many words of tripe at a penny apiece, drinking too much bad liquor, messing around with too many Greenwich Village girls. Waldham was close enough to the city and room and board are cheap.

"But I'd a thousand times rather have New York cops grab me for burning an orphan asylum when I was guilty and they knew it than fall into the hands of small-town gendarmes with bees in their bonnets. I've traveled around, Abelard, and I know a stranger under suspicion in a small community has three strikes called on him before the first pitch. I know of cases where innocent men have been lynched, railroaded to prison, beaten to death, driven crazy.

"When Amanda Holmes told me that girl had been murdered I knew the law would be around for me any minute. I've got a black mark against me in New York—a disorderly conduct rap that doesn't mean a thing, but would be enough to make these hicks think I'm a jailbird—and I wasn't going to let myself in for any third-degree stuff without a lawyer or a friend to talk up for me. I got out of the house so I'd have time to think. The chief had told me about the bloodhound so I headed for the bay. There was a dinghy with oars tied at the yacht club dock. I rowed out and made fast to the far side of an express cruiser and stayed there all night. I didn't intend to run away. I thought I could phone some lawyer in New York this morning."

"Did you?"

"No. I recognized you when I saw you yesterday. We're not pals, but we've met and we're more or less in the writing business together. I thought maybe if I could sneak past the room clerk downstairs I could make a deal with you. If I give myself up, will you see that I get a lawyer—a good one?"

Voss said, "You can count on me to do all I can. I know a good lawyer who will come on the run if I call him. But we'll wait and see. Maybe you won't need a lawyer."

"No such luck," Thael predicted gloomily. "I've got a hunch I'm going to be in this thing pretty deep. How about walking to the police station with me?"

They went together out of the inn, along the dirt road that circled the base of the hill, past the path and the gateway to the cemetery, to Main Street. Two blocks away, beyond the bronze Victory Monument on its circular pedestal, the center of a shaded green square was occupied by the gracious two-story frame building that was town hall, courthouse, police headquarters and jail.

Everyone they passed appeared to know that Thael was suspect. Men and women moved to the edge of the sidewalk to give them a wide berth; unfriendly stares followed them; faces pressed close to windows. When they went into the City Drugstore, where Thael filled his pockets with cigarettes and bought magazines in anticipation of a prolonged stay behind bars, the girl who waited on him trembled visibly.

Voss was sweating long before the ordeal was ended. He was used enough to being stared at, but not in this way. Fear and savagery were reflected in the eyes that turned upon them now, and while Thael was their chief target, there was still an overflow that made Voss as uncomfortable as he had ever been.

"My God," Thael said as they crossed the square, "it's like running a gantlet. These people are sold on the idea that I'm a kill-crazy nut. Maybe it's a good thing I'm going to be locked up."

Cornelius Proctor was poring over headlines in a copy of the *Daily Record* when they entered his dingy office. Marking his place with a thick forefinger he glanced up and saw Voss. He grinned wryly.

"'Murder Strikes Twice; Horror Writer Sought—'" he quoted. Then he saw Thael and stood up so suddenly he nearly upset his chair. "So you got him!" he gloated.

"No," said Voss. "Thael got me. He says he doesn't know anything about it, but he wanted time to arrange for a lawyer. He's written too many stories about the third-degree to need first-hand information."

Proctor looked sorrowful. "Third-degree?" he repeated. "We don't have anything like that here. We treat our customers like gentlemen." His big hands twitched, curling loosely into fists.

"I believe in handling things quietly, myself," Voss told the chief, watching those fists. "So does my friend Bergman, the big criminal lawyer. He'll represent Thael if Thael needs representation."

Proctor's sad eyes turned upon Voss. He flattened his hands on top of the desk. "If he's innocent he won't need a lawyer. If he killed the girl no lawyer can help him." His eyes narrowed. "I'm going to have to lock you up, Thael. Maybe I wouldn't have if you hadn't run out on us last night. Now I haven't got any choice. You'll be treated all right. Anything you want except guns and saws you can send out for. If you know anything you'd better make up your mind to come clean. I'll let you think it over for a couple hours, then I'll talk to you." He yelled, "Backus!"

The sallow young policeman Voss had seen the night before slouched into the room. His face, which had been apprehensive, sagged with surprise when he saw Thael.

"This is the guy you couldn't keep an eye on," Proctor said. "See if that talking-to I gave you did any good. Don't book him, but show him to one of our guest rooms—and don't forget to lock the door."

Thael glanced at Voss, his expression one of anxious pleading. "You'll take care of things, Abelard?"

"I'll take care of everything," Voss assured him.

When the door had closed behind Thael and Backus, Proctor asked, "Friend of yours, Voss?"

"No. I met him once in New York. I don't know much about him."

"I'm glad. Don't like his looks. Eyes too bright and shifty."

"Too much thyroid," Voss said.

The chief was interested. "That's the stuff that makes murderers write notes, isn't it?"

"That's thymus. The thyroid is a different gland. Hyperthyroids have bright eyes. They're apt to be crazy about sex, and when they kill they're brutal killers."

"Maybe you ought to send me that book after all. If it tells how to spot criminals like that . . ."

Voss grinned. "It isn't as easy as it sounds. The pituitary gland made me grow, but I'd probably fall more or less into the thymocentric class, and I'm neither genius nor murderer. You've got all the thyroid you need and an adequate pituitary, judging by the look of you. Everybody has glands and I don't suppose anybody has all of them in perfect balance. Thael kills hundreds of people with his typewriter, but I can't picture him actually murdering anything besides the English language."

"What about Dawson's glands?"

"Dawson is powerful, hairy, sullen. The adrenal gland has left its stamp all over his makeup. He could kill in a fit of temper. He'd be the sort to pick up a rock to do it with and he'd hit hard and several times."

"Well," Proctor said, "if he did it he's the coolest killer I ever met up with. Took him to Tom Wilkins's to view the body early this morning. Tom hadn't touched it, pending the autopsy. Blood was still there, black and clotted, and her eyes and mouth were wide open. I damn' near got sick. Dawson looked at her a long time and seemed as pleased as though someone had given him a quart of liquor. . . . But I'd talked with Cynthia's handy man, Athens Jackson, and he swore to Dawson's alibi word for word. So I let Dawson go home."

"How about fingerprints?"

"None." Proctor snorted with disgust. "Not even the girl's on the note. Went all through her room this morning without finding anything."

"How about handkerchiefs? Do you remember what kind she had?"

"She had some. Just plain women's handkerchiefs."

"Initialed?"

"I don't know. I suppose. Everybody has handkerchiefs with initials. What's on your mind, Voss?"

"Nothing. I was only wondering."

Proctor looked at him quizzically. "You wouldn't be holding back anything?"

"Nothing you could put your finger on. I'll admit I'm trying to build up some ideas. I feel really concerned about what's happened. It was dumped in my lap so neatly it might almost have been done for my special benefit."

"I wonder . . ." Proctor began meditatively. Then he shrugged. "Well, the only one I haven't talked to yet is Sue Lyons. I was about ready to call on her when you showed up. Want to come along?"

Voss said he did. Sue Lyons was the most fascinating and enigmatic figure he had encountered in Waldham thus far. He walked out of the town hall with Proctor, across the square and along Whitcomb Street toward the bay.

"They named this street for Terry Whitcomb's family?" he asked.

"For Terry's grandpa, Cap'n Henry Whitcomb. A whaler and a hell-raiser. Died eight years ago at ninety-seven, heartbroken because Terry couldn't hold his liquor. Squeezed the Whitcomb fortune out of whale oil and real estate—made the sea and the land pay him plenty." He pointed up ahead where the street ended against a huge white house topped by a square tower, close to the water's edge. "Built that place seventy-five years ago. Room in the center goes up three stories clear to the glass roof of that tower. Mainmast of his first ship is there, set in the floor, with yardarms and ropes and blocks all attached. The old boy used to get drunk and climb up the Jacob's ladder and think he was at sea. Took a fall off the ladder to finish him. He busted both legs and when they made him stay in bed he sort of pined away."

"Leaving his cellar to Terry."

"Terry's a baby. Gets the horrors on no more liquor than Cap'n Henry used to take to rinse out his pipes before breakfast. He can sail a boat, though; even when he tried to get himself drowned in that storm the day after Brewster Lyons was shot, he couldn't. He still sails a lot after dark. Sometimes I wonder if a guilty conscience didn't send him out that first time and every time since."

At Bay Street, a block from the Whitcomb house, they turned left. Proctor waved toward a broad, gracious mansion set back in a deep lawn among trees and shrubbery.

"Cynthia's place. She was engaged to Brewster and Terry was engaged to Sue, but Terry really wanted Cynthia. He took Cynthia out sailing with him the day before Brewster was killed, and Cynthia and Brewster quarreled over that, folks say. Maybe Terry killed Brewster, or maybe Terry just went to pieces afterward because he figured Brewster had killed himself on account of that boat ride. Anyway, Cynthia and Terry never spoke afterward. I don't know which had it in for the other."

"Does Terry get around much?"

"Haven't seen him in five-six months. He's just past forty, but his hair is pure white. He stays home and Jenny Midge buys the groceries. Funny thing—he and Jenny are supposed to hate each other like poison. Doc Manning's about the only one ever gets into the house. Every so often he gets called in to sober Terry up. Swears he's going to have him committed."

Sue Lyons's house was next to Cynthia Carrington's, but separated from it by a hundred yards of wooded lawn and nearer to the low stone building of the yacht club. It was a smaller and less pretentious house than Cynthia's, but picturesque and neat. Sue came to the door. She wore a scarlet blouse over a linen skirt and her cheeks seemed waxen in contrast. Her eyes were dull and haggard from lack of sleep.

"I've been hoping you'd call," she said, leading them into a living room that ran from the front of the house to the rear. "I wanted to see you both. You, Cornelius, to find out where I stand on your list of suspects. You, Mr. Voss, to ask if you'd be interested in going to the yacht club dance tonight. They always send me tickets."

"I'd be delighted," Voss said. "Nobody will dance with me, but I can sit on the veranda and listen to the music."

"I'll dance with you," she told him. "I'm pretty bad, but maybe you can manage me."

"Sue dances like a swan," Proctor declared, evidently meaning it as a compliment. "And, Sue, you aren't on my list of suspects at all. Far as I can learn you weren't out of Voss's sight all the time you were on the hill. That lets you out unless I start being suspicious of him, too."

She gave Voss a long penetrating glance. He knew she was remembering those four or five minutes when she had not been in his sight—was wondering whether he had really not mentioned them, and why.

"Sit down," she urged. "I suppose Mr. Voss has told you about our walk. I don't know what I could say that he hasn't."

"Just the same I'd like to hear it in your own words, Sue. It doesn't mean much, but it's routine. I've got to be able to say I've talked to everybody who saw her."

"It won't take many words. Mr. Voss and I had been to Brewster's grave and we went up the hill to the place where father found him. Evelyn Lister and the young man Thael were sitting there. We went on past without stopping, to the top of the hill, and admired the view for perhaps five minutes. When we came down they'd gone. I didn't notice anything, but Mr. Voss saw blood on the stone seat."

Not a word about the handkerchief with the "L" woven into the corner. Not a word about the motorboat.

"See anybody?" Proctor inquired.

"Jenny Midge was in the cemetery and went toward her house. Cynthia and Dr. Manning came down the path just before we went up. That odd-job man at the inn, Art Dawson, was painting a shed at the foot of the Hill."

"No one else?"

Again that penetrating look at Voss. He could read her mind. She was thinking of the outboard motorboat they had heard and of her own hasty trip back along the path to the point where she could see it.

And Voss realized for the first time that the noisy little craft could have carried the killer. Its sound had ceased while they were passing the little nook. If it had touched shore at that time an active passenger could have climbed the hill, killed the girl and returned in just about as many minutes as had elapsed between the stopping and restarting of the motor. He might have been the man in white Thael claimed to have seen climbing the hill, shielding his face with his right arm. He would not have known of Thael's presence, or counted on anyone being in the vicinity.

Sue took a long breath and replied to Proctor, "No one else."

It was positively uncanny that the high-pitched whine of an outboard motor should cut across the stillness at that moment. Voss glanced out of the rear windows of the living room and saw the boat coming from the direction of the Sea Crest Golf Club around the curve the hill made in the shore line of the bay. A man was crouched in the stern.

Voss left his chair and strolled to the windows, trying to seem disinterested. A second later Sue was at his side, her pale lips parted.

The boat drew nearer, crossing the bay. Voss thought it was headed for Terry Whitcomb's house, behind which a large sailboat was moored to a buoy a few yards out. Then it swerved and came directly toward the rear of Cynthia Carrington's garden.

Even before he could make out the features of the man at the tiller Voss divined his identity. Sue knew, too, and her figure stiffened and her face went white as death.

The nose of the boat lifted on the soft sand of the beach. Garth Manning, wearing gray trousers and a white shirt, hoisted the light motor from its supports with one hand, took the end of a long painter in the other and walked rapidly up the beach toward Cynthia's house.

5

A battered Buick roadster entered the parking lot beside the yacht club and nosed up to the fence. Abelard Voss noticed familiar fender dents. He said, "Here's the doctor."

"Doctor?" Sue echoed. "That's no doctor. That's Ralph Decker, the golf pro. Dr. Manning drives a Chrysler sedan."

A sturdy man of about thirty-five with brown hair and pleasant eyes got out of the Buick and smiled at Sue. She beckoned him over. She said, "This is Mr. Voss, Ralph. He thought you were a doctor. Now I remember how you tried to improve my golf and couldn't, I wonder if he wasn't right."

"Nonsense, Sue," Decker returned. "I'm proud of you. Women are rotten golfers ninety-nine times out of a hundred and you're the exception." He took Voss's hand in a friendly grip. "I've heard of you. Dr. Manning was telling me about your books yesterday. You've got something real to work on now."

"Not me," Voss protested. "I'm an innocent bystander at this stage of the game. I guess I saw Manning in your car last night and thought it was his."

"You might have. I loaned it to him. He came to the golf club by boat and got a phone call there about the murder. He had to get back in a hurry."

"I see." Manning had been in that motorboat when it stopped below the hill, all right, Voss reflected. The sound of the motor had been heard approximately half an hour after Manning and Cynthia had descended the hill, and meanwhile the physician would have had more than sufficient time to walk to Cynthia's and get the boat. This morning he had returned Decker's roadster and brought the boat back to Cynthia's.

Voss remembered Sue's breathlessness on the hilltop and her pallor when they had sighted the boat from her house. He stole a sidelong glance at her and saw pallor in her cheeks now, where a moment ago had been a flush of excitement.

Through the open windows of the clubhouse floated the muted throb of an orchestra. Cars were coming into the parking lot every minute. The wide veranda of the club was crowded.

The sun had set long before and the dusk was purple. The bay stretched out before them quiet and unruffled, its deepening shades overlapping like layers of mist until water and sky were lost together in a star-powdered haze. The inn on the slope of the hill was ablaze with lamps, but the opposite shore was dark.

Manning and Cynthia Carrington had already arrived and were on the veranda. Sue went up to them. She introduced Voss and immediately he was enchanted by Cynthia's cool, remote beauty.

Her eyes held him longest. They were deep-set, large and luminous and their color was the gray of the sea under a leaden sky, its placid surface shadowed with the memory of storms past and the knowledge of storms to come, its depths fathomless. They were still eyes, but extraordinarily alive.

Her face, framed in close-coiffed dark hair, was almost transparent in its whiteness. Her mouth was firm and straight. A soft blue gown clung gracefully to her slim figure.

Beside her Sue Lyons seemed gaunt and tired and old in her pearl-gray dress, although there could not have been more than two years' difference in their ages. Sue's voice was enthusiastic, however, exclaiming, "How sweet you look tonight, darling!"

Darling. Cynthia Carrington had come between Sue and her fiancé seven years ago. Cynthia had been mysteriously connected with the death of the brother Sue loved. Cynthia was in undisputed possession of Garth Manning—and in Voss's mind there was not the faintest doubt that Sue was desperately and hopelessly in love with Manning.

"I wish," Cynthia replied in a low husky voice, "I thought you meant it, Sue. I don't feel a bit sweet."

Manning's handclasp and tone were warm. "I've read your stuff, Mr. Voss. I like the way you analyze your criminals, being a student of psychology myself. Sorry we didn't have a chance to talk last night."

"It wasn't a time or place for talking," Voss said. "It was a nasty mess. Crimes of violence are always sordid."

Manning nodded in agreement. "For all our show civilization hasn't gone far beyond the Neanderthal man except in non-essentials. You look over those people on the dance floor, all of them your neighbors and more or less respectable according to common standards, and reflect that one of them may have just smashed a girl's skull. . . ."

Decker asked, "But haven't they got Thael dead to rights?"

"He had the opportunity," Manning said, "but where's his motive? He's only been here a week. Why would he leave a note referring back to something that happened long before he came? I'd be more inclined to suspect that hot-headed Dawson."

"Please let's talk about something else," Sue cried. "The orchestra isn't bad tonight. Will you risk a dance with me, Mr. Voss?"

"The risk is all yours," he assured her gravely.

They went into the main hall of the club building. It was a long, low-ceilinged room wherein white-coated musicians perspired amid potted palms on a platform at one end. Most of the presumably respectable people of Waldham seemed to be assembled there, on the floor dancing or watching from seats near the windows and on the veranda, and Voss recalled Manning's words. Guiding Sue through the slow steps of a waltz, he studied the faces of those they passed. One of them could be a murderer—or a murderess—he was thinking, and one the man—or the woman—who had written that unsigned letter with its hint of impending violence so promptly realized. And it was not altogether unreasonable to suppose that the same person might have written the letter and committed the murder—though it was far from clear why one who was planning the supreme crime should call in a practicing criminologist at the critical moment.

Eddie Braithe and Dale Parsons were dancing trickily to the conventional measure of the music, twisting and trotting and stomping. They were looking into one another's eyes and laughing and again Voss was struck by their resemblance.

Sue noticed them. She said, "Aren't they a pretty couple?"

"Pretty" was the word for them, he agreed.

When the dance ended Eddie came over. He asked Voss, "What did you think of the *Record* story? Was it gruesome enough?"

"Revolting," Voss said. "It might have been written by a veteran tabloid artist."

"It was. I phoned them so late, all I could do was give the dope to a rewrite man and let him use his imagination to fill in. But I put my own story on the wire today. Wait till you see it."

"Shocking?"

"Worse than that," Eddie boasted. "Stunning. I hope they put my name on it. It starts, 'George Thael, hack for the horror magazines, has at last produced a masterpiece. . . .' Then I have to qualify it, of course, to keep clear of libel. You know—'*if* what the police believe is true.' '*If* it develops he really did the job.'"

"*If* he didn't do it," Dale said brightly, "I hope he sues you for all the *Courier's* worth."

"He'd be better off at his penny-a-word writing," Eddie said. "The *Courier* is going to suspend publication one of these days if the advertisers don't start paying their bills, and I'm going to New York to hunt a job. But Thael did it, all right. Who else would?"

The music started again. Braithe promptly put his arm around Sue's waist and glided off with her, leaving Voss with Dale. He looked down at her ruefully.

"I'm afraid I can't do all those stunts Eddie was doing."

"Thank heaven," she sighed, moving into his arms. "Every time we go to a dance he wears me to a shadow. I only stand for it because it saves me the trouble of dieting to keep my figure."

He grinned at her. "I suppose you weigh all of ninety pounds?"

"Ninety-seven," she told him seriously. "But last winter in New York I got up to a hundred and eleven. I was positively vulgar. I don't know what I'd do if my mother and father didn't have this summer place here and if I didn't have Eddie to dance me around."

"Is that your only exercise?"

"Goodness no! Every afternoon I bundle up in sweaters and go around the golf course in the sun, if the sun happens to be shining. Didn't you notice I was ready to faint when I came up the hill with Eddie? He'd just driven me back."

He remembered that she had shown signs of faintness when she saw Evelyn Lister's body in the flashlight beam, but he hadn't attributed it to too much sun or exercise.

He inquired, "Did you see Manning at the links?"

"He came up from the dock just as we were leaving. He went to the clubhouse."

A bronzed hand on Voss's arm halted him. He looked into the smiling face of Irv Proctor.

"You may know a lot about crime, Voss," Irv said, "but you don't dance worth a nickel. I took pity on Dale and decided to cut in."

Dale moaned, "Oh, dear, another acrobat." She relaxed against the young policeman's chest and they whirled away.

Voss wandered out on the veranda. One end of it was screened by palms and appeared deserted. He strolled that way. The palms blocked the lights so that he did not see the woman standing at the railing, looking out over the water, until he was within six feet of her. It was too dark for him to recognize her, but the night could not conceal the lonely, forlorn quality that clung like living mist about her.

He turned back, but she called him and the voice was Cynthia's.

"Not dancing?" he asked.

"It's too warm." Her face was a pale blur in the gloom. "Mr. Voss, is it true that you came here to write about Brewster Lyons's death?"

He was vaguely disturbed, not so much by her question as by that intangible quality hovering in the air around her. He was at a loss to understand it; one moment he thought of it as a ghostly fragrance, somehow suggestive of delicate evil, and the next he fancied oddly that she wore an aura woven of the emanations of some deep spiritual unrest.

"Not necessarily," he replied. "I came partly for a quiet week end and partly to talk to the people who remember that case."

"If you do write about it," she said, "I'd like to see what you've written before it's published. I might be able to help you."

"I should think it would bring back a lot of unpleasantness."

"Bring it back! Mr. Voss, I have lived with horror and fear for seven years. When I go out in the street Jenny Midge shrieks accusations at me. Half the people I meet have that doubtful look in their eyes that speaks louder than shrieking. In the daytime I can force myself to think of other things, but at night I can't control my thoughts and I have hideous dreams. I've reached the point where I have to face reality or go insane."

"You won't go insane," he assured her. "The very fact that you recognize the danger is your guarantee."

"I made myself go back yesterday to the place where it happened. Just that act of walking up the hill helped me."

He knew suddenly what strange thing surrounded her. It had no name that he had heard, but he had encountered it in rooms where people were very sick. It was akin to the too-sweet smell of dying flowers, to the sigh of a person anesthetized. It betokened a mental or spiritual unhealthiness or maladjustment and was evil only in a passive sense insofar as it reflected evil.

He felt pity for her, tormented ceaselessly by circumstances over which she had no control; and he admired her, fighting valiantly to free herself, risking deeper hurts.

"After all," he said gently, "if you weren't responsible—"

Her hand fell on his sleeve, light as a leaf and as tremulous. She whispered, "That's it. I've never admitted it to anyone before, but . . . I have always believed *I* killed him!"

He looked at her in amazement while his mind groped back into the story Proctor had outlined. He protested, "You had no gun. The course of the bullet showed he couldn't have shot himself, but someone hidden in the bushes could have shot him, wiped the fingerprints from the gun and tossed it where it was found."

"That's the way the story came out. But there was something else—something I can't help feeling another person knows. Now, since the Lister girl was killed and that note was found with her, I have a new kind of fear. For myself. As though someone were working to ruin me, to make me take the blame—"

The palms rustled. Voss turned and saw Ralph Decker. The golfer's face was in shadow, but the line of his jaw was hard. He was watching them and he might have been listening.

"I've been hunting for you, Cynthia," Decker said. "I thought we could sneak a dance while the doc is absent. He won't poison me if he doesn't catch me at it."

Cynthia breathed, "Come tomorrow noon to my house, Mr. Voss. For dinner." She smiled wanly at Decker. "I'll share the danger with you," she said.

They went in, leaving Voss to scowl out over the bay, feeling himself completely caught up in the pattern of events and frankly fascinated by it. He wanted to help Cynthia. He wanted, for her sake, to expose Evelyn Lister's slayer and Brewster's, if that were possible at this late date.

Thael, Dawson, Manning, Sue—any of them could have murdered Evelyn, his reasoning told him. Then unwillingly he added the name of Cynthia, who might just conceivably have acted alone or in concert with Manning. Or an unknown could have done it, creeping through the screening woods.

Motives? The pulp writer would have been driven by swift passion or anger; Dawson by jealousy; Manning by the desire for revenge or the necessity of escaping further blackmail or scandal; Sue—or Cynthia—by the urge to protect Manning. Or any one of them, including the unknown and excepting Thael, might have been Brewster Lyons's murderer, and might have found it necessary at this late date to silence Evelyn for reasons of self-preservation.

The name of Thael was more persistent than the others in Voss's mind. Voss had phoned the New York police that afternoon and had talked to his friend Lieutenant Bob Saint-Amour of the homicide squad about the writer. Saint-Amour had checked with the record bureau. That disorderly conduct charge of which Thael had spoken had been an assault charge originally, brought by a girl. She had been Thael's friend and he had been taking her home from a Greenwich Village party. They had quarreled in her apartment, presumably over matters that had to do with her virtue, and Thael had broken her jaw in a fit of brutal temper. Later she had refused to testify against him. . . .

Sue Lyons came out of the ballroom, looking neither to right nor left. She went down the veranda steps and walked the length of the dock, which marched into the bay on stilted pilings and ended at a broad float made to rise and fall with the tides. For a minute her tall figure was silhouetted dramatically against the starry sky. Then she sank down on a bench.

Voss strolled to join her. She looked over her shoulder when she heard his footsteps. "I wondered where you were," she said. "It's too nice a night to be indoors listening to that racket. While you were dancing with that pretty child I went for a nice long walk."

He sat beside her. He asked bluntly, "Could Cynthia have shot your brother?"

"Could Cynthia . . .?" She balked at the notion. "Why, Cynthia wouldn't. She's gentle, kind. . . ."

"Murder is unnatural to most of us," he said. "Not deep down in the savage depths, perhaps, but there's an ingrained aversion to it in our civilized veneer. But fill the mildest person with an emotion strong enough to crack that veneer—a sudden storm of anger, a powerful dose of fear or greed—and that man or woman is almost always capable of murder. A doped rabbit will fight a fox."

"I don't believe Cynthia could have done it," she answered flatly. "It wouldn't have been possible for her under any circumstances."

"Do you like her a lot?"

"Probably more than anyone else. We've been very close since we were children in school. Oh, I know what people say—they say I'm a hypocrite, that I really hate her because she's more beautiful than I, because she broke up my affair with Terry Whitcomb, because her affair with Brewster ended so tragically. That isn't true. People can't help what fate does to them, and Cynthia has been mistreated terribly by fate."

He thrust his hands into his pockets and leaned back. He wondered whether she was as free of resentment as she pretended to be and perhaps tried very hard to be.

"I don't think she did it either," he said. "I was only trying to find out why she's so frightened."

"She has been afraid for years. I don't know what passed between her and Brewster just before he was killed except that they had quarreled about Terry. Perhaps she blames herself for that—for making Brewster's last hours unhappy. Or perhaps she believes Terry killed Brewster on her account, and yet can't be sure of it. If you knew her better you'd understand how those things would bother her."

He said, "They'd bother anybody. . . ." Then he forgot the rest of what he had been going to say.

Sue's hand, fumbling at the waist of her dress, had brought forth a handkerchief. Her fingers twisted the cloth idly. A ray of light from the veranda fell upon the handkerchief, briefly touching the embroidered letter "L" in one of the corners of the linen.

The handkerchief, if it were not the one he had picked up close to the battered corpse of Evelyn Lister, was certainly exactly like it.

He murmured, "The art of picking pockets has its fine points."

He never knew whether she heard him. At that instant she leaned forward. "Look," she said, pointing.

He could just make out on the edge of the bay at his right the mass of Terry Whitcomb's house and the bright dot of a single electric bulb, or a lantern, hanging beneath the sloping roof of the back porch.

What Sue was pointing out, though, was a tall gray shape that flitted soundlessly over the black water. It was a moment before Voss realized that he was staring at a sailboat without lights headed out toward the sound, leaning away from the faint breeze that blew over the bay.

"It's creepy," he said. "I suppose it's Terry Whitcomb?"

She nodded. "Poor mad boy. Quite often, from my bedroom window, I see his boat going out into the dark and I always think ugly dreams are driving him. Last night I watched him and remembered the time he went out in the storm—the evening before Brewster was buried—and came back a different person. It's terrible and tragic. I'm always relieved when I see the boat moored to its buoy in the morning, and yet a little sorry, too."

He said nothing. He did not know what to say to penetrate the strange mood that had come over her.

"Do you know what the name of the boat is?" she asked.

"No."

"It's the *Cynthia.*" She stood up, all at once very casual, and put the handkerchief out of sight in the folds of her gown. "I've got a beastly headache. Would you mind taking me home?"

They went around the veranda instead of ascending the steps again and so avoided meeting any of the dancers. Through the open door Voss saw Dale still dancing with Irv Proctor, and when they rounded the corner of the clubhouse Cynthia and Decker were walking aimlessly in Taylor Street, half a block away, beneath a street lamp.

A dark figure was hurrying toward them from the other direction. Voss recognized Chief Proctor before they met him in front of Sue's house.

"Going to the dance?" Voss asked.

Proctor looked angry and baffled. He said, "Yes. I haven't danced in twenty years, but I'm going. I'm looking for Manning and Irv—and you. Like a damned fool I let that fellow Thael out of the jug this evening and now I've got to put him back again."

"Something has happened," Sue gasped.

"You bet something has happened. Another murder has happened. Somebody got into Jack Miller's house half an hour ago and killed Art Dawson."

6

Voss feared at first that Sue Lyons was going to faint. Her whole body stiffened, her lips parted and her eyes grew wide. She did not look at either of the men; her expressionless gaze went into the shadows that engulfed Cynthia's house. . . . Or was she, Voss wondered, looking beyond it toward the mysterious castle in which Terry Whitcomb lived with his familiar devils?

After a second he touched her arm. "Don't let it get you," he said.

Her mind seemed to return from a far journey. She whispered, "Dawson. Why should it have been Dawson?"

"Who'd you think it would be?" Proctor demanded.

"Who . . . Why I never dreamed it would be anyone at all. But what could Dawson have done to deserve . . . that?"

"I can make a guess," Proctor said. "Dawson saw the girl killed and tried to blackmail the one who did it. A man who does that is always asking for a dose of the same."

"Or perhaps Dawson killed her and committed suicide," Voss suggested. "He couldn't face the fear of being found out."

Proctor shook his head impatiently. "Not from what Jack Miller told me on the phone, it wasn't suicide. Voss,

I've got to get over there. I sent Backus on ahead and he's not very bright. Coming?"

"I'll follow right away." He watched the policeman stride on toward the clubhouse and turned back to Sue. His fingers tightened on her arm. He repeated, "Don't let it get you."

She shuddered. "It's so ghastly. Everything has been so . . . ghastly."

"Did you know Dawson well?"

"I've hardly spoken to him. It isn't him or the Lister girl I'm thinking of. It's the fact of two murders in two days in Waldham, where there hasn't been anything of the sort in years. Mr. Voss, why should that girl have been killed on the anniversary of my brother's death, in the same place? Why should I . . . we . . . have been the first to find her body? Why should Cynthia have been so near?" She hastened to explain, "I don't mean I question her presence on the hill; I'm only wondering why the full horror of it should be added to her suffering."

"If there was any reason behind those things," Voss said, "we may never know it. Maybe it was only coincidence."

"That's too easy. There are substantial reasons behind most of the things we call coincidences. It isn't by pure chance that some lives are fortunate and some are tragic from beginning to end. . . . Do you know, when I hear of some awful crime, like murder, I often find myself feeling sorrier for the criminal than the victim?"

"The criminal is very often the real victim."

"This time I'm sure of it. Something wicked has been hanging over some of us in Waldham for a long time and now it has grown strong enough to seize an instrument. Some miserable person who can no more help what is happening than we can. . . . Oh, I know it sounds crazy!"

"It doesn't. A lot of sane minds have thought as you're thinking. You have some idea of the nature of this wicked thing?"

"No—none whatever." She sounded very eager to convince him. "It's merely an intuitive feeling that has hung on. . . . And here I am keeping you when Cornelius is in a hurry."

The unlighted windows of Sue's house were gloomy and forbidding. Voss did not know whether poverty or choice kept her living there alone without so much as a maid. The house would be haunted by the ghost of Brewster Lyons, whom she had loved, and tonight there would be other specters even more fearsome. Perhaps she would watch from her bedroom window while Terry Whitcomb's sailboat returned from its pointless voyage.

"Wouldn't you like to go back to the club till the excitement is over?"

"No, I'm not afraid. Not for myself. I'm not curious either, for a wonder. I can wait till tomorrow for details."

She went up the flagstone walk to the screened veranda, not glancing back. The door closed behind her with a little clap of finality.

Proctor and Irv were leaving the yacht club when Voss joined them. He crowded his tall frame into the back seat of Irv's small sedan.

"Where's Manning?" he asked.

"Called away," said the chief. "Someone phoned close to an hour ago and he went out in a hurry. I left word for him to come along."

Irv grumbled, "He's got a genius for being out of reach when he's needed. Last night for instance."

Irv pressed the starter button and the engine roared. They swerved into Taylor Street. Almost immediately Irv braked the car and leaned over his father's knees, peering at someone on the sidewalk at his right.

"Anybody been along here, Decker?" he shouted.

Voss caught sight of the golf pro and Cynthia Carrington. They had moved far enough from the street lamp so that their forms and faces were indistinct.

"Nobody special," Decker answered. "What's happened now?"

"Dawson," Irv told him crisply. "Somebody finished him." He released the clutch and opened the throttle as he spoke and the car jerked ahead.

Voss twisted to look back through the rear window. For a surprised instant he was under the impression that Cynthia and Decker were struggling together violently in the darkness. He was at the point of telling Irv to stop again when he saw Decker lift her, an arm beneath her knees and one around her shoulders, and go with swift strides back toward the yacht club.

She had collapsed, he supposed. The news would naturally have been a tremendous shock to her. But Decker would see that she was cared for, that Manning or some other physician was called if it were necessary.

The sedan fled past Hill and Main to Walnut Street and swung right perilously. Five or six men and women stood on the porch of the Miller house. Backus was among them, leaning against a pillar, his hands stowed nonchalantly in his pockets. He was smoking a cigarette, but spat out the stub of it when Proctor appeared.

"I been standing right here, Chief," Backus said confidently. "Nobody went in or come out. Everything's just like it was."

Voss could hear a muffled sobbing through the screen door. A woman near him murmured, "Poor Lila Miller. What a dreadful thing to come home to!"

Backus made a convenient target for Proctor's irritability. The police chief fixed his subordinate with a glare that was compounded of sad contempt and withering pity.

"How d'you know everything's like it was? There's two other doors and about forty windows to this house."

"Golly!" Backus mumbled, his jaw dropping. "I couldn't very well surround it all alone. Do you think—?"

"I think you better get right over to Amanda Holmes's house," Proctor said. "You know what I mean?"

Backus nodded. "I know what you mean." He straightened his narrow shoulders and started away.

Others knew what Proctor had meant, also. Someone whispered, "That writer fellow," and someone else supplied Thael's name.

A stooped scrawny man of middle age opened the door for the newcomers. He looked at Voss with eyes that were like gray marbles rolled in mud.

"Go on up, Chief," he said hoarsely. "It's at the back of the house just off the head of the stairs. I'll stay down with the missus. I seen plenty already."

"Just don't go away, Jack," Proctor warned, starting up the stairway. "I'll want to talk to you."

The sobbing of the woman, but of sight in a darkened room at the right of the entrance hall, seemed to fill the house. Voss's nostrils twitched uneasily at depressing smells of stale beer, stale cookery, stale tobacco smoke and—unless his imagination played him tricks—fresh blood.

The white-hot light of an unshaded bulb beat out of the doorway of a rear room beyond the head of the stairs. Proctor went ahead and stopped abruptly just within the portal, robbed of all animation. Irv, coming next with his tripod and camera case, pushed him. Voss reached the doorway just in time to hear Irv's hushed exclamation.

There had been nothing imaginary about that sweetish, sickish blood odor. It swept over Voss in a smothering wave as he ducked his head beneath the arch of the door, entering the room. It came from a wide double bed that appeared at first glance to be a tossing sea of crimson gore.

"He didn't kill himself," Proctor declared in thick tones. "Not by a—" The rest of his profane sentence was lost as Irv noisily raised the two window sashes near the bed.

Art Dawson's body lay sprawled face upward on the drenched counterpane. One glassy eye stared unwinkingly at the bright bulb dangling from the ceiling; the other had burst and marked the beginning of a jagged wound that had ripped the left cheek wide open. The corpse wore the clothes in which Voss had seen the painter dressed the night before, but they were sodden and torn where a dull blade had been driven through them a dozen times at the chest, the belly and the thighs.

Beside the bed on the shabby rag carpet lay the weapon that had killed him. It was a brass paper knife with a blunt five-inch blade and a grip cast in the shape of an owl, a crude and commonplace utensil of the ten-cent-store variety. From point to hilt it was stained with the evidence of the use to which it had been put.

Still swearing incoherently, Proctor tiptoed nearer the corpse and plucked a folded piece of paper from the half-closed fingers of the right hand. He read something written thereon and shook his head like a man trying to emerge from a bad dream. He held it so that the others could read, too.

Knowing a squeamishness and a dull anger that were rare in him, Voss looked at the five printed words clipped from a newspaper, pasted like a fragment of grim doggerel:

I knew
too much too

Irv took the paper from his father's hand. He folded it, handling it with great care. He placed it between the leaves of a notebook and put that in his hip pocket.

"A hate killer," Irv observed. He spoke quietly, but his self-control was obviously strained. "No one who hadn't hated him would have gone in for all that mutilation."

Proctor aroused himself. "What were you saying yesterday about glands, Abelard? About someone who would strike hard and several times?"

Voss smiled wryly. "That was Dawson himself. I'd picked him for the adrenalin type. It would be anger rather than hate."

"No, you said something about Thael."

"Thyroid. Thyroid people are often interested in sex and are brutal when aroused. Thael was arrested in New York for beating up a girl who wouldn't acquiesce."

"By God," Proctor said, "Thael's guilty. Me, too, partly, because I turned him loose."

"You've got to consider other angles. This wasn't either anger or hatred suddenly bursting its bonds; it was cold-blooded premeditation. The note shows that. The murderer might have been unnecessarily brutal just to confuse us or he may have had a streak of rampant sadism. There are a lot of things to think about." Voss pointed to two bulging suitcases, packed and strapped; to a barren clothes closet; to dresser drawers, open and empty. Last of all his gesture indicated a flat sheaf of banknotes weighted down with an ashtray on the otherwise clean top of the dresser.

Irv picked up the money and thumbed swiftly through crisp new bills.

"All fifties," he announced, awed. "Twenty of 'em. A cool thousand dollars."

Proctor said, "Dawson wouldn't earn that much in a year and wouldn't save it in a lifetime. Now how the devil—"

"Blackmail," Irv said promptly. "Dawson knew who killed Evelyn. He offered to leave town for so much money. He was all packed."

"I can find out from the banks Monday if anyone drew out a thousand in fifties," Proctor stated. "But if the one who was being blackmailed killed Dawson, why'd he leave the money behind?"

"He was rattled," Irv guessed. "He forgot it. All he could think of was getting away."

"And yet," Voss pointed out, "he remembered to leave the note. And when you come to check up, Irv, I bet he remembered to clean up his fingerprints, too."

Irv stooped over, his camera case without replying. Proctor exhaled his breath in a long sigh.

"You two look around," Proctor said. "I've got to see what Jack Miller and his wife know."

He went out hurriedly, like a man glad to escape.

"I wonder," Voss said, "which room was Evelyn's?"

"Next door," Irv told him. "I used to see her looking out the window when I passed. Dad went through her letters and stuff already without any luck. Think we should have another look in there?"

"I'd like one, if they haven't locked the door or cleared her stuff out."

They hadn't. The knob of the door turned easily under Voss's hand. The room was pitch dark and hardly any light filtered through from the doorway of Dawson's room. There were heavy odors of incense and cheap perfume. Voss searched his pockets in vain for matches and felt for a wall switch without finding one. Finally, waving his long arms at random, he touched a dangling string which, when pulled, snapped on a rose-colored ceiling light.

Judging by the appearance of the room its occupant might only have stepped out for a moment, intending to return and straighten things up. The bed was unmade, the blankets thrown back and the pillow and sheet still held the faint impressions of a head and body. Filmy pink undergarments were tossed across a chair. A small, rose-shaded lamp stood upon the dresser amid a litter of powder boxes and jars of skin cream and miscellaneous cosmetics. A drugstore calendar on the wall bore last December's dates, but its lithographed picture of a mother and laughing infant was timeless. A photograph of a grinning movie hero cut from a rotogravure was thrust in the corner of the big mirror.

Voss drew aside the chintz curtain that hid the clothes closet. Four or five pairs of shoes lay in disorder on the floor, three or four hats were piled untidily on shelves, six or eight dresses and two coats were draped on hangers.

The dress nearest his hand caught Voss's attention. It was of white linen with a printed pattern of tiny blue anchors and the skirt was torn from a little below the waist to the hem. A thin jagged streamer of cloth hung down from the rent. There were dirt-stains on the dress and a trace of cobwebs at one shoulder.

It suggested violence and a secret tryst. It seemed somehow characteristic of Evelyn Lister's sordid life.

Proctor's footsteps sounded again on the stairs, slow and reluctant. Voss went to meet him and was at once conscious of the man's increased bafflement.

Gripping the post at the head of the stairway with a big hand, Proctor recited tonelessly:

"Lila Miller and Jack go to the movies every Saturday night regular. She was upset about the Lister thing, but they went tonight anyway. Dawson was sitting on the porch smoking when they went away. He's their only boarder since Evelyn quit paying rent. The Millers came home at ten and saw his light and Jack hollered up the stairs that it was a pretty good show, and when Dawson didn't answer Jack came up and saw him.

"Folks next door saw the Millers go out and saw Dawson on the porch. They went inside about nine and Dawson was still there. He didn't talk to 'em, but they thought he was kind of fidgety. They didn't see him go into the house or anyone else go in or come out. They just weren't watching. They were playing Chinese checkers when they heard Lila scream. It was the only noise that had bothered them.

"So help me, that's every damned thing I could find out."

Voss was sorry for the chief. He searched his mind for some heartening bit of information and was forced to fall back upon generalities.

"Your murderer," Voss told him, "is a smart person, an extraordinarily brilliant person. One who understands the importance of perfect timing both for the security of the moment and the psychological effect. One who is clear-sighted, methodical, thorough—"

"Thorough enough to wipe up every fingerprint in the room," Irv broke in, coming to the other doorway. "I can't find a trace of any prints, not even Dawson's, nor anything else that looks as though it might help."

The hinges of Proctor's jaws bulged. "I've heard tell," he said softly, "that in the big cities they sometimes manage to get evidence with a piece of rubber hose. Now I never thought there was much sense in that, but I'm beginning to see . . ."

The screen door downstairs opened and slammed. There were shuffling footsteps and George Thael came up to the second floor, hollow-eyed and bewildered. Behind him came Backus, his coat thrown back, his hand resting on the butt of a revolver in a holster at his hip.

Thael appealed to Voss. "What's it all about, Abelard? I was sound asleep—"

"Never mind the talk," Backus snapped. "Get into that room." He gave Thael a push that sent him staggering to the lighted doorway. "Now what you got to say, looking at your dirty work?"

Thael had nothing to say. He merely moaned in abject terror, clutching the frame of the door. After one brief glance he refused to look at the dead man.

"I read about people breaking down at the scene of the crime," Backus said with immense satisfaction. "Now I guess you got him."

He looked to Proctor for some sign of approval, but the police chief was fairly apoplectic with anger.

"Who told you to bring Thael here?" Proctor roared. "Can't you get even the simplest idea through that thick skull of yours? I wanted Thael pinched—taken back to jail—locked up. Do you understand?"

"B-but—"

"But nothing! I was going to bring the bloodhound here to try to pick up a scent. Suppose the mutt tells us Thael was here now? Why, for all we know, it'll be because you brought him here—you moron!"

Backus shivered. "I never thought, Chief. I never remembered the dog at all. I can take him back. . . ."

Eddie Braithe appeared on the stairway. His face was solemn but his eyes glinted.

"Good copy," he remarked. "Dumb cop ruins only clue. Is it true that Dawson got it, Chief? I just heard something about it over at the club."

Proctor swore roundly and explicitly.

"It's true," Voss told the young editor. "He was stabbed six or eight times. I'd advise you not to look."

Braithe looked, despite the warning. He withdrew his head from the doorway a second later and his face was pale. "Golly!" he breathed. He wiped his brow with a shaking hand.

Proctor was questioning Thael. "You say you went to bed soon as I let you out of the cooler?"

"You bet I did. I was thirty-six hours without sleep in that filthy sweatbox. I'd like to go back to bed right now."

"Will Mrs. Holmes verify your story about not leaving the house?"

"I'm sure she'll say I was in my room all evening as far as she knew."

Backus leaned forward. "Sure she will," he jeered. "But Amanda Holmes wouldn't of known if you went out or not. She was at the movies, too, till after ten. She told me so."

"You're certain," the chief growled to Thael, "you don't want to tell us anything to make it easier on yourself?"

Thael closed his eyes and leaned wearily against the wall. He said, "I didn't do it. I swear to heaven I don't know a thing more than you do about it. Not nearly as much, in fact. When you let me out of jail I went to my room and to bed and I was still there when your hired man came to wake me up. I'd like to sleep for a long time. I don't care right now whether I sleep in my bed or in your jail so long as I'm not bothered."

The chief bit the end from a cigar. "Match?" he muttered to no one in particular. Braithe gave him a folder of matches, and Proctor lit the cigar and put the folder in his vest pocket. "Take him back where we had him before, Backus. See that he has a pillow and a mattress or as many blankets as you can find. Let him sleep. Don't try to think—just do as I say."

"C'mon," Backus ordered, grabbing Thael's arm. They went down the stairs together. Thael looked over his shoulder when they reached the bottom step.

"That lawyer, Abelard," he said. "That fellow Bergman."

"I'll get in touch with him as soon as I can," Voss promised. "I'll look you up in the morning."

Braithe sighed noisily. "What a night, what a night! Irv tells me they've turned Thael loose and so I have to ditch my girl and dash to the office and phone the *Record*. That ruins the hottest news story I ever wrote. And now I have to forget my girl again and tear back to the office and phone to say Thael's locked up, after all, and there's another murder on the fire. What a life!"

He started down the stairs, too. Irv called after him sarcastically, "That's sure tough on your girl, fella." Irv's face was not pleasant to look at in that moment.

Dr. Manning arrived a quarter of an hour later, nervous and bitter, with a story of having been decoyed two miles out of town on the Main Street road by a telephone report of an automobile accident.

"A queer, squeaky voice said a woman was dead and a man was dying," Manning told them. "Said the police were being notified. I nearly broke my neck getting out there. I couldn't find a sign of an accident of any kind and there weren't any houses within a mile where I could make inquiries."

Walking toward the yacht club alone, Voss wondered about that telephone call. There was little question that someone had called Manning at the dance; Proctor had learned of such an occurrence earlier. But why should the murderer—if it were he who had phoned—care whether Manning was at the yacht club or out on the highway when the crime was committed?

There was an obvious answer: The criminal had hoped to cast suspicion on Manning by leaving him without an alibi that could be checked easily. And there was an obvious speculation also: Could not Dawson have called Manning? Could not Dawson have tried to blackmail Manning? Could not Manning have lied about that accident business to forestall any questioning about his movements?

The orchestra in the clubhouse was playing a slow waltz. Although it was only a few minutes past midnight most of the cars had departed from the parking lot and Voss could see few dancers through the open windows. News of the tragedy seemed to have spoiled the fun. There had been an air of dark disquietude about the gathering crowd in front of Jack Miller's house and about the few late strollers

Voss had passed. He sensed an annoying reflection of that feeling within himself.

A single upstairs rear window in Sue Lyons's house was lighted dimly. She would be awake, unable to sleep. A strange, restless, frustrated woman, giving an impression of hardness and cleverness, yet decidedly likable.

She had nerve and determination, Voss reflected. She had shown genuine sympathy for whomever had been driven to the extremity of slaying Evelyn Lister and Art Dawson. She had a keen sense of past injustices. She was afraid, and she was holding back something, trying desperately to shield either herself or another person from suspicion.

Suddenly, as he cut through the parking lot toward the path that led to the grounds of the Bay View Inn, Voss wondered where *she* had been at the moment the owl-headed dagger was plunged into Dawson's heart.

7

Waldham's plague of reporters and photographers descended early Sunday morning. They came in coupes and sedans and three in an airplane from New York. They crossed the Sound by ferry from New Haven. There were half a dozen from Boston. The *Daily Record* sent four men, to Eddie Braithe's intense disgust.

They were young men for the most part, impudently inquisitive, incessantly active and eternally bored. They chain smoked cigarettes in Chief Proctor's office and drove with careless speed through the streets and button-holed everyone. They made pictures of the cemetery, of the Carrington house and the Lyons house and the Whitcomb house, of the hilltop nook where death found Brewster Lyons and Evelyn Lister, of the bed upon which Art Dawson's nightmare execution took place.

They took rooms in the Bay View Inn, the Waldham Hotel, Amanda Holmes's house, Jack Miller's and other private residences. They questioned everyone who would admit remembering that seven-year-old mystery of Brewster Lyons and set portable typewriters clacking with that ancient history, liberally interspersed with descriptions of the somnolent quaintness of Waldham. They lay in wait with lens and pencil for Dr. Manning. They sent notes into jail to Thael, who persistently refused to see any of

them and whose wish for privacy was respected by the
police chief. They gave the local telegraph and telephone
offices the busiest hours they had ever known.

They attended Evelyn Lister's funeral en masse. They
packed Tom Wilkins's simple chapel across the street from
Mrs. Holmes's house and formed an irreverent motorcade
behind Wilkins's shiny new hearse. They were the only
ones, excepting Irv Proctor, who heard the brief service
read at the grave by the Reverend Joseph Ling, for there
were no mourners and those whose curiosity brought them
to the cemetery kept at a decent distance.

Abelard Voss, who had been roused from sleep at seven
o'clock by the first flying wedge of reporters, stood on
the fringe of the little crowd of spectators with Cornelius Proctor. Both men paid close attention to the faces of
those around them, but saw no emotional display to which
they could attach any significance. Mrs. Holmes's was the
only face there that Voss recognized.

The grave was dug far west of Brewster's gloomy monument and not many yards from the fence beyond which
Jenny Midge's ancient house rotted in the midst of its
resurrected garden. Jenny Midge had come part way to see
the funeral; she sat on a fallen tree a little distance back
in the woods, so motionless that when he first caught sight
of her figure Voss took it for some misshapen stump or
abnormal forest growth.

Two modest clusters of roses were left beside the grave
when the coffin was lowered.

"Dawson cut the red ones in the garden at the inn,"
Proctor said. "Took 'em to Tom Wilkins's yesterday afternoon and said he'd pay for the funeral if it was cheap. Now
Tom doesn't know whether he'll get paid or not. Lila Miller sent the white ones."

Red for valor, white for purity, Voss thought sardonically. He polished his spectacles with a huge handkerchief and waited for the minister to finish his reading and

crumble a clod over the coffin. He felt an immense pity for the wretched girl whose slim body lay in the embrace of the democratic earth. She was better dead, very likely—but why all this hollow mockery?

"I've got an invitation for dinner," he said as soon as he could leave. "See you this afternoon, Chief."

He went away quickly, hoping no reporters would follow. It was a sultry, humid, overcast day and he sweated beneath his Palm Beach coat as he passed through the cemetery gate and strode along Hill Street. His wrist watch said five minutes to twelve when he climbed the steps to Cynthia Carrington's wide screened porch.

The sound of his feet brought a tall, stooped old Negro to the door. "Miss Carrington expects me," Voss said. He gave his name.

The Negro would be Athens Jackson, of whom Dawson had spoken. He was of a rich mahogany color with gray wool covering his head like a skullcap and wore baggy pants and a white jacket. He was nervous and worried, his face was lined deeply with the evidence of inner distress and his long arms twitched.

"Miss Ca'ington she not in, suh," he replied with a generous Southern accent. "Dat is, she in, but she too sick to see anybody. She come home not feelin' well las' night."

Voss watched the mahogany hands writhe together. "Is it anything serious? She didn't have an accident?"

"Ah dunno, suh. Dat is, ah don' think so. Ah guess maybe she be all right aftuh while."

Voss turned uncertainly, suspecting the darky of evasion. A sense of uneasiness was building up within him. He recognized Cornelius Proctor's car coming along the street and lingered. The car stopped in front and Proctor got out.

"So this is where you're eating," Proctor said. "Don't think I'm going to horn in. I'm on business."

Behind Voss Athens Jackson made a sound that might have been snuffle or gasp.

"She isn't feeling well," Voss said. "I'm heading for the inn."

"Who isn't feeling well? Cynthia? Too bad. But it's Athens I'm after. Stick around, Abelard, till I find out what he knows."

There was no mistaking the gasp that came from Athens's blue lips this time.

They went up on the porch. Proctor settled into a big wicker chair while Voss made room for himself in a swing that was littered with newspapers and magazines. The Negro remained standing, fearful as a guilty soul before the judgment seat.

"Who'd you see day before yesterday when you went to get milk for Miss Carrington and met Dawson on the way back?" Proctor demanded.

Athens blinked in surprise. "Who ah see? Dawson, suh. An' Mis' Thatcher who ah buy de milk f'om. Nobody else. Leastways nobody to talk to. Maybe somebody walkin' in de street ah didn' pay no 'tention."

"Who was on the hill?"

"Ah nevuh seed nobody but Mist' Dawson."

"Not Miss Lister or Mr. Thael?"

"Not nobody."

"Far as you know just Dawson was up there?"

"Fah as ah knows dat's all."

Proctor frowned. Voss understood he was trying to find out whom Dawson might have seen near the scene of the murder and tried to blackmail. If there had been such a person there would be grounds for suspecting him of Dawson's murder and Evelyn's as well.

"If you're holding anything back," Proctor warned, "you're only making trouble for yourself. If you hide evidence you're an accessory. Know what that is?"

"Nossuh. But ah ain' holdin' back nothin', suh. Ah sweahs to it."

"Accessory," Proctor explained relentlessly, "means you can go to the electric chair just the same as the one that did the killing. Where's Elsie?"

"Elsie she in de kitchen, suh. Ah go git her."

"Call her," Proctor said. "Stay where I can see you. I don't want you telling her what to say."

"Long as ah live ah ain' nevuh tol' Elsie what to say," Athens averred with a solemn dignity that disavowed any humorous intent. "Ah ain' stahtin' now in mah ol' age." He went toward the door to the house. "Elsie honey," he called.

Voss found a copy of Friday's Waldham *Courier* in the swing. He glanced at the front page idly and opened it. When Elsie came to the door he looked up from "Social and Personal" paragraphs, legal notices and innocuous articles about various town activities.

Elsie was short and plump and very black in her starched white apron and cap. The fearful intentness of her eyes was even more pronounced than in the case of Athens. She looked, Voss fancied, not as though she expected the worst, but as though the worst had already happened.

"Yo'-all want me, Mist' Proctuh?" she inquired.

The chief nodded. "What did Athens tell you about going for the milk day before yesterday?"

"He don' tell me nothin' till aftuh yo'-all see him yest'day. Den he say he met Mist' Dawson an' he think maybe yo' s'pect he kilt dat po' gal."

"Who else did Athens see?"

"He don' tell me nothin' else, suh. Eff'n he got anythin' on he min' he keep it to hisse'f. Ah ain' one o' dem wimmen got to known ev'y step a husban' take, suh."

Proctor sighed. Voss looked down at the *Courier* again, his attention caught by the title of a syndicated serial story, *Death Takes a Dare*. He scanned the columns idly.

"I guess," Proctor mumbled, "I might as well go home. If I could find anything at all to go to work on—"

Voss leaned forward so abruptly that Proctor was surprised. The tall criminologist's eyes blazed and his fingers tightened at the edges of the paper.

"Got something?" Proctor inquired.

"Look," Voss said, holding the sheet so that the policeman could see. "Halfway down that first column, two or three words cut out with a razor blade. Two more holes in the second column. Remember those notes?"

"Great jumping tadpoles!" the chief exclaimed, rising. He read what remained of the mutilated sentences: "'. . . there are seven of us to reckon with.' 'I will not stop until . . . who dares to stand in my way.' 'What if the police found the one person . . . and forced him to tell?'"

"We'll have to get another paper," Voss said. "Elsie, is there one in the house?"

"Yassuh," she replied, staring in perplexity. "Ah got Mis' Ca'ington's papuh in de kitchen. Ah don' know wheah dat one come f'om. We on'y gits de one ev'y week."

She disappeared, to return in a few seconds with another copy of the *Courier*. Voss opened it, took a pencil and an envelope from his pocket and copied words from the columns on the back of the envelope.

"There it is," he said.

Proctor read in Voss's neat handwriting:

> Counting myself
> I have killed everyone
> who knew about it

"Another one," Proctor said hoarsely. "Ready for another corpse. Here of all places!"

"A suicide note, by the sound of it," Voss pointed out. "We're supposed to find the missing words pasted on a slip of paper with the last corpse of the party—the third, or perhaps the fourth or fifth."

He thought fiercely, *Not Cynthia. It mustn't happen to her.*

"Suicide . . . Athens, what's the matter with Miss Carrington?"

The Negro quailed before the police chief's sternness. "Ah dunno, suh. Uh—dat is—" He looked helplessly at his wife.

"I want to see her this minute," Proctor shouted. "Do you hear, Elsie?"

"Y-yassuh. On'y ah cain' he'p yo'—"

A cheery voice hailed them from the sidewalk. "What's all the excitement?" Garth Manning came up the steps.

Voss said, "Athens and Elsie tell us Miss Carrington is sick and can't see anyone, but it's important that we see her."

"Sick?" Manning came up on the porch, frowning anxiously. "What's the matter with her, Elsie? Where is she—in her room?"

Elsie's black eyes rolled heavenward. "May de Lawd fo'give me, Doctuh. She ain' heah. She ain' been heah all night. Ah been 'spectin' huh all mo'nin,' an' ah don' wan' to tell nobody nothin' till she tell me what to say huh own se'f."

"Da's a fac'," Athens declared, his knees trembling. "Eff'n she don' come home befo' long we was a-goin' to tell de po-lice, 'cause den we know she in trouble—"

"Or past all trouble," Proctor said grimly. He showed Manning the mutilated newspaper and the words Voss had written.

Voss fought down a numbing dread; the thought of Cynthia lying dead somewhere with a folded slip of paper in her cold hand shocked him beyond anything in his experience.

Manning's face was suddenly white and drawn; the lines about his mouth were like lines etched with biting acid.

"She didn't do this!" he cried. "It's false on the face of it. God help her, she's been desperate enough to take her life a thousand times in the last seven years, but I'd stake my immortal soul she wouldn't dream of anything such as we saw last night."

Voss spoke slowly, choosing his words. "I agree with you. Anyway, if she had wanted to leave a note of this kind she would have written it out. But the message might have been intended for her—for whoever finds her, rather—by someone else."

"You mean. . . ?"

"Many a homicide has been disguised as suicide. . . . Understand, Manning, I'm not saying I believe anything serious has happened to her; I'm only pointing out a possibility. We've got to find her."

"Dat papuh," Elsie asserted, "ain' Miss Ca'ington's papuh. Somebody done lef' it heah."

"It would be easy," Proctor admitted. "Any visitor could have left it or any person sneaking around after dark. If the screen door was locked a piece of wire would unhook it. Maybe Irv can get fingerprints from the paper."

"Fingerprints don't show up well on newsprint as a rule," Voss said. "It's worth trying, of course. Elsie, when did you see Miss Carrington last?"

"She nevuh come back f'om de dance, suh."

Voss remembered his brief glimpse of Cynthia and Ralph Decker through the rear window of Irv's sedan. Decker had been carrying her in his arms. And before that Voss had seen what might have been a struggle.

He put down the impulse to voice the ugly suspicion that leaped into his mind, not knowing what inner prompting urged him to keep silent. He only said, "Decker might know where she went."

Athens spoke up hesitantly. "De boat—de rowboat—it gone f'om wheah it was, suh. Ah cain' fin' it noplace. De outboa'd engine in de garage, but de oars is gone, too. Ah ain' say she tuk it. . . ."

Manning said, "She did. I'm sure she did. She used to ask me to take her rowing sometimes at night when the bay was calm. Being on the water soothed her. She spoke of drowning as the easiest . . ." He did not finish.

"Manning," Proctor said with exaggerated matter-of-factness, "you couldn't break down and tell us anything we ought to know, could you? For a long time you've been closer to Cynthia than anyone else. You've also been close to—well, a lot of things that enter into this case. No sense my going into details. Maybe as her doctor, and maybe as just a plain citizen, you can tell us things you might not want to talk about ordinarily."

The physician was not deceived by Proctor's casualness. "If you were to break down and say exactly what's in your mind, you'd tell me I was one of your most promising suspects, wouldn't you?"

"Everybody's a suspect," Proctor said. "You've got sense enough to see that. I was just giving you an opening. If you haven't anything you want to tell us, say so. We've got plenty to do."

"Don't be silly," Manning chided.

They went into the house after that, peering into each room, arriving finally at Cynthia's bedroom on the second floor. Voss stood in the doorway and surveyed the chamber with interest, glimpsing a side of Cynthia's character that had been hidden from him until now.

It was a large, serene, lavender-tinted room, furnished simply, but with fastidious care. There was a shelf of books, some of which dealt with popular religious philosophies; there were three or four comfortable chairs and a long chaise-longue. The bed had apparently not been slept in the night before; its silken coverlet was as smooth as a sheet of glass. There was no untidiness anywhere, no toilet article out of place on the mirrored dressing table, no chair out of its logical location.

Voss guessed that the orderliness of the room was a part of Cynthia's defense against the jumble of her mind. In the midst of its perfect neatness perhaps she contrived to find moments of freedom from the tide of memories and fears that surged out of her subconscious whenever her vigilance was relaxed. It seemed to him a brave and pitiful—and quite hopeless—striving toward the illusion of a balance that would produce harmony out of discord, peace out of chaos.

He pitied and respected her more than ever, faced with that intimate revelation of her courage.

"I'll phone for the brains of the department," Proctor muttered. "Irv and Ben Thoad's hound. And I'll give Decker a ring."

They went downstairs together.

Manning said, "I'll be home all afternoon, Cornelius. You'll let me know the minute you find out anything?"

Proctor grunted.

The doctor looked at Voss. "If you aren't needed here, you and I might have that little talk. . . ."

Sitting at the telephone stand in the hallway behind Manning, the chief signaled furiously to Voss to accept the invitation.

Manning's small white house was in Whitcomb Street just around the corner from the Carrington mansion toward the center of town. The two men went up on a side porch where an unobtrusive sign said *walk in* and through a cozy tiled waiting room into the physician's consultation room. There were a glass-topped desk disorderly with papers, a glass-fronted case of books and a case of surgical instruments at either side of a clean brick fireplace, framed photographs on the smooth plaster walls, and comfortable chairs. Through a partly open door could be seen another room where there were tall lamps and an adjustable examination table equipped with clamps and brackets.

Voss lowered himself into a leather armchair, waved away a box of cigars Manning held out to him and glanced with appreciation at the bearskin rug and wrought-iron fire tools.

"I like it," he said.

Manning applied the flame of a lighter to the tip of a cigar and sat comfortably in the big swivel chair behind the desk. "It's been peaceful till today. Not too many patients this time of year. A neighbor woman comes to put things in their place and prepare meals when I feel like eating at home."

"I take it the reporters have been after you."

Manning exhaled smoke explosively. "All of them. I let the first one in without thinking. In fifteen minutes I had a dozen. 'Are you sending flowers to Evelyn Lister's funeral?' they wanted to know. 'When do you expect to marry Cynthia Carrington?' 'If you wanted to murder someone would you use a club or a knife or poison?' I finally kicked the whole gang out after offering to trade punches with a couple of the more impertinent. I suppose I'll catch hell in their papers."

"Your tactics are bad. Make it a point to humor them. Give some sort of answer to everything they ask, but don't say more than you mean. You won't be misquoted as often as you'd think. I had six or eight of them while I was dressing and eating breakfast."

"I guess I haven't the gift for doing the right thing," Manning said. "I tried to help the Lister girl. She came to me bawling, scared to death, going to have a baby. I was half tempted to take it away from her—but I wouldn't, of course. I treated her, though, for a venereal disease she'd picked up from one of the local lads, and because I felt sorry for her I tried to inject some sense into her. She used to come over to talk to me about her troubles. I advised her to make the man who was the baby's father marry her or at least support it. I got the surprise of my life when she went to the authorities and named me."

"In a way it was a compliment to you. She preferred you as a husband. Or if she couldn't get married she knew you would be the better provider."

"Compliment hell! It was opportunism plain and simple. The neighbors had seen her coming here. She knew they weren't above thinking I might have made passes at her, being a bachelor. They're always ready to believe the worst and swear to it."

"I suppose it was Dawson's baby?"

"It must have been. He'd been hanging around her a long time. I've got a hunch he told her to go after me as one man who couldn't afford a scandal. I threw a scare into him once telling him I was going to try to prove they'd got together to swindle me. He chased me with a gun that time.

"I'm pretty sure I wasn't the only victim, either. I have an idea she was killed because she tried the same game on somebody else."

"Somebody who refused to be the goat, eh?"

Manning nodded. "It's just an idea. I examined the body and she wasn't pregnant, but she could have said she was. Her chosen victim would remember the mess she'd dragged me into and wouldn't like to think of that happening to him."

"Has she been especially friendly with anyone in particular?"

"I wouldn't know." Manning paused, gnawing the end of the cigar. "There's that angle and sometimes I think it explains the whole nasty business. Then I think back seven years and all at once the whole picture changes in my mind and I see another figure behind it all. Maybe two figures."

"Jenny Midge," Voss hazarded, "and . . . ?"

"Whitcomb. His case is really tragic. He's killing himself with whisky and it's just as well. But meanwhile he's a schizophrenic if I ever saw one, a man torn to tatters between two terrible passions. Murder as an outlet for bottled-up fear or hatred would be right in his line. He's still clever, too, for all I suspect the alcohol has got at his brain cells."

"There are crimes of sudden anger," Voss said reflectively, "but neither of our murders was done on impulse. Nearly all other murders are committed to remove insupportable obstacles between the killer and something he wants. For instance a person who knows a man's guilt may stand between that man and his continued freedom. Or one from whom a man has suffered some terrible wrong or indignity may stand in the way of that man's self-respect or self-satisfaction."

"All right," Manning said. "Suppose Evelyn had known that Whitcomb killed Brewster Lyons in the hope of winning Cynthia—had known it from the beginning, possibly, or more likely just ran across some evidence of it. Suppose Dawson knew, too. Whitcomb has money left and naturally they'd be trying to blackmail him."

"How about Jenny Midge?"

"That's a little harder. She loved Brewster so it isn't likely she killed him. But she may have got the idea that Evelyn and Dawson were in some way responsible. Or perhaps Evelyn was desecrating Brewster's grave, to which Jenny devotes most of her life. You know they say Evelyn used to take the canning factory boys into the cemetery at night. She's been seen with men in the vicinity of Jenny's house, too—and that's a sacred shrine to Jenny. Evelyn may have used the house as a rendezvous. Jenny wouldn't need much more reason for murder than that."

"She's stark mad?"

"Stark is the word. I've always thought she was potentially dangerous and should be locked up."

"It's a puzzle," said Voss. "It's the most fascinating puzzle I ever ran across. Most dead men, whether they died in bed or with their boots on, are completely dead after a few years. When I first arrived in Waldham my interest was aroused because so many people spoke of Brewster's death in a way that showed it was as fresh in their minds as though it had happened last week."

"You say when you first came to Waldham. Do you know, Voss, I've been wondering why you came. Ordinarily you wouldn't be interested in Brewster's death unless somebody hired you to dig back into it—or unless you had some inkling these other murders were going to follow."

"I had no inkling," Voss told him. His bright eyes watched the doctor with almost inhuman intensity. "Neither did I undertake to investigate that earlier affair for anyone."

"Then," said Manning, "I'm still wondering. Of course I haven't any business asking."

"You're sure, Manning, you don't know more than you'll admit about my reason for being here?"

The physician's dark eyes were steady and expressionless, meeting Voss's. He waited a long minute before he said with a trace of hostility, "That sounds almost like an accusation, Voss. A pretty direct hint, at any rate."

Voss's smile was disarming, dissipating the sudden tension. "It wasn't intended to be an accusation. I was thinking of something altogether apart from the murders, possibly connected with them in some way, possibly not. I'm satisfied with the way you responded . . . I was trying to make up my mind, too, whether Cynthia isn't largely responsible for the fact that Brewster's ghost has never been laid. Every time she walks along the street people can see how she's been haunted—"

"I'd give all I own," Manning interrupted, "to take that memory out of her mind. She went through an experience very few people could bear. Her dreams and feeling of guilt are the result of her conscious and subconscious minds warring, the one trying to rid itself of a dreadful phantom, the other keeping it alive."

"It's a wonder she has managed to hold together."

Manning's voice softened. "I'll never forget that night I saw her stumbling along the path in the twilight. I spoke to her, but she didn't know me. I took her home and tried to get her to tell what happened. She couldn't talk. Brewster's father got worried later and went out with a lantern and found the body on the hill.

"Cynthia was in a hysterical coma for three days. It was a complete amnesia. She came out of it slowly and told her story, but there was very little in it the police didn't already know. By that time they had investigated and discovered there were no clues at all, no fingerprints, no witnesses. They soft-pedaled any suggestion that Cynthia might be guilty because it was the merciful thing, and no one really thought she had done it."

"A pity it should ruin her life."

"That's what I thought. People say I'm in love with her, but pity describes my feeling better. I'd devote the rest of my life to helping her if I thought in the end she could relax and be normal and be married. I mean be married to anyone."

"Ralph Decker would like to marry her, wouldn't he?"

Manning let slow heartbeats pulse away before he answered. "I haven't got to like Decker particularly in the two years he's been around. He's a nice fellow, probably, but I'd want to know more about him before I trusted him very far. Some secret sin or tragedy is weighing on his mind; that much I know." He clenched his fists and his voice became ragged. "If I find out he's taken Cynthia somewhere . . ."

A buzzer purred beneath the desk. Dr. Manning lifted the phone from its cradle and talked and listened. He said into the transmitter, "I'll be right over." He said to Voss, "Mrs. Bell's baby. Been expecting it for a week. We'll have to get together again soon."

He was preoccupied and impersonal as they left the house. He had slipped into a conventional pose as easily as a bright dagger slips into a velvet sheath.

But Voss did not forget—could not forget—the sheer animal ferocity that had stood forth naked in his eyes for one infinitesimal instant.

8

Jenny Midge came hobbling out of the cemetery. Her head was bent, the gnarled fingers of her left hand held the corners of her gray shawl together at her withered bosom, her right hand at her side gripped a pointed gardening trowel. Voss took a sidewise step out of her way, uncertain whether or not she had seen him.

"Good afternoon," he said.

She stopped, tipped her head over one shoulder and peered up at him with eyes so coldly bright that he felt a physical chill, standing there in the white sunlight. She did not speak or move.

"I saw you watching the funeral this morning," he said, not knowing what else to say. He felt foolish talking to her, as a man might feel talking to a dog or a stone or a picture, knowing perfectly well it would not answer.

He looked past her toward the mound beneath which Evelyn Lister lay and saw it covered with flowers, blue and yellow and red and white—many more flowers than Dawson and Lila Miller had provided in their scant offerings. He speculated on who could have strewn them there and what impulse of tenderness or grief—or mockery—prompted the votive act. Then he remembered with a start that there was fresh earth on the blade of old Jenny's trowel.

Her voice startled him more, coming forth deep and harsh as an angry man's from her bloodless lips.

"Why do you stay here, Abelard Voss, where blood has been shed and will be shed? You are not safe among these people who are marked for death. No one is safe except old Jenny Midge, who tends their graves after they have gone."

"Who are marked for death?" he asked.

"Go look in the Book of Fate. Their names are written there. But even if you knew you could not save them."

"Have you read the book?"

Her beady eyes were veiled swiftly. "Not I. What I know comes to me in dreams when the moon is full or when the storm is raging. Everything comes to me then, but some of it I forget."

"Who will die next?" he pressed. "Tomorrow or the day after or later in the week?"

"Ho, ho! It may be you, young man, if you are still here. It may be anyone. How should I know, with an old woman's memory playing me tricks? It may be my darling Brewster—but no, he is already dead." A gust of fury shook her like a sudden wind and her skinny fist brandished the trowel. "But the tortures of hell are eating the heart out of the one who killed my darling."

"I have never heard who killed him," he said persuasively. "Tell me, mother."

Her eyes darted at him like rusty lances. "You call me mother? A fine mother I am! Mother to the dead, it may be. He died by hands he trusted. Remember that when you hear the devil has claimed his own."

"I must know more than that. Give me a name, Jenny—something I can understand."

"I can tell you nothing. I have talked too much already. I am a very busy old woman. If you want to live you will go away and not come back." She huddled herself in her shawl, bent her shoulders and hobbled away faster than before.

He cried, "Wait!"

She gave no sign of hearing, but kept hobbling toward the village, toward Terry Whitcomb's house. Voss took a single step after her, then thought better of it. He shrugged and went into the cemetery.

Brewster Lyons's black marble shaft was a stubby thumb jerking upward from the rectangle of fresh-stirred soil. The flowering plants at its base seemed intrusive splashes of gaiety in a setting that was meant to be forever somber.

"He died by hands he trusted," Voss repeated to himself. The old crone might have meant the hands of Cynthia, whom Brewster loved. Or hands he had trusted might have been the hands of Sue, his sister, or of Terry Whitcomb, his friend and rival in love. Or those of Garth Manning, who had been on the hillside path when Cynthia came groping down through mists of horror.

Or even the hands of herself, Jenny Midge, Brewster's mad old nurse.

Voss shook his head irritably, wandering over the whispering gravel and hushed grass toward the newer grave. Why should he try to puzzle out the words of a lunatic? After all they had been highly fanciful words, incapable of any solid interpretation.

Meanwhile the disappearance of Cynthia presented a problem that could not be ignored. It was possible of course that she had merely lost her nerve, hearing of Dawson's murder, and had fled before the shadow of some terrible fear. And it was possible the shock had brought back the amnesia that had followed Brewster's tragedy and she had wandered off, not meeting Manning this time nor anyone who knew her.

But that left Decker unaccounted for, and Decker had been carrying her in his arms when Voss had looked back.

The notion struck Voss like an icy wave: What if Decker, who had left the dance floor some minutes before Dawson's murder, had guilty knowledge of the crime and Cynthia either shared that knowledge or suspected it? What if Cynthia had wanted to call after them last night as Irv's sedan drove away? Might not Decker have stunned or strangled her and borne her alive or dead to a place where no one would be likely to find her?

That disquieting theory would have been the more impressive had there not been a dozen others, each with its own peculiar recommendation. Manning in his conversation with Voss had gone further than he knew toward explaining why he might have slain Evelyn and Dawson. There were Sue Lyons, Jenny Midge, Terry Whitcomb, George Thael and others to be considered. . . .

But the time for speculation, Voss reminded himself sharply, was after all available facts had been garnered and sorted and weighed.

He paused for a minute or two beside Evelyn's grave. Cut flowers, long-stemmed and leafy, covered the earthen hill completely. Fresh-planted rose bushes, pruned and watered, were at either end of the mound. Jenny must have taken half the blooms from her garden, he thought, to deck the unloved girl's resting place so generously. She must have made several trips with her arms overflowing with their burden of beauty.

He saw, looking ahead, a place where the wire fence was so loose it sagged near the ground. Beyond it ran a narrow open trail, too overgrown to be called a path, through the woods toward Jenny's house. According to Dr. Manning, Evelyn had crept furtively along that trail on clandestine missions and had hidden secret sins within the four tottering walls of the structure.

The cool look of the woods helped Voss to make up his mind, together with the certainty that Jenny Midge was absent. He crossed the trimmed grass and the fence and plunged gratefully into the green shade dappled with pale flecks of sun. Instantly the world seemed to change, to become still and mysterious and solemn. Even the songs of the birds were sadder.

He walked without hurry. His white shoes became stained with the moisture of ferns and vines they trod down. In spots where the ground was bare and damp he could see the prints of the old woman's boots turned on their sides outward as her weight had distorted them. In a very short while the house became visible through the bushes, gray and desolate against the brown of the scarred hillside.

A haunted house, he granted, if ever there was one, set paradoxically in a sea of living flowers so profuse that he could not tell where the buds had been snipped to cover the new mound of earth in the cemetery.

The rich sweetness of blossoms mingled with the moldy odor of decay. The drone of bees vibrated through the birds' chorus. The air was still and warm and moist. Voss had the feeling of being bewitched as he walked around the house, noting the big padlock on the front door and the spiked planks, much newer than the building itself, that shielded the back door and the lower windows.

An upper front window was unboarded and broken, though. Having made up his mind during his walk through the woods Voss did not hesitate. Standing on tiptoe he could reach the edge of the sagging porch roof and twist his fingers through the rotting shingles to grip a timber that seemed strong enough. At considerable risk to his clothing and some to his limbs he drew his body up and threw a knee over the roof. He crept precariously along the expanse of crackling shingles until he could reach the window. The sash lifted without difficulty.

Dust and cobwebs were luxuriant within the room beyond the window. The walls had been plastered, but now
the laths were laid bare in great irregular patches. The
wide floorboards groaned mournfully when Voss set foot
upon them.

Dust and cobwebs were in the gloomy hallway and in
the two other upper rooms. The rickety stairs shrilled
warning as Voss descended them, testing each step before
entrusting it with his weight. He went slowly down into
thick dusk crisscrossed here and there by thin rays of gray
light filtered through the disintegrating walls.

It was easy to imagine the spirits of Jenny Midge's father and mother and two brothers, who had died beneath
this roof, stealing back sometimes and finding it only a
little less dreary than the confines of crumbling coffins.

From the back of the house came the faint smell of
wood ashes and meals cooked in recent days. The living
room had been made habitable for one who was not fastidious. There were two or three broken chairs and a table
upon which was a half-burned candle thrust into the neck
of a ketchup bottle. An ancient sofa, leaking cotton stuffing, had been drawn in front of the cold fireplace and two
or three greasy blankets were folded upon it. A fat gray
spider was its only occupant at the moment, but apparently that was where Jenny Midge slept when for one reason
or another she did not stay at Terry Whitcomb's.

Fully conscious of the fact that he was committing
what might be construed as a criminal offense Voss opened
doors and peered into corners. On the floor of a shallow
closet he found his first object of special interest, a bundle made up of a man's rubber-soled canvas tennis shoes
bound together with a thin white belt studded with tiny
blue anchors. The belt was a part of a girl's dress—a part
of that same soiled and torn linen dress he had noticed in
Evelyn's room at Jack Miller's, Voss was certain.

He picked up the bundle and a metal disc fell out of one of the shoes and tinkled on the floor. It was a copper lucky penny stamped on one side with the words *Souvenir of Niagara Falls* and on the other with a design purportedly representing the famous waterfall itself.

Voss put the coin in his pocket and tucked the bundle under his arm and continued his circuit of the room. He was peering into an empty flower vase on the mantel when he felt one of the bricks of the hearth rock beneath his foot. He stooped and pried it free and uncovered the end of a small metal box such as fishermen use for tackle. Two adjoining bricks came up easily and he had the box in his hands and was relieved to discover that it locked only with a simple catch.

He carried the box to the table and raised the lid. First of all were revealed three cracked and yellowed photographs, one of a man and a woman of middle age, one of two young men and the other of a young and pretty girl. He surmised immediately that the first two were portraits of Jenny's mother and father and brothers, who had been wiped out by typhoid. It was with a distinct shock, however, that he recognized similarities in the features of the third portrait and those of the shrunken hag he had met outside the cemetery. It was Jenny Midge's picture, logically enough, made forty or more years ago—but somehow he had never thought of her as having once been young and comely and it was difficult for him to think of her that way now.

Beneath the pictures were a number of letters in envelopes. Reluctantly, Voss looked at the postmarks of the first few and read dates in 1902 and 1904. Relieved, he dismissed the lot of them as irrelevant to any of the matters in which he was interested.

The bottom layer of the box's contents drew a surprised whistle from him. It was a deep pile of banknotes, tens and twenties, some of them of the old large size and some newer. Gold certificates were among them. He made no effort to count the bills. He could see that there were hundreds of dollars there, perhaps thousands.

He had a cheerless conception of Jenny crouched within the shuttered house in a blurry circle of candlelight counting her hoard of dollars, savings of a thrifty lifetime, and fondling her pitiful mementoes of tragedy.

He replaced everything except the shoes and belt and the souvenir coin. He negotiated the perilous stairs again and peered from the upper window, making sure no one was within view. He slid over the porch roof, dropped to the ground and hastened away from that unearthly place through the woods and the cemetery to the streets of reality.

While he was still a block away Voss caught sight of a concentration of people, some of them with cameras, on the walk and the lawn outside police headquarters. A spindly young man detached himself from the group and came to meet him, walking with nervous strides.

"Hey, Voss," he cried. "Remember me—King of the *Record?* I've been looking for you."

Voss remembered him from two or three casual meetings. He said, "Hello, King. How are you getting along with your local correspondent?"

"You mean Braithe?" King grinned and jerked his head back toward the gathering. "He's leaning against that tree sulking. Thinks the paper should have left everything in his hands. Why, he's hardly got brains enough to gather up the personals for his own little paper, let alone cover a big yarn like this for New York."

Voss looked. Braithe did appear to be sulking. His head and shoulders were slumped rebelliously and his hands were jammed deep into his trousers pockets.

"He thought this was his big chance to make good as a newspaperman," Voss said. "Now you and the rest of the

gang have taken it out of his hands. Give him something
to do if you can."

"I've kept him busy trying to get to Thael all morning.
The chief wouldn't let any of us into the jail. But he's
questioning Thael now and he promised to give us some
dope soon as it's over. Therefore the assemblage." King
looked at the shoes under Voss's arm. "You wouldn't be
bringing in evidence, now, would you?"

"These?" Voss laughed. "An old pair of tennis shoes. If
you can hook them up with a murder you'll be doing well."

"Maybe I can, Voss. They don't look big enough for
you. You haven't said no, anyway, so I'll keep them in
mind. I don't suppose you could tip me off to anything I
could print?"

"I've been going in circles," Voss told him. "This is
probably the damnedest case I was ever mixed up in, and
that takes into account some beauties. I'm going to get to
the bottom of it if it takes me the rest of my life. But so
far I haven't even scraped the surface."

He pushed through the crowd, ignoring questions
called to him, paying no attention to cameras that focused
on him and clicked. Backus was at the door keeping the
reporters out. He admitted Voss with a self-important
smile.

Irv Proctor was just leading Thael from the chief's
office into the corridor that led to the cell block. Thael
looked at Voss with an expression of deathly weariness.

"For God's sake, Abelard," he called, "can't you do
something to get me out of this flea bag? They're hound-
ing me to death while the murderer is getting ready to
polish off somebody else. Just because I had a lot of gin
one night and slapped a drunken tart they're sure I killed
a girl I'd just met and a man I'd never so much as spoken
to. How about that lawyer?"

Voss said truthfully, "I called Bergman's house first thing this morning and was told he was out of the city and couldn't be reached. But he'll be in his office tomorrow."

Thael started dejectedly down the corridor. "I may not be alive tomorrow," he said.

It would have been comical, under other circumstances, to see Thael's look of disgusted weariness so perfectly reflected in Cornelius Proctor's face. Voss did not feel like smiling, however, as he went into the office and sat down across the desk from the chief.

"I wish you'd clear this thing up, Abelard," Proctor growled irritably. "You heard Thael say he was at the end of his rope. That goes double for me—only Thael's going to get out in an hour and I've got to stick."

"You're letting him go?"

"He doesn't know it," Proctor said with some satisfaction. "He was so nasty I sent him back to cool his heels for an hour or so without telling him. But he didn't kill Dawson. He was home in bed like he said."

"What makes you so sure?"

"Betty Wilkins, the undertaker's wife, went to call on Amanda Holmes at half-past nine last night. Amanda wasn't home, but Mrs. Wilkins knocked till Thael stuck his head out the window to see who was there. He was so sleepy he didn't remember it, but she saw him, pajamas and all."

"That's a load off my mind. I was feeling sorry for the poor devil. I can't find the slightest excuse for thinking he did it."

"Except that he was with the girl about the time she was killed."

"Plenty of people have been with her. Any of them could have been as close to her as Dawson was without being seen. Thael's story about leaving Evelyn sitting alone sounds logical. If it's true it would take the other fellow—

or the other woman—only five or six seconds to pick up that rock and strike with it."

"The other woman," Proctor said. He let the words stand by themselves, to wear whatever meaning Voss chose to clothe them in.

Voss placed the shoes and belt on the desk. He said, "It was Evelyn's belt, I think, and her boy friend's shoes. They're nines, of a popular make. It's just possible we can trace them through the store that sold them to the man who bought them. More likely Ben Thoad's bloodhound can sniff out the answer for us."

"Where'd you find 'em?"

"In Jenny Midge's house, I climbed in a window. Manning told me Evelyn had been seen keeping some of her dates there."

Proctor nodded. "How do you know the belt was Evelyn's?"

"It matches a dress in her closet. The dress is torn and dirty. If Evelyn and her friend were in the house and Jenny or somebody else came around they might have had to leave in a hurry. The man might have forgotten the shoes—he'd probably been carrying them after playing golf or tennis—and she might have lost her belt and torn her dress sliding out a window."

Proctor put the articles in a drawer of his desk. "We'll check up. It might give us a new angle and it might not. I doubt if it'll prove murder, though."

"You very seldom prove murder," Voss declared. "Not absolutely. The evidence is nearly always circumstantial, since the killer seldom invites witnesses. You get a jury properly indignant and show them enough circumstantial evidence and you get a conviction. Or else you trick your man into betraying himself or scare him with the electric chair till he decides to cop a plea in the hope of having it called second-degree murder or manslaughter."

"It's a lousy business, isn't it?" Proctor glanced up quickly as many feet scuffed in the corridor. "What the hell!"

Backus opened the office door. "In here, boys," he said to what appeared to be a multitude outside.

"Hey!" Proctor exclaimed. "I didn't tell you to let 'em in, Backus."

The ill-starred policeman turned pale. "But I heard you tell 'em you'd see 'em soon as you got through with Thael. And I seen Thael go out of your office just before you told Mr. Voss you was goin' to let him go, but wanted to make him cool his heels a while first—"

"Shut up!" the chief roared, his face crimson. He gripped the edge of his desk tightly, fighting doggedly for self-control while reporters and cameramen streamed in, some of them grinning at what they had overheard, all of them firing questions at once.

9

Violence flared sharp and swift as saw-toothed lightning in the town square next morning, rewarding the patient vigil of the reporters lounging beneath the shade trees.

Eddie Braithe started it without quite intending to. He was hurrying into police headquarters at the moment Irv Proctor was hurrying out. They collided and halted, regarding one another without much friendliness.

"Well," Irv said mildly.

Braithe smiled. "What's all the excitement today?"

"No excitement I know of."

"I guess there wouldn't be. Nothing could be exciting for you after Saturday night when I gave you that break with Dale Parsons. Man, is she a cuddly little armful on a dance floor or parked in a lonesome lane!"

Braithe talked loud enough to attract the attention of all who were within earshot. Somebody snickered.

"I ought to shove your teeth down your throat," Irv said with quiet ferocity. "That's a hell of a thing to say."

The young editor's smile broadened. It was taunting and so was his voice.

"You wouldn't want to trade for a share in my girl, would you, Irv? You tell me everything that goes on at headquarters and I'll turn her over to you Tuesday evenings—"

Irv hit him hard in the face. Braithe took two or three steps backward and sat down.

Somebody yelled, "It's a fight! Gather round, boys!"

Braithe was game and capable. He shook his head once to clear it and then he was on his feet dancing confidently toward Irv. He feinted with his right and drove his left over Irv's guard, hitting Irv's chin, tipping his head back. This time Irv went down, his heel catching on a stone and tripping him.

A roar went up from the swelling crowd.

Braithe crouched and waited for his opponent to rise. He was still smiling and swearing softly to himself at the same time. His stance was good, his movements were eager, his eyes alight with the joy of battle.

The policeman was up a second after he had struck the earth. He walked into Braithe savagely, driving right and left. They were about evenly matched, Proctor having the advantage of strength and weight and Braithe the advantage of skill.

They traded solid, soul-satisfying punches for a full minute. The crowd was delirious. Bets were offered and taken. Three or four photographers were busy with their Speed Graphics getting action shots of the bout.

Then Cornelius Proctor appeared. He strode ominously between the fighters, taking one of his son's stray blows on his big shoulder. He grasped each of the youths by the shirt front and held them apart.

"Plenty of places to fight," he rumbled. "Why pick this one? What's the matter with the woods?"

"Irv couldn't wait," Braithe panted.

"Hell of a lot of business either of you've got trying to fight," the police chief growled in disgust. "Both of you winded at the start. You better shake hands and make up."

Irv backed away. "No hand-shaking for me." A thread of blood trickled down his chin from a cut lip.

"Then I'll have to arrest you both for disturbing the peace," said Proctor. "I'll have to put you in a cell to think it over."

Braithe's fingers caressed the region of his right eye, which was pink and swelling. "Both in the same cell, Chief?"

Proctor nodded.

"That would be worse than the third-degree," Braithe said. "Come on, Irv—you know you couldn't stand it. We'd better shake. I'm sorry I got you started. Guess I was jealous or something."

He held out his right hand. Irv hesitated a moment, then took it. The clasp was brief and Irv's face remained perfectly blank.

The crowd broke up slowly.

Abelard Voss missed the action, but George Thael painted an enthusiastic motion picture of the fight for him half an hour later when they met on Main Street.

"Fighting is my favorite sport," said Thael. "Watching fights, I mean, in alleys or barrooms or Madison Square Garden. Braithe is one of the best amateur boxers I've seen in a long time. If he'd go into training I could make plenty managing him."

Thael was in better spirits than Voss had ever before found him. He had been set free early the previous evening and had slept long and well at Mrs. Holmes's house. The morning papers had been kind to him as though to make up for their earlier sensationalism in describing his arrest.

"You think he'd have licked Irv in the end?" Voss inquired.

Thael considered. "I wouldn't want to give odds. Trouble with Irv, he wouldn't know when he was licked. He's got the guts to take a lot of punishment and the strength to stick through and his punches carry a lot of weight. He was clean out of his head with blood lust. I think it would be worth money to see 'em fight to a finish."

Thael went into the Elite Café for a late breakfast and Voss went on to Cornelius Proctor's office. He found the chief alone, his chin propped up by one hand, moodily drawing circles and triangles on a desk pad.

Proctor's face brightened. "Been trying to phone you, Abelard. Been finding things out, but they don't make head or tail. Maybe they'll mean something to you."

"About Cynthia?"

"In a way. Decker found her boat adrift off the golf club this morning. One oar was dangling from the lock. The other oarlock was ripped out and there was a gash along the gunwale as though something had run her down in the bay."

Voss waited anxiously. Proctor bit the end from a cigar. "Match," Proctor said.

"I haven't any. What did Decker say about Saturday night?"

"Thought I told you. I talked to him yesterday. Said she fainted when she heard about Dawson and he started to carry her to the club, thinking Manning would be back. She came to and insisted on sitting down and resting. Then she wanted to go home and made Decker leave her in front of her house. Wouldn't even let him come up on the porch."

"He didn't hang around?"

"No. He thought she'd go right to bed. He got his car out of the parking lot and went home without seeing anybody, he says. That means his alibi is reasonable, but there's no one to back it up."

"That," Voss stated, "is the weakness in Manning's alibi, too."

"You got a match, Abelard?"

"No."

Proctor felt in his vest pockets. He brought forth four books of matches and placed them on the desk. He found five other books in his coat pockets. He chewed the end of the cigar without lighting it and made a pile of the match folders.

"She could have gone out in the boat to think things over, as Manning suggested, and been run down," Proctor said. "She could have rowed out and drowned herself and the boat could have drifted against something on the tide and been battered. If she drowned herself then that suicide note wouldn't be hard to explain. By the way, Irv couldn't get any fingerprints at all off that newspaper."

Voss imagined Cynthia Carrington's delicate hands cutting significant words out of the *Courier* and pasting them in order on a sheet of notepaper. There was something very wrong with the idea.

"What we found yesterday indicated more than a suicide note," he told Proctor. "It was a confession of murder. If you can see Cynthia murdering Evelyn and Dawson you're a better seer than I am."

The chief snook his head in perplexity. "That's just it. I can't. She could have run away, or tried to, because of fear instead of guilt. You know Manning's name keeps coming to me. She was so friendly with him, she might be linked to the killings in some way and still be innocent, if he did them. And getting back to where we were before, what if she was head over heels in love with Manning and found out Evelyn was planning some new scheme to hurt him?"

That last was an argument, Voss decided, which might be applied also to Sue Lyons.

He said, "There's no question that Cynthia was in the boat?"

"Practically none. We got Gardenia to follow her scent and it went right to the edge of the water."

"Did you try the hound with Decker's scent?"

"No. We should have, maybe, but we didn't. Pretty late to try it now. I'm going to have another long talk with Decker today. He seems a nice fellow, but nobody knows much about him. Came here two years or so ago. Keeps to himself a lot. Walks in the country. And he's crazy about Cynthia."

"What about the Dawson blackmail angle?"

"If there was blackmail," said Proctor, "that thousand dollars on the dresser didn't have anything to do with it unless Dawson blackmailed somebody for it six weeks ago. Dawson deposited that much in the Long Island National Bank on April twenty-seventh and drew it out Saturday morning."

"How about the tides, Proctor? What's it like when people drown in the bay?"

"If Cynthia drowned last night, after midnight, it's not likely we'll ever find her body. The tide causes an under-current. It would carry a body out into the Sound, and usually that's the end of it."

Voss was silent.

"Ben Thoad's coming over with the hound this afternoon," Proctor said, breaking the pause. "We're going to try to get somewhere with those shoes. We'll let Gardenia smell 'em and then lead her around town to see if she'll pick up a trail."

He opened the desk drawer in which he had placed the shoes and the belt. He stiffened. He swore roundly, opened other drawers and looked wildly about.

"Gone?" Voss asked.

"Gone." Proctor raised his voice. "Backus!"

The sallow policeman shuffled into the room apprehensively.

"What did you do with those tennis shoes I put in my desk yesterday?"

Backus wet his lips. "I don't know nothing about 'em."

"Who was here when I was out?"

"Nobody. Or everybody, I guess I should say. All them reporters. You know how folks drift through here."

"It's the first time anybody drifted through my desk drawers," Proctor said. "Get out." He rested his chin in his hand and took the cigar from between his teeth and put it back again. "Match?" he said.

Voss pointed wordlessly to the folders of matches on the desk. Proctor opened one, tore out a match, struck it and lighted the cigar. He put the folder in his vest pocket. He picked up a pencil and began to draw new triangles and circles on the desk pad.

"I've got some pencil work to do myself," Voss said, rising. "It's high time I started making a list of the things we know, such as they are."

"What good will that do? Thael might be able to imagine the missing information and make a story of it, but we've got to deal with facts."

"Not altogether. Thael's work isn't so very different from a good detective's. A story has to have certain psychological elements and a certain continuity of mood to hang together, and so does a crime. Both form a pattern which is more or less conventionalized, although capable of infinite variations. If you can get enough of the elements of a crime in their proper relation to one another sometimes you can guess pretty accurately at the rest."

"I wouldn't know about that," Proctor growled. "I'm just a small-town cop, too old to learn anything. Good luck to you, just the same."

The sky had become overcast, promising rain, when Voss left the town hall. He was at the edge of the square when he heard someone running across the lawn after him. It was King, the *Record* reporter.

"Slow up those long legs," King puffed. "I'm hunting Thael. You seen him?"

"He went into the restaurant half an hour or so ago."

"I know. He told the Greek there he'd just found out who the murderer was. He tried to phone you and beat it in a hurry."

"He's rooming just around the corner."

"I've been there. No dice."

"You'll catch him," Voss said. "In Waldham you meet every able-bodied inhabitant once every two hours. Probably he's only got a hunch that isn't any better than another person's hunch."

But he felt his interest mounting, just the same, as King hurried away. With all his Greenwich Village sophistication and glib phraseology Thael wasn't given to false alarms. It was not beyond the realm of credulity that he had happened on some pertinent if not vital information.

Voss changed his direction and went toward the café. It was an hour before lunch time and the only person visible inside was Joe, the swarthy proprietor, deep in the perusal of that morning's *Record*. Voss seated himself on a stool at the porcelain counter, twined his legs around its base and called for coffee.

Joe's face and tongue became animated when he recognized his customer.

"You seen that writer guy Thael? The cops let him loose again. He's lookin' for you. Claims he's got evidence that'll convict the guy what done the murders."

"Who is his candidate for the electric chair?"

At the coffee urn Joe shrugged. "I asked him but he wouldn't say. He was lookin' at this here paper and all at once he jumps up like he set on a stove and says he's doped it all out. He jumps clear to the phone and tries to ring you. Then he goes out without payin'."

"Put it on my check."

Joe shook his head vigorously. "Nix. He's gonna come back and pay. He's just excited."

"How long ago was it?"

"Half an hour, maybe. No longer."

Voss sipped his coffee and looked out the window. A thin drizzle not much heavier than a mist had started. He left his cup half full, laid a nickel on the counter and went out. He hurried, hoping to get to the inn before the rain increased. As it was his clothes were sodden and his hair was plastered dankly to his head when he entered the lobby.

The room clerk said, "A message for you, Mr. Voss." He pushed a slip of paper across the counter. Someone had penciled on the slip, "Mr. Thael phoned 10:35—will call again."

Voss bought a *Record* at the desk and went up to his room. He removed his damp clothing and wrapped his bony frame in a purple silk dressing gown. He stretched himself on the bed with his head propped upon two pillows and his heels balanced on the crossbar at the foot and took up the paper.

The front-page headline said:

RICH BEAUTY MISSING;
FEARED KILLER'S 3RD

The rest of the page was given over to a large picture of Cynthia, obtained evidently from some friend, and smaller pictures of Evelyn Lister and Art Dawson.

The murder story told Voss nothing he did not already know, nor was there anything else in the paper that in his opinion might have given Thael his inspiration. Voss read it carefully, not skipping the comic strips or the lovelorn column or the back-page sports picture of two boxers, the left-handed welterweight champion and the title contender, facing each other in their fighting postures. Then he tossed the paper on the dresser, put on another shirt and a tweed suit, combed his hair and went downstairs to lunch.

The drizzle continued, not increasing in intensity or cooling the atmosphere appreciably. Voss returned to his room, cleared off the writing table and arranged sheets of paper upon it. With a fountain pen he began to outline two separate theoretical explanations of Waldham's recent murders, treating them as a single crime. One theory began with the death of Brewster Lyons; the other ignored that mystery as being unrelated to the newer tragedies.

In connection with the first line of thought he wrote down the names of Terry Whitcomb, Jenny Midge, Garth Manning, Cynthia Carrington and Sue Lyons. In his second list he included all those and also the names of George Thael and Ralph Decker, who had come to Waldham since Brewster's death.

He meditated, then added the names of Jack and Lila Miller to both lists. After further deliberation he placed Eddie Braithe's name along with Irv Proctor's at the bottom of the second list.

There was hardly a decent alibi among the lot of them, he reflected. Thael had the best alibi for the time of Dawson's death. Irv could probably produce witnesses to his presence elsewhere on both fatal occasions. The Millers might have the word of their neighbors and others that they were at the movies Saturday night and Braithe could presumably show that he had phoned the *Record* by long distance from his office that same evening. But as alibis went not any of them seemed definitely puncture-proof.

The phone rang. It was not Thael, but Cornelius Proctor wanting to know about Thael.

"I heard how he was shooting his mouth off," Proctor said. "What was there to it?"

Voss explained that he did not know.

"I'll send somebody to look him up," Proctor said. "I've just been talking to Decker. Couldn't get two connected words out of him. The man is crazy—literally crazy—on account of what's happened to Cynthia. . . . And now I guess I've got to go to Dawson's funeral, rain or no rain. It's at two if you feel like taking it in."

"No, thanks," Voss declined.

He tried to get back to his paper work after that, but the task seemed pointless. He could not carry either line of thought to even a tentative conclusion until he knew what had become of Cynthia. She had run away or had drowned accidentally or had taken her own life or had been murdered. It seemed imperative that he know which, as much for his inner peace of mind as for his hope of bringing a killer to the end of his destructive run.

He paced the room restlessly and then stretched out on the bed once more. It was hard to understand why Thael had not phoned a second time. Thael might have been prevented, of course. Joe the Greek had probably talked to people who had talked to everybody, including the person Thael suspected.

It was nearly four by Voss's wrist watch when the rain stopped and pale rays of sunshine slanted out of the west. He left the inn and walked down the dirt road toward Hill Street intending to find Thael. He had, strangely, an inexplicable conviction that something more important than Dawson's funeral had happened that afternoon. There seemed to be tension in the very air that hinted at things happening.

The coolness was noticeable now. The soft earth was springy under Voss's rubber-shod feet. There was a fresh sweet fragrance in the light breeze. The grass was greener than it had been.

Close by the clump of alders that screened the entrance to the hillside path Voss spied an object that did not belong among the tall weeds. He went nearer, his pulse quickening as he recognized the shape of a carpenter's claw hammer. He stepped over it, his eyes probing the shadows beneath the alders. He saw almost at once the thing which, he realized suddenly, he had expected all along to see.

George Thael was sprawled on his belly on the wet earth, his arms and legs outflung. His head was turned sidewise so that the left cheek was hidden. The right side of his face was masked from temple to chin with bright blood which had run down to stain the dead leaves beneath.

10

The clank and rumble of ponderous machinery came around the curve of the road. Voss stepped into the ruts and saw a big gray dump truck jouncing toward him. He held up his hand and as the machine slowed down he read the insignia of the county department of public works. A wizened little man craned his neck around the spattered windshield.

"No riders," the little man yelled. "Get off the road!"

Voss lifted his voice above the clatter of the motor. "I don't want a ride. I want help. I want to get word to the chief of police and the medical examiner."

The driver's eyes bulged. "What happened? Another one?"

Voss bent his head impatiently. "Don't stop to ask questions, man! You can come back and find out all about it."

"I get you. You want a cop, eh?" The man squirmed back behind the wheel.

"I want Chief Proctor. And tell him to send Doc Manning."

The truck roared down the road past the cemetery gate and careened into Main Street. Voss pushed his way back into the dripping alders to kneel beside Thael. There was little doubt in his mind that the writer of mysteries was dead. He knew how terribly effective a weapon a hammer could be.

Yet, when he lifted one of Thael's arms, stirring the whole body, there was a fresh flow of blood from the great wound in the skull. And when he turned the limp form over and felt beneath the wet shirt over the heart there was, incredibly, a faint pulse.

Voss looked about him, considering. The inn was more than a hundred yards away and the yacht club nearly as far. He could have lifted the injured man and staggered under his weight to one building or the other, but he was not sure the carrying might not injure Thael further. He contented himself finally with stripping off his own coat, raising Thael's head gently and arranging a makeshift pillow for him.

That done, the criminologist studied the ground and the bushes for signs of a struggle. There were broken twigs where Thael had crashed through the alders and there was one spot near the hammer where feet had scuffed up the roots of grass. But the slow rain, which had helped the would-be killer by driving potential witnesses indoors, had also obliterated any clear footprints there might have been. It would not make it easier to bring out any fingerprints on the handle of the hammer, either, if the person who wielded it had been careless enough to leave any.

It seemed a long time, although it could not have been over ten or fifteen minutes, before a small sedan came out of Hill Street and turned into the narrow road. Voss saw Irv behind the wheel and his father hunched beside him. The car skidded in the ruts and stopped and both men jumped out.

"Who is it?" the police chief demanded, his face haggard. "Not Cynthia?"

"It's Thael," Voss said. "He's still alive, but I wouldn't be surprised if he's done for."

"Alive!" Irv uttered the word as though he could not believe it. He touched the hammer with the toe of his shoe and stared intently through the branches at the unconscious man. "The truck driver said he'd been killed."

"Is Manning on the way?" Voss inquired.

"Hell no," replied the chief. "We didn't take time to stop for him. Like Irv says, we thought it was all over. Abelard, why don't you take the car and get Manning while Irv and I look around?"

Voss got into the sedan instantly, crowding his knees beneath the wheel. He turned the ignition key, started the motor and swung the car around. He drove to Manning's house as fast as he dared with his long legs cramped uncomfortably over brake and clutch pedals.

He left the motor running in front of Manning's house and sprinted for the open door where the sign said walk in. He did so, his soft shoes making no sound against the tiled floor of the reception room.

Through the closed door of the doctor's office came a woman's voice speaking his name, bringing him to an abrupt halt.

"I think," Sue Lyons was saying within the office, "Abelard Voss suspects us both."

Dr. Manning's voice, replying to her, was unworried. "What if he does? He may be as smart as some people say, but he still can't prove we killed anyone."

"He must know you were in Cynthia's boat close to the scene when the Lister girl was killed. I recognized you going away after I'd heard the motor stop as though you might have landed for a little while. I saw the body about the same time and was so frightened I dropped my handkerchief and had to pick Voss's pocket to get it back. Garth, I—I was sure you had killed her."

"Sue!"

"I didn't blame you. I thought she deserved it. I wouldn't have said a word to save my life. Anyway I haven't forgotten I owe you my life."

"You don't. If you'll remember the circumstances you'll recall that the only thing I could have done was die with you." Manning was still for a space while Voss breathed stealthily, waiting for the next words from beyond the door, not wanting to eavesdrop, but unwilling to miss overhearing what he might be able to learn no other way.

"What happened Friday—" Manning continued finally, "I borrowed Cynthia's boat because I'd been playing tennis and it was hot and the water looked too cool to pass up. I'd promised to get over to see Decker. I was around the bend in the shoreline just below the hill when the motor went dead. I don't know why I didn't think of the gas tank right off. I fooled with the ignition and the carburetor for a few minutes before I found out the fuel was used up. There was a can of gasoline in the boat, luckily, and I filled up and went on. Meanwhile I'd drifted almost into shore."

"I'm glad to hear it," Sue told him. "You don't know how worried I've been. Not so much because of my own ideas as because of what Voss might think. He must know you were on the hill when Brewster was killed because he knows you met Cynthia there, but I wonder if he suspects I was with you when the shot was fired?"

"It's all funny and mixed up. You know it's only by the grace of God I didn't kill Evelyn. I was considering it seriously. . . . Don't jump like that. . . . I'd been steering clear of her, but I guess she needed money pretty badly because she came around and tried to borrow some and when I wouldn't lend it to her she threatened to sue me again for exactly the same thing. Even if she couldn't win another case, she said, she could make plenty of trouble for me and ruin my practice.

"She could have, too, and I believe she would have. And I was filled up to the neck with scandal and black-mail. I'd have murdered her in a minute and risked prison or the electric chair before I'd have gone through another siege of it."

"I understand perfectly," Sue murmured. "It would hurt Cynthia terribly to have you get into another scandal. . . . Oh, don't try to tell me again you don't love her—"

Voss coughed. He rattled the knob of the outer door and trod heavily on the floor. He called loudly, "Dr. Manning!"

The physician opened the door of the office. He looked angry. He said, "Voss! What the devil—?"

"Someone tried to kill George Thael," Voss interrupted. "Broke his head with a hammer. He's still alive over by the inn. I've got a car outside."

Sue had appeared at Manning's shoulder. Voss watched both their faces. He saw there surprise, confusion and uncertainty.

Manning controlled himself. "Wait till I toss a few things in my bag." He ducked back into the office.

"How much do you know about it?" Sue asked, eyeing Voss searchingly. "Have you got the one who tried to kill him? Do you have any idea who it was?"

"I just found him. Proctor and Irv are there now looking for clues. If he lives he'll probably be able to tell who was after him."

She repeated, "If he lives."

All at once Voss thought, *What if Manning used that hammer? Wouldn't he have a beautiful chance to finish the job now!*

Then, looking past Sue into the office, Voss forgot all else seeing in the cold fireplace a half-consumed wad of paper. In itself the charred object was innocent enough—a copy of the *Courier*, still displaying its masthead in Old-English type. But it had not been there yesterday, and the logical way for Manning to dispose of a newspaper he no longer wanted would seem to be to toss it into the capacious wastebasket beside the desk. And, regarding the desk again, Voss was startled afresh to observe a second copy of the same paper neatly folded atop a pile of other periodicals.

Why, he asked himself, had the doctor burned an extra copy of the *Courier* so soon after that other extra copy had been found on Cynthia's porch with those ominous words trimmed out of its columns?

"No time to waste," Manning said, bringing his black bag and jamming a felt hat on his dark head. "You'll excuse me, Sue? We can get together tomorrow to talk about—about those headaches of yours."

"Headaches" was an apt word, Voss told himself, leading the way to Irv's sedan. He slid under the wheel and waited for Dr. Manning to get in and shut the door. He drove furiously, mindful of the precious minutes that had elapsed.

"The vultures are gathering." Manning pointed ahead where several cars were stopped. A restless little group had surrounded the alders. Voss recognized King and some of the other reporters. Braithe hung around the edge of the group, considerably subdued by the presence of experts in the business of crime reporting. Braithe's right eye was an angry streak of red in an area of blue and swollen flesh.

Voss braked the sedan and they got out and pushed their way through the crowd. Proctor was bent over Thael. Irv was working hard trying to keep reporters and photographers back from the motionless form.

"How d'you expect us to find any footprints or anything if you track up the ground?" Irv was pleading. "You can get pictures without stepping on him."

He nodded briefly to Voss and Manning and let them pass. Manning opened his bag, plugged the tubes of a stethoscope into his ears and unbuttoned Thael's shirt. He stooped and examined the wound, which was high in the side of the skull above the hairline. He poured some colorless liquid on a piece of gauze and wiped the blood away.

"Will he live?" Proctor asked hoarsely.

"How can I tell?" Manning's voice was testy. "He's alive, but his pulse is very low. There'll be concussion certainly and fractures for all I know. I'll have to see X-rays before I can be sure."

One of the reporters cried the question, "He's not apt to die tonight, is he, Doc? I've got to know. I've got to wire a story to my paper within an hour. If it's going to be another murder we'll want it in headlines."

Manning looked around at all of them.

"He won't die if I can help it. Not under my care. If he does half the people in town will swear I killed him." An expression of dismay came over his face as he saw one of the young men scribbling. "Hey—I don't want you to print that!"

Voss said, "They'll print it. Save your breath. If I were you and thought there was real danger I'd call in another consulting physician in self-defense."

Manning swore bitterly. "When there's a wrong thing to say or do I'm always Johnny-on-the-spot."

King drew Voss aside. "I wouldn't want the other papers to get this before the *Record* prints it," he said. "I went from door to door trying to get a line on Thael. An old lady in that house"—he pointed to a small white cottage opposite the cemetery gate—"told me she thought she saw him heading toward the inn about noon. I went to the inn thinking he'd called on you, but the clerk said you hadn't had any visitors or calls. So I thought maybe the old lady was mistaken."

"Thanks," Voss said. "It may mean something if we can find out that somebody else headed that way about the same time."

"That's what I was thinking. I'm going to keep up the door-to-door business. I'll compare notes with you if you'll give me what breaks you can."

"I won't hold back a thing I don't have to, King."

The chief and Irv Proctor were lifting Thael as tenderly as possible. Braithe was standing by his Zephyr sedan, the biggest car there, holding the door open. He had spread a robe over the rear seat. The two officers laid Thael on the seat and Manning got in beside him and Braithe drove away.

Proctor glanced ruefully at a dark stain on his sleeve. "They're taking him to Manning's office first," he informed Voss, "for emergency treatment and examination. After that they'll take him home or to a hospital, whichever seems best." He added after a moment's silence, "Or else to Tom Wilkins's morgue."

"Find any clues?"

"Not a sign or smell of one. Irv says there isn't a print on the hammer. For all the trail the slugger left he might have been Brewster Lyons's ghost."

"You know he might have been, at that," Voss said. "You've heard of discarnate spirits taking over a man's physical body and directing it?"

"Not me. Every time anybody started to talk about that sort of rot I put my fingers in my ears and beat it. Don't tell me you take it seriously."

"Not literally. But I've seen the memory or the example of dead men—which are their ghosts in a very real sense—inspire living men to murder. It amounts almost to the same thing."

"Now," Proctor mumbled, "I know why you're such a slick detective and I'm such a dumb cop. You're crazy. Too bad I wasn't dropped on my head when I was a little shaver."

"It wasn't a fall," Voss told him. "It's the way the ductless glands work in me. They're said to be the seat of psychic perception, by the way. Especially the thymus, which gave me my imagination, and the pituitary, which made me tall and skinny and ascetic."

"I haven't got a gland in me and I'm proud of it," Proctor retorted.

Irv was packing his photographic paraphernalia, with which he had made pictures of Thael and the scene of the assault.

"I'd rope off the spot if we had a man to watch it," he said to no one in particular. "But if Thael lives we'll have to keep somebody guarding him day and night till this is cleared up and that will leave us shorthanded. What we need is a bigger police force."

"And a better one," stage-whispered someone in the ranks of the newspapermen.

The sun was down below the hilltop now and the shadows were long and chill. The brown path twisted up the incline ahead of them, dusky and mysterious. Voss shivered and picked up his coat. It was too soiled with mud and gore to put on and he stood holding it away from him.

Irv said suddenly, "Listen."

After a second or two Voss heard it—a rhythmic scuffling, a gentle wheezing, beyond a turn in the path. It came nearer, sounding plainer in their ears. Their eyes were centered with one accord at the point where the path was lost in the undergrowth.

One second the spot was vacant; the next it was occupied by a fantastic hunched shape, solid gray except where dark eyes blazed. All around Voss men caught their breath sharply and he was as startled as the rest of them, although he knew even before the queer figure emerged from the shadows that it was only Jenny Midge.

She came on toward them without hesitation, dragging one foot after the other with that odd gait that just missed being a limp. She paused beside the alders and looked knowingly at the crimson stain against the leaves. She raised her old arms in a gloating gesture for all the world like a witch out of a weird tale.

"The devil is claiming his own," she said in her deep harsh tones. "Soon all of them will drown in blood."

Here and there in the little group were quick movements. Cameras pointed at the insane creature. Shutters clicked.

11

"I should have pinched her," Cornelius Proctor muttered wildly. "I should have slapped Jenny Midge right in the cell Thael came out of and told her she wouldn't get out till she talked sense." He rumpled his sparse hair with his thick fingers. "But my God, Voss, I'd go off my nut completely if I had her on my hands! I couldn't stand the glare in her eyes and the croaking way she talks. Do you blame me?"

Voss shook his head with more than a trace of sympathy. He was perched on the edge of the chief's desk. Irv sprawled in a chair in a corner of the office. An hour had passed since Thael had been taken to Manning's cottage and they were waiting restlessly for some definite word of his condition and his chances for recovery.

"Even if she pretended to be sensible we couldn't believe her," Irv said. "It would have made things a lot simpler for us if the murderer had picked on her in the first place—if she isn't the murderer. Nobody would have cared much."

Proctor frowned at his son. "That's no way to talk." He began to make meaningless pencil marks on the pad before him. "In New York they'd have locked her up," he went on. "They'd figure she must have seen Thael lying there when she went up the path even if she didn't lay him out. She'd

be guilty of something or other just because she didn't
report it. But in New York she'd be sent to Bellevue and a
gang of doctors and nurses would be put to work on her.
She wouldn't have a chance to drive the cops screwy."

Voss said, "Let her alone for a while. If Thael comes
through all right he may clear up the whole business. We
can be pretty sure he was attacked because he'd been saying he knew the killer—"

"Or because he was guilty and wanted to make sure we
wouldn't suspect him any more," Irv put in with unexpected savagery. "How do we know he didn't hit himself with
that hammer? That kind of thing has been done."

"It has been done," Voss admitted, "but seldom that
thoroughly. Remember he was hit twice and either blow
would have put a man to sleep. I'd like to be sure he'll
have a bodyguard from now on."

"He'll have Backus," the chief said. "I'd hate to have
my own chances for living depend on Backus, but I can't
spare anyone else. I gave him a long lecture that maybe
will keep him on his toes for the next day or two."

The phone rang. Proctor sat up straight. "You want to
bet it isn't bad news?" he asked. He reached for the phone
without waiting for a reply.

They could all hear a girl's voice in the receiver. Irv
arose and said, "For me?" His father gave him the phone
and Irv held the receiver so tightly against his ear that the
voice over the wire was no longer audible to the others. He
said, "Hello," and listened. His face brightened. "Right
away," he said. He hung up and left the office without a
word, closing the door behind him.

"What's a murder," Proctor inquired sarcastically,
"when a youngster's got a girl on the brain?"

Voss stretched out a spindly leg and hooked his toe beneath the rung of the chair Irv had occupied, drawing it

close. He sat in it and rested his elbows on the desk and his chin in his hands.

"Do you know why I came to Waldham?" he asked Proctor.

The policeman looked up sharply. "I know you told me you were thinking of writing up Brewster Lyons's demise." His eyes narrowed. "I didn't believe that was all there was to it. I think somebody hired you to come down here—somebody who had an idea things were going to happen."

"You're partly right. A person sent me five hundred dollars as a retainer and wanted me to find out who killed Brewster, if anyone did. That person didn't give his name or any details, but he said I might save an innocent life by clearing up the old mystery." Briefly Voss described the letter he had received in New York. "It's a secret as far as anyone else is concerned," he finished, "but I thought you might be able to give me an idea of whom it could be."

"You mean to say you'd take on a job without knowing who you were working for?"

"I haven't taken on a thing. Not having anything better to do I came to Waldham to look the situation over. I got here just in time for a homicide, although I doubt whether Evelyn's was the innocent life the writer of the letter believed was in jeopardy. When I find out who wrote that letter and why, I'll decide whether or not I've been working for him."

"*If* you find out."

"I will. The answer is bound to show up along with the other answers."

"You're going to see it through regardless, then?"

"Yes." Voss's tone was so self-assured as to be almost boastful. "I've never looked into any criminal case I didn't see through. I've never failed to get the right answers one way or another. This time I'm in it to my neck, and you can see how deep that is." His gray eyes twinkled. "If I have to work without a fee—if I have to give back the five hundred I've already been paid—it will just be my tough luck."

Proctor stroked his nose reflectively. "Damned if I can think who'd write to you. That is, it could be almost anybody who was anxious to see the thing cleared up. Of course, you being an expensive proposition, it wouldn't be anybody poor. Sue Lyons, I understand, is close to being dead broke, with no prospects—"

"I doubt if it was Sue."

"Terry Whitcomb is our richest man. He used to be a playboy, but now he lives like a tramp and leaves the handling of all his affairs to the bank. Cynthia Carrington probably comes next. In fact there are quite a few people here with money enough for private investigators."

"We won't learn much by measuring bank accounts."

"Maybe not, but how else can we get started?"

"Let me see your notes. Maybe we can find a starting point there."

"Notes!" The police chief was indignant. "Abelard, it's all I can do to keep my records straight. I don't scribble for amusement like you authors. The only notes that bother me are my promissory ones in other people's hands."

"Then it's time you had a lesson. Take that pad and tear off the sheet with your pretty pictures of stars and moons. Write at the top of the first clean sheet 'The Crimes.'"

Proctor did so reluctantly, looking rather foolish. He said, "Go on."

"Now write what I tell you." Voss dictated slowly. "'Evelyn Lister was murdered Friday, July seventh, about seven-thirty in the evening at the spot where Brewster Lyons was killed seven years ago. The criminal struck her a single fatal blow with a rock and left an obscure note purporting to give a reason for his act.'"

"I know all that already," Proctor grumbled. "I've written it, though."

"You might add a note to the effect that the time is uncertain. We think she was killed in the interval between Sue Lyons's and my first passing of the spot and our return. She might conceivably have been dead when we first saw her, however, since neither of us saw her move. Thael might have heard us coming and propped up a corpse for our benefit."

"Good Lord, Voss, I never thought—"

"Don't think of it now. It's a very remote possibility. Make a new paragraph. Write, 'Arthur Dawson, her sweetheart, was murdered Saturday, July eighth, at nine-thirty in the evening in his bedroom. The criminal stabbed him several times with a dime-store paper knife and left a similar note.'"

"Got it." Proctor scribbled rapidly and with concentration.

"'George Thael was assaulted with murderous intent Monday, July tenth, shortly after noon, while presumably on his way to give important evidence regarding the foregoing murders. The criminal struck him twice with an ordinary claw hammer. There was no note, which may indicate that the assault was not planned in advance, but became necessary to the criminal quite suddenly.' That's all for that sheet."

The policeman stared gloomily at the paper. "I can see how this would help if a man didn't have a memory."

"You're only at the beginning," Voss explained. "As you work over your notes you'll add a good many details about each crime. Some of them will strike you as significant in the light of your other notes."

"There's more, then?"

"There's a lot more. Start another sheet. Write at the top 'The Motives.'" He waited. "Now take this: 'It is almost certain Evelyn was killed by someone to whom she presented an insuperable obstacle that could not be removed by ordinary, safer means—'"

"Spell 'insuperable,' Abelard."

"Leave it out. What I mean is, she was in the way of something the criminal had to have or she was a menace to the criminal's life or liberty. The theory of blackmail would fill the bill."

"I get you."

"New paragraph. 'It is possible Dawson was killed for the same reason, but more likely he died because he knew the criminal and so became a new obstacle in his own right.'

"New paragraph again. 'Thael was undoubtedly assaulted because he had mentioned possessing information that would expose the criminal.'"

"Okay. It sounds reasonable enough, Abelard."

"You're only starting. Write at the head of another sheet of paper 'Character of the Criminal.'"

"Ah! We're getting somewhere now."

"'He—or she—is utterly ruthless and dangerous. There is every evidence of unhesitant action timed so perfectly it must have been planned to the last detail. He or she has a morbid imagination that delights in mysterious gestures as exemplified by the notes left with each of the two corpses, plus arrogance and considerable self-esteem. Very probably the criminal is in evidence every day, pretending to want to help solve the crimes or taking what would seem to be a normal interest in them. . . .'"

"Don't stop now. We're getting down to brass tacks, Abelard."

"We're getting to the heart of the pattern. Things are beginning to take shape. If you've got the idea we'll go on to the fourth page. That might be headed 'The Criminal's Next Steps.'"

"You mean you've doped out what he'll do next?"

"Some of the things he'll do are fairly obvious. In all likelihood there will be another attempt to kill Thael if it turns out the first try was a failure and the necessity for silencing him remains. And the evidence of a third note already prepared seems to indicate pretty conclusively that one of two things is planned—the suicide of the criminal, ending the series of crimes, or the murder of still another person, dressed up to look like a suicide. I'd say we ought to look out for murder."

"Cynthia. . . ."

Voss's lean face grew hard and grim. His big fists clenched slowly. "I hope not, Proctor."

"So do I, Abelard. I'd rather be killed myself than see it happen to her. But what can we do?"

"We can take another sheet of paper," Voss said. "We can make a list of suspects and suspicious facts in connection with them. Give me the name of someone you've been suspicious of."

"Manning." It was Proctor's turn to be stern.

Voss took a leather-covered notebook from his pocket and found a certain page. "'Garth Manning.'" he read. "'Was made the goat in a sordid scandal by Evelyn and may have been facing a second experience of the same kind.'" He remembered the conversation he had heard through the door of the physician's office and mentally changed the "may have been" to "was." He continued, "'He was close to the hill when Evelyn was killed, if not on it. He might have been the man Thael saw ascending the hill. . . . He was away from the yacht club the night Dawson was killed and cannot produce witnesses to substantiate his story of where he went. . . .'"

"I haven't checked yet on his movements this afternoon, Proctor, but I have compared his characteristics with some of those I have ascribed to the criminal. In a good many ways they're alike."

Proctor growled, "If I was a grand jury I'd give you an indictment right now."

"Try another name."

"Jenny Midge."

Voss found another page and glanced at it. "She was close to the scene of Evelyn's demise," he said, following notes but not reading this time. "Evelyn had trespassed on Jenny's sacred ground in the cemetery and in the old house beside the hill. Jenny is filled so completely with hatreds and carefully nourished thoughts of vengeance that what might be an ordinary dislike to another person could easily become a motive for murder in her disordered mind. Having started on a career of murder she would be apt to continue till she had destroyed everyone she considered deserving of death, or until she was stopped.

"She is fairly well educated and doubtless very clever in her unbalanced way. She has practically every one of the characteristics the criminal has."

Proctor's jaw dropped. "By God, I believe you're right! She was a bright girl when I was a youngster, but always queer. . . . Abelard, it's those characteristics I can't seem to spot. I can sometimes tell whether a person is a shady sort or one I can trust, but that's about as far as I can go in analyzing people. Is there some simple rule I could follow?"

"Use your eyes, your ears and your head," Voss told him. "Cultivate that sixth sense people call intuition. Take a university course in psychology and go beyond it, paying special attention to abnormal manifestations. Read Freud, Krafft-Ebing, Jung and the others. Keep track of all crimes as they happen and make records of their significant points and compare them. Learn to observe scientifically—"

"Hold everything! I can handle our local traffic violators with no more college diplomas than I've got now, which is none. That's all I have to do most of the time. If we don't have murders oftener than every seven years in

Waldham I'll call you in when they happen and give you full charge. When my old car breaks down I don't start studying mechanics; I call an expert."

"I guess you could call me an expert," Voss murmured with a trace of vanity. "I'm pretty good on murders. Not that I didn't have to work hard to get good. . . ."

"Tell me one thing," Proctor broke in. "Haven't you got a pretty good idea who did the killings?"

"I have," Voss told him gravely. "One person, more than any other, seems to me to fill the bill in all particulars."

"Well, then, what are we fooling around with this stuff for? Tell me who he is, Abelard. We'll go to work on him in a big way. We'll find some excuse to lift him out of circulation, to keep him in jail—"

"Not this person." Voss's eyes narrowed and his lean jaw hardened. "You'd have the whole town up in arms if you made the arrest I'm thinking of without plenty of proof. You'd make it impossible ever to get a conviction. If the case could be handled your way, do you think I'd let a murderer run free a second longer than I had to?"

"You could at least give me some idea."

"Not now. I don't want the culprit to have the faintest notion we're suspicious. I want you to think along the lines I've indicated and see if you can arrive at the same conclusion I have. You might just happen to hit on the one thing I've missed—the weakness in the murderer's plan that will give us the advantage we need."

Proctor sighed. "All right, Abelard. I'll keep on with these notes. Damned if they aren't beginning to look like something. I'll put down in the list of suspects—let me see—Manning, Jenny, Terry, Decker . . . yes, and Sue and Cynthia in the bargain. That's six. Maybe I'll think of some others. I'll check all their alibis again, such as they are."

"First of all," Voss warned, "try to give yourself a picture of how the criminal should look and act. If you haven't any scientific foundation, imagination is the best substitute. Build up the picture as much as you can. Then compare it with each of your suspects and see if you can modify it to fit him—or her—without destroying any main characteristics of either."

Proctor grinned. "I'll do it," he said. "By God, I will!"

There were footsteps in the corridor. Someone opened the office door and held it and Dale Parsons came in timidly. Voss got to his feet and smiled. Proctor stared at the girl in undisguised astonishment.

"Come in and sit," Voss invited, placing the chair for her. "I've been hoping for a chance to talk to you."

Irv appeared in the doorway behind her. He said, watching her anxiously, "Dale phoned me to meet her so she could tell me things that may be important to our investigation. I convinced her she ought to tell you, too. She doesn't want to make trouble for anyone who may be innocent and I promised to keep her name put of it as far as possible."

"We're used to keeping secrets," Voss said. "It's part of our stock-in-trade. Sit down and stop worrying, Dale."

She was worrying considerably. Her eyes were frightened and her face was pale. She was quite unlike the poised, carefree young thing Voss had danced with Saturday night before anyone had begun to realize how black a pall of horror was settling over Waldham. Yet for all her nervousness she was still as pretty as a figurine of Dresden china.

"I've been thinking an awful lot about the . . . murders," she told them, sitting straight on the edge of the chair. "It came to me I might know something—not anything definite—but something that would help. . . ."

"The good Lord knows we need help," Proctor rumbled sententiously.

"What I say won't hurt anyone who might be innocent?" she asked.

"No one will ever know you told anything about him," Voss assured her. "We're not going to accuse anyone till we have actual proof."

She appeared to be satisfied. "I was on the golf course Thursday afternoon, the day before Evelyn Lister was killed," she began. "I was trying to get in eighteen holes—"

"And get rid of two ounces of your ninety-seven pounds," Voss supplied.

"That's it." She smiled at him and relaxed a little. "Well, after the fourteenth hole I saw I'd have to hurry to meet Eddie, who was going to call for me, and I went back to the clubhouse. I saw Ralph Decker and Evelyn Lister talking together, almost hidden by the corner of the building. Neither of them saw me."

"Just talking?" Proctor inquired.

"Decker was mad. His face was red and furious. He talked so loud I couldn't help hearing him. He said, 'Why, you little tramp, I ought to shoot you!'" She paused. "Only he didn't use the word 'tramp—'"

"That's all right," Voss said. "What else did you hear?"

"Nothing else. I went into the locker room for a shower. When I came out fifteen or twenty minutes later Decker was sitting on the steps alone with his face in his hands. He didn't even look up when I went past him."

Proctor stated solemnly, "Evelyn was up to her old tricks."

"There's another thing about her," said Irv. "Tell it, Dale."

"All right. . . . This was a long time ago, two months or more. I'd come home on the late train from a show in New York. There was a bright moon. I passed Evelyn on the street—she didn't speak, but I knew it was she—and she was going toward the Whitcomb house. I looked back a minute or two later and saw her going into the house. I was only about a block away, so I couldn't have been mistaken. . . . Oh, I feel like an old gossip telling these things!"

"They may be more important than you think. Did you see anything else?"

"That was all."

Irv was inexorable. "There is something else. Tell them about that—about Eddie Braithe."

"Oh, Irv, he was just talking to hear himself." She appealed to Voss. "You know how these boys are, always trying to make an impression."

Voss grinned. "You'd know that better than I. Just the same I'd like to know what he said."

"It was so silly. . . . We were driving past the cemetery and Eddie pointed to Brewster Lyons's grave and said, 'That fellow must be right at home in hell. He was a devil incarnate. He killed himself in such a way that others will have to bear the burden of the blame all their lives.' I wasn't sure what he meant and I didn't ask him. Eddie is always trying to work out his own explanation of things and he always believes he's right till someone proves he isn't."

"He must have been riding on his own imagination," decided Proctor. "He couldn't possibly know anything about it first hand. He was in college when it happened, staying through summer school to make up some credits. I remember because Irv was there at the same time for the same purpose."

"Braithe might have been guessing," said Voss, "and he might have been guessing right. If Brewster actually did something like that it would explain a lot of things that have been bothering me. In fact I've been working out some such theory of my own."

"Theorize all you want," grunted the chief. "We'll never know."

Voss disagreed. "I think we will. I'm sure we will if we try hard enough to find out."

"Maybe we ought to ask Eddie Braithe to join our detective division and—"

Someone coughed outside the open office door. Proctor ended his sarcastic suggestion prematurely and glowered toward the sound. Voss was acutely aware of the embarrassment of all of them as Braithe came into the room.

Braithe's right eye was grotesque, but the rest of his clean-featured face was grave. The flippant humor that had seemed so much a part of him was no longer in evidence.

"I've been listening for three minutes," he said. "Couldn't resist the temptation when I heard my name spoken. I guess you're all thinking I might have done the murders, aren't you?"

Dale would not look at him. She cried in a small voice, "Eddie, you don't think—?"

"I don't think anything you wouldn't want me to, Dale. With murders happening all around I think everybody should tell Proctor and Voss everything they know and everything they suspect. What you said about me was true and I still think I've got it doped out right."

Proctor cleared his throat. "Listening outside my office," he growled. "Sneaking around like a spy. What business have you got here, anyway?"

The corners of Braithe's mouth twitched. "Manning sent me. Said you'd be glad to hear Thael isn't hurt as badly as we thought. He's conscious."

"Did he tell anything?" Voss asked.

Braithe shook his head negatively. "He was vague. The shock was worse than the wounds. He has a concussion but no fractures. Manning thinks it's an amnesia."

"Then," Proctor said, "he won't ever be able to tell who socked him?"

"Manning wouldn't know about that. Amnesia may last for a few hours or a few days or a lifetime."

"I'll bet a quarter," Proctor said, "this amnesia will last a lifetime. Everything else that has happened so far has been bad luck for us. It would be too much to hope Thael would clear the whole thing up with a dozen words. . . . Braithe, what's all this rot about Lyons killing himself to make trouble for other people?"

"It's an idea of mine. I can't prove it. But if you'll remember, Brewster was a queer sort of duck. He was shy and afraid of people. He had an awful inferiority complex. He was sick. He was so jealous of Cynthia he couldn't see straight.

"I couldn't say how he did it, but it would be like him to commit suicide and to do it in such a way that suspicion and fear would be left behind. He'd want to think people would worry about his death and keep worrying as long as they lived. . . . Do you follow me, Voss?"

"I follow you. I'll go a long way toward agreeing with you."

"My idea can be carried a lot further. I've got a hunch Dawson and Evelyn were killed because of the suspicion and fear Brewster left behind. Sweet little Evvie would be scheming day and night how she could make money out of it, suspecting some particular person, and her boy friend would be hand in glove with her. They'd finally have that person ringed around with so many threats and so much half-baked evidence that even if he didn't kill Brewster he'd be afraid of being arrested and tried for it and possibly convicted. So he'd kill them, wouldn't he?"

"Who would?" Irv demanded.

Braithe shrugged. "I'm guessing. You can put in a name as well as I can. There are a lot of crazy people in Waldham besides Jenny Midge."

Irv stood up. "I need air," he said. "Shall we go, Dale?"

She looked at Braithe inquiringly.

The young editor smiled. "Run along, Dale." He said to Irv, "I don't mind your taking her home this time."

Irv balled his fists and looked Braithe in the eye for a long half-minute. Proctor sat forward in his chair and placed his hands flat on top of the desk. Voss tensed his lean muscles, ready to intervene at the first sign of a blow being struck.

But Irv at length only said, "Thanks." He said it sardonically. He looked at Dale and she got up and they went out of the office together.

The chief said, "Damn it, Braithe—you love trouble, don't you?"

"No, I don't. You've got me wrong. Irv needs lessons in holding back his temper and holding up his guard in a scrap. I'm willing to give them to him. . . . Voss, if I wait outside, can I have a word with you when you're through here?"

"I won't be two minutes," Voss said.

Braithe left. Proctor said, "Cocky little brat, isn't he? That punch in the eye didn't do him much good. Hope he tangles with Irv sometime when I'm not around to stop it and Irv takes him apart."

"Eddie has a good head on his shoulders, Proctor. Unfortunately he has a lot of ego along with it. He'd like to be important in this little epidemic of murder and the fact of the *Daily Record* superseding him with grown-up reporters has hurt his vanity. But I wouldn't be surprised if he'll be of use to us just the same."

"Hard to think of him being of any use to anybody. . . . Abelard, guess what I've been thinking about Manning and Thael."

"I wouldn't dare."

"I've been thinking Manning might have given Thael some sort of drug that would keep him from remembering what happened. Is a thing like that possible?"

"Yes. Scopolamine—truth serum—in certain doses can produce amnesia. So can a number of the barbituric and morphia preparations. They have to be administered by a man who knows what he's doing."

"Manning would know. I'm going over to his place and have a look for myself."

Braithe was waiting outside the entrance to the police station, leaning against a tree, lost in gloomy thought. He greeted Voss with an unaccustomed and unfeigned diffidence.

"I've got a favor to ask you, Voss. I'm like the little kid who couldn't bear to be left out of whatever was going on. My job as reporter for a big New York paper has dwindled to next to nothing. How about letting me help you catch the murderer?"

Voss tried hard not to grin. "I'd be tickled to have you or anyone else help me," he said. "Have you any notion what you might do?"

"One. Somebody ought to do some sleuthing around Terry Whitcomb. I'm a nosy guy, Voss, and I've found out just enough about Terry to know that things go on inside that big old house of his the devil himself couldn't improve on. It wouldn't surprise me a bit if Terry was your killer."

"I've had him in mind, Braithe. I intend to do some checking myself and I'd be grateful for the results of any checking you do. But remember, whatever you do is strictly on your own responsibility and you can find out more by legitimate means than by prowling and housebreaking. It's all right with me if you want to play detective, but don't get too enthusiastic."

"I'm no burglar," Braithe said. "You don't have to worry about me getting into trouble. . . . And there's another thing. Proctor thinks I'm screwy and he's sold on Irv, so I wouldn't want to tell him. Don't think I'm sore or jealous—but do you know who was playing around with Evelyn Lister a few weeks ago? Irv. They hung around Jenny Midge's house."

12

All the heat and humidity of the last four days seemed to have been gathered together to make Tuesday a day to try the patience of all men. The sun beat down from a sky that glittered at the zenith and darkened toward the horizon. The water of Waldham Bay was as glassy and oily as a swamp puddle, unruffled by any breeze.

"Storm's on the way," Dr. Manning observed to Abelard Voss when they met at the City Drugstore. "It can't come a minute too soon to suit me. The winters are fine; they bring me lots of business and the cold keeps my blood circulating the way it should. But damn July and August!"

Voss was balanced awkwardly on a stool at the soda fountain sipping an iced drink through a pair of straws. He had removed his coat and his pink-striped shirt was wet and clinging. He had compromised further with discomfort to the extent of loosening his tie and unbuttoning his wilting collar.

"Sit up, Manning, and have one of these concoctions," he invited. "When you've drunk it you're worse off than you were before, but it cools you going down. How's the patient?"

Manning slid to the stool beside Voss. "I'll try anything once. The patient isn't going to die. He isn't going to talk for a while, either, by the looks of things. Most of the time he's in a comatose state, which is natural enough for the time being, but even in the intervals when he seems wide awake his mind is as blank as a new sheet of paper."

"You're giving him drugs, of course."

Manning looked sidewise at his companion. "Sedatives. They're practically necessary. But they wouldn't make him forget his own name."

"I take it he may snap out of the fog almost any time."

"He may. I hope he does. Our police chief believes I've doped him purposely so he can't remember. That means the chief thinks I used that hammer on him."

"Did Proctor say so?"

"Not in so many words. But he hung around till midnight last night asking me what I was giving Thael and putting a lot of leading questions. Proctor never bothered to learn to be subtle. I think he firmly expects to send me to the electric chair before this is finished."

"Did he give Thael a police guard?"

"That fool Backus is sitting on my porch, littering it with cigarette stubs and ashes and matches. He was shooting craps with some of the reporters till he lost the two or three dollars he had to his pocket. If I wanted to kill Thael I wouldn't in the least mind having him guarded by Backus."

"How about a nurse? Does Thael need one?"

"He's got one. Mrs. Holmes asked for the job and I gave it to her. She's a practical nurse. Strangely enough she's taken quite an interest in Thael. He's the first writer she ever boarded and she considers it a romantic calling."

Voss asked, "Have you come to any conclusion about Cynthia Carrington?"

Manning's face darkened. "Yes. I'm convinced Cynthia is dead. How—whether by her own hand or someone else's or by accident—I don't know. It doesn't matter much in a way, from my point of view. If someone killed her I'd like to strangle him with my own hands, but there wouldn't even be much satisfaction in that."

"It's easy to see you thought a lot of her. I haven't given up hope of finding her safe, if that's any comfort."

"It isn't. . . . Yes, I thought a lot of her. I was never in love with her, although everyone in town will tell you differently. But I wanted to help her more than I ever wanted to help anyone. I've sacrificed time and money and effort to try to cure her of something no medicine can reach. I had a tremendous stake in her, professionally and personally, and if I could have pulled her through I'd have considered myself more richly rewarded than if I'd made a million dollars out of my practice. I thought I was winning. And now . . ." He made a gesture of futility.

"You never thought of hiring detectives to cure her, did you, Manning?"

The physician's dark eyes regarded Voss without expression. "You're not trying to sell yourself to me, are you?"

"Would I have to do that?"

Manning slid off the stool. "I'm not sure what you mean. I am sure I've got to get back and see how Thael is making out. Drop around when you have a chance."

He went out, leaving his iced drink untouched. Voss gazed after him for a moment, then selected a fresh pair of straws from the container before him and reached for the drink.

Ben Thoad and Gardenia basked in the adulation of a large and appreciative audience that trampled the lawn of the small house in Franklyn Street, behind St. Paul's Church, where they lived by themselves. The sergeant's face wore a beatific smile that indicated to Voss, while he was still half a block away, that the joke about the bloodhound's name had been received with kindliness if not with hilarity.

The audience consisted entirely of reporters and photographers. In deference to the latter Thoad had arrayed himself in full uniform and had hooked the inadequate stiff collar tightly around his flabby neck. Perspiration stood in shining beads on his bald scalp, ran down his forehead into his eyes and slid over the bridge of his long nose to drip on his bulging coat front. He made a square-shouldered, pompous, ridiculous little figure in front of the cameras.

Gardenia took it more calmly, showing unmistakable signs of boredom. She sprawled at full length on the grass, her tongue lolling, hardly bothering to watch the proceedings.

Thoad's smile broadened when he saw Voss. "Hang around and you'll learn things you never knew before, by thunder!" he cried. "I been telling the boys how a smart bloodhound has twice the brains of any human detective ever lived. They're going to print a piece about her and some pictures of both of us. That'll be real news, mister!"

One of the reporters prompted, "You were telling about that boy who ran away from home and was gone two days."

"So I was. Well, sir, this little feller—Johnny Kurtz his name was—had gone to China far as his folks knew. They'd hunted everywhere for miles around. Finally as a last resort they came to me and asked would I put Gardenia to work on the case.

"Well, we let Gardenia smell some of the little feller's clothes and promised her a nice bit of boiled liver if she delivered. She started out of the door of that boy's house and trailed for half an hour right in the backyard, showing us every move the fugitive had made. All at once she lit out for the barn and when we got there she was trying to climb the ladder to the haymow.

"They'd looked in the haymow already. But I boosted Gardenia up and she went right to a big pile of loose hay at one end and started to dig. And all of a sudden, by thunder, there was Johnny, scared to death he was going to get whipped for playing hooky. He'd hid out there two whole days, sneaking into the house when everybody had gone to bed to raid the icebox and the pantry."

"What's that story I've heard you tell about his trailing a man in an automobile?" Eddie Braithe wanted to know.

"Now that was really a rare case and I don't say even Gardenia could do it every day in the week. But it just happened a burglar had gone through the Collingfords' house while they were visiting up in Maine and the neighbors saw the open window next morning and called the chief. Well, that burglar was pretty dumb because he left just the sort of clue Gardenia and I work best with. He'd put on one of Mr. Collingford's suits and had left his old pants behind.

"Those pants told Gardenia all she wanted to know. She started out of the house and made a beeline for the highway. She went along the side of the road where there was a ditch with some rainwater in it and for a long time I couldn't figure out what she had on her mind. Four miles out of town, though, she turned up a side road and sure enough we found our burglar in a shack with all the loot right there.

"Both him and us were surprised when we got the whole story. It seems this burglar had heard about Gardenia, but had never guessed she could trail the old Ford car he used for his getaway. But it was an open job and his body-scent just rolled out of it as he drove along and clung to that wet ditch. There wasn't any wind to blow it away or probably she wouldn't of been able to do it."

King, of the *Record*, said, "This is good copy, Sergeant. It'll make a nice hot-weather feature to take the curse off the heavy reading. What else has she done?"

"Plenty, mister. I could fill a lot of books with stuff about her. You've heard how crooks with bloodhounds following 'em take to the water to hide their trail? Well,

Gardenia don't worry no more about water than she does about solid ground. There was another boy missing two years ago—the little Barnes boy—and we got her trailing him. She went straight to the swimming hole in Waldham Creek and swum out to the middle and stopped there. And sure enough the boy was at the bottom, drowned. His smell came right to the surface and there wasn't enough current to sweep it away."

"I suppose," King said, "a great many bloodhounds could duplicate Gardenia's feats."

Thoad scowled. "Darned few, by thunder! There's one I trained her in specially I bet not ten dogs in the world can do. Usually a dog remembers a certain scent just as long as it's on the trail and forgets it an hour or so later. But not Gardenia. Why, in practice I've had her trailing men and pulled her off the trail before she got to the end. Next day I'd take her back and try to make her remember, without giving her any garment to smell or anything. Now she remembers as long as two or three days at a time. Once she gets after a man she doesn't forget what he smells like till she gets her boiled liver. Then she knows it's all over."

Braithe looked at the bloodhound with new respect. He said, "You know, Ben, I'll bet she'll be the one to solve this murder mystery in the end."

"Give her a chance and she'll solve it," Thoad asserted stoutly. "Just let the murderer leave one thing lying around we can be sure is his and let her get its scent. Then all we got to do is get all our suspects together in one place and call her in. She'll go right to the one we want."

"Suppose she should make a mistake?"

"She won't. I tried her a hundred times or more. When there was a roomful of people I'd borrow a handkerchief from one of 'em and give her a whiff of it outside. Then I'd take her into the room. She never yet missed going right plumb to the one who owned the handkerchief."

"Voss, you'd be a world-beater if you had a nose like that," King chuckled.

Voss mopped his face with his handkerchief. "I've got the nose," he said, "and I'm a world-beater without using it. If Gardenia gets to the murderer ahead of me I'll pine away with mortification."

He strolled on.

Sue Lyons was coming out of the Main Street Grocery carrying a huge paper sack of supplies. Voss lengthened his stride to overtake her.

"Good heavens," he said, "you'd never get home with that load in this heat. Let me have it."

She surrendered the burden gladly. "There's a condition attached to it," she told him. "You're to come to my house for dinner at seven tonight. Garth Manning will be there. I told him I'd ask you if I could get in touch with you."

"I'll be glad to come," he said, "if you'll let me make a condition, too. I'm devoured with curiosity to know why you owe your life to the doctor. Tell me that here and now and I'll accept with thanks."

She halted and faced him. "You *were* listening outside the office door," she accused.

"I was. I don't do those things often, but I couldn't help hearing you talking about me the minute I came in. I felt like a secret agent in the movies, standing there, but I thought I was justified and I still do. You understand there have been two murders and an attempt at a third and one of the surest things I know is that there will be at least one other attempt."

"On whom?"

"If I knew that I could relax. Thael is in danger, of course, but we're taking precautions to protect him. I'm convinced the killer will strike at someone else, but I don't know the party's name and address."

"Perhaps he has struck already."

"Are you thinking of Cynthia? Perhaps—but I doubt it. It may be just a feeling in my bones, but somehow I'm quite satisfied she'll come through. Her death doesn't fit into any pattern I can conceive."

"Tell me about your patterns. I met Proctor and he was enthusiastic about them, but not very clear."

"You're evading. Tell me about owing your life to Manning."

"Oh, you could have found that out from anyone. A little before Brewster died I was swimming in the bay and got out too far and couldn't get in against the tide. Garth was on the yacht club pier and saw my trouble and kicked off his shoes and came after me. It was a foolish thing to do; he should have taken a boat. He got to me, all right, and we were just about to drown together when someone did manage to reach us with a boat."

"It was a courageous thing for him to do. I can understand how you must appreciate it."

She walked for a dozen paces in silence. He saw strain and indecision in her face and knew from past experience that he was about to be entrusted with a confidence. He waited.

Sue said abruptly, "Yes, you can understand. Sometimes I think you have more understanding than any other person I ever met. I don't mind your having listened last night; I only hope neither of us said anything unfriendly about you, which we might have. And I want to tell you something else, because I suspect you've guessed it already. You'll regard it as strictly between us?"

"I'm like a priest that way."

"You must have guessed that I'm terribly fond of Garth."

"It isn't a guess. I know you are."

"We should have become engaged years ago. But he was having a struggle to make ends meet when he first came to

Waldham and I guess he didn't feel that he could afford to get married. Things dragged on and finally I became engaged to Terry, although I never really expected to marry him. I was a lot younger in those days and most of the girls I knew counted on being engaged at least three or four times before they were married.

"Garth took that engagement seriously, though. He kept away from me—till that day I almost drowned, that is—and then, when he thought we were both done for, he told me he loved me. He called me darling and kissed me, and I was almost glad I was going to die if that had been necessary to make him speak.

"After that things were different. I didn't definitely break my engagement to Terry; I was willing to let it die a slow and painless death through neglect. I went out a lot with Garth and Terry began paying attention to Cynthia, which worried Brewster more than any of us suspected. Garth and I were walking along the hill path when Brewster was killed. We didn't know what was the matter. All Garth realized was that something terrible had happened to Cynthia and being a doctor he took charge of her immediately."

"And he's been looking after her ever since."

"That's it, Mr. Voss. For seven years Garth and I have been the best of friends, but since that day we've never spoken of anything more than friendship. I'm afraid—I think he's fallen in love with Cynthia and hasn't the heart to hurt me by saying so."

"He says he hasn't. He says he pities her personally and finds her a challenge professionally. I think if he could ever get her straightened around he'd feel free to neglect her, but pending that time he doesn't dare."

She sighed. "That's what he tells me. Probably he believes it. But I believe he's mistaken. I suspect that if I deliberately stayed away from him—let him know I'd lost interest in him—he'd marry Cynthia. . . . I'm telling you all this hoping you'll advise me whether I shouldn't do that."

Voss was embarrassed. "I wouldn't dare advise you. I've been consulted on a good many problems, but never before on one of that kind. You've paid me one of the biggest compliments I've ever had. . . . Or if I were to advise you I'd only tell you to sit tight and wait. I think we're going to have our murderer pretty soon. I think when we get him, if not before, we'll know pretty well what happened to your brother. That may make a tremendous change in you and Cynthia and Manning, too."

"It's good advice," she admitted. "It's what I've been telling myself. Only I've been trying for so long to make up my mind it seems I can't wait a day longer. . . . Do you think I'm a fool, Mr. Voss, or a mental case?"

"I think," he said, "you're one of the sanest women I've ever met. You've been in torment for seven years and you've taken it like a heroine. Now matters connected with these murders are nearing a climax, by all psychological rules, and in some degree everyone in Waldham is conscious of the strain. Not only the murderer, who is the worst sufferer, but you and I and all the rest feel the end of our patience and safety drawing near. The tension you are under is many times greater than it was. That's why you feel like cracking up. Don't do it."

She said, "Next to Garth I admire you most." It was a simple, almost childlike statement, made without coquetry.

"You're all right, too," he said clumsily. "I'm hoping for you and betting on you."

They were in front of Sue's house when Voss's ears caught a hoarse, prolonged cry. It was a moment before he realized it was a drunken man singing raucously at the top of his lungs.

"Terry," Sue informed him. "He was like that all last night. It's one of his spells. Maybe the last one."

"Is he often this bad?"

"Four or five times a year. He always needs Garth to straighten him out, because it always leads to delirium tremens. Hell die sooner or later in one of those spells, Garth says, and it will be just as well for him and everyone else. He hasn't a friend in the world. I wanted to be one, but he won't let me set foot in his yard."

"If I were Manning I'd get him into a sanitarium and have him kept there for a year or two. It might bring him around."

"Garth has been threatening to do that. Maybe he will this time. I'll take the groceries now. Don't forget, seven tonight."

"I'll remember."

She started toward the house and then turned back impulsively. She said swiftly, as though it were something she had to say, "I used to believe in the creative power of prayer and faith. I always thought one could get or bring about any reasonable thing he wanted badly enough. For years I tried to keep firm in my belief in two things—that Brewster's death would be cleared up and that . . . my own problem would be solved. But just lately I've discovered I had no prayers or faith left. I'm beginning to be terribly afraid for myself as well as for other people. . . . Mr. Voss, from my standpoint whatever happens will have to happen soon."

"It will," he told her. "It will happen very soon."

13

The storm held off with maddening deliberation throughout that sweltering afternoon and struck with a vengeance at six-thirty. It came with a muttering of thunder, a minute or two of dull and sluggish lightnings, a quick massing of sullen clouds that enveloped Waldham in premature darkness. A hot breeze went through the streets and over the fields where no breath of air had stirred all day. Then the big drops clattered, raising white puffs of dust, and immediately the rain was a solid wall of rushing water whipped by a cold wind. The skies exploded and bellowed; the lightning flashes were blinding swords slashing wet blackness.

Voss was in Whitcomb Street close to Manning's house on his way to Sue Lyons's. He had brought a raincoat, but it gave scant protection against the deluge. He fled toward Manning's side porch with the coat flapping against his ungainly legs.

The house was dark. Voss tried the side door with its hospitable sign, but it was locked. It came to him that Manning had already started for Sue's. He wondered how long the intensity of the storm would last and whether it were worth a thorough drenching to be on time for dinner.

A car crept toward him through the rain from the direction of the Whitcomb place. Its fender-sunk headlamps were blurred spots of brightness in the gloom. It stopped with a jerk in front of Manning's cottage and someone inside cranked down a window.

Eddie Braithe's excited voice pierced through the roar of water. "Voss, is that you? Come here, will you?"

Thankfully Voss plunged head-down through the slanting lines of rain. The door of the car swung open and he scrambled into the spacious interior of the Zephyr.

"I'll soak your cushions," he warned.

"To hell with that," Braithe said, and there was a queer vibrancy in his tone, "Voss, how would you like to catch the killer in the very act? I was on my way to headquarters, but I'd rather have you than Proctor."

Voss's jaw tightened. "Tell me about it while we're on the way."

Braithe accelerated the sedan, swung it in a sharp U-turn at the corner and sent it rolling back the way he had come. He crouched over the wheel to peer through the streaming windshield on which the automatic wiper made no impression whatever. Voss noticed that the youth's hair and shirt and trousers were thoroughly wet.

"Somebody's outside Terry's house with a gun," Braithe said. "Somebody in a raincoat with the collar turned up and a slouch hat pulled down over his eyes. I saw him not three minutes ago."

"Doing what?"

"Same thing I was doing—peeking in windows. Terry's been raising the devil all day and I've been keeping an eye on him. Soon as it got dark I sneaked into the yard. And I saw this fellow and beat it before he saw me, because I didn't dare tackle him alone. . . . Got a gun?"

"Not with me."

Braithe opened the glove compartment in the instrument panel and took out a small, nickel-plated revolver.

He handed it butt first to Voss. "You hang onto it. I never had much use for them and I'd probably shoot myself. It's only a twenty-five, but it may come in handy."

Voss took the weapon, broke it part way and glanced at the brass rims of cartridges in the cylinder. He put it in the pocket of his raincoat. He said, "I never shot a man, but I've spoiled a lot of targets."

The car slowed and stopped while they were yet half a block from Terry Whitcomb's place. Braithe switched off the lights. "Nothing for it but to get wet," he said. "It wouldn't do to take the car closer. I guess we're wet enough already so it doesn't matter."

He got out and Voss followed him. They ran toward the negligible shelter of a ragged hedge that marked the boundary of the Whitcomb lot. The rain was merciless; it made a sodden mess of Voss's expensive Panama, guaranteed waterproof, and sluiced beneath the collar of his raincoat, soaking him to the skin. Water squirted from his shoes at every step.

But Voss did not mind. Creeping through a broken place in the hedge and following Braithe through the knee-high grass, he was conscious of a heady thrill of danger that made his blood race exultantly. He was nearing a crisis, a turning-point in the unholy plot he was tracing; he knew it with an inner assurance that had little to do with reason or logic, but was overwhelmingly convincing.

Braithe halted, practically invisible beside him, and grasped Voss's arm. "Look!" he whispered, pointing ahead.

Voss could see the gray wall of the big house with its black windows a hundred feet away. Masses of dark shrubbery huddled against its stone foundation and writhed and swayed in the wind. But he could see nothing else through his watery spectacles.

"What?" he asked. "There's no one—"

"Down!" Braithe shouted, forgetting caution. He flung himself flat on his face and tugged with one hand at Voss's trouser leg. "Get down, you idiot!"

A thin red flame stabbed out of the shrubbery straight at Voss. A gun barked wickedly against the thunder of the storm. Voss dropped beside Braithe, panting, realizing the bullet must have missed him only by inches. He could see nothing from where he lay except the bent and moisture-laden stems of the grass in front of his face; could hear nothing except the beat of the rain.

"I'm game to take a chance," Braithe whispered. "If you'll keep watch I'll crawl on my belly and come up toward the bushes in a roundabout way. Soon as you see a movement or hear me call, yell as loud as you can and have your gun ready. But be sure you know what you're shooting at."

"Go ahead," Voss said grimly. "I'll keep my eyes open."

Braithe disappeared at Voss's right, slithering with lithe agility through the weeds. Blue-white lightning bathed the scene with spectral brilliance before he could have been thirty feet away, yet Voss could not see him. Darkness closed in again and Voss moved hurriedly to the left. He threw himself down a dozen yards from where he had been. The move had placed him considerably closer to the house.

Almost at once Braithe screamed, "Voss!" and there was a thrashing in the bushes. The gun spoke twice more, its sound merging with the roll of mighty thunder, and darts of warm flame licked out of the foliage as before. There was a wild yell. Feet drummed against sopping earth.

Voss lunged erect, holding the small revolver in his hand. He ran toward the bushes. Lightning flashed again when he was within ten feet of them and showed him plainly that whoever had been at that spot had gone. There were only footprints made shapeless by the pounding rain.

He tripped over a stake driven firmly into the earth and fell headlong. The left leg of his trousers was torn by a nail in the stake. He lay with the breath knocked out of him for a brief space and the lightning came again and this time he caught sight of a tall figure in a dark raincoat moving toward the rear of the house. The collar of the coat was turned high and the brim of a shapeless hat was pulled low to meet it.

The figure turned the corner of the house as Voss struggled erect and immediately there came another scream from Braithe. "Voss! Hurry!"

And the flat, jarring concussion of a fourth shot.

And silence.

Braithe was huddled in the grass. Voss nearly stumbled over him. He knelt and asked, "Are you hurt, Eddie?"

The younger man nodded. Looking closely into his face Voss saw that it was twisted savagely. He saw also a spreading dark stain across Braithe's shirt front.

"I'll carry you to your car," he said.

Braithe shook his head. "I'll be all right. It's only my arm," He held his right forearm out, exhibiting the bleeding groove that cut across it. Voss understood that the blood on Braithe's shirt had come from the arm.

"That isn't so bad," Voss told him. "We'll get it dressed right away."

"Just a scratch," Braithe said tightly. "It doesn't hurt too much. But it scared me half to death. I was never shot before. It might have finished me." He took a deep breath and got to his knees. "I'll wrap my handkerchief around it and hunt up Manning or somebody. Did you see the guy?"

Voss helped him to rise. "I saw him for a second from the rear. Who was he?"

"Golly, I wish I knew. I got a punch at him, but not a single good look. Voss, if you want to stick around you needn't go with me to hunt a doctor. I'll be all right."

"It's less than a hundred yards from here to Sue Lyons's. I think you'll find Manning there. If not you'll find a phone and Sue will probably have mercurochrome and bandages."

"Don't worry about me," Braithe said. "Worry about yourself." He stumbled away into the darkness.

Voss hesitated. Once more lightning blazed while he was looking toward the water. Through a mist of rain he could see a small sloop—beyond a doubt Terry's *Cynthia*—dancing at her mooring past the end of a rickety dock.

The back door of the Whitcomb house creaked on rusty hinges. Voss heard shuffling steps and made out the dark blob of a person coming from the house into the night. It was not the tall, slouch-hatted man; this was an old woman, short and fat and grotesque, who wheezed loudly and hustled along with a peculiar gait that fell just short of being a limp.

He watched Jenny Midge vanish into the storm in the direction Braithe had taken. He tried to imagine what kind of errand might call her forth in this weather, and debated whether he should follow her.

Then from within the house came a screech of laughter so uncontrolled, so brittle with insanity, that Voss's nerves stretched with it. Suddenly he felt that he must see the unhappy man who lived there. He sought for a reasonable excuse to enter the black rectangle of the doorway, which Jenny Midge had not closed, and found two: First to discover whether Terry Whitcomb was safe from the tall gunman who had skulked through the bushes, and secondly to make certain that the gunman and Terry Whitcomb were not one and the same person.

He stepped lightly up on the low porch and into a narrow hallway in which the rushing sound of the storm was stilled. He groped forward, keeping his left hand against the wall and his right on the revolver in his raincoat pocket.

A flicker of lightning showed a corner of a big room in the center of the house.

Voss reached the narrow entrance to that room and paused. Thunder rolled overhead and lightning came again, revealing a scene that might have been lifted bodily from a nightmare.

The blue light filtered into the square room through a flood of water that clattered over a skylight three stories above the floor. It glistened upon the smooth oak of a tall ship's mast that raked from the skylight to the floor, bearing spars and cross-trees and cleats and taut ropes. And the floor was like the scrubbed and sanded deck of a ship, with a large brass wheel set abaft the mast and a brass compass case beneath it and coils of rope spread over the planks and a scuppered rail against either wall.

At the foot of the mast, resting his left hand against it, bracing his feet wide apart as though to accommodate the roll of a vessel fighting heavy seas, stood a man whose back was to Voss. The man was gaunt as a skeleton, his unshorn hair was pure white, he wore a soiled white shirt and soiled canvas trousers rolled up above bare feet. With his right hand he lifted a black bottle to his mouth and drank.

In the instant before the light died out the illusion was complete and shocking. Voss thought fancifully of a phantom ship racing over a phantom sea, bearing Terry Whitcomb into realms of deeper madness.

In the blackness Whitcomb bellowed, "Sink, damn you—sink!"

He must have hurled the bottle from him, for there was a crash of glass against one of the walls and a jangling of fragments on the floor. The laughter screeched again. Bare feet padded toward Voss.

He shrank against the wall, relinquishing his grip on the revolver, drawing his right fist out of his pocket. If the frail madman should attack him he would have no need of a gun. . . . But Whitcomb evidently did not know there was another person in the house. He collided with Voss, staggered back and after clawing at the wall for support continued his uneven progress down the hall toward the back door.

Voss followed him into the storm. He saw Whitcomb trot to the end of the rickety dock and plunge into the swirling water of Waldham Bay. He thought the man would surely drown, but as he reached the dock a gleam of lightning revealed Whitcomb clambering with unexpected ease over the side of the tossing sloop.

A second or two later the *Cynthia* swung out from her mooring before the gusty wind and drifted toward the Sound.

A flashlight beam cut through the streaming night and sprayed over Voss's gangling form. He turned, blinking into the glare. Garth Manning said, "Oh, it's you." The beam dropped from Voss's face and swerved toward the bay. Manning came to stand beside the investigator on the dock.

The beam picked up the *Cynthia* sixty yards out from her mooring. On her forward deck a white-haired, white-clad skeleton was tugging at a rope, hoisting a slim foresail to a naked mast. The canvas stretched and shuddered in the wind.

"Maybe this will be his last trip," Manning said. "No sane man would put up sail on a night like this. Voss, what was that shooting?"

Voss looked at Manning carefully. The physician was hatless and wet and in the reflected glow of the light his face was streaked with dirt and one side of his suit was plastered with mud.

"Braithe went looking for you," Voss said. "Did you see him?"

"I didn't see anybody, I was running for Sue's porch when I heard shots. I started over and fell down on the way. I was hoping Terry had killed himself."

"He hasn't. Braithe was shot in the arm. Somebody aimed three bullets at me and missed. I saw a tall man, about your build, wearing a raincoat and a soft hat."

"About my build, eh?" Manning swept the light over the water. "You know, I was wondering what that was out there. It might be a rubber coat and a hat."

Voss glimpsed the dark objects floating fifty feet out and getting farther away. There was no possibility of recovering them; no other boat was within convenient reach and no ordinary man could swim out to get the garments, if garments they were, and be sure of returning.

"Probably you're right," Voss said. He thought about Braithe and decided there was no need to worry about him. The youth's wound was not serious. He could find another doctor, or even have it dressed at the drugstore. He glanced at Manning.

"Don't look at me," the doctor said. "I wasn't wearing those things. I didn't throw them in the bay. . . . Voss, we can't go to Sue's this way. Let's go to my place and phone and get a drink—"

Voss held up his hand for silence. His sensitive ear had distinguished a low moan beneath the noise of the storm. The moan grew in volume and climbed the scale until it screamed a shrill alarm over the village.

"Fire siren," Manning informed him.

"Fire, too," Voss said. He stared across the tip of the bay, past the Bay View Inn, to where a red glow was distinct against the sky. As they looked a yellow tongue of flame leaped high and sank again.

"There isn't anything over that way," Manning said slowly, "except Jenny Midge's house. The lightning . . ."

"Where's your car?" Voss demanded. "In front of Sue's?"

Manning nodded. He started to lead the way, walking, and presently broke into a run. Voss trotted at his heels. They were both short of breath when they reached the Chrysler.

From the porch of the house Sue called, "Wait, please! I want to go along." She came running out with a slicker over her shoulders. Voss helped her into the front seat with Manning and climbed into the rear.

"Dinner will keep," Sue said. "I heard the shots and guessed neither of you would be on time and was able to salvage most of it. What happened?"

Voss told her in the fewest possible words while Manning guided the car through flooded streets. She made no comment, but her eyes showed increasing fright.

Other cars were crawling toward the scene of the blaze. Manning pulled to the curb to let Waldham's lone fire truck splash past with its clanging bell and whirling red lights.

"A lot of good that outfit will do," the doctor said, "The closest it can get to the house is the cemetery. Even if there were hydrants those two hose lines wouldn't throw as much water as is coming out of the sky."

They drove into the cemetery until they had to stop where a dozen other cars were parked at the end of one of the gravel lanes. They got out and began to walk toward the broken place in the fence where the path led to Jenny Midge's house, past tombstones reflecting the radiance of headlamps and flashlights and lanterns.

It was at once apparent, as they entered the ruddy glow that surrounded the burning house, that no human agency could save it. Red and yellow flames licked out of first-floor windows and climbed the walls to the roof, where narrow blue streamers wavered back and forth over the sodden shingles. Vast billows of brown smoke rose to meet the lowering clouds. The rain hissed viciously as the heat turned it to steam, but it did not retard the destruction noticeably.

Chief Proctor, standing as near to the blazing structure as the fierce heat would permit, was arguing indignantly with a circle of newspapermen.

"Nonsense!" he expostulated. "It's a lightning fire pure and simple. Who in hell would try to commit murder by burning a house when no one was inside? I saw Jenny Midge with my own eyes heading for the Whitcomb house just before the storm."

Voss watched for an opportunity to speak to Proctor alone. He felt that the policeman should know as soon as possible about the happenings at the Whitcomb house. He began to edge away from Sue and Manning, who were too intent upon the spectacle to notice him, when he was brought up short by the sight of a man with a bandaged head coming through the path from the cemetery.

"Thael!" he said. "In the name of all that's holy, what are you doing out of bed?"

The writer was pale and worried. He wore the clothes in which he had lain beneath the alders the day before. They were drenched and so were his bandages. He grasped Voss's arm and leaned heavily upon it.

"The doc must have given me a lot of dope," he said; "I feel fuzzy as a caterpillar. But I'd rather die on my feet than in bed. Abelard, somebody tried to shoot me through the window of Manning's house."

"Somebody *what?*"

Thael repeated patiently, "Somebody tried to shoot me. Amanda Holmes had to go home. Backus was in another room reading funny papers. The windows were closed to keep out the rain. The window across from the sofa I was lying on broke and a hand came through with a pistol. Just one shot was fired. I rolled off the sofa to the floor, trying to get out of range, and I guess the gunman beat it. There's a bullet hole in the wall three inches above the spot where my head was."

"Great Scott! What did Backus do?"

"He looked goofy and ran to the phone to try to call Proctor. He was still trying when I decided to put on my clothes and slip out. I heard the siren and thought I'd like a little excitement."

"Who slugged you yesterday?"

Thael shook his head. "I didn't see him. He was hiding in the bushes. I heard him jump out and I started to turn around and that's all I remember. I seem to have had some sort of idea of who did the murders, too—I was on my way to tell you about it—but to save my life I couldn't think of it now."

"Yet you recall everything else clearly?"

"Not everything. I couldn't remember my name this morning. Things have been coming back a little at a time. But I'll get it all pretty soon. I feel fine, except for being dizzy and weak."

"You shouldn't have come here alone. You're begging for killing."

"I thought it would be better than staying— Oh, my God, Abelard—*look!*"

Voss spun on his heel as a dozen other voices gasped, *"Look!"* His eyes followed the horrified stares of a hundred people at the upper front window of the house above the porch roof.

Behind the broken window the head of Jenny Midge lifted into view. Her dark eyes bulged glassily, her hair was a snaky tangle, a bandage covered her mouth. Her arms and hands seemed to be pinned to her sides. The head moved jerkily, as though Jenny were struggling to come nearer to the window. In her sweat-streaked face was a look of such piteous pleading that several men in the crowd moved forward, only to be driven back by the merciless heat.

Then the head disappeared.

Proctor shouted, "She's tied and gagged! It's murder!" He started toward the house. Men grabbed his arms and shoulders, holding him. Proctor swore half tearfully and tried to fight against them.

Voss saw the hopelessness of the old woman's plight clearly and was sickened by the thought of her agony. There was nothing to be done. Jenny Midge would keep no more graves fresh and fragrant and no one would bother to beautify her own. The violent death she had predicted for so many others had come at last to her.

Sue screamed, "I can't stand it!" She leaned against Manning and went limp in his arms. He held her, looking wildly about for a dry spot where she might lie.

Proctor was bawling, "You're letting her die like a rat! You're a bunch of yellow cowards! You're—"

The roof collapsed with a crash that drowned out his voice and many other voices. A geyser of red sparks shot far above the crackling pyre and scattered on the wind.

14

They took what was left of Jenny Midge out of the smoking ash heap of the old house in the morning when the rain had slowed to a gentle patter and the wind had died. They found the note then, too, or rather a small boy found it, water-soaked and pulpy, fastened in the split end of a stake at the edge of the trampled flower garden.

The note was similar to the others except that its wording was:

> I knew
> I never told
> I should have

The words had been cut out of the most recent installment of the *Courier's* serialized mystery story *Death Takes a Dare*. Wafer had softened the paste with which they were attached to the sheet of notepaper and Irv resolved to attempt to analyze it.

The morning newspapers from New York achieved a new high note of hysteria. Before noon the corps of reporters and photographers had doubled as newsmen came from Washington and Baltimore and Philadelphia to write first hand of the spectacle of a whole village terrorized by a seemingly insatiable killer.

Leland Padgett, the district attorney, arrived in Wald-ham by an early train and brought with him a state po-lice detective. A gray-haired, pink-jowled veteran of many political campaigns, Padgett made it plain from the begin-ning that he meant to take full charge of the case and, if possible, full credit for its ultimate solution.

In Proctor's office Padgett listened impatiently to what the police chief could tell him of the investigation.

"Trouble with you small-town officers," the district attorney diagnosed, "is you're afraid of hurting somebody's feelings. When murder happens you've got to take off your kid gloves and forget friendships. You've got to be tough with everybody."

Padgett swung in his chair to face Voss. He was slightly more respectful in addressing the famous criminologist from New York City, but still loftily self-important.

"First of all we want Thael back here," he said as a busy man might order his first course in a restaurant. "I'm told he walked out of the doctor's house without saying any-thing and was seen talking to you at the scene of the fire just before he vanished. Did he say anything that might make you think he intended to run away?"

Voss's expression was quizzical. He did not like Leland Padgett, but his quiet frankness might have been mistaken for friendliness.

"When we were walking back from the fire," said Voss, "Thael told me he was thinking of returning to New York. He asked me to advise him."

"And did you?"

"I told him there was a train leaving in fifteen minutes. I advised him to catch it without even waiting to pack."

"Why in the devil did you do that?"

"For several reasons. He wasn't under arrest and in my opinion shouldn't be. He was a sick man. The police were supposed to be looking out for him, but someone came within inches of killing him. I knew he would be safer in New York."

"Bosh!" Padgett snorted. "Do you want to know what I think? I think he's the man who wounded Braithe and shot at you last night. I think he killed Jenny Midge and those others. I think he hit himself on the head and faked amnesia and fired that shot into the windowsill to keep suspicion away from him. Who else could have done all those things?"

Proctor muttered, "Manning could have."

Padgett did not try to conceal his contempt of the suggestion. "I know Manning. I've met him half a dozen times. He wouldn't run around killing off his neighbors. I'm going to ask the state police to try to locate Thael at his New York address. If he's run out on us I'm going to hold you personally responsible, Voss."

Voss smiled. "Do you intend to limit your investigation to one suspect?"

"I'm not exactly an amateur at this sort of thing. I'm going to interview every man, woman and child who might have had the slightest connection with what's happened. I'm going to take Williams, who is a hard-boiled detective, with me and I'm not going to stand for any nonsense. The situation seems to have grown too big for you local people and someone has to take it in hand."

He glared at them impressively before he stood up and stalked out.

Proctor mopped his furrowed forehead. "And I was afraid to pinch Jenny Midge! I could have stood her better than I can stand that red-faced windbag. But I suppose she'd have been murdered in jail and that would have made it worse. . . . Abelard, will they find Thael at home?"

"I'm almost sure they won't. He'd be a fool to go there."

"Well, until he's found, Padgett will be convinced he's the one who murdered them all. That will keep him from sending you or me to the electric chair and that's something."

They found Cynthia Carrington that same day at noon.

Ralph Decker was driving from the golf club to the village when he sighted a small sloop pounding against the bottom of the bay at the far side of the hill. The vessel's sails were torn to shreds and she threatened to break into pieces at any minute in the heavy swell that remained after the wind had gone. On her forward deck lay the inert figure of a white-haired man whom Decker recognized half a mile away as Terry Whitcomb.

Some men went out in a launch during a lull in the rain and took off Terry. He was in a drunken stupor. The men took him to his home and put him in his untidy bed and called Manning, who administered a hypodermic and phoned to New York for a male nurse.

Meanwhile the launch went back to tow the *Cynthia* to her mooring. One man went aboard to steer the damaged vessel and while they were crossing the bay he heard a muffled moaning up toward the bow.

The man finally located the source of the sounds, smashed a padlock that secured the door of a tiny sail locker and found Cynthia Carrington curled up there, bruised and tattered and semi-conscious. He hailed the launch, which immediately took her aboard and rushed her to her home. Elsie put her to bed and Manning was summoned from Terry Whitcomb's side.

Manning ran all the way to Cynthia's house through the rain. Proctor and Voss were on the porch when he dashed past them. His face was white and dreadful.

Proctor said to Voss, "If Terry Whitcomb should be murdered today or tomorrow we wouldn't have to look very far for a likely suspect."

Padgett and the thickset man who was Williams, the state police detective, came up on the porch a minute or two later. Williams was glum and uncommunicative, but the district attorney had reached a new conclusion too exciting to keep to himself.

"We've got our man," he announced jubilantly. "That fellow Whitcomb will burn if he lives through the DT's. They tell me he's loony as a bedbug. What beats me is why you fellows didn't get on to him sooner."

"You're ready to exonerate Thael, then?" Proctor asked.

"I think so. I hadn't been told about Whitcomb when I was thinking about Thael. Not very much, anyway. . . . But look at the case we have now. Whitcomb intended to kill Miss Carrington. He was going to drown her, undoubtedly, but he passed out before he got around to it. He went batty years ago and he's been working up to the point of murder ever since, egged on by a combination of liquor and disappointment in love."

Voss lounged back in the porch swing. "You get your answers fast, don't you, Padgett? If I were you I think I'd go into the detecting business in earnest. I suppose you've got all the evidence you'll need to convict Whitcomb?"

Padgett eyed him suspiciously. "Evidence? We'll get around to it fast enough. There are plenty of ways of finding out facts. Just you wait and see."

Decker came running up the walk. He hurried past the group on the porch without a glance and started up the stairs. At the landing he encountered Manning, who was coming down.

"You can't go up there," Manning said loudly enough for those on the porch to hear. "She needs to rest."

Decker's voice was strained. "I just heard about it. I've got to see her. I can't believe it till I see her."

"Nothing doing," Manning snapped. "That's final. I forbid you and I'll break your neck if you try it."

"Listen, Doc," Decker pleaded desperately; "I love Cynthia more than you could ever understand. I only want to look at her for a second. If you don't let me I'll go nuts!"

There was a pause. When Manning spoke again his tone was softer. "All right. I'll open the door and let you look in. You mustn't make a sound, though. I've given her a sedative and she can't be disturbed."

They went up the stairs together. In less than two minutes they were back on the porch. Decker was subdued and self-conscious. He hesitated a moment, not looking at any of them, and then strode away without a word.

Padgett asked, "How soon can I question her, Doctor?"

"Question her?" Manning was amazed. "Why, man, you can't question her at all as long as she's in this condition. She won't be awake all day or all night, except to take a little nourishment, if I can help it. I don't know what her nerves will be like tomorrow. She may have suffered a severe shock."

"Is she injured in any way?"

"She's bruised from being shaken up in the boat. She's scared half to death. That's all I can be sure of."

"We'll have to question her, you know. It's a necessary formality. It isn't a matter of personal like or dislike—"

Manning broke in coldly, "I'm her physician. I'll tell you when she can see visitors and how much talking she can do. If I find you making any effort to disturb her without getting my permission I'll make so much trouble you couldn't get elected dog-catcher in November."

The district attorney dropped his eyes before Manning's icy anger. "We don't want to annoy a sick woman, of course. What about Whitcomb? We've got business with him, too."

Manning smiled and his smile was more awful than his fury. "I wouldn't care personally if you started giving him the third-degree this minute. But, speaking professionally, you wouldn't get a thing out of him. He's in a coma you couldn't crack with dynamite. He'll probably be worse tomorrow. I wouldn't be surprised if he'd die. But dead or alive he'll be available for some days to come. He's in no condition to kidnap anyone else or run away."

"Then I suppose we'll have to mark time." Padgett was inclined to be fretful. "I'd go home if I hadn't already told the newspapers I was going to stay right here till everything was settled." He addressed the detective sarcastically, "Williams, maybe we can kill time solving that mystery the baldheaded police sergeant was trying to interest us in—the mystery of who tried to poison his decrepit bloodhound." He laughed.

Walking away from the house with Proctor, Voss observed, "Padgett may have had something there and not known it. Did somebody try to poison Gardenia?"

"Looks that way. This morning Ben Thoad noticed little patties of raw hamburger scattered around his yard. White powder'd been sprinkled over them. He took it to Manning and the doc said it was arsenic—rat poison or bug poison. What do you make of that?"

"It proves what I've suspected for the last two days. Our murderer is on the run, Proctor. He was the aggressor to start with, but now he's on the defensive. He underestimated us and overestimated himself. The fire is hotter than he thought it was going to be and he's afraid of us all and of that bloodhound."

"Maybe he'll quit killing people."

Voss's eyes glittered. "Don't bank on it. A scared killer is ten times as dangerous as one who's sure of himself. Fear will make him take chances he'd never dream of otherwise. The worst of it is he'll never get rid of that fear as long as he lives. That's the most terrible thing about murder and that's why you can't afford to let the man who has committed it remain at large. He'll murder again—he can't help murdering again—as often as he feels himself threatened."

"I'd sure like to catch this murderer," Proctor muttered. "I'd give a year's pay to grab him before Padgett does."

"You have a good chance. He has already overplayed his hand. If you don't have him in one of your cells within the next day or two it will be because he's dead."

"Do you still think you know who he is, Voss?"

"I've been practically certain since yesterday. It wouldn't do any good to tell you, though, because you couldn't ever prove it by ordinary means. But he'll betray himself as most criminals do. By the very nature of things he can't help it. . . . Let's walk around by Jenny's house. I'm afraid the thing I want to get will be gone, but it's just as well to be sure."

They had gone a block down Whitcomb Street. They turned right in Hill Street and walked the two blocks to the cemetery. Brewster Lyons's grave was an unsightly splotch of wet clay and the roses on Evelyn Lister's grave were broken and bedraggled. The mound beneath which Art Dawson had been buried at a little distance from Evelyn's was the neatest of the three; it had not been touched since the sexton had placed the last spadeful of earth and the rain had only smoothed and settled it.

The path to the spot where Jenny Midge's house had stood was muddy and water dripped from the trees. The stone chimney rose above the ruins like a clumsy monument. All about it was a pile of damp ashes, with thin blue smoke still rising from one corner.

Leaving Proctor, Voss waded through the blackened debris. The acrid smell of the charred timbers caught in his throat. The ashes were heaped thickly upon the hearth, but he found a half-burned plank and shoveled them away. He stooped and pried up some of the bricks and found the tin box undamaged.

"Take charge of the money," he said to Proctor when he returned, smeared to the knees and elbows with dirt and slime. "I haven't counted it, but what I'm really interested in is the letters. Maybe they'll tell us something and maybe not."

He emptied the box and handed the banknotes to Proctor. The chief swore in amazement and began to count them.

Voss riffled through the letters. The postmark dates of the top envelopes ran from 1902 to 1907. It was difficult to think that anything written so long ago could have a bearing on what had happened during the past week. And then at the bottom of the pile was an envelope that literally jolted him with surprise.

"Great horned owls!" Proctor breathed. "Abelard, there's over three thousand dollars here."

Voss did not hear him. He was staring at the envelope. He drew out the folded sheets it contained and ran his eye down the careful handwriting and studied the stylized signature in faded black ink at the bottom.

He said exultantly, "Here's what you've been waiting seven years for, Proctor. Look it over."

Proctor took the envelope. "Addressed to Sue Lyons . . . posted in Waldham on July seventh, nineteen thirty-two. Why, Abelard, that's the day Brewster was killed!"

"Read the letter."

The policeman did so. His face was inscrutable when he had finished, but his eyes were hard and bright as glass.

"Good God, Abelard—then she did kill him! What a hellish thing. I can hardly believe it."

"It must be true. It explains everything. Proctor, it goes a long way toward explaining these later murders, too. Let's go!"

"Where?"

"First of all to find Sue Lyons. We'll steal a march on your friend Padgett yet."

"You've been making mud pies again," Sue said to her callers with weary flippancy. "But come in and bring your mud with you. I can tell by your faces you've found out something."

Voss halted in the vestibule. "No sense in our tracking up your living room. We won't stay long." He showed her the envelope. "Do you recognize the handwriting?"

The color fled from her face. She stared at the address and then at the date. She sat down abruptly in a straight chair that stood against the staircase.

"It's Brewster's. It's a letter to me I never received."

"It's his last letter," Voss told her. "It explains something that should have been explained a long time ago. Jenny Midge has been hiding the truth. Would you like to read it?"

She smoothed her hair back from her forehead with a childish gesture of bewilderment. "You read it to me, please. I'm not sure I could. I've been quarreling with the district attorney and some thug who goes around with him. I'm all worn out."

"This will hurt you," said Voss, "but I think it will make you glad, too." He read:

> "'Dear Sister:
>
> "'When you receive this I will be dead by Cynthia's hand. Killing me will be the most merciful thing she has ever done. It will be better than madness and I have been going mad for a year, slipping a little further from sanity every time I caught her looking at another man. I know it's wrong to be so jealous, but I can't help myself.
>
> "'You are the one person I can trust. You always seemed to understand me better than anyone else. I am going to tell you exactly what will happen, but you must keep it to yourself except in one extremity. If they

should decide to electrocute Cynthia for killing me you must show this to prevent it. I
want her to suffer as I have suffered, to live
and not know the mercy of death for a long,
long time. . . .'"

"But I don't understand. How could he know beforehand that she would kill him, if it's really so?"

"The letter explains itself. Listen—'This evening I will
take her for what used to be our favorite walk on the hill.
I will take a revolver with me, concealed under my arm.
The revolver will be ready to fire and a thread will be tied
to the trigger. While we are sitting together I will turn the
revolver beneath my coat so that it is aimed at my heart. I
will tie the end of the thread to some part of her clothing.
When she moves she will fire the gun and end my suffering. No one will believe it suicide because the thread will
slip off the trigger and there will be no fingerprints of
mine. . . .'"

"Oh, poor Cynthia! What a hideous thing to do to her!"

"'. . . She will never dare tell what has happened, but
will go through life knowing she has sent me to my death.
Her friends will suspect her and avoid her. She will never
be able to give herself wholly to any man, remembering.
She will never sleep peacefully at night. But I will rest the
more peacefully, knowing she is not in the arms of Terry
Whitcomb or Garth Manning or any of the men she went
out with after I had begged her to be true to me.

"'Keep this until you are sure she will never be convicted of murder. Then destroy it. I do not know whether you
will approve of my request, but I know you will respect it.
I am your brother and this is my last earthly wish. Good-
by.' It's signed 'Brewster.'"

Sue's hands were twined tightly together. She whispered, "How horrible! My own brother. I loved him, but I

should have known there was something wrong with him. He was never healthy. He'd been studying too hard for the bar. . . . No wonder Cynthia has been so miserable! She must have suspected what happened, but she knew no one would believe a story so fantastic. The worst of it was she could never be sure herself. . . ."

"Jenny was with your people when the letter came," Voss said. "Brewster was her pet. She recognized the handwriting and opened the letter and knew you would never do what he asked. So Jenny simply kept the letter. It seemed quite right to her that anyone who had made her darling suffer should suffer in turn."

Proctor muttered, "We can blame Jenny for everything. A pity she didn't die when her folks died. Think of her keeping that grave fresh all these years just to torment Cynthia . . . accusing Cynthia every time they met . . . trying to make the girl as crazy as she was." He knotted his fists. "But she'll be all right now."

Sue smiled with difficulty. "Yes. I can't tell you how glad I am. Now at last Cynthia will be free."

15

Dr. Manning phoned Voss at the Bay View Inn early Thursday morning. "The best medicine I can give Cynthia is a look at that letter," he said. "I've just seen her and she's much stronger. Could you bring it to my office?"

Voss permitted himself a self-congratulatory smile. He had been expecting that call since the evening before. He told Manning, "I really shouldn't. It's information I was asked to get by an anonymous client. I was directed not to show it to anyone till I contacted him. It might mean losing a fee."

"Damn the fee, Voss! I'll pay it."

"Would you ask me to go back on a client?"

Manning's voice was nettled. "You know darned well I'm that client. You've known or suspected it all along. Well, I acknowledge that anonymous letter now. You won't have to put an ad in the *Courier*."

"I'll be right over," Voss said.

He skipped breakfast and walked to the doctor's house in cool, bright sunshine. He found Manning with Sue Lyons in the consultation room. Her face was radiant.

"Believing in faith and prayer again?" Voss asked her slyly.

She blushed and looked at Manning with pride and possessiveness.

411

He handed Manning the letter. Seated at his desk Manning held it between his fingertips and glanced at Voss. "May I read it now or must we talk business first?"

"Read it. I'd like to know whether you think you've had your money's worth before I stagger you with my bill. You see, I consider myself a specialist in my line and I charge like the Park Avenue medical specialists in New York."

Manning read the letter slowly. He read it a second time. He smoothed it out on the blotter before him.

"We've had three murders here in six days," he said, emphasizing each word with care. "The man who committed them was only a minor criminal compared to the man who wrote this and planned the thing behind it. You'll forgive me for saying it, Sue; I'm not talking about your brother so much as the insanity that took possession of him."

She bent her head. "I love Brewster as I remember him during our childhood. I hate the man who did that to Cynthia."

"You've produced what I asked for," Manning said to Voss. "I hoped it would turn out this way. It will do Cynthia more good than a million dollars' worth of doctoring. I was afraid the answer might be different and that's why I made my letter anonymous and asked you to tell no one about your findings until you had contacted me."

"What would you have done if it had been different?"

Manning shrugged. "It depends. If you had found proof that would convict a living person of murder I might have wanted to suppress it. If it had developed that Cynthia had killed Brewster in a fit of madness—perhaps without knowing what she was doing or remembering it later—I would have insisted that it be suppressed."

"And if I wouldn't keep still?"

"I was going to try to buy you off. If you couldn't be bought . . . well, I'm not prepared to say what I would have done. I toyed with the idea of poison."

"I admire your frankness. You were thinking of Cynthia all along, weren't you? Hers was the innocent life you thought I might save?"

"Yes. She couldn't have hung onto sanity much longer under the circumstances. If she had lost her mind I would have considered it the greatest failure of my career. The fact that she needn't now is worth any reasonable fee. How much shall we say?"

Voss considered. "My regular fee is steep for some people. I came into this realizing I might not get anything beyond the five hundred you advanced and it wouldn't ruin me to have that come true. I'd be willing to skip it if I thought it would hamper any—er—matrimonial or other plans you might have."

"It won't." Manning smiled thinly. "You sound as though you're going to make it stiff, but I think I can stay with you. I'll put my cards on the table and throw myself on your mercy. Lately I've been averaging better than ten thousand a year, for a wonder, and I haven't spent all of it. I've been careful about investments."

"Two thousand dollars," said Voss. "That's my fixed charge for any investigation lasting not longer than a month. You've given me a quarter of it. You owe me fifteen hundred."

Manning appeared relieved. "It's a lot, but you had me afraid it would be more." He pulled out a desk drawer and produced a large checkbook. He wrote a check for fifteen hundred dollars and handed it to Voss. "We're square," he said. "I'm a thousand times obliged."

"So am I." Voss folded the check and placed it in his wallet where four of the five hundred-dollar bills still reposed. "I'm two thousand times obliged. This is returnable, by the way, if I find it necessary to send you to the electric chair. I've never yet taken money from a man for that."

Manning saw no humor in the suggestion. "I suppose you mean you're going to keep after the murderer till you catch him, but have no idea who he is."

"I have a good idea. There are still some things I'd like to have explained, though. One of them is a half-burned copy of the *Courier* I saw in your grate Monday. There was another copy on your desk. That was the day after we found that paper at Cynthia's with some words cut from it."

"Garth wasn't trying to hide anything!" Sue exclaimed indignantly.

Manning's jaws clamped together. "Yes, I was, too. I get the *Courier* every Friday, but Sunday night I found an extra copy in my waiting room. I remembered that one at Cynthia's and looked and sure enough some words had been cut out. I thought there were enough suspicious facts against me without adding another."

"What were the missing words?"

"The ones intended for Jenny Midge."

"That leaves one note still unaccounted for. If the pattern is carried through it means one more corpse to come. What chance would a man have of killing Terry Whitcomb?"

"No chance at all unless he dynamited the house. I asked for the toughest male nurse I know, a fellow named Sontaag who trained at Bellevue and has had experience in prisons and asylums. I warned him there was apt to be trouble and lent him a gun and promised him double pay."

"You think he's protection enough?"

"He's worth ten like Backus. He has a telephone. If I wanted to worry about Whitcomb I'd worry about his dying of alcoholic poisoning before he can get well enough to tell us all he knows about the events of the last few days."

"You're pretty sure he knows something about the murders?"

"I wouldn't be surprised if he knew everything. . . . And now I want to have another look at Cynthia. If she's as well as I think she is it's time she read this letter. I'd like to have you come along, Sue—and you, Voss, if you don't mind waiting downstairs for a little while."

Voss said, "I'm anxious to hear what happened to her if she's able to tell it. Suppose I run over to the restaurant and have some breakfast and then call at her house?"

"That will be fine," Manning said.

They all got into Manning's car and he drove Voss to the Elite Café and went on with Sue. Inside the café Irv Proctor was sitting at the lunch counter hunched moodily over a cup of coffee. He did not look up when Voss sat beside him, but when he heard Voss's voice ordering ham and eggs he swung around swiftly.

"Hey!" he said. "I thought you'd be in jail."

"What for?"

"Padgett said he was going to lock up everybody who refused to co-operate with him. He came near locking me up."

"You'd look funny in your own jail."

"It was Braithe's fault. He told Padgett I'd been hanging around Jenny's house with Evelyn Lister. I ought to thrash the so-and-so again."

Voss grinned. "Again? I thought that last scrap was stopped before either of you got thrashed. . . . Was Braithe telling the truth?"

"I went walking with her once or twice," Irv admitted, his face turning a dull red. "We sat on Jenny's porch one day, but we didn't go in. I didn't care much for her. I'd thought it might be nice playing around with her on the sly, but when I got close to her she was too obviously on the make."

"I see."

"Not that I'm any saint. Don't get that idea. But . . . well, she gave me the feeling she only wanted to get something on me. I thought of Manning, of course."

"You were wise. About Braithe—do you think you'd have trouble licking him?"

"I'd break him in half. I'll admit he's a tricky fighter, but it's not so much skill as the fact that he's left-handed and learned to box at college under a left-handed instructor. A left-hander's stance always makes it awkward for a right-handed opponent."

"And vice versa?"

"Not so much. The left-hander, guarding with his right arm and slugging with his left, is used to boxing right-handers as a rule."

Voss ate silently, "I've got a gun of Braithe's," he said at length. "He lent it to me the other night and I haven't had a chance to return it."

"He'll never miss it. He's got thirty or forty of 'em, old and new. Collecting them is a sort of mania with him."

"Yet he was never on the wrong end of one till night before last."

Irv sniffed. "And was he a baby about that! I was in the City Drugstore when he came in to have it dressed just before the fire siren let go. He had a handkerchief wrapped around his arm and he'd poured about a quart of iodine on the scratch and I guess it did hurt like hell. I hope so. There were powder burns around the wound and he was scared to death of blood poisoning. I asked him if he wanted to ride to the fire with me and he said no, he was too weak and was going right home to bed."

Voss pushed back his empty plate. "If you're not doing anything important today you might stop at the Whitcomb place from time to time. I don't think Terry would be safe even if he were dying. It's just a hunch—neither Padgett nor Manning nor your dad will take me seriously—

but I wouldn't be surprised if he'd have an unwelcome caller before midnight."

"Oke," Irv said. "I won't be doing much else besides dodging Padgett. I'll call on the stew-bum every hour or so."

Ralph Decker sat in the swing on Cynthia Carrington's porch, gnawing his lip and tapping one foot restlessly. He gave Voss a furtive glance in which was so much unhappiness that the lank investigator could not help being sorry for him.

"Are Manning and Miss Lyons here?" Voss inquired.

Decker grunted affirmatively. Voss sat beside him, noting that the golfer was unshaven and his hands were shaking.

After a minute Decker burst out rebelliously, "They're up there fussing around about something unimportant and making me wait to see her till they're damned good and ready. Manning isn't a bad fellow in some ways, but he's too officious to suit me. What harm would it do if I were to see her just for a minute?"

"You'll see her. I wouldn't be surprised if you'd see a lot of her from now on. She ought to be a different woman after today."

"If anything happened to her I could never forgive myself," Decker said. "I scared her into running away. I didn't know she'd do that, of course. I heard her talking to you, saying she was afraid she'd been responsible in some way for Brewster Lyons's death, and I tried to tell her how dangerous it would be if she let herself get mixed up in anything like that. I shouldn't have frightened her. She was already on edge about the murder of Evelyn and she fainted when she heard what happened to Dawson."

"So I gathered." Voss plunged abruptly into the matter that had been on his mind since the night Dale Parsons had been in Proctor's office. "By the way, you were friendly with Evelyn at one time, weren't you?"

Decker sat up straight, wary and belligerent. "What makes you think that?"

"I heard you'd had a row with her the day before she was killed. You called her a name and said she ought to be shot."

For a moment Decker's drawn face was furious and he seemed on the point of striking Voss. Then he slumped back in the swing like a man who knows utter defeat.

"You're guessing right, so why shouldn't I tell you?" he said bitterly. "I was living alone in the pro's quarters at the club and Evelyn started hanging around and we got chummy. No intimacy, you understand—no sex; I knew what sort she was and I didn't care to involve myself with her. But I didn't mind talking to her when no one else was there.

"Well, she came to see me last week and said she was going to have a baby and would blame me if I didn't pay her off. She wanted five thousand dollars at first and then she came down to a thousand. I guess I could have settled for five hundred or less except that I knew she was lying and I'd have killed her before I'd have given her a nickel."

"Good Lord," Voss said, "she must have tried that game with everybody in town! Somebody apparently paid her a thousand. I don't know where else Dawson could have got that much money."

"You see, don't you, that to have given in to her would have queered me definitely with Cynthia?"

"Yes."

"Besides," Decker confided, "I didn't have any money to spare. I've saved some, but Cynthia is well off and it will take all I have and all I can make to hold up my end with her."

"Are you sure she's in love with you?"

"I think so. Something has been keeping us apart. At first I thought it was Manning and then I decided it must be the Brewster Lyons business. Eventually that will be cleared up and then I'm positive everything will be all right."

Manning came to the head of the stairs and called, "Voss, are you down there? Come on up."

Voss told Decker, "It will be cleared up very quickly now." He went upstairs to Cynthia's lavender-tinted room.

Her face, raised up on big pillows, was wan against the fanlike spread of her dark hair, but her smile was warm and colorful. She wore a sheer nightgown of apricot silk that left her smooth throat and her rounded arms bare. She stretched one of her arms toward Voss as he entered.

"Thank you for giving me back my life," she said. "I can hardly believe it. For the first time I'm convinced I was altogether blameless."

"We were sure of that all along," he said, taking her hand in both of his.

"All I did was go for a moonlight sail with Terry and a party of others and dance a few times with Garth," she pointed out seriously. "I never realized how badly Brewster was taking it. Of course that was because he was insane. I can forgive him everything, knowing that."

"So can I," Sue murmured. "I know how fine and brilliant he really was before . . . everything happened."

Manning interrupted, "We've said all those things. The real reason I called Voss up here, Cynthia, was so you could tell us how Terry shanghaied you. We spent four ghastly days worrying about you and had about given you up for dead. We'd like to know what really happened."

"It was awful," she told them. "I hate even to think about it. I was terribly frightened Saturday night at the yacht club. When I heard what had happened to Art Dawson I collapsed. When I came to it seemed that I just couldn't bear to stay where people were or to go home where there were no people except Athens and Elsie. Something told me to run away while I was still able to. I think I was nearer to being crazy than I had ever been. . . ."

"I should have watched you more closely," Manning said.

"You couldn't have helped, Garth. I was beyond your reach or anyone's that night. I made Ralph go away as soon as we got near my house. I didn't go in. The bay was so still and calm I thought perhaps being on the water would soothe me. I thought, too, that if I decided I had really lost control of my mind I would drown myself. I got the oars out of the garage and took the boat, making no more noise than I had to. . . ."

Voss's imagination, always susceptible, presented to his mind the cool whisper of the water against the sides of the boat, the breeze ruffling her hair. It would be dark and peaceful out there—almost as peaceful as being dead, once she had stopped rowing and shipped the oars and let the small craft choose its own unhurried course.

And then the tall gray ghost of the sloop bearing down upon her unseen. . . . It might have been a monstrous coincidence or Terry might have set his helm deliberately to run her down. All she knew was that she had heard the creak of a rope against a cleat and had looked up to see the lean bowsprit thrusting through the air above her and had tried to scream and could not.

The shock of the collision hurled her into the water, but she managed to grasp one of the bowsprit stays. Somehow she dragged herself to the forward deck, not knowing the sloop was the *Cynthia*, and crawled aft to the cockpit. And there was Terry Whitcomb, his white hair disheveled, drunk and mad, but in a way quite pleasant and courteous.

Terry had said, "We've waited for this night, Cynthia, my boat and I. I've known for a long time I couldn't die till you were ready to die with me. We'll stay together till the big storm comes and all three of us will sail out and never come back."

She had thought he was making a bad joke, he seemed so calm and nice about it. But before he moored the sailboat he seized her with a great deal of gentleness and a great deal of strength and bound and gagged her and put her in the sail locker. After that he left her alone each day to suffer in the unrelenting heat and visited her each night, bringing food and giving her the freedom of the cabin. He permitted her no opportunity to escape or cry for help, but neither did he attempt to harm her or force his attentions upon her.

"I became resigned to death," she told them, her voice hushed with the horror of it. "I thought this must be the inevitable ending I had feared for seven years without quite knowing what I was fearing. I began to pray for the storm that would set me free. I was glad when I heard the thunder and the rain and felt the wind strike the boat."

Voss and Manning had witnessed the beginning of that last hazardous voyage without suspecting that Terry had a passenger aboard. Once the *Cynthia* was under sail Terry released his prisoner from the locker and from her bonds. But while he was struggling with the wheel she tried to jump into the water and Terry became angry and thrust her back into the tiny prison.

Hours later she felt the keel of the sloop strike against the bottom and begin to pound. She did not feel the bruises that covered her body as she was tossed about inside the locker. She sank into a state of half-consciousness and saw nothing significant in the fact of men lifting her into another boat and taking her ashore. It was like a dream, being carried into her own house and undressed and put to bed—a pointless dream before the end. . . .

Manning must have seen it all as vividly as Voss had, listening to Cynthia's halting tale. A shudder went through his erect frame.

"Terry will pay for it," Manning declared with deadly earnestness. "I'll do my level best to pull him through so that he can be sent to prison for kidnaping and attempted murder. I'll see that he goes to the toughest prison in the state for the rest of his worthless life—"

"No, you won't," Cynthia broke in firmly. "We've all forgiven Brewster because he was mad and unhappy. Terry is just as mad and miserable. If he lives, Garth, he'll go to a sanitarium or an asylum. If the proper treatment can make him well again, so much the better. I'll never bring charges against him. I'll even lie—say I went with him willingly—to prevent anyone else from bringing charges."

Sue leaned forward and touched Cynthia's hair impulsively. "Oh, Cynthia," she said, "I was hoping you'd say that. You can't know how much I was hoping it. It shows there is no bitterness left in you when you have every right to be bitter, and that's the most wonderful thing in the world!"

Manning shrugged irritably. "You women! Of course you'll have it your own way, Cynthia. Only I think we'd better let you rest now."

"I don't want to rest. I'm full of life and energy. And before I forget, don't tell anyone else the story I've told you. Above all, don't tell Ralph."

Voss shook his head. "We won't. It will be better if he never hears it all, if Whitcomb lives. Did you know he'd been waiting downstairs all morning for a chance to see you?"

"Send him up," Cynthia directed. "Send him up right away and leave us alone for a little while."

Manning turned and opened the door and Ralph Decker was standing just outside in the hallway.

16

Downstairs the doorbell pealed musically. Athens's dragging footsteps slid across the floor and the porch. A strange voice was heard asking for Dr. Manning.

From the head of the stairs Manning called, "Here I am, Sontaag. What's the matter?"

The answering tones were stolid and matter-of-fact. "I went to your office when I got your call fifteen minutes ago, Doctor. Your housekeeper said you were over here."

"My call?" Manning was puzzled and petulant. "I didn't call you."

"Somebody did. He sounded like you and he said he was you. Wanted to know if the patient was asleep and I said he was. Told me to leave him and go to your office right away."

"I wonder who in the—?"

Voss pushed past the doctor and started down the stairs. "Come on," he urged. "We've got to get over there."

Sontaag was a stocky, phlegmatic young man with the scarred face of a fighter and a glimmer of slow intelligence in his blue eyes. Just now he was worried. "You think something's wrong?" he asked Voss.

"A little matter of murder, perhaps," Voss said in passing.

He began to run around the house and through the yard toward the Whitcomb place, which was almost directly behind Cynthia Carrington's. He heard Manning and Sontaag running behind him. It took them three or four minutes to reach the screening hedge that marked Terry's boundary line.

A small sedan was at the curb and the front door of the house stood wide open. As he dashed up the steps Voss saw a man back in the dim hallway. The man was Irv Proctor and he was coming slowly toward the door, staggering a little as one drunk or bewildered. When Voss entered Irv stopped and a foolish grin came over his pasty face.

"I dropped in like you suggested just a minute or two ago," he said. "Terry's in there." He gestured vaguely toward the big room in the center of the house.

Voss strode to the doorway of that weird room and halted, shaken despite the fact that he had prepared himself for something like the sight that met his eyes. Behind him Manning cursed and Sontaag gulped audibly.

Terry Whitcomb dangled lifeless from his own yardarm. A thick rope had been lashed to the lowest spar of the tall oak mast and its free end was noosed around his neck. His feet swung eight inches above the floor and near them lay an overturned chair that had been brought from another room. Terry wore pajamas that might have fitted him when he was fleshier, but were far too large for him now. His face was a grotesque purple mask, bloated and splotched, with the open eyes bulging and the open mouth disgorging a swollen tongue. His body turned sedately from side to side as the rope twisted and on his chest was pinned a sheet of paper.

Manning regained a semblance of composure. He went across the room and grasped one of Terry's hands. The dangling arm flapped loosely. Manning said, "He's dead, all right."

"How long?" Voss asked.

"No time at all. Five minutes at the inside, fifteen at the outside. He's not only still warm—he's still feverish from the alcohol he put away."

"Where's the phone? We'll have to get Proctor. Padgett, too, I suppose."

"They're on the way," Irv said. "I called dad first thing. There's a phone in the hall and an extension in Terry's bedroom at the front of the house."

Voss was reading the note pinned to the dead man. "Here are the missing words from the paper we found on Cynthia's porch. *'Counting myself I have killed everyone who knew about it!'*" He picked up a newspaper that was spread on the floor and scanned its pages. "And here's the paper that furnished the words for the note found in Evelyn Lister's fingers—*'I was only fifteen when it happened but I knew too much.'*"

"That doesn't mean a thing," Manning stated vehemently. "One of those mutilated papers was left at my house and one at Cynthia's. It only means the murderer was scattering around clues that would point to other people. Otherwise he could have made all his notes from a single copy of the *Courier* and then burned it. He simply left one here when he got through with his dirty work."

"Sure," said Irv. "Unless Whitcomb killed himself that's what happened. Could he have killed himself, Manning?"

"Yes, he could have. That is, he would have been able to walk in here and climb on a chair and put the noose around his neck. I wouldn't think it likely, though."

A car stopped outside the house. There were sounds of people mounting the steps. Proctor and Padgett and the thickset state police detective entered the room.

Something very like a snarl twisted the district attorney's mouth and his pink face was pinker than ever. "The Dutch act, eh? Got a hunch I was on to him and slid out from under before I could grab him." He read the note and looked at the paper that had lain on the floor and listened to Voss's concise statement about the phone call to Sontaag. "Well, I guess this closes the case. If the state is saved the expense of a prosecution, so much the better." But he sounded disappointed, as though he were thinking of headlines that might have been in the course of a long and spectacular trial that would never be held.

Voss said, "Aren't you jumping at conclusions? It would be a lot more convincing if he had written a suicide note and confession in his own hand."

"Nonsense, Voss. You can't expect a crazy man to behave rationally."

Voss pointed to a table scarf that lay in a rumpled heap on the floor. "That must have been brought from another room. I can't think why, unless someone used it to wipe his hands and rub away fingerprints."

"You're only trying to complicate matters. Doctor, was he strong enough to get out of bed and hang himself?"

Manning nodded. "He was stronger than you'd think. The only way I could keep him in bed this morning was to give him sedatives. They wouldn't hold him down long." He looked at Sontaag. "Was he restless?"

"He was raving," the nurse told them. "He was begging for whisky, I gave him a drink and he went to sleep."

"Or else he pretended to go to sleep," Padgett suggested. "Where were you when you got that phone call, Sontaag?"

"I was in the kitchen heating water when the phone rang. I answered it in the front hall."

"And went right out?"

"First I looked into the bedroom to see whether he was still asleep. Then I went out."

Padgett said decisively, "He called you himself from the extension. He got the operator and asked her to ring this number back and talked to you, disguising his voice. Then he hanged himself. . . . What do you say to that, Voss?"

The criminologist made a grimace. "Too far-fetched."

"You bookish fellows are the far-fetched ones. You're always looking for something obscure. You miss the truth because it's so simple. I wonder where Whitcomb kept his private papers, if any?"

"I've got 'em," Proctor answered. He had been rummaging in the drawers of a built-in desk in a corner of the room and had brought forth and opened a metal box. "I've got 'em and I've got something else that makes your idea sound better, Padgett." He held up two sheets of paper.

Voss read them over the district attorney's shoulder. The first was a simple receipt for a thousand dollars signed with Evelyn Lister's name and purportedly witnessed by Jenny Midge. It was dated April 25.

The second document, which bore similar signatures, was written shakily in a stilted hand. It said:

> I hereby affirm of my own free will that on this date and previous thereto I do not know or have not known of any unlawful or wrong act ever committed by Terrence Whitcomb; and that whatever I may have said to the contrary was false; and that I have no claim upon Terrence Whitcomb whatsoever and never had any claim upon him; and that Terrence Whitcomb has never been my lover or in any way intimate with my person.

"It's Terry's handwriting," Manning declared. "Sounds like his wording, too. He had a sharp mind when he wasn't more than half drunk. I'd say the papers were genuine."

"That cinches it." Padgett was beginning to feel better. "Now we have absolute proof that the Lister girl blackmailed Whitcomb, threatening to drag him into the clutches of the law in connection with the Brewster killing and on a trumped-up charge of rape and seduction. He knew she could make a hell of a lot of trouble, even if she didn't send him to prison, and so he paid her off. But she probably kept after him and he saw he couldn't trust her, so he watched his chance and sneaked up on the hill one day and killed her.

"Thael saw him, but didn't know who he was till later when he happened to get a peek at Whitcomb through one of the windows. In some manner Whitcomb learned of Thael's knowledge and waylaid Thael in the rain. Jenny Midge most likely knew all about it, which made her the next to be killed when Whitcomb began to get scared. And Cynthia Carrington—well, he just wanted to kill her because he was in love with her and she wasn't in love with him. . . ."

Padgett smiled at the detective, who smiled back. "Fast work, eh? Williams, we've got it solved twenty-four hours after our arrival on the scene."

Proctor turned to Irv. "'Get your cameras and stuff," he ordered. "Let's finish up in here in a hurry so we can cut him down. And while you're out pick up Ben Thoad and his hound and bring them back with you."

"What do you want with a bloodhound now?" Padgett demanded. "We've got everything figured out for you."

The police chief was very grave. "You've got me half convinced," he admitted, "but on the other hand I've got a lot of respect for Voss's ideas. If there was a murderer here and if he used that table scarf it may be the dog can trail him. I think it's worth a try."

"Well, you're the boss cop here," Padgett said. "'You can do what you like. Don't blame me if it doesn't get you anything except a razzing from the newspapers."

Ben Thoad marched in ten minutes later, his dark eyes glowing fiercely. "Gardenia," he said, "we're after the fellow who tried to poison you. We got to find him, by thunder, if he's the last fellow on earth!"

Under the amused regard of Padgett and the interested attention of the detective the little sergeant went through the solemn rigmarole of interesting the bloodhound bitch first in the jar of boiled liver, then in the soiled table scarf. Gardenia sniffed and looked at Thoad and wagged her tail.

Thoad took a tight grip on the animal's leash. "Find 'em, Gardenia," he commanded.

There was little doubt that Gardenia had become aware of an individual scent. She went toward the front of the house, her claws sliding and scraping over the floor as she tried to move faster than Thoad conveniently could. She went into a doorway that opened off the front hall.

Padgett chuckled. "I told you it would be wasting time. That's Whitcomb's bedroom. She's trailing Whitcomb backwards."

Gardenia spent only three or four seconds in the bedroom, however. She came out and headed back to the center room and through it toward the rear door, sniffing vigorously at the floor boards as though to separate a particular scent from a medley of others. She went across the back porch and down into the yard with the men following her, all excepting Irv, who was busy inside with his cameras and fingerprint apparatus.

"This isn't Whitcomb's trail," Proctor told the district attorney. "Not unless it's an old one."

Padgett did not reply. There was an expression of dismay on his face as though he were afraid his ingenious theory might after all be disproved.

Voss remarked, "A man could have entered and left by this door without much chance of his being seen." He jerked his head to indicate the hedge that blocked the view from the rear of the Carrington and Lyons houses.

The trail led around the far side of the house, where a man would have been invisible except to a watcher on the bay, to the point where Whitcomb Street branched sharply to the right almost at the water's edge. There it ended.

"Whoever it was got into a car here," Thoad said in a tone of grievance. He was a comic and tragic little man standing there beside the ungainly hound with the leash in his hand. "The gravel is scuffed by tires and there's drops of oil. Gardenia can't go any farther."

"How about the time she got that burglar who traveled by car?" Voss asked.

"Conditions were different. It was an open car and we had a ditch with water in it beside the road and there wasn't any wind, by thunder—"

"We're making fools of ourselves," Padgett said brusquely. "In the first place we have no assurance that any murderer handled that table scarf. In the second place I've heard time and time again that bloodhounds can't be relied upon. In the third place I'm still willing to let my theory stand as the final answer in the case. In the fourth place I've got an appointment with a number of people at Miss Carrington's house."

Manning spoke quickly. "What's going to happen there?"

"I phoned her," Padgett said, "and she told me she was up and around and it would be all right. I asked all the people who might possibly have had any connection with the murders to be there. At that time I didn't know the solution of everything was so near."

"Whom did you ask?" Voss wanted to know.

Padgett consulted a slip of paper. "Miss Carrington, Miss Lyons, Miss Parsons and Decker. I meant to include Dr. Manning and Irv Proctor. And of course you're invited,

Chief, and you, Voss." He glanced at his watch. "We've got twenty-five minutes."

"What's your idea in getting them all together?" Manning inquired.

"Well, originally I intended to satisfy myself that there wasn't any more likely suspect than Whitcomb in the bunch. Now I'm not interested in suspects. I'm going to tell them how I have it figured out and ask them to come forward with any information they may have to bolster my case. Not that I really need any more proof. . . ."

The corner of Voss's mouth twitched. "We'll all be there. But first I'd like to have Sergeant Thoad take his dog once around the block to see if she can't pick up that scent again. She has a habit of remembering, Thoad says. Want to wait, Padgett?"

The district attorney snorted. "No, thanks. I'll look for you at Miss Carrington's at eleven-thirty sharp. Come on, Williams." He went away hurriedly with the detective following.

"He's a big bluff," Manning remarked, "but I'm glad he's got it settled. You know, the more I think of it the more I'm becoming convinced Whitcomb did kill himself. A good thing, too, in a lot of ways. . . . But I've got to see Cynthia before that horde descends on her. I think Padgett had a lot of nerve, picking her place for his confab after I warned him."

Proctor watched the physician stride down the street. He took a cigar from his pocket and gripped it between his teeth. "Match?" he said.

"Use your own," Voss retorted.

Proctor thrust a hand into his coat pocket and brought it forth full of match packets. He selected one and replaced the others calmly. He lighted the cigar.

"Go ahead," he directed Thoad. "Give us a yell if you find a trail, which you won't. . . . Do you still think you know the murderer, Voss?"

"That's what makes it so hard to take," Voss muttered. "I know him very well. I've sat and discussed his handiwork with him several times. What I don't know is how I can prove him guilty so thoroughly there will be no question of his wriggling out of it. He's been slick, Proctor. None of the clues he has left are conclusive so far. . . . He has alibis and he has been careful about details."

"Why not accuse him and have a try at it anyway?"

"If you'd stop to think a minute you'd know why. If he goes to court and is acquitted because of insufficient evidence he's in the clear for the rest of his life. A man can't be put in jeopardy twice for the same alleged offense."

"Then you're going to let things drag on?"

Voss shook his head slowly. "No, I can't do that. He's all through with this particular series of murders. Terry Whitcomb's death completed the design. It gave the false answer Padgett leaped at, which is the answer the murderer planned from the beginning for us all to accept. But as I said, a man who has got away with murder once is apt to try it again. We can't afford to let him remain at large."

"Well, what in hell are you going to do? Sneak up on him after dark and shoot him?"

"'Nothing so drastic. I'm only going to see if I can't steal Padgett's party and make my man give himself away."

Proctor scowled. "It's done in the ten-cent detective magazines, but I never heard of it working in real life."

"It works, all right. Remember my telling you very few killers are ever convicted by policemen or prosecutors? Most of them convict themselves with a little encouragement. They're tricked or frightened into making damaging admissions till there's nothing left for them to do except confess and try to justify themselves."

"Here's hoping you can do it," the chief said dubiously. "It'll be worth watching. But I thought you said yourself we were up against a really smart customer."

"He was smart enough. Inevitably, though, he has been getting panicky. I have three or four tricks that are bound to surprise him—bits of evidence that might not mean much in court, but will look bigger to him than they really are. Once we find a way to shake his self-assurance, his egotistical faith in his own scheming, we'll have shaken him to the core."

"I'd give my shirt to see Padgett crawl. I don't suppose there's any way I could help?"

"I'm counting on you—first of all to have Ben Thoad and Gardenia parked somewhere near Cynthia's, then to produce them when I give you the nod."

"Still thinking about that table scarf?"

"It's a good bet. It would be stupid to overlook it."

"You wouldn't tell me your suspect's name beforehand?"

"I'd rather not. I intend to play for a strong psychological effect. It's amazing how much pressure is exerted on a man with a guilty conscience when a number of pairs of eyes suddenly start accusing him."

"All right, Voss. It's your circus. Just give me the chance to make the pinch, will you? What do we do first?"

"You arrange things with Thoad. I'll wander around for a few minutes and show up at the proper time."

"The psychological moment, hey?"

"I hope so."

It was after all a forlorn, desperate hope, he reflected grimly as he ambled down Whitcomb Street toward the heart of the village. If the person he had in mind ever suspected how flimsy a structure of genuine evidence he had built up it would be unquestionably a lost hope.

Many cars passed him, speeding toward the Whitcomb place. Tom Wilkins's hearse was one of them. The others carried newspapermen who had just become aware that a fourth link had been forged in Waldham's chain of murders.

He saw a shiny Zephyr coming toward him and his eyes lighted. He waved and Braithe stopped for him. As he got into the car Voss noticed that Braithe's right arm was heavily bandaged.

"How is it?" he asked.

Braithe made a face. "It didn't hurt when it happened, but I thought I'd go crazy with pain yesterday. I can use my arm all right, though. . . . What's all this talk about Terry Whitcomb being killed?"

Voss told him what he could as they drove along. "It happened just in time to give the *Courier* a fresh lead for tomorrow's edition, didn't it?"

"The heck it did! By the time the afternoon and morning papers get through with it the *Courier* will be a pallid copy of them. Folks won't read my paper for the big story; they'll read it, as always, for the gossip paragraphs. 'Mrs. Limpus entertained at a luncheon bridge Tuesday. . . .' That's why I want to get away from Waldham and go to work in a big city where they do things in a big way."

"Take a quick look and come back out," Voss suggested as they stopped in front of the Whitcomb house. "I can give you all the dope. Keep it from the other reporters, but in about ten minutes the brains of the investigation will get together at Cynthia Carrington's to compare notes. You ought to hear something interesting there if I can get you in."

"You're a pal," Eddie said. "I'll have to hurry, though. This is my busy day, putting the paper together for the press." He got out of the car and ran up the steps. He was back in less than five minutes, looking unhappy.

"I don't know why I always have to see the corpse," he complained, starting the Zephyr. "I haven't got a strong stomach for that sort of thing. . . . Do you think you're getting a line on the murderer?"

"Padgett has it all doped out. He'll fight the man who says Whitcomb didn't do it. He says it was Whitcomb's plan all along to commit suicide when he'd killed everybody he had it in for."

"Padgett and I think alike," Braithe said, "only I didn't have to wait for that note pinned to Terry's pajamas to figure it out. I suspected Terry from the start."

"Then who was the man we saw prowling around Terry's?"

Braithe pursed his lips. "I thought for a while it was Manning, and then I decided it must have been Terry himself. He'd seen me poking around. He put on that hat and coat and came out and tried to kill us. Then he went back to his booze."

"You and the district attorney!" Voss scoffed.

They pulled up in front of Cynthia Carrington's and got out. Athens let them in, his dusky face troubled. They entered the big living room where nine people were seated in chairs and on sofas.

Padgett, who occupied a big chair in the central position with the detective at his right, scowled at Braithe. "No reporters," he said shortly. "When this conference is over I'll have a statement for the press."

Voss pushed Braithe ahead of him into the room. "He's here in a dual capacity, Padgett. He offered some time ago to help me in my investigation. He was with me the night I was shot at. I think you should have invited him as a witness in the first place."

Padgett glowered, but offered no further protest. He said gruffly, "Well, then, let's get started. I was just going to tell these people, Voss, that everything is settled. The murderer has been discovered and the case is closed." He put his fingertips together and puffed out his pink cheeks. "The murderer, ladies and gentlemen, is—or was—your unfortunate neighbor, Terry Whitcomb."

He paused for effect. Voss lowered himself into a vacant chair in a corner near the door and studied all their faces. Cynthia, wearing a flowered blue wrapper and sitting beside Decker on a sofa, was startled and incredulous. Sue Lyons, who sat in a big chair with Manning perched on its arm, gave Padgett one disdainful look and turned her face from him. Irv and Dale Parsons appeared embarrassed and watched the pattern in the rug as though they expected it to come to life at any moment. Braithe sat beside Voss, smiling expectantly. The rest of them were non-committal, waiting for Padgett's next words.

Those next words were a challenge. "Does anybody here disagree with that statement?" Padgett thrust out his jaw, seeming to dare any of them to speak.

Voss thrust his hands in his pockets and stared hard at the polished toes of his tan shoes. He was annoyed to discover that he felt self-conscious and clumsy. He told himself it was now or never; he could either take the plunge and risk his reputation for infallibility or remain silent and see justice cheated.

He said in tones that were intentionally sharp and impatient, "I disagree. Your statement is ridiculous, Padgett. If you'd had any training at all in criminal psychology you'd know very well it wasn't Whitcomb."

17

Leland Padgett could not have been more completely flab-bergasted if he had been hit in the face with an egg. The pink in his cheeks deepened to crimson. He opened his mouth as though to emit an indignant roar and closed it again with an effort. He seemed close to strangulation over the comparatively restrained words he finally selected for utterance.

"Perhaps you would rather bore us with your wild theories than listen to mine?"

"I would." Voss's gray eyes flashed behind their spectacles. "I think it's high time we had a comprehensive look at all the facts in this case. I can put them before you very briefly if you care to hear them."

Proctor appeared suddenly happier than he had been for days, sitting on the sofa beside Decker. Braithe had taken a pencil and a wad of paper out of his pocket. He whispered, "Nice going, Sherlock."

Padgett cleared his throat. "Of course you have no official standing. However you have some sort of reputation as an amateur in criminology." He stressed the word "amateur." "If you will make your statement as short as possible and if these good people don't mind having their time wasted, I suppose we could listen."

"I don't mind," said Proctor promptly.

Manning seconded the chief. "I'd like to hear it."

One or two of the others nodded.

The district attorney waved a manicured hand. "Very well, Voss. I'll give them the official verdict when you've finished."

Voss grinned faintly. "I hope you give the right one." He looked around at his audience again. "I suppose you've heard about the letter Brewster Lyons wrote seven years ago, which was delivered yesterday."

They all had, apparently.

"Well," Voss said, "as I see it these recent crimes are only connected with the strange death of Brewster as an imaginative murderer tried to make them seem connected. He used that earlier case as a smokescreen to hide his real motives, knowing better than most people the full extent of the evil Jenny Midge was perpetuating."

Padgett said testily, "No one has maintained that Whitcomb killed young Lyons, if that's what you're getting at."

"You would have, Padgett, if that letter hadn't been found. . . . But to get back to the motives, we must start first of all with the charming character of Evelyn Lister. Delicacy does not permit a full description of her way of living, but I think we all remember her as a scheming lady without morals or conscience, who would not withhold herself from any man who could be made to pay for his fun later. She was bad and unscrupulous and dangerous—and not so uncommon, either, in this mercenary world."

Sue Lyons spoke up angrily. "She was a cheap hussy."

"'Cheap' isn't quite the word. She collected a cool thousand from Terry Whitcomb not very long ago. That's an isolated instance.

"She hit upon her career as an extortionist when she was going to have a baby. She found herself wishing the father had plenty of money and could be made to pay for her inconvenience and the wish grew into the plot.

Art Dawson, her paramour, may have encouraged her. She looked for a likely victim and chose Dr. Manning because he was good-looking and well-to-do, was known to have taken an interest in her and could hardly afford a scandal for professional reasons. She offered him an opportunity to make a cash settlement. When he refused she took a chance and went into court and won her case so easily she was pleasantly surprised.

"It was so good a plan she didn't see why she couldn't use it again and again. Suppose she coaxed you to go walking with her, Proctor, and later threatened a similar scandal and you remembered what had happened to Manning. You'd think of your job and your reputation. You'd be tempted to buy her off, wouldn't you?"

Proctor colored. "I'd be tempted to wring her neck!"

"Ah, that was another common reaction. Ralph Decker was heard to speak of shooting her. . . ."

Decker squirmed uncomfortably.

". . . Irv didn't miss getting caught by much, although he showed good judgment in looking before he leaped. . . ."

Irv bit his lip and his shamed eyes avoided Dale's amused ones.

". . . Terry paid her to avoid a lot of grief. Dr. Manning had cause to fear he was going to be victimized again.

"But one intended victim who had been with her surreptitiously decided he wasn't going to pay blackmail and wasn't going to get into a scandal either. As I've already suggested to Chief Proctor this person was a not uncommon glandular extremist, a thymocentric. The man with too much thymus may be a terrible, grown-up child. A cruel, cunning and dangerously childish nature inhabits his adult mind. The scientists say he commits seventy percent of all murders. Often any kind of motive—even a whim—is enough for him. Frequently he makes elaborate plans, scattering meaningless clues and trying to make trouble for as many people as possible. He's playing a horrible game all the time. His greatest weakness is that his ego makes him write notes, generally of an obscure and fantastic nature. And his chief identifying mark is that, being a coward, he strikes in the dark or when he has disarmed his victims by pretended friendliness."

Braithe's whisper was exuberant. "This is swell, Voss! It's a scoop for the *Courier*—"

"Our thymocentric chose the anniversary of Brewster Lyons's death as a starting point because it would seem to lend significance to ensuing events," Voss pursued. "He made a date with Evelyn on the hill, perhaps promising to bring money for her. He drove to the foot of the hill to a spot where he could not be seen either from the village or the golf club and where bushes would hide him from the sight of anyone on the bay. As he climbed up, George Thael, who was more or less an interloper, had just a glimpse of him with his right arm thrown across his face to protect it from the branches. The killer had picked up a stone on the way. Evelyn saw him, of course, and judging by the expression on her face she knew what was coming before he struck her, but she didn't have time to cry out.

"I might state parenthetically that the point of evidence Thael noticed is now in my possession. I didn't tell you, Padgett, because you seemed more interested in conclusions than facts, but after I advised Thael to take that night train to New York I telephoned my friend Lieutenant Bob Saint-Amour of the homicide squad there to meet the train. You've heard of Saint-Amour, of course. He took Thael to Bellevue and last night he telephoned me at the inn to tell me Thael finally had remembered what that knock on the head made him forget."

For the first time there was an expression of misgiving in Padgett's, face. And for the first time Voss saw out of the corner of his eye a fleeting shadow of uncertainty cross the face of the killer, and felt tremendously heartened.

"It wasn't altogether coincidence that I arrived in Waldham that first day," Voss said. "There were disturbances about that time that impelled a certain client to send for me. One of those disturbances was Evelyn Lister, who either had become very ambitious or needed money very badly for some special purpose, since her demands had become nervier and had included more people than ever before. Another was the obvious fact that Cynthia was nearing the end of her strength. And by the same token, it being the anniversary of Brewster's death, it wasn't a coincidence that Dr. Manning chose that particular time to make her face the bogey of her fear.

"Before he killed Evelyn our thymocentric had prepared at least two of his notes—the first and the last ones to come to light. They were the alpha and omega of his plan. The first would seem to link Evelyn's death with the death of Brewster and the other, hinting at suicide and a guilty conscience, would purport to solve the puzzle to the satisfaction of the duly constituted authorities." His gaze swung toward Padgett, who wet his lips nervously.

"Then," Proctor supplied, "he distributed the papers he'd cut the words out of around at various places, just to worry people."

Voss assented. "It was a rather foolish attempt to muddle things. . . . The first hitch in the murderer's neat plan was caused by Dawson, who must have known of Evelyn's date and tried to blackmail the man who made it. So the murderer, faced with this unexpected threat, made a date with Dawson also, promising him a certain sum of money if he would leave town. The appointment was made for an evening when it was known Dawson would be at Jack Miller's house alone. Meanwhile the murderer pasted another note together. We know the rest of that episode.

"Then Thael suddenly became aware, through witnessing a certain gesture, of the identity of the man who had climbed the hill through the wood. He was foolish enough to blurt it out in the restaurant. The murderer heard of it and watched Thael till he had a chance to slug him with that hammer. That time the necessity was so great there was no time to prepare a note.

"And finally, with the town overrun with reporters and things getting too warm for comfort, our man hurried to complete the design. It seemed advisable to kill me in such a place and manner that Whitcomb would be blamed for it, and he wasted three bullets in the attempt. That same night he failed in a second attempt to kill Thael and he went after Jenny Midge, either because she had seen him with Evelyn or because she had seen him lurking around the Whitcomb house. He followed Jenny through the storm to her house, knocked her out and bound and gagged her and set the place afire. He may have thought the flames would burn away the ropes and gag or he may not have cared whether they were discovered or not.

"He had too much self-confidence. His faith in his own plan was so great he could not let Terry die of his own accord. He had to murder Terry as a final masterly touch. He phoned the nurse, pretending to be the doctor. . . ."

"It makes a pretty story," Padgett said judiciously. "In the main it follows my own line of reasoning. In fact, it makes me more certain than ever that Terry Whitcomb was our killer."

The small clock on the mantelpiece whirred and began to strike rapidly. Braithe jumped up.

"Noon already!" he exclaimed. "I've got to be getting back to the office. Voss, the *Courier* will go to town in a big way tomorrow. If only you could pick out the man as you've picked out the pattern!"

Here was the ultimate test. Voss drew a deep breath and sat up straighter in his chair.

"I can," he said quietly.

In the living room doorway Braithe whirled. "What the devil! Here I was going to miss the best part of it!"

Something rang metallicly on the floor at his feet and Abelard Voss bent and picked it up. "You're losing your luck," he said, handing a bright copper disc to the young editor.

Braithe took it and grinned. "I'd feel naked without it in my pants pocket," he said, putting it there. Then his blue eyes flickered and he took the coin out of his pocket and looked at it. "Why," he said, "this isn't mine. I had one something like it, but mine came from Washington and this is from Niagara Falls."

Dale stared thoughtfully. "Yours was from Niagara Falls, too, Eddie. I remember your showing it to me and saying we'd spend our honeymoon there and my saying no, we wouldn't."

He rubbed his chin. "Maybe you're right. Anyway I lost the thing a long time ago and I've forgotten. I could have lost it anywhere and I suppose there are any number of them around. Everyone's been to Niagara Falls and Washington. . . . But why are we wasting time? Who's your candidate, Voss?"

"He'd visited Jenny's Midge's house at least once with Evelyn Lister," Voss said. "He lost that lucky coin there. He forgot a pair of tennis shoes there and she forgot a belt. I wouldn't be surprised if Jenny caught them and they had to leave in a hurry. I took the shoes to the police station, but the murderer got them back before we could trace them. They were size nine."

"Half the shoes in this county are size nine," Padgett growled.

"He found a tin box in Jenny's house," Voss hurried on. "In it was that last letter Brewster Lyons wrote. He read the letter and knew Brewster had committed suicide and told certain people without revealing how he knew. That's another thymocentric trait—he talks more than he should.

"I wondered why he hadn't destroyed the letter before starting his extravaganza of homicide, because its discovery would have destroyed the illusion he was trying to create. I decided Jenny must have hidden her tin box in another place after she found him in the house and he couldn't locate it. That would give him a reason for adding arson to his other crimes. The box would have been destroyed with its contents if it hadn't been buried."

Braithe still smiled, but his face was bloodless and he held himself rigidly. Everyone in the room was watching him. He said, "You'll have to come to the point pretty soon, Voss. I can't wait. The paper will be late as it is."

"Better call your printer up and tell him to go ahead without you," Voss suggested. He nodded slightly toward Cornelius Proctor and the police chief got out of his chair and went purposefully from the room, his eyes hard and cold.

"You're razzing me," Braithe said. His voice was thin with strain. "You're trying to get my goat."

The front door opened. Proctor came back into the room and Gardenia, the bloodhound bitch, entered, dragging the solemn-faced Ben Thoad at the end of her leash. Her head was up, her nostrils inquisitive. She sniffed at Braithe, putting her wet muzzle against his flannel trousers. She looked at Thoad and wagged her tail confidently.

Words in the animal's mouth could not have made her meaning clearer.

"I don't like dogs," Braithe said, backing away.

"I don't blame you," said Voss. "This one has been following a scent that started with a table scarf in Terry

Whitcomb's house—a scarf that had been handled by Terry's murderer. The trail has led straight to you. Gardenia is even with you now for trying to poison her."

Dale came to her feet, her hand against her breast, her mouth open. "Eddie!" she gasped. "Eddie—"

"You can't pin anything on me!" It was a frightened scream torn from Braithe's throat. "There isn't a bit of proof!"

"I know you killed them," said Voss. "We all know it. I knew it when you drove me to Whitcomb's place the night of the storm. Even your clever ruse of handing me a revolver didn't fool me. You had another revolver lashed to a stake and a string laid through the grass so you could fire that first shot from the shrubbery while you lay beside me. You sneaked around and put on a raincoat and hat you had hidden and shot twice more at the place where I had been lying—only I had moved. You got behind the house and threw the coat and hat in the bay and shot yourself in the right arm—being left-handed—and threw the gun away. I'd have grabbed you then if I'd had proof enough to send you to the electric chair.

"Thael knew you killed them when he saw you fighting with Irv, with your right arm shielding your face. The man who climbed the hill to kill Evelyn shielded himself from the branches with his right arm. A right-handed man uses his left arm for that purpose almost always, especially if he has been trained to box. Being a boxing fan Thael saw the connection while he was looking at a photograph of a left-handed prize-fighter in the *Record* right after you and Irv mixed it up. . . . But again it wasn't the kind of proof you can depend on in court.

"And you saw me take your tennis shoes from Jenny's house to Proctor's office. You were with the reporters at the door. You came and went pretty much as you pleased around the police station. It was easy for you to get them back."

Braithe fought for self-control and achieved it in a measure. He spoke softly and tensely. "Listen, Voss—all of you—those things are tiny threads. You can't convict me and you know it. I'm innocent. You'll only make trouble for yourselves by trying to make it for me. If you take me to court you'll be a laughing-stock—"

"There are threads enough to make a strong rope," Voss interrupted. "I haven't begun to tell you all of them. You may not have realized that we'd cover every inch of the side of the hill for footprints, lint, anything that would show you climbed up to kill Evelyn while you were on your way to meet Dale at the golf club. You didn't think we'd analyze the paste from those notes to compare with the paste you used at your office, or that we'd examine the floors and stairs of the Miller house and trace the hammer that was used on Thael and go over the soft earth of Jenny Midge's garden where the note was left. There ought to be fingerprints or traces of perspiration on the table scarf in the Whitcomb house and tracks on the floor that will match the soles of your shoes.

"And you'll be our best witness. The thymus gland makes cowards. You'll crack any minute. You can't help it. . . ."

Eddie Braithe cracked then. His lower lip contracted, baring his teeth. He wheeled and lunged toward the door, straight-arming Ben Thoad. The fat sergeant was just getting the little jar of liver out of his pocket; he went against the wall with a thud and the jar smashed on the floor.

Dale screamed and clung to Irv, holding him back when he would have leaped at Braithe. Cornelius Proctor reached into his hip pocket and took out a snub-nosed revolver.

There was a rumbling growl, a streak of tan, a weird cry from Braithe and the thump and clatter of his falling.

The bloodhound crouched watchfully over him, her fangs unsheathed, snarling a warning.

Proctor unclipped handcuffs from his belt, fitted the steel to Braithe's wrists and pressed the shackles into their ratchets. He put the revolver back into his hip pocket and helped Braithe to stand.

"Excuse me for beating you to the arrest," he said politely to Padgett and the detective from the state police.

Ben Thoad said, "All right, Gardenia." The bitch forgot Braithe, wagging her tail as she looked at her master expectantly. Beaming with pride, Thoad began separating the boiled liver from the bits of broken glass. He fed it to Gardenia a scrap at a time.

Braithe was breathing hard. "A hot bunch of cops," he muttered, sullen and defiant. "You're a phony, Voss. The mutt is smarter than any of you. I'll make fools of you in court."

"Do you think a jury will let you get away with four cold-blooded murders?" Padgett asked. "Do you think anyone will overlook the burning alive of a helpless old woman and the fatal beating of a young girl whose lover you had been? The whole country will howl for your life. You'll be lucky if you're not lynched."

Padgett was altogether pleased with the way things had turned out. His eyes were bright with anticipation and his pink jowls quivered in a smile of complacency, as though he could already see the murder trial headlines.

Proctor touched Braithe's arm and they went out the door and across the porch together. Irv patted Dale's shoulder and left her, following them. Padgett and the detective got up.

"Thank you all for your excellent co-operation," Padgett said. "Thank you in particular, Mr. Voss. You've been very helpful and I'll see that you share in the credit.

If you'll call at the town hall in a little while I'd like to
get a statement from you. It would help me in preparing
the state's case."

"I'll be there," Voss assured him. "I want to go to the
inn first and pack. I'm anxious to get home."

Padgett and the detective left and Ben Thoad and Gardenia went with them.

Dale Parsons stood at the window beside Voss, watching the little group go down the street. At the corner an
ancient roadster with six young men clinging to it swerved
perilously and stopped with a screeching of tires. A second and a third car pulled up behind it. Prisoner, police, Padgett and Gardenia were swallowed up in a frenzied
horde of reporters and cameramen.

"Tomorrow," Voss predicted, "Eddie will realize a great
ambition. He'll write the lead story in the *Daily Record*
under a byline. It will be a weird jumble of fact and fancy
intended to justify him in the eyes of the world. He'll get
ten thousand dollars for lawyers and all the publicity he
wants and neither will save him."

Dale shivered. "It scares me to think of how I went out
with him, danced with him—even kissed him. I used to
like him a lot." Her earnest blue eyes looked up at Voss.
"Please don't tell Irv."

"I won't," he promised, not smiling. He did not feel
like smiling, even though it was all over and he had been
triumphant. The sordidness of murder invariably persisted to the bitter end, he reflected, and then left an ashy
aftertaste.

He saw Cynthia's hand move and Decker's hand close
over it. There was no fear in Cynthia's face any more
nor any haunted look. She had never loved Manning, he
thought; she had been dependent upon him and he had
been drawn to her by her need. Now there was no depen-
dence, no need.

And Sue Lyons's face would never again betray that wistful hunger. The things she had prayed for and believed in had come to pass. She seemed younger, fresher, more alive than ever.

The terrors that had darkened all their lives were dissolved. No ugly mystery lay beneath the black marble shaft in the cemetery around which grass would now grow. The hatreds Jenny Midge had nourished were dead with her. The mad voice that had shrieked blasphemies from the old Whitcomb place was stilled.

Some of those things must have been in Garth Manning's mind. He said, "Voss, we all owe you more than we can ever pay. You've lifted a cloud. I'm supposed to know a little about psychology, but I'd never have suspected that playful Braithe youngster. None of us who knew him would have. You've worked a miracle."

"No miracle," Abelard Voss said modestly. "I've studied enough criminals to know that what is one man's cross is another man's motive. I take the known facts and do a lot of guessing and make notes and shuffle them till I've got a shoe that fits someone. It's easy when you get the hang of it."

"Easy!" Decker scoffed.

"Well," Voss conceded, "a little luck always helps. And there is something to be said for prayer and faith."

ABOUT THE AUTHOR

Donald Clough Cameron (1905-1954) skipped college and jumped into the newspaper field at the age of seventeen (as a crime reporter for the Detroit *Free Press*), working in that field before becoming a freelance writer in the 1930s. His middle name came down to him from the English poet, Arthur Hugh Clough. He wrote short stories, comic book stories (co-writing the story that introduced Alfred as Bruce Wayne's butler), and six detective novels before he died of cancer. He was survived by his wife, Eva, and a son. Three of his mysteries featured criminologist Abelard Voss. (The third of these, *And So He Had to Die*, 1941, has a renewed copyright.)

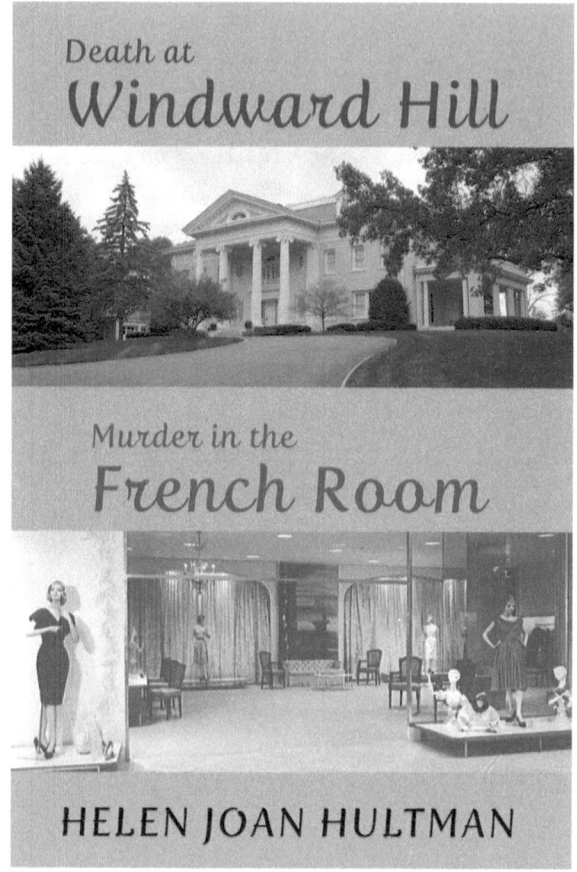

Death at
Windward Hill

Murder in the
French Room

HELEN JOAN HULTMAN

SALLY WOOD

MURDER
OF A
NOVELIST

DEATH
IN LORD
BYRON'S
ROOM

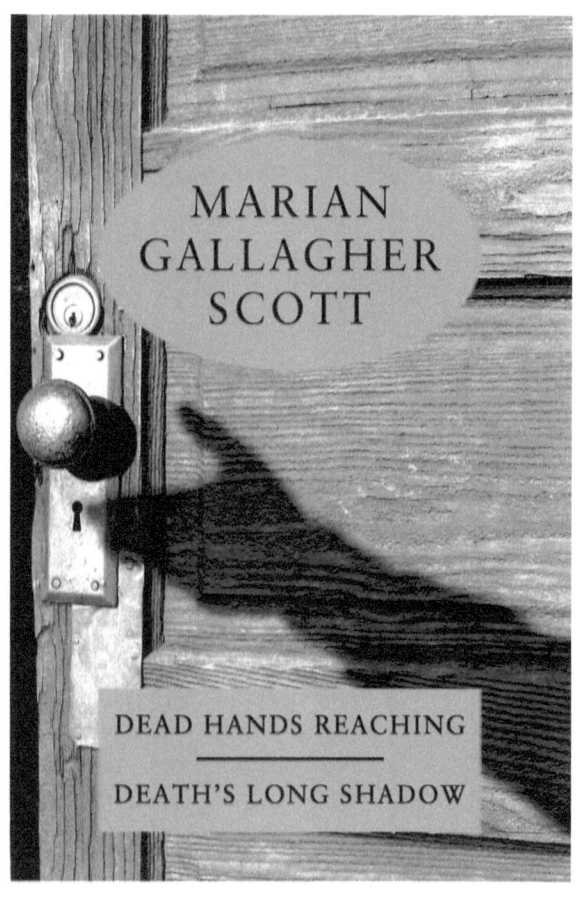

MARIAN
GALLAGHER
SCOTT

DEAD HANDS REACHING

DEATH'S LONG SHADOW

PATTERN
IN BLACK
AND RED

FARADAY KEENE